W.A. SIMPSON

TINDERBOX

This is a **FLAME TREE PRESS** book

FLAME TREE PRESS
6 Melbray Mews, London, SW6 3NS, UK
flametreepress.com

US sales, distribution and warehouse:
Simon & Schuster
simonandschuster.biz

UK distribution and warehouse:
Marston Book Services Ltd
marston.co.uk

Publisher's Note: This is a work of fiction. Names, characters, places, and incidents are a product of the author's imagination. Locales and public names are sometimes used for atmospheric purposes. Any resemblance to actual people, living or dead, or to businesses, companies, events, institutions, or locales is completely coincidental.

Thanks to the Flame Tree Press team.

The cover is created by Flame Tree Studio with thanks to Nik Keevil and Shutterstock.com.
The font families used are Avenir and Bembo.

Flame Tree Press is an imprint of Flame Tree Publishing Ltd

flametreepublishing.com

A copy of the CIP data for this book is available from the British Library and the Library of Congress.

HB ISBN: 978-1-78758-750-2
PB ISBN: 978-1-78758-749-6
ebook ISBN: 978-1-78758-751-9

Printed and bound in Great Britain by Clays Ltd, Elcograf S.p.A

W.A. SIMPSON

TINDERBOX

FLAME TREE PRESS
London & New York

CHAPTER ONE

The vermin of the earth had long claimed the corpse of the witch, but Isbet recognized the old woman right away, despite her head being severed from her body. Death had taken her, yet her voice and her blood cried out for justice from beyond the veils that separated the living from the deceased and other creatures that roamed the places in-between. Isbet knelt in the rich loam and laid her staff, Gaemyr, beside her, not noticing that his carved face was in the dirt.

"A fine way to treat me."

"Hush." Isbet's voice was harsher than she intended. She reached to her right and turned the staff over, although he could quite easily do so himself.

"Who did this to you?" Isbet removed her backpack from around her shoulders and laid it aside. The lifeless pile of bones could not answer, at least not on their own. Isbet closed her eyes, willing something to come to her, an image, a face, anything. However, her power as a diviner was tenuous, and she often needed talismanic help. Isbet could feel her fingers curling into the dirt and the power burning in her veins. *I will kill you. I will make you suffer for what you have done.*

It was not until the burning reached her eyes and she felt stinging tears pooling within them that she breathed in, fighting for control. Now was not the time for this. She must find out – she must know—

"Isbet." Gaemyr's voice brought her out of her turmoil. "See where she is."

The witch's body lay near the ancient hollow tree, a great-grandfather in an old forest that had survived the many wars and other follies of man. Isbet knew what was underneath its tangled roots. She had played here as a child, spending many a lazy summer afternoon at hide-and-seek in the catacombs, not with mortal children like her but with the Children of the Earth.

She wondered where they were now.

"Do you suppose—" Isbet's brow furrowed, and she tugged at one of the myriad thin braids she wore. "She wouldn't have gone into the cave. She couldn't—"

Isbet went to stand, her legs stiff from kneeling. *The Box*, she thought. *It must be....*

"It would explain much," Gaemyr said.

Isbet did not want to leave the remains there, but she had to see what was amiss. She approached the tree and investigated the gaping hole in its trunk, large enough to allow a grown man to descend into the cave underneath. Even with the sun high as it was, shadows lay across the rough walls. Still, Isbet had a sense that something was not right. When she went to boost herself into the hole, Gaemyr said, "Shouldn't we see to her first?"

His words caused her to pause. Gaemyr was right. It was difficult to tell how long the remains had lain there. If not properly laid to rest, they would taint the place as her body decayed. So would her Gift. It would continue to flow from her body, spreading like a plague to steal the life of the woods. "Yes."

When Isbet knelt again, she reached for her pack. Inside she kept everything she needed to send the old woman to rest. Once she finished here, Isbet would see to other things.

Isbet plunged Gaemyr into the soft earth. The red jewels that served as his eyes glittered. That face reminded her of the old spirits that lived in the trees, which made sense since the wood of the staff came from the Celestial Vine, which climbed into the heavens only to fall by the Woodsman's Ax. Isbet had visited the forest where the Vine held sway; its twisted limbs were the home of innumerable mythic beasts and beings.

Isbet's eyes settled on the corpse again.

It was a moment before she noticed the wetness on her face as the tears escaped. She swallowed the stone that had lodged in her throat.

"Old Mother, forgive me for being away for so long. I was not here to save you."

The urge returned – to throw herself to the ground and weep. To scream curses. But Isbet forced the bitter loss down. There would be time for grieving later.

First, she would find her grandmother's murderer.

From the pack, she drew what appeared to be a cameo pin. Anyone not trained in the arcane would see the profile of a young creamy-skinned maiden, but those with the Gift saw the face of the Duine Shee, her eyes black within their sockets, her mouth opened in a soundless scream.

Isbet laid the cameo on what remained of the witch's breast, her movements practiced. She climbed to her feet, brushing the decaying leaves from the knees of the trousers she wore. Unlike other maidens, Isbet did not hinder herself in dresses and robes. There were too many evils in the realm to risk capture because one tripped on the folds of a skirt.

Her gaze skimmed the surrounding area until she found what she searched for, resting at the base of the tree.

"It was a mighty blow," Gaemyr commented. Isbet didn't bother to respond.

The witch's skull stared at her. Isbet lifted it and made her way back. She positioned the skull above the body. Isbet sat cross-legged. All was in readiness, but she didn't act. She stared at the eyeless sockets of the skull of the woman who had taught her the secrets of the realm.

"Isbet?"

Isbet drew in a labored breath. She had yet to perform the ritual and already she felt the weight of exhaustion in her bones. Despite that, Isbet stretched her back, reached out one slim hand, and set her palm down over the cameo.

She spoke the name.

The face on the cameo came to life. A scream burst from its thin lips and a wind not felt by Isbet whipped the lifeless gray strands of the Duine Shee's hair into distress. The wailing of the death talisman did not disturb her as its agonized cry filled the air around her, nor did she feel any concern at the unseen presence that approached the veil between the mortal and the ether.

Isbet reached out again. Another gift of the students of the arcane was the ability to move the veils aside to allow a spirit entrance into the mortal realm. Often, the unschooled assumed that the spirits would have the greater power and be able to move aside the veils themselves. Isbet never corrected the speaker when she heard such things.

The spirit of the old woman touched the remains – not in a physical sense but with the intangible presence that gave life to the beings walking the mortal realm. It had many names – essentia, quintessence, or soul.

There was a violent jerk of the body and the Shee's scream quieted. The eyeless sockets of the skull glowed with cold white light. The jaw hung ajar.

Isbet wasted no time. "Grandmother, who has done this to you?"

"A man." The voice seemed to travel from many miles away. "One who is a coward at heart, yet he wears the guise of a soldier."

"Do you know who this man is? Where he is?"

"He is at the seat of power in this land."

Isbet worried her lower lip. A soldier to a king? She realized with gnawing apprehension that there was only one way that could have occurred.

"He has the Box."

There was a pause as though the voice feared to give its reply. "Yes."

Isbet swore. "Stupid man," she muttered to herself. The Box, a source of magic long passed down through the generations, was the key to commanding three of the most powerful entities in the known realm. To the ordinary – the ones without the Gift – they were a source of terrible fear. Three mighty hounds, all sinew and bristling fur, claws, and jagged teeth. Where the Box had come from and how the dogs became enslaved to it, was a secret lost to history.

However, to Isbet, who had played with them in the catacombs, they were protectors of both her and her grandmother; they were friends.

"He doesn't realize what he faces upon death?"

Her voice filled with mirth, the witch replied, "He knows nothing of the consequences."

Perhaps that would be enough. "Shall I leave him, Grandmother?"

"He is cunning, this man," the witch said. "He will figure a way to prolong his life or discover immortality and have safeguards on himself and his possessions. No one will give him challenge as long as he holds the Box."

The dogs could well bring him Apples of Immortality or many items that could stave off death for him if he hadn't commanded them to do so already. Could she steal the Box back and command the dogs to take his life or kill him herself? Either way, he would die without punishment. Isbet knew that he would have to answer for the murder of the old mother, but would that be enough?

An idea was forming in her mind. "So, even if I were to get the Box back, it would be futile. He would live a long life and when he passed on not face the consequences."

"My dear granddaughter, there are always consequences to every action."

"True." Isbet nodded. "And if he searches for immortality—"

"You are scheming, granddaughter."

Isbet smiled. Even in death, the old woman knew her. "Here is what I propose to you, Grandmother. I will not kill this man. I will find him and ingratiate myself into his world to find the things he holds most dear and I will rip them from him. And then when he is at his lowest, I will reveal my intent to him. Then, I will have the dogs take him."

Isbet could sense the old woman's approval. "It is a fitting punishment for his crime."

"Grandmother." Isbet swallowed as the grief threatened on the fringes of her heart. "How did this happen?"

Again, there was a pause. "Trusting fool that I was, I thought the soldier would show decency to an old woman. I no longer had the strength to retrieve the Box. I thought if I offered him a treasure—"

"And that wasn't enough for him?" One man could not be so

avaricious. Even as the thought occurred to her, Isbet knew that it was more than just possible. "You didn't tell him about the dogs?"

"It was his treacherous nature." The ghost spat out the words. "Which I did not see until it was too late. I refused to impart my secrets, and he slew me for it."

"I am sorry I was away so long," was the only response Isbet had.

"Nonsense, child." The witch's voice told Isbet of her fatigue. "Were you lollygagging about? Were you neglecting your studies? I see the staff, so I know you were not. It was to be your reward."

"I impressed my teachers." Isbet managed a tired smile. "I will miss you, Grandmother, and I will do this thing for you. This man will suffer for what he did."

Isbet felt the presence recede behind the veil. "Use your cunning and guile and guard your secrets well."

The veil slipped back into place. Isbet drew in another breath as the loneliness crept upon her. Again, she stared at nothing until Gaemyr, silent through her exchange with the ghost, spoke. "How will we do this?"

The simple question brought Isbet from her musings. "How?"

"It is one thing to seek retribution, quite another to get it."

Isbet chewed on her thumbnail. "And there is the matter of the dogs."

Isbet lapsed into silence again, but it was momentary. "As they say, first things first." She rose on her stiff legs, brushed down her trousers again. "We'll need things from the cottage. I will give her a proper burial before dark."

"Disturbing that no one has ever found her remains."

"I'm certain someone did but those damnable superstitious villagers—" Isbet pursed her lips into a thin line. "Never you mind. Unless they can provide me with information about the king, they're of little use."

Isbet shouldered her pack, then approached Gaemyr and yanked him from the earth.

"I'm hungry," he whined.

"Do you see another soul out here?" For an aged mystical talisman, sometimes he behaved like an insolent child.

"Why not let me devour the king?"

"And have us put to the stake? Are your appetites worth that risk?"

Gaemyr shuddered next to her palm. "I suppose I can manage."

Isbet started back down the dirt road. Although it was early spring, there was a nip in the air and night still descended. She kept a brisk pace as she walked and let her mind ponder the situation.

Having promised her grandmother, she would punish the man who murdered her, but she needed, as her talisman pointed out, a means to do so. There were few ways for a commoner to become a king's confidant.

As though sensing her thoughts, Gaemyr spoke. "Monarchs often take mistresses."

"I will not even dignify that with an answer."

Gaemyr snorted as though put out. "There are worse ways to pass an evening."

"How would you know – ow! Blast you, you piece of rotting—" Isbet held her palm up and looked with annoyance at the splinter lodged in her thumb. Gaemyr grinned at her from where she had dropped him in the dirt.

"Serves you right."

Isbet supposed it did. Gaemyr often made a point of reminding her he had not always been in his present condition, although Isbet didn't know what he was before his transformation or why he was in his wooden prison. She was certain she didn't want to know. Since she needed the staff and the power he possessed, Isbet thought it wise not to antagonize him further. "My apologies, I meant no offense."

"Yes, well," Gaemyr grumbled, "mind yourself."

Isbet rummaged through her pack for a pin and wasted precious time removing the splinter. The sun was beginning its descent by the time they reached the cottage.

The old witch had built her home off the main road, hidden within the forest just out of view. It appeared as many expected the home of a village witch to be. Humble yet serviceable. What the people didn't see were the many wards and safeguards around the cottage. They were already fading with the witch's death. Isbet would have to see to this.

Despite her years, her grandmother had kept the thatched roof well mended; the gray stone facade remained without cracks, put together so well there were no noticeable seams. It was possible through a mixture of magic and help from the Children.

Sunlight glinted off the panes of glass in the square windows, reflecting the light back, making them appear mirror-like. There was no need for curtains as the glass held enchantments that prevented anyone from seeing inside. Isbet started up the stone path.

At the threshold, Isbet leaned down and spoke in whispers to the lock. Locks had power all their own and were vital to many a spell casting. At the sound of the click, Isbet pushed the door open with her free hand.

The cottage was as Isbet had left it earlier. She stood just inside the door and for the third time that day felt the grief in the bottom of her soul well like a river swollen at spring thaw. It surprised Isbet, the childlike whimper that escaped her lips. Everything in the common room was in its place, but Isbet's eyes fell on the old rocker beside the fireplace. In her elder years, the witch needed the warmth to soothe her old bones, as she was so fond of saying. She would sit there, wrapped in a quilt. It was a gift from a villager in gratitude for her delivering a healthy baby boy.

Isbet propped Gaemyr against the wall and closed the door.

"Here now, what's this?" the talisman demanded.

Isbet approached the chair and picked up the quilt. She wrapped it around her much as her grandmother had done. It had a musty, comfortable smell – one of home. She kept it around her as she made a slow circuit of the room. The cottage was much larger inside than outside. Shelves lined the opposite wall filled with dusty tomes of many sizes. Isbet had read them all. She let her fingers brush across them and experienced their sparks of power.

The sturdy table sat in the middle of the room, polished to a shine. Two chairs. It had always been that way since Isbet had arrived. There was a matching cabinet made by the same hands, artisan's hands. Within were stacks of mismatched dishes and crude utensils, yet they served their purpose.

Isbet avoided the flight of stairs that led to the second floor and her old room. She didn't wish to go there, although it had been as warm and rustic as the rest of the cottage, and she would not go into the witch's bedroom.

The kitchen was next. The old wood stove sat against the far wall. It was cold now, the remains of the witch's breakfast in an iron pot. Dried herbs, flowers, and fruits hung from the ceiling, or were stuffed into baskets affixed to the wall. They filled the kitchen with their various scents.

Sacks and barrels overflowing with vegetables from their garden sat in the corner to her left. There was a chopping block used for food and for making potions. There were more shelves against the right wall, where tiny bottles sat, holding many salves and liquids. There was another cabinet taking up the remaining room, made up of dozens of tiny drawers containing more tools and examples of her grandmother's craft. There was no great black cauldron as many people thought witches owned. It was a ridiculous notion. What did one need with such a thing? her grandmother had always said. She had a small one, squatting on the chopping block.

Isbet left the kitchen and her eyes fell once again on the rocking chair.

No longer able to keep her grief at bay, Isbet crossed the room and went on her knees before it. She could imagine the old witch filling the space, her ample girth holding scents of potions and spices, her voice carrying strongly to fill the room and Isbet's mind with her secrets.

She was a witch. An ugly old crone, some had whispered behind her back. A dangerous woman who incited fear and revulsion, yet the hypocrites came to her to cure their ills and solve their problems. To them, the old witch was a tool. To Isbet, she was her only family.

The girl was no longer the witch Isbet, but a woman who had lost. She laid her arm across the seat, buried her face in its crook, and wept.

CHAPTER TWO

An overwhelming silence filled the library as Bram watched the aging envoy sign the surrender. Slim fingers, rough and mottled with age, moved without rush across the sheet of vellum. His name was Esten Tallan, current advisor and prince-regent of Avynne. The entourage of six men and women who had accompanied him on the supposed peace delegation huddled in the left corner of the room, not daring to disturb the quiet.

The only reason Bram was present was that Wilhelm Stark, current ruler of Rhyvirand, had commanded him. Wilhelm had conquered Avynne, as he had Bram's own country of Tamrath. It seemed forever ago and yet only yesterday that Bram stood in this room as a hostage for their conqueror – to ensure that his beloved Tamrath would surrender. Watching his brother, Jaryl, bent over the same document.

Bram had begged Jaryl not to do it. He had told him that his life was not worth their people losing their country to Wilhelm. Jaryl was now the ruler of Tamrath – a duty he did not expect so soon or want. The war, more like a mild skirmish, had ended with Bram stripped of his identity. He was no longer the Arch-bishop and Prince of Tamrath. He was a pawn of their enemy.

It was over. Bram had barely noticed, but there was no welcome release of tension for him or anyone. The old man held himself with an air of dignity. Even if his people were now the vassals of their enemy, he considered himself the better man.

Not that it matters here, Bram thought.

"Why did not King Wilhelm himself meet us?" Tallan eyed the corpulent man sitting on the other side of the table with annoyance. Ancer Fallor was Wilhelm's supposed advisor, although Wilhelm never went to him for counsel. He was merely a figurehead. Someone to do the unpleasant chores of the kingdom. Yet Ancer was convinced of his importance.

"Why ever should he?" Ancer raised an arched brow. "You are a servant required to perform a simple task."

There was no reaction to show his insult, save the twitch of a muscle beneath Tallan's right eye. Bram's hands fisted at his side, and he bit down on the inside of his lower lip to stave off any harsh comment.

A polite knock at one of the opulent double doors drew Bram's attention away. It opened moments later. Two guards entered, followed by a woman – a nurse, Bram guessed by the make and pristine cleanliness of her uniform – who led a boy of about six years before her.

"Ah!" Ancer turned in his armchair. "The boy is well?"

"Yes, my lord," the nurse replied. She gave him a gentle push. The boy approached the table, glancing at Bram before his attention returned to Ancer.

Bram remembered his own examination. Strangers prodding at him while asking him questions that had made him blush with shame. They pronounced him healthy and fit. Triune forbid they would say otherwise.

"Your name is Seth, is it not?" Ancer smiled to endear himself to the boy, the duplicity of it easy to hear.

The boy fought to control his fear. He drew himself up, yet his hands remained balled into fists at his side. "I-I am Prince Seth Oran of Avynne, son of King Alir Oran. Y-you will show me the respect I am due."

Bravo. Bram liked the boy prince. Tallan didn't speak but Bram noticed his lips upturning in a slight smile. His eyes filled with pride.

"Now see here, young man—" Ancer started but seemed to think better of it. He laughed nervously. "Your fire will impress my king. I hope you realize what a wonderful opportunity he has awarded you." Ancer nodded to Bram. "Bram here can tell you. Wilhelm is working to unite all the kingdoms as in centuries past. You should be proud to be a part of that."

"I—" Seth began, his voice strengthened. "I want to go home."

A change in the tone of his voice showed Ancer's ire at Seth's continued defiance. "You are home. You will call Wilhelm father, and you will be his son."

Just liked he'd done to Bram. He hated calling Wilhelm father; it was bitter on his tongue every time he said it. Bram didn't know what sickness of the mind caused Wilhelm to continue to exert power over him.

"I won't call him father!" Seth's whole body stiffened, resolute. "I am not his son!"

Bram's lips went up in a self-satisfied smirk. Each passing moment impressed him.

"Cease this foolishness." Ancer waved in a dismissive gesture. "You'll mind your elders or face punishment."

"You can't punish me! I am a prince of—"

"Seth." All eyes now fell on Tallan. "You are a prince of the realm. Behave." The words, although an admonishment, held a note of familial affection.

"But Uncle—"

Uncle? His throat constricted. Often important officials were close relatives. Who else could you trust?

"Come here." Tallan turned in his chair and held out his arms.

"Now wait—"

"Lord Ancer." Bram refused to keep silent any longer. "Is there any harm in the two saying goodbye?"

Ancer's mouth opened as though to give further protest. Bram gave him a look that made him close it again. The only good that had come out of his situation was that Wilhelm made it very clear that Bram was now a Prince of Rhyvirand, and the kingdom would treat him as such. That gave Bram some freedom to move about the estate as he liked.

Uncle and nephew conversed in whispers. After a time, Seth's eyes welled with tears. His uncle touched the tip of Seth's nose and leaned close, continuing to share perhaps secrets or simple advice as Seth nodded. The boy sniffled once then composed himself with much effort. A grown-up endeavor that took more strength than a boy his age should need.

"You will make your father proud, agreed?"

"Agreed, Uncle." Seth wiped at his eyes with the back of his hand. He then turned to Ancer, bowed and said, "At your service."

Bram could watch no more. He turned and strode from the room, ignoring the surprised stares, not caring what they thought. Bram didn't walk far, halting at the first cross-hall he came to and leaning against the wall, his hand splayed against his face.

Despite the surrounding opulence, Bram hated this place. What did it matter they treated him well? That he had power to exert as he had when he ordered Ancer silent? This was not his home. Bram had only visited the manor once before, when his father had been invited by the old king and queen before their deaths.

The palatial estate was a grand old building of gray stones set at the far border of Rhyvirand's capital, Faircliff. Wilhelm insisted the interior be pristine. Not fortified for battle as the castles of old were, it was more a place to show off wealth and power. After visitors crossed the threshold, as the heavy oak doors remained open during the day, they would find themselves in the front gallery with a high-domed ceiling made of stained glass. Sunlight poured in, throwing patterns and shadows. The glass ceiling depicted dogs, sitting at attention on top of three massive treasure chests. From there were hallways, at four points of the compass. The North Corridor led to the Great Hall, where Wilhelm went about the affairs of business every day.

The second floor had many receiving rooms for guests and the king's parlor where he often entertained. At the West Corridor, was the library where Bram had been. The third floor was for the royal family alone. They decorated the rooms in different themes but always tastefully. The beds were large and plush, the sheets silk with downy quilts and piles of pillows. Bram's room was there, although he seldom enjoyed it. It was a place to lay his weary head after a day of self-recrimination and guilt.

If Bram was here, despite the circumstances, protocol demanded, as Tallan had reminded Seth, that he behave in a manner befitting a prince, never showing his true feelings – anger, frustration, and humiliation.

"Protocol be damned," Bram muttered, although even as he spoke the defiant words, he would continue to behave as expected. Years of tutoring and drilling on how princes should conduct themselves had been ingrained into his being.

It was a few moments before Bram realized he heard footsteps. He straightened away from the wall as Tallan and his entourage moved down the corridor, accompanied by the two guards. Bram had a twinge of irritation. Just what did Ancer believe Tallan would try to do?

As they approached, Tallan caught sight of him. "Hold one moment."

Seeing Bram, the guards made no protest. Tallan moved to stand before him. "Prince Greyward," he whispered, using Bram's family name, "would you grant me a favor?"

The request surprised him. As much power as he had, it only went so far.

"Would you," Tallan said, "look after my nephew?"

Words eluded him. "Me, sir?"

"Can I trust you to take care of him and to keep him from harm?"

"No one will harm him," Bram said. "I can assure you of that." Then, knowing he was taking a risk, Bram added, "He's of no use to the king injured or ill. He will receive well treatment."

"Perhaps, but—" Tallan hesitated. "I don't want him corrupted. There are things he needs to understand and things he doesn't."

"Yes." Bram knew all too well. He tried to smile. "I will look after him."

"Thank you." Tallan extended his hand and Bram grasped it. He realized by the rough quality and firm grip that Tallan was no soft politician but had a fighter's experience and will. "Good fortune."

"Indeed," Bram said. "To both of us."

The young prince watched as the entourage continued. The guards would keep with them as far as the border, where Tallan would return to a kingdom bereft of its heir. Bram waited alone in the corridor until he again heard footsteps. The nurse was leading Seth by the hand. Bram experienced a twinge of guilt for leaving the boy alone with Ancer, curious what the advisor might have said. Bram stepped in their path. "That will be all for now."

"Yes, Highness." She bobbed a curtsy and hurried off.

Seth looked at him with large dewy eyes, deep blue over an upturned nose and full lips. Dark curls were in a permanent state of disarray and Bram imagined whoever cared for Seth had a time getting his locks to behave. Bram smiled down at him. *He will break many a maiden's heart when he grows up.*

"Seth—" What to say to the lad? He ran his hand through his hair as he searched for the right words. "Let's go for a walk."

Bram held out his hand and Seth, after a moment's hesitation, slid his small and soft hand into Bram's larger callused one.

Bram led the boy through the halls and, as any child would do, Seth looked about with unbridled curiosity at everything around him. When they came to a set of doors also in stained glass, this time depicting a scene of dogs surrounded by flames as they devoured the king's supposed enemies, Bram shuddered as he reached for the brass handle. Before them lay an enclosed garden that served as a haven from the cold stone and metal. Arrangements of exotic flowers – orchids, calla lilies – followed the curve of a circular path set in the gray stone. A peach tree stood at its center; its new buds were just beginning to open. It was early spring, cool but comfortable. Bram led Seth to one of the two cast-iron benches on either side of the circle.

"I will not say either of us is fortunate because we are not," Bram began. "But I promised your uncle I would look after you and I will."

"I know," Seth whispered.

"I think we should be friends, Seth."

He looked up and something akin to hope gleamed in his eyes. "Can we? I'd like that."

"So would I," Bram said.

"You won't leave me, will you?"

Bram laid his arm across Seth's shoulders. "I'll try not to."

Seth moved over and leaned against Bram. "I want my father."

"I know." Bram rested into the boy in kind. How would Seth feel if he were to return home to find nothing was as he had left it? He hoped Seth never found out what his father had done. How he had abandoned his kingdom and his people to become the pawns of a foreign invader wearing the guise of a friend.

"There you are!" Ancer came huffing up to them. Like Seth, Bram had been defiant to the man on sight. "I've been looking all over for you."

Since the open garden was close to the library, Bram doubted that was true. "I'm giving Seth the time he needs to adjust."

Seth had latched onto the sleeve of his shirt and hid his face against Bram's forearm. Bram patted his hand, hoping to convey his thoughts: *Don't worry, I said I wouldn't leave you.*

"The king has granted him an audience in his private study," Ancer said. "You'll come with me now, young man."

The grip on Bram's sleeve tightened. "I will escort him," Bram said.

"Prince Bram, I don't—"

"Lord Ancer, is there an issue with my escorting him? Was there some reason you needed to speak with the king?"

There wasn't and Ancer knew it. Seth was showing more maturity than Ancer.

"Very well, Highness."

Bram didn't miss the inflection on his title. It seemed Ancer had scored a point. As Bram walked by, Ancer reached out and grasped Bram by the shoulder.

"Don't be so smug in your supposed power, Bram."

"I have power over you, at least," Bram shot back, "and don't you ever put your hands on me again." Un-princely of him, he knew, but the fear in Ancer's eyes was most gratifying. Bram jerked his shoulder away and pulled Seth indoors.

"Bram?"

"What? Yes, Seth?"

"You – you won't get into trouble because of me, will you?" The boy looked up at him with plaintive eyes.

Bram worked to quell his temper, knowing he shouldn't upset the lad because he let Ancer rile him. He knelt before Seth and mussed his hair. "No." Then in a conspiratorial fashion, Bram whispered, "Ancer is just an old windbag."

Seth giggled and pressed both hands to his mouth to stifle the sound.

Bram grinned at him. Seth blushed but looked pleased to be sharing a secret with an adult.

As they continued down the hall, Seth asked, "What is the king like?"

Bram realized he had to choose his words. As much as he wanted to tell the boy the true nature of the man who he would call father, any unflattering remarks would have repercussions.

"He is a very—" Bram sighed. "He will not behave like we suppose a king should. He will be open and does not require you to kowtow to him overmuch. He will speak to you as a confidant and treat you as one unless you cross him and then – well – while he shows mercy, he will clarify that the punishment for betrayal is severe. People note him for his flamboyant generosity to those in his confidence and how he wishes to surround himself with beautiful things." *Like the two of us.*

Various emotions came and went on Seth's innocent face. They ranged from confusion to fear to curiosity. "Is he much like my father?"

A tremor passed through Bram. "Yes. The king is like your father."

They were silent for the rest of their walk.

Bram could walk to the king's study blindfolded, having been summoned there enough times. The two guards nodded to him as they approached. One turned and knocked, then opened the door, allowing them entry. As he did so, music floated from within, filling the hall with the dulcet notes of a piano. It seemed the king was entertaining.

"I can play," Seth whispered.

"Really?" Bram said with interest. "Will you play for me, sometime?"

"Yes."

As the two stepped into the room, Seth's eyes widened in astonishment. Bram couldn't help but smile at the boy. He had the same reaction when he first took in the king's study.

Tall arched windows allowed the sunlight to bathe the room in its warm glow and the occupants to witness a spectacular view of the city as its buildings created a patchwork quilt of color. To the left was the king's work area. There was an enormous desk, surrounded by shelves lined with leather-bound tomes. The desk itself was cluttered with various papers and ledgers waiting for the king's perusal.

Placed around the room were other methods of entertainment. The space boasted a billiard table, dartboard, and a card table, along with comfortable chairs and sofas plush and soft, waiting for a weary traveler. There was also a sideboard and well-stocked liquor chest. Even the floor beneath their feet reflected opulence – tiles of pale marble veined with gray.

There was a ruddy-skinned young man around Bram's age playing the piano. Bram had seen him wandering around the estate, but no one had thought to introduce him. He was quiet and often kept to himself. There were rumors about what purpose he served. It was common knowledge that the king was not faithful to the queen. Even more astonishing was that the queen didn't seem to care.

The royal couple sat at a lunch table next to one window, playing a game of tiles. Dressed in a silk high-necked shirt, dark trousers, and soft slippers, the king gave no sign of his station unless you counted the signet ring he wore.

His wife preferred to appear in public dressed as was befitting her station. She wore a scoop-necked ivory gown with a flared hem and embroidered with gold thread. Her blonde hair was piled atop her head and secured with gold needles. A choker band encrusted with pale onyx encircled her creamy throat. A matching ring adorned her finger, where there should have been her wedding band.

Bram often wondered if the queen loved the king at all. Rumor had it she didn't, but loved to be queen. And if her royal husband kept her in comfort, she saw no reason to make a fuss over his dalliances.

Many rumors surrounded the man. Since Bram had lived at the estate, the king's appearance had improved. When Bram first laid eyes on him, he'd had a tanned face, showing the first signs of age, with a craggy roughness of the common soldier the people thought him to be. Now the tanned complexion glowed with the smoothness of youth. His hair had been showing the first hints of gray and receding at his forehead. It was now black and lustrous, much like Bram's own. It was as though he was losing years – becoming a young man again. There were whispers in the night of dark magic and talk of strange goings on in the cellars below the estate.

"My dear," the king was saying, "I believe you've been practicing in secret."

The queen smiled at him. "And if I have, my husband?"

"Then I shall have to do the same," he said. "You've trounced me in how many games? What do I owe you?"

"A few baubles and trinkets." She inclined her head to Bram and Seth. "Good afternoon, Bram."

Bram bowed. "Good afternoon, Your Majesty." Then he turned to the king and inclined his head. "Prince Seth Oran of Avynne, as you commanded, Father."

"Splendid." The king grinned. "Bram, I'm pleased you came. I would have summoned you. I have a task for you but right now— Approach me, Seth."

Seth looked up in question at Bram. The king's smile faltered.

"Seth, it's all right. Don't be frightened." Bram nodded.

"I understand your fear, Seth," the king said. "Trust me when I say you find yourself in a fortunate position. My name is Wilhelm, but I would like for you to call me father."

"Yes, sir." Seth looked at his toes.

"He is a handsome young man," the queen said. "Do you play rune tiles, Seth?"

"Yes – Your Majesty."

"Then perhaps you can give me more of a challenge than my husband." She smiled at the lad.

"All right."

Wilhelm rose. "I suppose our talk can wait." He mussed Seth's hair much like Bram had done. Seth took Wilhelm's place at the table.

"Walk with me, son." Wilhelm laid a hand on Bram's shoulder. Bram, however, couldn't stop himself from looking back at Seth, but the queen had his attention. Bram wasn't certain how he felt about that. He realized he wanted to be Seth's only friend and confidant, which was absurd, he knew, but since he had no one else he could confide in, Bram realized he needed the boy in his life.

Bram knew the queen seemed patient with children but preferred to be free. The royal couple didn't have children by birth, which fueled the rumors that the queen was barren, or the king was unable, but no one discussed it.

Wilhelm led Bram onto the terrace. The air had that crisp scent of coming spring. Of life renewing itself and waking from its long winter slumber.

"As you know," the king began, "we have been in talks with both Chirilith and Chira. Chirilith is proving to be a challenge to have them come to our way of thinking but considering the size of the kingdom, we must take care. Now, Chira is another matter altogether."

Bram tried to feel empathy for the kingdoms and their rulers, but he found it difficult. He couldn't stop the flush of embarrassment over his emotions.

The king placed his hands on Bram's shoulders. "You are not supportive of either country. Good."

Damn you, Bram wanted to shout, *using my emotions against me this way!*

"I want you to travel with the next envoy to Chira." Wilhelm held Bram's gaze, which always made the prince uncomfortable. Something in Wilhelm's eyes made Bram and others want to obey. Again, Bram recalled the whispers of dark magic. "Tell them of how well you get on here. How you are being groomed to rule your kingdom."

Lie for you so they will find favor with you. "Yes, Father."

"And I will tell you, my dear boy, that Chirilith is not willing to help Chira, any more than they helped Tamrath, despite the history that their peoples have. All that bad blood and such."

"Yes, of course."

"Chira is being difficult, and their queen is listening to many unsubstantiated rumors about our person and our land."

Unsubstantiated – gods, how he hated this man.

"Use that undeniable charm of yours, son." Wilhelm tapped his chin with one finger. "A pity she is so much older than you. Perhaps an offer of marriage— Oh, don't look so contrite! She's an old maid not even worthy of you.

"However," the king turned away from him, "we have to consider a suitable bride for you, but that is a talk for another time."

"Yes, sir."

"You will leave in two days' time."

"Overland?"

Again, the king regarded him. "I trust there will be no issues for you traveling through Tamrath?"

Bram's throat tightened and he swallowed. Gods, Tamrath – Jaryl! He couldn't – couldn't. Not there. Wilhelm had to realize it would destroy him.

"It will be a confirmation of your loyalty." Wilhelm walked along the terrace rail and traced the intricate carving with one finger.

"Will I – be calling upon the patriarch?" Bram forced the words past his lips.

"No." Wilhelm leaned in a casual stance with his back against the rail. "This is none of their concern."

It mortified Bram to feel his eyes burn with unshed tears. "As you wish, Father." An idea occurred to him. He didn't want to leave Seth alone for as long as the journey would take. "Father, may Seth accompany me?"

Wilhelm lifted one arched brow. "Hmm – a good idea. Yes, take Seth along. That will give you time to coach him."

"Thank you." Bram couldn't hide his relief. At least that went in his favor.

"Let's rejoin my wife and your young charge," Wilhelm said. As protocol dictated, Bram stepped aside so the king could precede him. Even with Wilhelm's back to him, Bram kept his face schooled. Eyes followed him everywhere.

His thoughts, however, were tumultuous.

So, I am to be your instrument of betrayal now. You are a coward, Wilhelm of Rhyvirand. Someday you will receive your due.

CHAPTER THREE

Isbet set the little doll on the dressing table and opened its jointed mouth with a deft motion of her finger. As with the Duine Shee cameo, the doll appeared as something ordinary at first glance, a child's toy with a cherubic painted face and straight black hair, clothed in a flower print dress.

"And just who will have an interest in our affairs?" Gaemyr was leaning against the small circular table where Isbet had spread a map. Although she didn't want for money, she had chosen one of the poorer inns of the city for various reasons. Isbet had no desire to become the latest mark for any thieves or cutpurses; although she could defend herself, it was such a bother. She didn't want someone to remember her face, considering what she planned to do.

Now, with the doll on her dresser, there was no chance of someone overhearing.

"Are you certain you're not tired?" Gaemyr asked. Isbet knew he wasn't asking because of her welfare.

"I am, but I'll sleep later." Isbet leaned over the map, tracing the borders between the kingdoms of Rhyvirand and its nearest neighbors, Avynne and Tamrath.

Isbet had learned many interesting things in the village of Wicayth, which her grandmother called home.

She remembered the last time she saw her grandmother's cottage, the day she set out on her current journey.

★　★　★

After spending a fitful night in the bed she'd slept in as a child, Isbet had awakened to a dismal gray morning that matched her mood to perfection.

Her first task was to see the magistrate and demand an explanation concerning her grandmother.

Isbet moved through the cottage on the pretense of gathering the things she felt she needed. This took no real thought on her part. She opened secret compartments and hideaways as she chose the best talismans, potions, and magical implements to aid her in her task.

Yet even as her movements were methodical, Isbet would pause every so often to touch a treasured memento or some shiny trinket, and the memory behind it filled her mind and caused a smile to come.

The villagers never entered the cottage out of fear, so all her grandmother's possessions remained safe. What she couldn't take with her she took to the catacombs underneath the great tree.

Isbet knew even without looking that the thief had stolen the most important item.

The Box.

Gaemyr leaned against the wall next to the front door, his eyes closed. He appeared to slumber but Isbet knew the staff didn't want for or ever need sleep, and as a testament, his eyes opened as Isbet set her much heavier backpack down with a thump.

"Will you have me destroy this place?"

She sighed. "We must. The wards are fading. Soon someone who is not dumbstruck by superstition will come and—" Isbet didn't even want to consider someone entering her grandmother's home.

"I will have to feed once I am done."

"You will," Isbet said. "I will see to it."

It took some time for her to position the pack, which was uncomfortable with her jacket and gloves. Once the last frost passed, she wouldn't need the cumbersome thing.

Isbet grabbed Gaemyr, who muttered a protest. She didn't look back as she closed the door behind her.

Her feet trod the dirt path one last time. When she believed she was a safe distance away, she drove Gaemyr into the ground once again.

Isbet sat and took a few moments to arrange the folds of her coat. She reached out with her Gift, touching on the patterns and lines of light that made the wards around the cottage, dispelling them with a touch of her essence or a whispered word. Gaemyr breathed through his mouth, dispelling what appeared to be a cloying mist. Isbet knew it was something altogether different. It poured from his lips and spilled onto the earth, seeping into the richness. There was the smell of the forest – of fertile loam and decaying leaves, of the crispness of autumn and the newness of spring.

Then the earth began to tremble.

The first sign that Gaemyr was at work was the groaning of the old wood that made the walls of the cottage. There was a crack, and the wood splintered as though struck with a mighty ax from within. Isbet sensed that, underneath the foundation, the earth was splitting; a tangle of vines forced their way through the dirt, tearing the floorboards asunder, filling every space, nook, and crack, breaking through stone and wood and metal. Roots plunged deep into the earth, birthing a nimble sapling, which matured with impossible speed.

Branches burst through the roof, spreading their ever-strengthening limbs to the sun, shredding the tiles like vellum until it caved in with a violent crash. On the path, new grass burst forth, growing tall and supple, wiping it from existence.

Isbet wasn't aware that she was biting her lower lip so hard it bled. She pushed herself from her position, stumbling from the stiffness in her legs. She forced herself up again, wiping at her tears.

Stop it! she admonished herself. *Stop being such a child. You have a task before you!* Still, Isbet didn't return to the clearing until the sounds of destruction had faded into silence.

★   ★   ★

Isbet walked into Wicayth in the late afternoon. It was a good-sized village with a steady commerce. She was no stranger to the place. Still, people didn't recognize her since she had been abroad for a few years. Although she received a few nods, most noticed the purpose in her expression and her pace, and they left her alone.

The magistrate's office was in the center of town in a cul-de-sac of official buildings with a communal pool and garden at its center. Children splashed about in the water under their mothers' watchful eyes. As Isbet strode by, some of the children stopped in their play to watch her pass. Isbet winked and the children fled with excited squeals and giggles.

The doors to the magistrate's office stood open, welcoming all who wished to see him. Unlike in the larger cities, the magistrate's office was in his home. He received visitors in the front room, with the living quarters closed off to anyone not invited.

"May I help you?"

Isbet hadn't noticed the young woman sitting at a desk in the entrance hall. She, however, noted Isbet's dress and her staff. Her eyes widened.

"Forgive me, my lady, did you come to visit the magistrate?"

"Celine, who's there?"

Before the girl could answer, a young man stepped through an entryway to her right. He was not the magistrate she remembered, who was a plump old man who loved his food and his ale. This man was only a few years older than Isbet, with an unruly mop of red hair and deep green eyes, a rarity in this part of the country – unless one had the Gift or were fey. Still, he was attractive.

He studied Isbet for a moment before saying with a slight inclination of his head, "My lady witch."

"Good day," Isbet said. "Is Magistrate Dobbins in?"

"Magistrate Dobbins passed away some time ago," the man said. "I am Magistrate Edolin. You have been away for a long time."

Now Isbet studied him. "I don't quite recall—"

"You wouldn't," he said. "I take it you're here about the wood witch?"

"Why were my grandmother's remains left to rot in the forest?"

Isbet heard Celine draw in a breath. Edolin glanced at her. "Celine, would you fetch my lunch, please?"

"Yes, sir." It didn't take one with the Gift to sense the girl's relief at escaping.

"Please follow me." Edolin stepped aside and motioned Isbet inside the room. "Please sit. Would you like some tea?"

"No, thank you." Isbet removed her pack and set it at her feet before she sat in one of the worn yet comfortable chairs.

Edolin didn't take a seat, however, and moved about the room as he spoke. "You must excuse me if I perform some breach of protocol. This is the first time I have hosted anyone of the Gifted."

"You have my word no ill luck will befall your house."

"I've not been long in this position, and you'll find I'm much more tolerant than the older citizens of this town."

"I am glad."

"Have you heard anything of the goings on in Faircliff?"

"No," Isbet said. "I have been on the other side of the continent."

"Quite a distance."

"Indeed."

"We are uncertain who murdered the wood – your grandmother," Edolin said. "But there have been many strange occurrences in the land and the people think the culprit to be someone with the Gift or their like, and those who would have buried her stayed away in fear. I'm sorry, that was before I came here."

"Your color suggests you're from somewhere much further north."

He smiled at her. "Correct." Edolin moved over to a fireplace and ran a finger along the mantel, frowning at the dust he found there. "I think you'll find your answers in Faircliff. A new king lives in the palatial estate."

"The old king passed away?"

"Executed, as far as anyone here knows."

"For what crime?"

Edolin shook his head. "No crime. They say a usurper killed both the queen and king and forced their daughter into marriage. Others say the princess conspired with a common soldier to commit regicide and they set themselves up as king and queen." He walked to the window. "The land prospered under them so there was no dissension. The king has…annexed both Tamrath and Avynne, and how he accomplished this has a variety of explanations."

He turned to face her. "Some say it is dark magic. People are of two minds – if the kingdom prospers, what should it matter? So what if there are some strange beasts in the forest or ghost lights hovering over the lake? Others—"

"And of what mind are you?" Although Isbet could venture a guess, as his body language told her of his confusion and uncertainty.

"All I know is—" Edolin didn't seem to realize he'd wandered off on a different path, "—whoever killed your grandmother, they were no parlor magician, but I'm sure you know that."

"You think this man who is king may have had something to do with it?" Isbet said. "Yes, it would make sense to destroy your rivals in magic to ensure your place."

"Mistress, if you go there, I advise not to show your true power." Edolin blushed. "Please forgive me."

Isbet stood and gave him a smile. "I take no offense. Thank you for your concern and your time."

"You're welcome," he said.

"Now I have something for you." Isbet undid the strings on a pocket of her pack. From its recesses, she pulled a gold coin. "Keep this always. It will bring you great luck."

"Thank you." Edolin took her hand and raised it to his lips. "I wish you a safe journey."

Isbet left the magistrate's house with her thoughts in turmoil. Her grandmother's spirit said her murderer was in a position of power. This supposedly common man accomplished the impossible without help or disruption of the veils. A foolish mortal dabbling in magic where they had no training or knowledge could cause disturbances of the fragile balance between the mundane and supernatural. A misspoken word or incorrect inflection could cause any spell to go awry, and continued use of a magical talisman giving nothing in return could bring about chaos.

Edolin, for all his being a country bumpkin, was correct. Isbet would find her answers in Faircliff.

★　　★　　★

Isbet rolled the map and secured it with string. "I must get near Wilhelm."

For once Gaemyr didn't comment. Before they arrived in Faircliff, they had the good fortune of coming upon a prison cart trundling down the road in the opposite direction. There were seven men inside the cage, two of whom were going to the chopping block. Gaemyr had pointed out one of them. "His soul is so black that he would be better off devoured by me."

Isbet followed the cart for a time until the driver stopped to relieve himself. She stole alongside it and before the prisoners' cries could summon the guard, Gaemyr feasted with relish, and had been lethargic since.

It was dusk before she arrived at the city gates, so Isbet asked the guard directions to the nearest inn, deciding not to waste time finding an out-of-the-way place. The one she chose was reasonably cheap and the room clean and serviceable. All the walking was catching up to her and after removing her boots, she stretched out across the bed.

"If you do not wish to be the king's mistress," Gaemyr said, "you must gain his confidence." His words were followed by a yawn. "Perform some tasks for his benefit? Save him from assassination?"

"Now you speak absurdities." Isbet sat down on the bed. "And yet these countries, Tamrath and Avynne, must have some faction planning rebellion. Don't they have their own Gifted ones? Even with the dogs, how did Wilhelm accomplish their capture without the force of arms?"

"There are places where you can find out."

"Yes." Isbet's lips upturned in a thoughtful smile. "Then let us visit them."

It was full dark when Isbet went out into Faircliff and as with others Isbet had visited in the past, all had their places of disrepute. Though there were many present with the Gift, most refused to speak with her at all. Even that told Isbet much. It was the citizens without the Gift, the ones who stood to lose the most, who provided Isbet with the answers she sought.

CHAPTER FOUR

There were at least fifty people in their entourage. Bram was of two minds regarding his position in the group. He was glad Wilhelm had given him full authority; even more so that he didn't insist Ancer come along. However, in true form, the king had made certain that each person represented his interests and his alone.

Besides himself and Seth, there was the nurse who had seen to the boy – Bram learned her name was Omiri – and his own personal valet, an older man named Evarran, who spoke little and replied to questions in a lifeless monotone. Bram knew he would perform his duties to the utmost, but he dared not confide anything to him. Evarran had been in Wilhelm's service from the start of his reign.

He also found himself saddled with the king's guest, the olive-skinned man who would serve as Bram's clerk. He introduced himself as Rajan and seemed friendly enough, but Bram had to question his motives. There was a steward to handle the food, an apprentice equerry for the horses, a captain, along with a handpicked group of soldiers as bodyguards, and two young women to serve as courtesans. Bram did not intend to take advantage of their services. There was also an assortment of courtiers and servants assigned various duties, few of which Bram remembered.

He did not trust even one of them.

He shared the captain's opinion that the entourage was much too large and would attract unwanted attention. Her name was Isadora Maive and although Bram wouldn't bring himself to trust her, he did respect her. She was an older woman with almost masculine features and steel-gray eyes, whose gaze had people scrambling to carry out her orders. He knew she had been in the service of the old king before Wilhelm came to power. In fact, she was present the day the king and queen perished. Bram didn't interfere with how she commanded her soldiers.

They left the capital with much fanfare. It annoyed Bram. Captain Maive seemed to share his opinion. Once they were out of the city and Bram rode alongside Seth's pony, he began to relax a little.

He was glad Seth was along. Unlike some adults, he didn't mind the boy's endless questions and tried to answer them. That the boy was an accomplished rider didn't surprise him. They had sat Bram on a pony at that tender age and now he rode like the Crown Equerry himself.

The weather remained mild and clear, although the ground beyond the paved road was muddy, and splattered the horses' legs and their riders' expensive boots. Bram, unlike the other courtiers present, had dressed for travel and instructed Seth to do the same. Bram thought with an inward smile, *He's a little boy, mud isn't a problem for him.*

They covered a lot of ground thanks to Captain Maive, or at least what Bram considered a lot. Often, they stayed in towns willing to accommodate them because the courtiers complained when forced to sleep out of doors. Bram spent his evenings with Seth, playing tiles or draughts, while Evarran served them. Rajan went over Bram's schedule and whom he would meet with once they arrived in Chira. Customs were similar there, so Bram didn't worry about offending anyone.

The towns and villages they passed through were all prosperous. There was little poverty in Rhyvirand thanks to the king, but there was something false about the supposed prosperity. People appeared happy but there was always that current of unrest in every spoken word and every smile.

During the entire journey, Bram tried to keep the prospect of returning to Tamrath in the darkest corners of his mind, but as he neared the border, his apprehension grew. It didn't help matters when Captain Maive announced they would travel on Patriarch's Walk, the main thoroughfare through the capital city, which would take him in view of the palatial estate – his true home.

Bram fidgeted in his saddle as the terrain became familiar to him. He sensed the scrutiny of those around him and he knew that some of them were hoping he would try to escape so they could claim responsibility for his capture in hopes of reward.

Bram wasn't successful at all in hiding his feelings, for as they neared the border Seth said, "This is your home, isn't it?"

He looked down to where the boy rode beside him. "Yes."

"Will they let you see your mother and father?"

Bram smiled. "My mother died when I was little. My father—" Bram swallowed; the wound was still raw, "—died a few years ago, in battle."

"I'm sorry," Seth whispered. "Who is king?"

"My older brother, Jaryl," Bram said. "I haven't told you about him, have I?"

Seth shook his head.

"Tamrath is a theocracy," Bram said. "My brother's title is Patriarch."

"What's a – what was that word?"

"The-oc-racy," Bram enunciated. "It means the ruling body is the church."

"Was your father a patriarch, too?"

"Yes."

Seth was silent for a moment. "You said your father died in battle. Did he come for you?"

Bram gripped the reins, the leather biting into his flesh. He let his eyes drift closed as he worked to compose himself. "Yes, he did. The battle he fought was to rescue me."

Seth seemed to ponder this as he worried his lower lip. "Don't feel bad, Bram."

Bram's expression softened as he gazed on the prince in affection. "Sometimes I do, Seth."

"You shouldn't," Seth said. Then he looked away and whispered, "My father didn't come for me."

How to respond? "I'm sure he wanted to, Seth."

"No, he didn't." Seth's lower lip protruded. "I know he ran away."

Bram pulled his mount to a stop and reached down, grabbing at Seth's reins. "Who told you that?"

"The queen," Seth whispered. "She said I shouldn't be ashamed that my father is a coward."

Bram muttered a curse under his breath. Although he was certain the queen had not acted out of malice, he wished she would exercise sensitivity.

Their entourage was slowing, and the captain turned her horse to approach them. Bram released a frustrated breath.

"Come here, Seth." Bram reached out and pulled Seth up onto the saddle in front of him as Bram's own father had done when he was learning to ride. Bram then called to the equerry, who took Seth's pony into his care.

"All is well, sir?" Maive asked.

"Yes," Bram said. He drew Seth against him, and the boy whimpered, snuggling into Bram's chest. The elder prince allowed him to cry.

They rode the rest of the way without speaking. As they approached the border, Bram straightened in his saddle. He was uncertain what or whom he hoped to see. An escort was there to meet them. The sight of the twenty-four mounted men and women in their crimson and gold uniforms brought an ache to Bram's heart. It reminded him of his own uniform, which Wilhelm had confiscated after his capture. As a second son, Bram had worn the rank of Arch-bishop, or more a Prince-bishop, in his country. It was the most prestigious of all the titles he'd held. In Rhyvirand, Bram was free to worship as he pleased, but everything else that he was Wilhelm stripped away. He was a prince now in the king's eyes and nothing more.

The twenty-four saluted and turned in practiced formation to flank the party of riders. The captain approached Bram on his horse. He was no one Bram recognized.

"Your Highness," he said and saluted, which Bram returned. For a moment the captain seemed at a loss, as his mouth worked trying to find the words. "Welcome home."

Triune give me strength. "Thank you."

"I am Captain Tamair," he said. "I have orders to escort you to the northern border. We will at one point take an alternate route as there was a fire in a large part of the city."

"Triune, was the loss great? How many hurt?"

"The loss was great. Many died, others were injured or are without homes." There was an edge to the captain's voice. An almost accusatory tone that filled Bram's heart with guilt, despite knowing there was little he could have done.

"I am sorry," Bram said. "The Patriarch – is he well?"

"Yes, although affairs of church and province weigh on him."

Bram decided to keep his own counsel. What good would it do to call the captain out? "Let's be off then, shall we?"

Tamair bowed in his saddle then turned his mount and signaled to his company.

"Bram?"

Seth had been napping and Bram decided not to disturb him. "Yes?"

"Why do they have gold triangles on their shirts?"

"It symbolizes the Triune," Bram said as he guided his horse forward. "My people believe in three deities who personify the natures of existence."

Seth yawned. "Will you tell me more?"

"Later," Bram said. They had crossed the border into the capital and Bram focused all his attention on his surroundings, drinking them in like a man dying of thirst. The people – his people – would pause in their everyday tasks to stare with mild interest as his party went by, but not long afterward, they returned to their lives. It was as if a knife plunged into his heart. Had his people forgotten him already, or like Tamair, did they despise him for his absence? Perhaps they blamed him for not fighting back and providing the means for their enemy to rob them of their independence.

Bram forced his gaze ahead as they passed the palatial estate.

They came to the burnt-out section of the city sometime later. Barricades blocked other routes, and two guards directed them to a side street. Laborers were busy repairing the damage, and curious despite himself, Bram observed for a time and sighed as he turned away.

The side street was narrow, causing the group to reorganize the line into a double column. Captain Maive directed her soldiers to reposition themselves, one man to every Tamrathi soldier.

The columns started forward as the people pressed themselves against doorways. Children sidled alongside them, staring with bright, curious eyes.

They passed three girls playing skip-rope. Bram couldn't say why they caught his notice. There was something different about them compared to the other children present. Flaxen hair curled and framed porcelain faces smooth and delicate with doe's eyes, upturned noses, and bow-shaped mouths. Their dresses were of white silk tied at the waist with a scarlet ribbon. They resembled dolls more than little girls.

One turned to Bram as she leaped and sang:

Two are the princes of Tam-rath.
Bound by blood and loy-al-ty
Turn the hand of the captive prince
Shroud thee from thy en-emy.

★   ★   ★

Bram startled awake or at least he came back to awareness without realizing he'd been – just what had happened? They were away from the column. It continued as though they didn't exist any—

Merciful Triune, the horses and their riders were passing right through Bram, Seth, and their mounts as if they were insubstantial as smoke.

His gaze tore away from the sight as the girls began to laugh. It was an unpleasant sound, the hysterical cackle of someone close to insanity. Bram gaped as their forms began to blur, becoming enshrouded in fog. He saw images within the gray fog of things with burning eyes and malevolent souls that he'd rather not see.

Bram dug his heels into the horse's flanks, but his mount refused to move. The girls' faces melted into the image of wizened crones with gnarled hands that reached for them.

"Seth! Oh, Triune!" They surrounded him. Everywhere hands grabbed, pulling Seth from his arms.

"No! Foul ones, keep off him!" Bram held on, but the witches had inhuman strength. One dragged Bram from his mount with little effort.

One girl pushed Bram to the ground and was on him, grinning with sharp teeth. She grasped him by the chin, squeezing until his mouth opened. She kissed him.

His breath left his lungs in an agonizing rush, and it seemed forever but was only moments before he plunged into oblivion.

CHAPTER FIVE

"Well, this is interesting," Gaemyr commented.

"Indeed." The veils whipped unseen as though caught in a silent storm. "The spell will incapacitate the caster for some time."

Isbet had taken to the rooftops to follow the prince's procession. At one point she had surprised a washerwoman hanging out clothes and with some slight manipulation, Isbet had gotten her to reveal the 'secret plan' to kidnap the prince. Now Isbet sat at the roof edge, her long legs dangling over the side. She rocked back and forth, the backs of her boots striking the stone.

"Do they have a Gifted here?"

"They do," Isbet said. "If I remember, they use a sorceress, although this is a theocratic land."

"Oh, dear." Gaemyr didn't like the meaning behind her words. "You're certain you want to risk her ire?"

"No," Isbet said. "But as I stated, she is more than likely in deep sleep. This spell took much of her power. Utter foolishness for Wilhelm to send them through Tamrath without some magical warding, unless...."

"A test of loyalty?"

"Precisely."

"This mortal has an odd way of doing things."

"If we are to believe this, he seems to want to trust Prince Bram but to what ends?" Isbet tugged on a braid. "He has Bram's kingdom. He doesn't plan to return him to his place?"

Gaemyr yawned. "I don't understand mortals."

Isbet sat spying for a while longer. Even after the spell ran its course, the procession moved on as though nothing had occurred. The courtiers present, into their own schemes and machinations, noticed nothing until their missing princes came to the attention of one of the Rhyvirand soldiers.

"Fortunately for us, spells such as this leave an obvious trail."

"What will you do?" Gaemyr muttered around his doze. "Steal him away from his kidnappers?"

"Hardly," Isbet said. "This is a volatile situation. I must find out who has stolen him first, before I decide what to do." Isbet swung her legs back over the ledge and stood, stretching the aches from her back. "Let us see where the trail leads us."

★   ★   ★

He was drowning. His chest burned, craving air as his mind screamed for it, forcing him to take that final step. To take that breath that would mean his end.

Bram came awake with his chest aching as though a fire burned within it. All around him was darkness, save a single candle flame.

"My Lord, Arch-bishop?"

Captain Tamair leaned over him. Bram came to realize he lay on a bed. He realized other things as well – the desk on which the candle sat, the chair where Tamair had lounged and the door, which showed a line of light from underneath.

"Why am I here?"

"Please, Highness." It took a few moments for Bram to realize that Tamair's attitude towards him had changed. The man smiled at him with friendship in his eyes. "I will explain all, you have my word."

"Seth, where is Seth?"

"The boy? He's fine, and has quite an appetite," Tamair responded. "The sylphs frightened him. We are sorry but it was necessary."

"Sylphs." Bram moaned and covered his eyes with one hand. "Then it was Coline."

Tamair had the grace to blush. "Yes, Your Most Revered."

Things were making sense now. Bram sat up on the edge of the bed. "How is she?"

"Resting, but she assured us she would be fine." Both Tamair and Bram turned to face the door when someone knocked.

"Enter," Bram said.

The tall, handsome man stepped into the room and grinned at Bram. Despite being dressed in the common garb of a laborer, he still carried that air of command that garnered instant respect. He represented the religion of Tamrath but to Bram, he was more.

"Triune save us all." Bram stood on legs that he was certain would never support him. "Jaryl?"

"Brother." Jaryl's expression melted into one filled with the love and admiration that Bram so missed. The Patriarch of the kingdom of Tamrath began to weep. "Welcome home."

Bram crossed the room, caught his brother in a fierce embrace and kissed him on the cheek. Words tumbled from his lips, all broken on the heaving sobs coming from his throat. He'd been so empty until this moment, existing but not living, bereft of his father, lost to his brother for what he thought was forever, and now Jaryl was here. The man who had looked after him, who had told him all the things he needed to learn about being a man when his father was too busy with affairs of state. He loved his father, but Jaryl was his brother and his friend.

"Bram," Jaryl said as he pulled away, "thank the Triune it worked."

"Jaryl." Bram shook his head. "My loving, foolish brother, what have you done?"

Momentary bewilderment crossed Jaryl's features, then understanding came. "That coward Wilhelm will never find out."

"Don't you think he'll assume—?" The thought of something happening to his brother frightened him. "Do you think I'm able to bear losing both father and you? Wilhelm has spies everywhere."

Jaryl framed Bram's face with his hands. "We've ferreted most of them out," he said. "And even if Wilhelm finds out, what will he do? Coline has assured me—"

"The dogs." Bram shuddered even mentioning them. With Jaryl's hands on his face, Bram felt a shiver pass through his brother.

"I won't let them have you again."

Bram laid his forehead against his brother's. "Jaryl." It had always been like that between them growing up. Unlike many of his peers, Bram had always gotten on well with his older brother. Bram had no real aspirations to the patriarchal seat and ever since they were tiny, Jaryl had sworn that he would always protect Bram no matter how old they became.

"Let's go out, shall we?" Jaryl turned to the door. During their reunion, Tamair had left the room and closed the door behind him. "Your young ward was worried for you. He made it clear – that is before he discovered who I was – that if I so much as brought you to harm, he would kill me in honorable combat. He is of Avynne?"

"Yes."

"He knows about his father, then."

"The queen told him. I thought to hide it from him, but now I wonder if I was mistaken."

"No help for it now," Jaryl said.

Tamair waited outside the door. He straightened away from the wall when Bram and Jaryl exited. Tamair saluted and Jaryl waved the action away. "No need for that."

Outside the door, the hall branched left and right. With the sparse design and decorations, Bram had a good idea of where they were. "This is one of the safe houses."

"Yes." Jaryl smiled. "I think the palatial estate would have been a tad obvious."

"Indeed." Bram had always enjoyed his brother's wit. "Triune, I missed you."

"I missed you, too." Jaryl embraced him again, but mindful of Tamair's presence, he made it brief. "Come, I'll take you to Seth."

★   ★   ★

The safe houses were all over the city of Bishop's Lane, used during times of crisis so that the religious leaders would have a place to find sanctuary. They also harbored guests of the Patriarch who were seeking asylum. They were nondescript, with no special markings to make them stand out from any other house around them, but every member of the ruling family knew their exact location. Only the most trusted of retainers stewarded the houses, usually relatives. A prestigious and comfortable position, the steward, and his family, if applicable, lived in the house without rent and with all their needs provided for.

Bram followed Jaryl to a sunny alcove off the kitchen. Morning sunlight streamed through the open windows. It was homey and comfortable with plush chairs and shelves full of books. A grandfather clock sat in the corner, telling him it was just past nine in the morning.

A light repast, set up on a sideboard, had Bram's stomach growling in response, despite his worry.

Seth was sitting at the table, devouring a plate full of eggs, crisp bacon, and griddle cakes. Bram examined him for a time, relieved to see him well. Across from him sat a young dark-skinned woman whom Bram recognized from way back. A distant cousin, he thought. She was plump with a round and dimpled face and deep-set dark eyes. Like Seth, she'd dressed in a morning robe and slippers and was sipping from a china cup as Seth spoke with animation.

"Seth?" Bram found he didn't want to interrupt, but Seth was concerned about him.

"Bram!" Seth shot out of the chair like an arrow. Bram scooped him up in a hug. "I'm so glad you're safe!"

Bram said, "Are you all right?"

"Those things scared me," Seth said. "But they looked funny to begin with."

"What do you mean?"

Seth's tiny brow furrowed. "They didn't seem like…they were girls."

Bram remembered how they had seemed flawless. "I think I understand."

Meanwhile, the woman had risen from the table and she approached them. "It's good to have you home, Lord Arch-bishop."

Her name came to him. "No need for formalities, Lady Ellyn."

"So, you remember."

"I remember your face."

"You should," Ellyn said. "I remember that kiss you stole during the summer festival when we were twelve."

Jaryl chuckled and Seth's face screwed up. The whole incident became a clear image in his mind, and with it came the memory of the incessant teasing he had endured from his male relations.

His face warmed, Bram replied, "It was a very pleasant experience." He felt a ridiculous measure of satisfaction when Ellyn blushed in kind.

"Come and sit," she said. "We have much to discuss and you are hungry."

Bram moved over to the sideboard and filled his plate. The scents made his stomach growl.

Once seated facing the window, Bram gazed out onto the city. The direction in which the house faced made it impossible for any passerby to glimpse someone at a window. "It's good to be home."

Bram saw Jaryl and Ellyn exchange glances. *They're thinking I'll continue to go along with this.* As much as he wanted to stay, Bram loved his kingdom and his people too much to place them in such danger. "Where are Wilhelm's people?" Bram asked as he sipped flavored coffee.

"Tucked away at the palatial estate," Jaryl said. "Aune is taking care of them."

"How is she?" Along with his first cousin Aune, Jaryl and Bram found themselves in no end of trouble as youths. Daughter of his mother's brother, she had the same mischievous streak as the two of them.

"Very well and taking to her new responsibilities," Jaryl said. "I suppose we all must."

Bram suddenly found himself without appetite. "This is my doing."

"What?" Jaryl and Ellyn said in unison.

"If I hadn't allowed myself to be captured—"

"Stop it," Jaryl said. "You will not blame yourself, do you hear?"

"And just what were you supposed to do?" Ellyn fixed him with a severe gaze.

"Die." Bram shoved back from the table. He turned away, unable to look at them. "Die in combat, a brave man like my father."

He heard the sound of a chair scraping back, and felt familiar hands on his shoulders. "At least you were there," Jaryl said. "You faced the dogs. I allowed an illusion to lead me astray."

"Our mother," Bram said. "How could you not follow?"

"And I lost Father and you," Jaryl said. Then all at once, his gaze turned fierce. "But you're home now and I won't lose you again. Sit, brother, and we'll tell you of our plan."

Bram returned to the table. He smiled at Seth, who seemed upset by his outburst. As they spoke Bram listened, but even as he did, he decided he would have to return to Wilhelm. He didn't have a choice.

"We've already received word from the Duchess in Bale province," Jaryl said. "She agreed to give you temporary asylum."

"Triune, I thought she'd never agree to help us." Bram paused with a forkful of eggs halfway to his lips. "What made her change her mind?"

"Riel didn't expect Wilhelm to take Avynne. Now that he has, well, she's no longer willing to leave things to chance." Jaryl took a sip of coffee before continuing. "Once we have firm positions, I'll send for you." He looked at Seth. "Riel will keep your young charge safe."

"I'm not leaving Bram," Seth said, through a mouthful of griddle cake.

"Seth, it's impolite to speak with your mouth full," Ellyn chided.

The boy looked contrite and swallowed before saying, "I'm sorry, Lady Ellyn."

"You'll have to leave, Highness," Jaryl said. "When Bram is here, he will need to be able to concentrate on the battle. He will need focus. With you to safety, we will have a much better chance."

"Is that true, Bram?"

"Yes, it is," Bram said. "I want you safe." Perhaps he should try to fight again. With Riel on their side, perhaps—

Footsteps sounded in an urgent rhythm and the door burst open. Tamair, drenched in sweat, his chest heaving from a mad flight, his face pale and etched with desperation, said, "Your Majesty, you must leave at once!"

"What is it? What has happened?"

"Damn our enemies," Tamair said. "We've been betrayed."

★   ★   ★

Isbet sat cross-legged on the floor as she stared into the crystal sphere and allowed herself a slight smile of triumph.

"You will be pleased with yourself for many seasons, won't you?"

Isbet ignored the staff, which kept watching over her captive. The young soldier lay prone in the bed. He was snoring.

"Perhaps next time you'll trust my instincts," she said.

Gaemyr snorted.

Isbet had watched the sudden mad rush of the prince and the members of the resistance that had blossomed in Tamrath not long after Wilhelm seized power.

"But they are following a path to failure," Isbet mused aloud. "The Patriarch moved too soon in his desperation. Still, his loyalty and adoration are commendable." Isbet knew of royal siblings constantly at odds, nurturing their petty jealousies and battles, with some hiring assassins. Although she loved her grandmother, Isbet often wished for a brother or sister to share her life. Isbet had acquaintances, not friends. As much as she respected others with the Gift, Isbet trusted few people.

The man next to her emitted a sleepy moan. Isbet had given him a very pleasant dream. It had been much too convenient to catch him, but Isbet had learned to use every advantage.

The trail of magic from the enchantment led Isbet to a section of the city bordering an immense lake. Often sea creatures would wash up onto its shores, much to the delight of some and the chagrin of others. Eager for winter to be over, people gathered around the lake to walk, fish, and play games.

The house where the trail ended looked like every other one on the avenue. It would take weeks for Wilhelm's soldiers to search them all, but then again if the king was so inclined, he wouldn't have to. The dogs would follow the trail. Once she found the house, she placed a marker on the threshold and returned to the site of the enchantment.

Upon inquiring, Isbet learned that Wilhelm's people had demanded escort to the palatial estate. The Tamrathi guards feigned innocence, but their lieutenant agreed. Isbet followed and waited outside the back gates, making a few coins playing the flute. It was near dark by the time her target appeared.

A group of seven Tamrathi soldiers emerged, on their way to the local tavern, laughing, joking, and seeming smug as they swaggered down the avenue. The youngest made the biggest racket and Isbet decided he would be her mark.

Isbet clutched Gaemyr while she followed them at a safe distance, although it wasn't necessary. They weren't paying anyone else the least bit of attention.

"It's strange how, despite being captives in their own land, they still go about their lives as though nothing has changed," Gaemyr said.

"Why is it so strange?" Isbet replied. "What else would they do?"

The soldiers ducked into a lit tavern overflowing with the scents of food, liquor, and exotic perfumes. Isbet wrinkled her nose, preferring the earthy scents of the woods. It was too early in the evening for the patrons to be drunk, although several were well on their way.

When Isbet stepped inside, a familiar sight greeted her: full tables, harried servers and a line of men and women lounging at the bar. The soldiers were just disappearing into a room to her left, and when Isbet stepped across the threshold, she observed the patrons at various games. Cards, billiards, and darts were just some of what she saw, but what caught Isbet's eye was the curtained doorway at the opposite end of the room. She was almost certain of what was within its dark confines.

"May I help you, mistress?" A young server approached her. He looked to be about sixteen, a little old for a server; most boys his age were joining the guard or working the docks. Perhaps it was his appearance. His light coloring and shoulder-length hair gave him an air of femininity that would get him beaten or worse in the rougher parts of the city. "Did you wish to set up a table? The fee is twenty." Educated.

"Yes," Isbet said.

"What do you do? Tell fortunes and futures? Make potions?"

"Both." Isbet was already rummaging in her pack. The lad's eyes widened when he saw the coin and its worth. "The rest is for you and make certain you get it. Come to tell me if the landlord tries to cheat you."

"Yes, my lady!" He straightened with importance. "I'm Kyliel. Call me Kyle. Were there other services you required?"

"Yes," Isbet said. "Can you find me information on the condition of the court sorceress?"

Again, his eyes widened, but he said, "I'll do my best, my lady. Come, I will show you to a table."

To her good fortune, the table was near the one where the soldiers now sat drinking. Isbet set her pack on the bare wood floor with a loud thump, drawing their attention.

In most cities across the Riven Isles, many inns provided patrons of the arts with spaces to ply their trades instead of chasing them away as a nuisance. The performer had to pay a onetime fee for the table then give the proprietor a percentage of whatever they made. There were strict rules governing this so there was no chance of the proprietor cheating. They faced heavy fines if a performer discovered any deception that could be proven in court.

With her staff and the items placed on the table, it was easy to tell what Isbet was and what trade she plied. Some items she used just for show, like the crystal ball. It was what most people seemed to expect when she divined for them. Cards and gems also seemed to be popular. In fact, various items for readings were as common as stones.

It wasn't long after Isbet settled that people began to approach her table. She observed that the soldiers were attempting to goad the youngest one of them into approaching her and he relented.

"My lady, witch." The boy ran his hand through his dark-brown hair in a nervous gesture. He wasn't handsome. His face was pockmarked, and his features were aquiline, further marred by a noticeable overbite. "Would you divine my future?"

Isbet motioned to the chair across from her. "Five, if you please."

The soldier handed over his coins.

"What is your name, young sir?"

"Quillin, ma'am."

"You are a soldier of Tamrath," Isbet said matter-of-factly and Quillin nodded. "You were just in a skirmish, were you not?"

He gaped at her. "How did you know?"

"I have the Gift." The incident was common knowledge throughout the city, the tale spreading like wildfire; however, her response only made her more fascinating in the soldier's eyes.

"Now, Sir Quillin, close your eyes, please, and lay your hands flat on the table. Yes, that's it." Isbet laid her hands atop his. None of this posturing was even necessary but again, it was all for the show. Isbet would never understand where the common person got such notions. "What do you envision for your future?"

"Well...." Quillin licked his thin lips. He leaned forward to stare at the sphere, and quick as a cat Isbet wrapped him in a veil. He went still, his eyes unfocused. Isbet knew his friends were watching, but if she made no threatening move, they wouldn't intervene. Quillin would see nothing in the orb but mist since he didn't possess the Gift.

"Open your mind and soul, Sir Quillin." Isbet peered into the orb and frowned.

Divination was not an easy task for a witch, being more in the realm of the sorcerers. The best Isbet could do was move aside certain veils that would allow her glimpses before blinding her should she see too much. It was up to the witch to fit together the pieces of the puzzle, which was why divination was often vague and filled with half-truths and supposed futures, and not because the witch wanted to seem mysterious or had some hidden agenda.

She first saw Quillin much older as an officer, it appeared. There were no children and Isbet wondered why. Further probing revealed her answer and what Isbet saw disturbed her. There was a woman, a neighbor, or a relative of Quillin's, and he had been in love with her for quite some time. She was exquisite and Quillin worshipped her. However, she was vain, selfish, and cruel. Quillin was to marry her by a prearranged agreement. Isbet saw a life of pain and loneliness while the girl ignored her husband unless she wanted for some trinket, and indulged in various dalliances.

And Quillin? Isbet moved the veils and what the glimpses revealed about his nature confirmed her thoughts. He was a decent man, rather naïve and eager to please, yet for the right woman he would be a fine spouse. It angered Isbet that he would spend his life fettered to an unworthy whore.

Isbet tried to manipulate the veils, to steer Quillin on a different path, but a mere witch had not the power to shape destiny. As she tried, she felt the life drain from her and she ceased her meddling. Sorcerers had some influence over the veils but attempting any real change exacted a heavy price. If the sorcerer didn't perish outright, they risked a slow death trapped in a body damaged beyond healing.

Should I tell him what I've seen and try to convince him not to marry her? Isbet dismissed the thought the moment it occurred. She had enough experience to know the trouble that would bring. A witch gives a divination or warning that angers the recipient and the next thing they find themselves imprisoned or tied to a stake. *You must tell them what they want to hear, not what they need to know,* her grandmother once said. Therefore, Isbet coated the truth in honey and every word left a bitter taste in her mouth.

When she released him, Quillin's face beamed. "Thank you, my lady. I will tell my companions to partake of your services so they may also benefit."

As Quillin rose to leave, he paused, his gaze settling on his fellows, who continued to goad him. Uncertainty showing on his face, Quillin turned to her again. "Um, my lady…would you care to dine with me?"

Isbet raised an eyebrow. *If you continue to make decisions only to impress your friends, you will have an unhappy life.* "Join me, Sir Quillin," she said.

At the very least, she would grace him with her company.

CHAPTER SIX

"Bram, please, listen to reason."

"No." Bram held Seth to him. The boy whimpered against his neck. "Take Seth. Get away. I'll give myself up to the guards."

Seth's voice was soft against his ear. "I want to go with you, Bram."

Bram loved Seth too much to hurt him with angry words, but he wished Seth would just do as he said. "Jaryl...." Bram stood facing his brother. The passageway was dim and smelled of mold and gave Bram an uncomfortable feeling of claustrophobia. "No one knows about these passageways, Jaryl, yet they keep finding us. That means—"

"Yes," Jaryl said, his voice grim. "I know what it means."

"Sire?" It was Tamair. He had gone ahead with a few of his soldiers to see if the way was clear. "We may have found an alternate route."

Bram gave Jaryl a questioning look. Jaryl's brows rose, his unspoken reply plain on his face. *Tamair? Surely not.*

"My Lord Patriarch? Arch-bishop?"

"There are so few of our enemy," Jaryl looked pleadingly at Bram. "We'll take them prisoner. If Wilhelm sends reinforcements, we can say you never arrived here or perhaps got waylaid on the road."

"No."

"Bram, please—"

He leaned forward and kissed his brother on the cheek. "There was a storage room some ways back. Lead the guards there. We'll wait for them."

Jaryl's throat worked as he swallowed. Tears brimmed as he struggled to keep them from falling. He stood for a moment before turning and striding away. "Follow me," Jaryl barked to Tamair.

"Bram?"

"Yes?"

"I'm sorry."

Bram snuggled his cheek against Seth's. His own tears ran in salty tracks down his face. "Thank you."

★　　★　　★

Leaving Tamrath behind was not the most difficult thing Bram would ever do in his life, but it ripped a piece of his soul away just the same. He only hoped Jaryl would be able to ferret out their betrayer before they undermined the resistance from within. He prayed to the Triune for his family's continued health and safety.

Captain Maive was apologetic, but she didn't grovel, which increased his respect for her tenfold.

"I advised against traveling through Tamrath without a Gifted escort," Captain Maive commented as they rode. "However, it was the king's feeling that they wouldn't try to reclaim you."

Bram knew that wasn't the reason, but he didn't comment.

"I doubt since we retrieved you that the king will take any action against Tamrath." There was a note of reassurance in her voice. Bram had feared just that. "But more than likely he'll want to investigate. It's a pity you didn't recognize your kidnappers. We assumed firstly that your brother and his sorceress had made the attempt."

"My brother wouldn't be that reckless," Bram muttered.

"My apologies, I meant no disrespect."

Bram was too weary to feel insulted. "I know, Captain."

Their journey went on as before, the only difference being that neither Bram nor Seth spoke much, and the guards scrutinized their surroundings and all those who approached them. The courtiers went on as though nothing had occurred.

★　　★　　★

Galil-Galith was much like Bishop's Lane, although there were many examples of the pantheon of gods and goddesses worshipped by the people of Chira. Their beliefs were like those of their sister country, Chirilith. It looked to Bram like there was a deity representing all aspects of life, and the symbols of their existence were in each building and on every street corner.

There had been a time in their mythos that the Riven Isles were one great continent worshipping the same gods, until the Celestial Vine fell by the Woodsman's Ax and broke the land into its many pieces. It had been one of Bram's favorite bedtime stories. There were those who believed the Celestial Vine existed and others, like Bram, who relegated it to a whimsical fairy tale.

Galil-Galith's palatial estate sat atop a hill overlooking the city, accessible only by a single main thoroughfare. The sheer drop down its east-facing side into a crescent-shaped lake below made for the perfect way to repel invaders. The cliff face was impossible to climb, as there was no shore to land on and the lake met the rock wall.

One could try to swim the lake, but from Bram's understanding that was a bad idea, as those who tried found themselves pulled down to either never surface again or surface with limbs missing. There was an inner compound surrounded by a wall of stone where the extended family members of the royal house lived and worked. Captain Maive presented their credentials to a burly guardsman and a group of five Chir soldiers joined them.

Despite himself, Bram again took an interest in his surroundings. He had been to Chira before; however, it was several years before, and he noticed the changes that had taken place in the inner complex. The burly guardsman had taken the lead to escort them to one of the small but opulent homes reserved for royal guests. Bram's immediate party and their guards would stay there. The courtiers were deposited at a local inn. Bram needed the respite.

Once their bags were inside the house, the captain of the guard announced, "The queen will summon you at her leisure," and he and his men departed.

"Well, he was a pleasant fellow," Rajan remarked. He had affixed himself to Bram's side again. Seth regained some of his exuberance as he continued to explore the house.

Since 'at her leisure' could mean anything from a few hours to a few days, Bram took Seth out and explored the city. Evarran was helping him dress for dinner and Rajan was pointing out some spots of interest he might want to visit when Captain Maive called on him.

"Will you be going about town tonight, Your Highness?"

"Yes, and I'll be taking Prince Seth with me," Bram said. "If you wish to relieve your soldiers and take the night off yourself, Seth and I can manage—"

"My Lord," Maive sighed, her expression one of embarrassment, "I would rather not leave you unattended."

Evarran never looked up from his ministrations, but Rajan was studying Maive.

"Yes," Bram said. "We'll have dinner and if you don't mind, I'll take Seth to the theater."

A brief change in her features told Bram of her relief. "Thank you, Your Highness."

The moment the captain departed, Rajan commented, "Can we even trust her to perform her duties after bungling so?"

"Would you call Seth to me, Rajan?" Bram didn't hide the annoyance in his voice.

Rajan sniffed, put out at being ordered about, but did as instructed.

Moments later, as Bram accepted his wallet from Evarran, Seth came bolting into the room.

"Don't run like that, boy, it's unseemly for a prince!" Rajan followed behind him.

"Don't order him about that way," Bram rounded on him. "He is a prince of the realm. Respect him as you would do me."

Seth had come to an abrupt halt when Rajan yelled at him and his eyes had gone wide with hurt, but when Bram spoke for him, his face pinched in confusion.

Rajan looked as if he had prepared an insult but changed tactics and said, "My apologies, Highness." He inclined his head to Seth, who looked questioningly at Bram.

"A good ruler will accept an apology given," Bram told him. A part of him ached to instruct Seth to enact some mild punishment, but Bram figured he was much too young to have that responsibility. "Besides," it pained Bram to say so, "Secretary Rajan is correct. A prince does not run about so." Bram turned to the side, out of Rajan's view, and winked at Seth. The boy caught the action and understood. Seth pressed his lips together, trying not to smile. The attempt was almost comical.

Seth turned to Rajan. "I accept your apology."

"Shall we go out?" Bram grinned at the young man.

"Oh, yes!" Seth's excitement was infectious. It washed over Bram, making him forget his troubles for a little while.

Captain Maive was waiting for them by the front door with two of her soldiers. They saluted and allowed Bram and Seth to go before them.

"Where will we go first?" Seth asked.

"I thought to find a gift for the queen," Bram said. "Why don't we visit the crafter's shop?"

"Can we?" Seth said with such hopefulness that Bram chuckled. Despite being well into his twenties, Bram enjoyed the crafter's shop as well.

Rajan's directions to the crafter's shop were precise. After much ducking and weaving through the crowds, they came upon the shop, set back from the street between a bakery and a wine steward. The crafter's shop had a green and tended front yard where the owner had set up a playground. When Bram set his young charge on the cobbled walk, he caught the look of longing on Seth's face. Bram released a breath of distress as much for himself. As a noble, he'd only played with other children closer to his station and that had been as little as he would have liked. How many days had he looked out the window with longing at the servants' children playing stickball, tag, and hide-and-seek?

Bram took Seth's hand. "I know, Seth." The young prince leaned against him as he walked. With the captain and the soldiers both flanking and behind, they drew more attention. The children stopped their play to watch their passing, while the adults bowed or curtsied. Bram wished they wouldn't.

Inside the shop, there were myriad sounds and motion from the toys, knick-knacks, and baubles. Seth's eyes got very round as he went to each shelf and tabletop.

A wizened old man leaned over a table, carefully applying paint to an apple-cheeked doll. A young girl, her chestnut-brown hair in two braids, gave Bram a gap-toothed smile.

"Good afternoon, My Lord, is there anything I may help you find?"

"We're just browsing, thank you." Bram returned the smile and the girl blushed. "This is a fine shop you have here."

"Thank you," she said. "You and the young sir grace it with your presence."

Now Bram blushed. "Well, I don't know about that."

"Perhaps a bauble for a lady friend?" The girl reached beside her, where a glass-enclosed case held miniature dolls. "They are popular, more so than jewelry. We can paint the doll to match the recipient's features."

"Really?" Although there was no 'lady friend' for him, Bram wondered if the queen would enjoy such a gift presented by Seth. "Is it too much to assume you have some in the queen's likeness?"

She grinned. "You are fortunate, sir. We have dolls made in the queen's likeness down to the fine ball gown she wore to the Belian Festival. We also have a dara of your royal father."

"Dara?"

"A male doll."

"Oh." Bram frowned. Something was whispering at the back of his mind just out of his range of hearing. It was like a soft voice humming a familiar tune that he needed to recall.

"Sire, are you feeling well?" the girl asked.

"Your pardon?"

"You're pale."

"Do you hear that?"

"Pardon?"

"Music."

Bram turned left and right, trying to locate the source of the sound. It didn't occur to him why it should matter so much. Just that he wanted – needed – to know.

Captain Maive had positioned herself at the door. The two guards stood on either side of the room near the open windows.

"Captain, where is that music coming from?"

"Your Highness?"

"That music, it—" In an instant, he forgot the music and everything else. The children within the shop rushed to the door, trying to get out. Parents scolded and pulled, but the nimble bodies squeezed past reaching fingers. All the children gathered there – save one.

Seth was missing.

CHAPTER SEVEN

Isbet watched the children halt as one in confusion at the front walk of the crafter's shop. She had perched her nimble body atop a tether rail and had a clear view to observe the prince. People paid little attention to her. She was yet another performer plying her trade as evidenced when Isbet lifted the flute to her lips once more.

"It is foolish of them to travel without a Gifted one in their group," Gaemyr commented.

Isbet caught the attention of the group of children. They rushed across the lane, unmindful of the traffic, and gathered before her like an adoring litter of puppies, except for one.

The young Prince Seth stood off to the side. He watched Isbet with mild interest. Making a slight change in the inflection of the notes, Isbet surrounded the young man with her enticing song, making it all for him.

His face and stance didn't change. He yawned, scratched the side of his nose, then turned away.

Isbet lowered the flute in surprise, to many protesting voices. She stared open-mouthed as Seth walked away.

"Well, isn't that a damnable thing?" Gaemyr muttered.

Curious, Isbet hopped off the rail and followed, stowing the flute in her shirt.

Seth rounded a corner with Isbet in pursuit. Where did that little urchin think he was going? She knew a scant moment later. Children will be children.

The vendor had his cart between two buildings at the entrance to an alley. Much to her chagrin, Isbet found her own mouth watering at the scent of sweet dough, fried in a vat of grease that she was certain was several summers old. The vendor handed Seth an oily paper sack and Isbet cringed as Seth reached into his jacket pocket and drew out a celestial. As she expected, the vendor's eyes bulged from his head. The boy had shouted to the rooftops that he was an easy mark.

"Quite a bit o' coin ya got." The vendor took the coin, knowing full well it was enough to buy him meals and drink for days, and that it was far too much for one bag of greasy sweet bread. "I'd git yer arse home before ya git knocked."

"All right." Seth didn't understand his meaning.

"Go thataway." The man motioned to the alley.

Isbet stepped forward. "Seth!"

The boy turned back, his innocent face contorting in confusion.

The vendor stepped in her path. "Mind yer busi—" His eyes traveled up and down her form and took in her clothes and Gaemyr in her grasp. "Oh, shite!"

Isbet made a simple motion. It seemed like nothing to those around her, just a flick of her hand in a dismissive gesture when she took hold of one veil and wrapped it around his face.

"Gods!" he cried, and Isbet didn't wait for the nightmare he saw to play out. She was at the face of the alley and grasped Seth's wrist, pulling him back onto the sidewalk as a dagger glinted in the sunlight. Isbet parried the blow with Gaemyr and turned the staff's face to their assailant. Gaemyr devoured him with little effort.

"Witch!" The others in the alley made their escape.

Isbet watched them go. She wondered if a curse would be worth the trouble; decided it wouldn't be.

"Miss?"

Seth was looking up at her with wide, frightened eyes. Isbet realized she still had hold of his wrist. She gentled her grasp. A crowd was gathering around the vendor who now sat slumped against the cart spouting terrified gibberish. It would be a long time before he accosted a child or anyone again.

"Come, let's get you to safety." With the veils masking their presence, Isbet moved away from the disturbance.

"Was – was that man – did he try to kill me?" Seth asked in a small, frightened voice. Tears pooled in his blue eyes and his lower lip trembled.

Isbet sighed, but refused to honey-coat her words. "Yes," she said. "Your mistake was showing them the celestial. It made you an easy target. Never show lots of money out in the open. It attracts the wrong attention."

Seth swallowed but nodded his understanding. "He called you a witch."

"I am a witch," Isbet said. "And so are you."

His face scrunched in a comical expression. "I can't be a witch. I'm a boy!"

Isbet laughed. "Well, to be fair, the male equivalent is a wizard. You have the Gift, Seth. To be honest, I'm uncertain if you're a witch or not. You could be many things."

"I can do magic?"

"Again, I'm not sure, so we need someone to test you." Isbet realized they had arrived back at the crafter's store. She also remembered the veils still had them hidden, which provided further proof of Seth's possession of the Gift. "Perhaps we should go inside, I'm certain—"

"You there!" The voice had Isbet turning. "Don't move!"

The female guard commander was striding towards them. "You are under arrest."

"What by the Vine for?"

The guard captain ignored her question. "Your Highness, did this woman take you?"

"Take me? No. She—"

The other two guards were approaching and from the corner of her eye, Isbet caught sight of Prince Bram plunging through the crowd towards her.

"Will you come along peaceably?" The guards flanked her on either side, their swords drawn.

"Seth!" Bram came to a halt. "Move away from her!"

"But Bram—"

"Seth, come here, now." His voice was sharp, more from concern than anger, Isbet knew, but Seth would think otherwise.

"Don't yell at the boy that way. He won't understand," Isbet admonished him, which was unwise, she supposed, but she felt it necessary.

"How dare you!" Bram forced the words between clenched teeth.

"Bram, please don't!" Fat tears spilled down Seth's cheeks.

"Do not resist. Relinquish your staff, witch."

Isbet sighed. This was becoming much too complicated. Without protest, she handed Gaemyr to one guard. "Behave."

By now, they had attracted more attention. Chir city guards were approaching, adding to the crowd. The guard commander got hold of her wrists. One of the Chir guards approached with iron manacles. Isbet tensed. She had wanted to avoid an escalated confrontation, but if the guards attempted to touch her with them—

"What are you doing?" the female captain said. "You can't bind her with iron. Get a rope."

The guard looked put out by a foreign captain giving him orders, but knowing he had to obey, retrieved a rope from the saddle of a nearby mount.

"Thank you," Isbet said.

The captain grunted a reply. "It is good you didn't fight, witch or no."

Isbet stood as the guard bound her wrists. As they led her through the crowd, she noticed the stares and frightened whispers.

"Do not fear," the guard captain muttered. "It is illegal to accost Gifted in this city."

Isbet had already known that, but too often she had seen how stability and the law often fell to mindless panic.

★   ★   ★

Seth shook off Bram's guiding hand. He stomped across the threshold, his tiny fists clenched, his cheeks puffed out within a face flushed scarlet.

"Seth, you're not behaving."

Seth turned. "You lied to me!"

"What?"

The tears came again. "You said you'd always listen to me."

"I will."

"Then why did you let them take her? I tried to tell you!"

"Who?"

"The witch lady!" Seth cried. "S-she d-didn't take me!" He hiccupped and his voice broke. "S-she saved me! She's my friend!"

Bram gaped at his young charge. Had they accused an innocent? Bram could only remember how infuriated he was when the woman had admonished him – not because he was a prince but because she had been correct.

"The boy is hysterical from his ordeal." Rajan had come out to meet them when they'd arrived. Bram frowned, wondering how Rajan seemed to know there had been an 'ordeal'.

"I'm not!" Seth stamped one tiny foot.

"Seth," Bram said, "your appearance is inappropriate. Go upstairs, wash your face, and change your clothes. Then we'll see about straightening this out."

Seth sniffed and drew his sleeve across his nose. Bram didn't bother to admonish him. "Thank you, Bram."

"Really, Your Highness—" Rajan began.

"The Chir guards can accompany us." Captain Maive, being the senior officer, had escorted the witch to the nearest guard station. "They'll know where they took her."

"The witch cast a spell on him to make him believe they were friends," Rajan protested. "You can't trust anyone with the Gift."

"You had better not let the queen hear you speak such. Her cousin is the court sorceress."

Rajan blushed under his ruddy complexion. "Of course, Your Highness."

"No, I don't believe Seth is under a spell," Bram said. What he didn't add was that he wanted to speak with this witch himself. Something about the woman in their brief meeting intrigued him.

*　　*　　*

Isbet stretched out across the straw mattress, her arms behind her head, and occupied her time counting the cracks in the stone ceiling. She only rose from her place when a young guardsman brought her a meal of tough meat and bread drenched in over-spiced gravy. He surprised Isbet by stammering, "My apologies – did you want – I mean the meat—"

"It's fine." Isbet took the offered tray, then, when the boy turned his back, she gave him a luck touch. It was nothing elaborate but at least he'd win at cards tonight and make enough to buy a certain maiden an inexpensive ring.

She didn't bother making the meal into something more suited to her taste, even though she was talented with home craft. If her situation didn't improve, she would need every dram of magic she possessed to escape and retrieve Gaemyr.

Isbet had just finished her meal and was sopping up the last of the gravy with her bread when the door opening brought her head up.

"Lady witch!" A tiny body launched itself at her and Isbet had scant enough time to lay her plate aside before catching Prince Seth in her arms.

"Did they hurt you? Shall I challenge someone to a duel?"

Isbet graced him with a kind smile. She was taking a liking to the child. "No, they have treated me fairly."

Seth seemed satisfied.

"You know," Isbet said. "I never introduced myself. I'm Isbet."

"You already knew my name," Seth said, puzzled.

"Who doesn't know the kind and wise Prince Seth Oran of Avynne?"

Seth blushed. "I'm just a little boy."

"You are much more than that," Isbet said. Movement at the entrance drew her attention as a tall figure stepped across the threshold.

"My lady, I must offer my apologies." Prince Bram inclined his head. "Had I listened to Seth, we could have avoided this. Please allow me to make things right."

Before she could reply, Seth said, "Can Isbet come dine with us?" He looked at Isbet in entreaty. "Won't you come to dinner, please?"

"How can I refuse such a gracious request?"

Both looked at Bram.

"Very well," Bram said.

Isbet stood and straightened her clothes. "This is unexpected. Two princes of the realm visiting a wandering witch under arrest?"

"The people will look upon my concern as a benevolent action," Bram said. "And I wouldn't have trusted anyone else to handle this."

"I see," was all Isbet said. Still, she thought, how odd. Bram could have sent a servant to retrieve her.

Their captain, whom Isbet learned was named Maive, waited for them in the entrance area of the guard station while Bram made the final arrangements for Isbet's release and Gaemyr's return. The staff had a great deal to say, which Isbet ignored.

A coach waited for them outside, its door emblazoned with the queen's seal.

"They have provided us more comfortable means of transportation," Bram smiled.

The queen's coachman climbed down and opened the door. Isbet knew it was proper to offer her hand to Bram, although she could climb into a coach by herself. When their hands touched, the first impression she received was of a man torn apart inside. A man who saw his entire world twisted into a falsehood. The intense sensation halted her, one foot on the step.

"Something wrong?" Bram smiled, but it didn't take a witch to see the sadness in his eyes.

"No," Isbet said. "Thank you."

As she settled herself on the seat, Isbet frowned at a twinge of guilt. She'd planned to use Bram for her own ends, and despite some less-than-pure denizens she'd associated with, she had the rather annoying habit of being honorable when the occasion called for it. *How I wish I could rid myself of that bothersome emotion*, she thought. Isbet wasn't even certain if she meant the guilt or the morality.

Isbet almost missed Bram instructing the driver to take a turn around the city. "We have some time and I wanted to talk to you," he said by explanation.

"What did you want to talk about?"

"First let's stop for an appetizer, shall we? I've already told the coachman."

They rode for a time, listening to Seth chatter on about his home. Isbet could sense Bram's regard although she kept her attention on Seth. The coach stopped after a while and when Bram drew back the curtain and pushed the small window open, the coachman handed them in three bags, each filled with plump cherries.

Seth tore into his and soon after his hands and face were smeared with juice. Isbet reached into her backpack and pulled out a handkerchief. "Seth."

The boy looked up and allowed Isbet to scrub his face and hands.

"You seem to like children," Bram said.

Isbet wiped her fingers with the cloth. "Why wouldn't I?"

Bram had the grace to blush. "Well – that is – I heard—"

"That witches hate children? That we enjoy cooking them in ovens?"

"Lady Isbet!" Bram nodded to Seth, who looked up. He hadn't heard a word Isbet had said.

"That, my dear prince, is a myth."

Bram leaned back and popped a cherry in his mouth. "So, what else is a myth? Is it true, witches can't cross water?"

Isbet had to bite her tongue to keep from laughing aloud. Of all the myths she had to endure, that was the most ludicrous. "No. Water is of the realm from where witches draw their power. We are most proficient with lakes, rivers, and streams. If you want to do something like change the tide you need a sorceress, and even that takes immense power."

"Why?"

"No magic worker has dominance over nature." Isbet frowned. "You have been in contact with magic workers?"

Bram turned his face to the coach wall. "There was never any need to learn such things. Coline...." His voice trailed off.

"I was away for a long time," Isbet said, her voice soft. "The Riven Isles have changed much since I left."

"Where were you?"

"Being schooled," was all the answer she would give him. Her eyes dipped to where Gaemyr lay across the coach floor. Isbet held the staff in place with the tips of her boots. He was her reward for completing her training.

"I wanted to know if everything is right with us?" Bram said. "My worry over Seth had me acting rashly."

"As I said, I accept your apology," Isbet said. "Do you believe me a person who would curse you after the fact?"

Again, Bram blushed, but said, "I know little about you at all except that you rescued Seth and for that, you have my gratitude."

"I am what you see," Isbet said. "A wandering witch, skilled in herb and hearth lore, divination, objects, and realm-speak."

"I've heard of realm speak," Bram said. "When you speak the language of birds and beasts."

"Not so much as speak. It's just to determine the beasts' wants and needs," Isbet said. "I am not the best at it."

"Will you tell me more?" Bram ran his hand through his hair in what Isbet thought to be a nervous gesture. "You…I find you fascinating."

"I don't see why," Isbet said. "Your story is far more fascinating than mine."

Bram snorted in a most impolite way. "Everyone knows my story."

"Wilhelm does not have the Gift."

Bram tugged at his collar in obvious discomfort. "Not as far as I'm aware."

"Yet the rumors—"

"Don't."

Isbet matched Bram's intense stare for a time before reaching into her pack and removing the doll. She set it on the seat beside Bram and opened its mouth. "You may speak now."

"What? How?"

"I told you, I am proficient with magical objects."

Seth had stopped eating long enough to stare at the doll. "It looks strange."

"It will to you." Isbet nodded to him. "What you see is its aura. Once you learn to use your Gift—"

"Triune, what did you say?" Bram demanded.

Isbet's brow creased in puzzlement. "Is there a problem, Your Highness? I'm certain you heard—"

"Never mind that, woman, did you say Seth...has the Gift?"

"He does." Isbet was not at all pleased with his referring to her as 'woman'. "I assumed you knew of it."

"No, I did not," Bram groaned the words. "Triune, no."

"Bram?" Seth reached over and laid his tiny hand on Bram's knee. "Are you mad at me?"

"No, Seth." Bram rubbed his eyes then tried to smile. He patted Seth's hand.

"You seem upset at the knowledge he is Gifted." Isbet's voice was ice.

"What?" Bram seemed to notice Isbet was there and her volatile mood. "No...you don't understand."

"Enlighten me, please." *Before I curse you.*

"Like me, Seth's had his life stolen, a pawn in Wilhelm's game," Bram said. "When he finds out Seth is Gifted—"

"Yes." Isbet let her body sink into the cushioned seat. She crossed her arms at her chest and nodded in understanding. Wilhelm would use the boy.

"You must tell no one he has the Gift," Bram said. "Please, I'll do anything."

"Not that simple," Isbet replied. "His power will manifest itself whether or not Seth wants it to." Isbet inclined her head to Seth. "Do you understand, Seth?"

"Yes." His attention was on the two adults now.

"You said you were uncertain Wilhelm has the Gift. Is he a skilled mentor?"

"No," Bram said, "that I can say for certain."

"First someone needs to determine what aspect of the Gift Seth possesses," Isbet continued. "He could be a witch, or wizard as we call male witches in some lands. He could be a sorcerer, diviner, necromancer, or one of the many offshoots."

Now Bram leaned into the seat and closed his eyes. He rubbed his temples. "Then I will have to tell him. Convince him that Seth needs a teacher and it will be someone of his choosing. Someone who will try to manipulate Seth to—"

"Bram, can't Lady Isbet teach me?"

Bram's eyes flew open. "Seth, that's not polite."

"But why?" Seth looked at Isbet with pleading eyes. "Would you teach me, Lady Isbet?"

"Seth," Bram reproved, "Lady Isbet must be about her own affairs. It isn't polite to coerce her into assisting you."

Isbet felt a stab of annoyance. As well-meaning as the prince was trying to be, he was only making her appear heartless.

"Don't you like me, Lady Isbet?"

"Seth!"

"Your Highness," Isbet said in the same tone she'd used to admonish him earlier, "I am a wandering witch. I returned here to see my grandmother only to find she had passed away. I have no pressing business of late. If Seth would like me to be his mentor, I may for as long as I am able. I leave the decision to you."

"Please, Bram?"

The Arch-bishop of Tamrath sighed in defeat. "I can't promise anything. I'll send a post to Wilhelm and he may say no. If he does, I won't be able to keep Lady Isbet."

"Yes, I understand. Thank you, Bram." With the matter settled, Seth went back to eating the cherries.

"You'll try your best to convince him."

"Of course," Bram muttered.

CHAPTER EIGHT

"Your Highness, the message has arrived." Rajan stepped into the breakfast room, holding a sealed envelope.

"Please read it, Rajan." Bram reached for a china bowl, where a towel soaked in warm lemon-water waited for his use. He wiped syrup from his fingers.

Rajan broke the wax seal. "Yes, the queen wishes us to report to the palace to tea with her this evening at four. Casual dress, it says." Rajan raised an eyebrow. "Shall I purchase an appropriate gift?"

"If you would."

"Bram, can Lady Isbet come with us?"

"I don't believe they included her in the invitation, Seth." Bram went to sip on grape juice.

"Well...sir, she was."

Bram paused with the glass half raised. "You're jesting? They included Isbet?"

Rajan sat and passed the invitation to him. "We are being watched, then."

"Understandable," Bram mused. Still, it puzzled him why the queen wanted Isbet to be there. "Where is she?"

"In the garden," Seth said. "May I be excused? I'll go tell her."

"Very well."

Rajan poured himself a cup of flavored coffee. "I still don't trust the witch, Your Highness."

"Did I say I trusted her?" Bram stabbed with his fork at a piece of sliced melon on his plate.

"She has no credentials to prove that she is anything but an ordinary herb girl," Rajan said. "Why didn't she escape the guards yesterday?"

"I'm relieved that she didn't," Bram said.

"We don't even know if she is who she says she is. She could be a spy, or an assassin sent to kill you, the boy, or both." Rajan's voice rose to an almost hysterical squeak. "Keshta, she could be after Wilhelm!"

"Don't you think I've considered all that?" A thread was holding Bram's temper. "It's doubtful Wilhelm will—"

Bram bit back his remaining words when Isbet entered the room with Seth grasping her hand. Bram rose from his chair at her approach and glared at Rajan until he followed suit. Whether she was a spy or no, Bram demanded courteous behavior at his table.

"Good morning, Your Highness," Isbet said. "I understand I am to accompany you to your audience with the queen?"

"Please join us if you haven't eaten." Bram motioned to the table. "And yes, you are." Bram blushed and said, "Good morning."

Isbet carefully laid a napkin on her lap, choosing some sweet griddle cakes with strawberry compote and a few slices of crisp bacon.

"You eat meat?" Bram blurted, then cringed.

"I am not a fey, Your Highness."

"Oh." *Blast it all, I've never had a woman make me blush as much as she does!* "It's just that I heard Maive admonish that guard about the iron shackles."

"Those with the Gift are not always fey but man's iron can harm us," Isbet said. Her brow creased in thought. "Some of man's devices hurt the earth, and because our power comes from the earth, we do as well, yet because we also live in man's world, we have a slight immunity. It would have marred my skin and made me ill. I would have been a long time healing."

Bram wasn't certain he understood, but he nodded.

"So, tell me, Lady Isbet," Rajan intertwined his fingers and rested his chin atop them, "where are you from?"

A raised eyebrow. "Do you mean where was I born? I have no idea."

Bram had trouble swallowing and he held the china cup in a white-knuckle grip. How could she be so nonchalant about it? Losing his parents had devastated him. He could see her almost dismissive words affected Seth.

"I never knew my parents, so I cannot miss them," Isbet whispered as she inclined her head to Seth.

"A pity," Rajan said, not seeming the least bit sympathetic. "Then where have you lived?"

It was a ridiculous question since she had stated that she was a wandering witch. Wandering was an occupation for some, although not accepted by polite society. However, there were people who simply could not find a steady trade or preferred not to, so they wandered from place to place to make their living.

"Nowhere per se." Isbet sipped the coffee she had poured. "I have traveled throughout the Riven Isles."

"Hmm," Rajan said.

Bram thought Isbet was very gracious to be answering Rajan's questions, which amounted to an interrogation. He was wondering if he should curtail Rajan's prying when the man fell silent. But Bram's relief was short-lived.

"To whom do you pledge your loyalty?"

"Rajan!"

"Your pardon, Highness, but it is a legitimate question if this woman is to be a teacher to young Prince Seth," Rajan said. "And might I be so bold as to remind His Highness that as the king's private secretary, it is my duty to ask such questions."

Private secretary, my ass. "I'm aware of your duties, Rajan."

Rajan blushed. Bram had made the true meaning of his words clear. "Highness—"

"A witch's loyalty is to the land," Isbet interrupted him. "To the realm that gives them their power. This is common knowledge. Yes, there are ones with the Gift who pledge their loyalty to a monarch or noble, but I am not one of them."

"You realize," Rajan regained some of his fire, "that you will have to pledge your loyalty to Wilhelm if you are to teach Seth. He will demand it."

Isbet lowered her cup and gazed at Rajan. In an instant her entire being seemed to change. The intensity of her gaze was enough to send a shiver along Bram's flesh. There was something dark in her eyes, knowledge of the shadow side of the arcane. It frightened Bram.

Then, as if the change had never occurred, Isbet was herself again. "I'm afraid I'll disappoint the king if he requires this of me."

Rajan did not comment but Bram saw terror in his eyes and in the pallor of his face. As for Seth, he was frowning in confusion, his stare traveling to each adult, but he seemed otherwise unaffected.

Bram thought, either his Gift grants him immunity or Isbet cares enough about him not to subject him to her anger.

But why would such a comment anger her?

★ ★ ★

"You must learn to control your temper," Gaemyr admonished her. "It's no concern of yours what the mongrel pup thinks."

"Yes, I know." Isbet sighed. She held up the formal jacket that had been purchased for her. The first choices of the servants sent to shop were very inappropriate for her needs. There were many frills, laces, and pastels and Isbet sent the servants running with one well-placed glare. The black waist jacket, bodice, and trousers trimmed in the red and blue of Chira fit well enough. Isbet was not some noble's daughter concerned with fashion and cosmetics. When she needed to dress – for example, if she were performing at some wealthy patron's home, and that was seldom – the lady of the house always supplied what she considered appropriate.

She never had a choice in the matter, but since the prince had made no sign of what he wanted her to wear besides telling her to dress casually, she'd taken the initiative.

"What will you do concerning the sorceress?" Gaemyr asked.

Isbet blew out a frustrated breath. "She must not suspect that I plan some harm to Wilhelm." The witch smiled. "Not that she would care. She may consider my injuring the king as a favor."

"Indeed."

Seth came to collect her, bouncing on his heels, and Isbet found herself caught up in his excitement. When they had replied to the invitation, they had asked that the court sorceress lend her expertise in determining which aspect of the Gift Seth possessed. As Isbet descended the stairs with him gripping her hand, she teased him that perhaps he would be a witch.

Bram and Rajan awaited them. Isbet had to admit the prince looked handsome, even in his casual dress, still tailored, made from silks that had come from Rajan's homeland far across the sea. Unlike Isbet, he wore the royal colors of Rhyvirand – scarlet and gold. The long greatcoat fit around his broad shoulders; the trousers outlined the muscles in his legs. Even Isbet couldn't help but appreciate the view. Being a witch did not make her immune to mortal desires, nor would it have required her to maintain her virginity.

Bram noticed her regard and his face flushed, an endearing trait, one that had the maidens swooning.

"You look...very becoming," Bram muttered.

Rajan's lips pursed in disapproval. "Highness, will her dress do? The queen will expect more conventional dress."

"Rajan," Bram warned.

"Remind me to devour him when the moment presents itself," Gaemyr commented.

Seth chuckled then flushed as Bram had when all eyes turned to him. He'd heard Gaemyr's comment.

"If my dress is unsatisfactory, please say so, Highness," Isbet said, turning the attention away from Seth. Without the Gift or a spell from Isbet, neither Bram nor Rajan could hear Gaemyr speak. "But I will not prance about in frilly skirts. They're not practical."

Bram bit hard on his lower lip; his face went red again and clenched in a comical expression as he held back the laugh.

I'm willing to wager you haven't laughed in a long time, have you? Isbet felt a little sorry for him. She had lost her grandmother, but he had lost his entire family, his kingdom, and worst of all, his identity.

Bram composed himself. "Let's be off, shall we? We don't want to keep Her Majesty waiting."

Seth filled the silence with his chatter, asking Isbet many questions, which as usual she didn't mind answering. She loved that the boy wanted to learn. Again, Isbet teased him about being a witch, much to his pouting and denial.

Bram, who had been silent to that point, spoke up. "You say he might be a witch," he said. "Since he's a boy, wouldn't that make him a warlock?"

"In some circles," Isbet said, "*warlock* is a derogatory term. Men who take that title are ones who practice the darker arts."

"I see." Bram smiled at Seth. "Then I guess you are a witch."

"Am not!" Seth huffed.

Isbet took pity on the lad. "Remember, we use *wizard*, Seth."

"Well, that's fine," Seth said.

They were all silent for a time before Bram said, "Lady Isbet, would you teach me as well?"

Isbet raised her eyebrows. "What is it that you wish to learn?"

"Everything," Bram said. "I am responsible for Seth's care. Wouldn't it make sense that I at least have the knowledge of the Gifted? It's not as if I can do anything with it. I just want to…understand."

"I'll teach you as well…if Wilhelm allows it."

Bram smiled at her. He had a nice smile that lit his whole face. "Thank you."

Isbet sank back against the cushions of the carriage. "When we have an opportunity, I will place a spell on you that will enable you to hear my staff."

"Hear your staff?"

"Her staff talks," Seth said.

"You're jesting."

"My staff is sentient. He will be instrumental to Seth's teachings, so it makes sense that you hear him too." Isbet noticed Rajan was looking from her to the staff, his expression ranging from confusion to disgust to disbelief, but for once, he didn't comment.

Bram was shifting in his seat with obvious unease. "Is that necessary?"

Hadn't she just explained that it would be? "Is there a problem, Your Highness?"

"I'm just not…" Bram turned his face away to stare out the coach window, "…comfortable with magic used on my person."

"Yet it is necessary"

"Very well."

The silence following was not comfortable.

The coach slowed and the occupants knew they neared their destination. Isbet smiled at Seth as the boy stretched to look out the window. She had to admit to her own curiosity. She'd never been to the palatial estate of Chira. The coachman opened the door, bowing low as Bram stepped out. He turned and offered his hand to Isbet, who took it in her grasp. Again, there was that underlying grief. She would have to remember to weave him a pleasant dream.

Although they all were guests of the queen, the guards who served as escort led them not to the main entrance but to a smaller side entrance within the queen's private garden. Two more guards met them at the gate and led them through rooms made cool in the shade by magical means until their escort deposited them in a sunny parlor filled with plants and flowers.

Liveried servants had set out tea for them and now stood behind the set table awaiting their queen's arrival.

"Can I have something to eat, Bram?"

"*May* I, Seth. In a moment. It's polite to wait for our hosts first."

The wait was not what they had expected. Isbet often waited days before seeing the lowest valet in an estate but she always made the best of it, being provided for with food, clothing, and a roof over her head.

The glass-enclosed double doors on the other side of the room opened. All stood as Her Majesty, Queen Aimeli Galith entered the room, followed by her cousin, the court sorceress, Lady Briwyn Galil. The men knelt before her, took her hand, and kissed it. They likely expected Isbet to curtsy, but that was never something she did unless the noble in question demanded it. Queen Aimeli smiled at Seth and spoke to him first before motioning the rest of them to their seats.

The years had not been unkind to the queen. She was still a beautiful woman with a sculptured face and piercing chocolate eyes. Her cousin was equally lovely, although a little plump in her features.

The servants served the queen first and she encouraged Seth to help himself. Lady Briwyn's eyes never left their young charge.

"Your Majesty," Bram began, "I thank you for this opportunity. I know how valuable your time is. On behalf of my father, King Wilhelm Salk of Rhyvirand, I give greeting and wish you good health."

"Greetings returned." Her voice was rich and regal. "We are glad to see you. There is much we have to discuss, and I doubt Wilhelm would listen."

"I don't understand," Bram said. "That is why I'm here. My father also feels we have much to discuss and has concerns that our noble neighbors don't feel comfortable in discourse with us."

"We don't." Briwyn turned to Isbet. "I'm glad you are here. You can corroborate our information."

"I, milady? There must be others—"

Briwyn gave her a familiar smile. "I knew your grandmother."

Isbet said, "So you know she has passed away."

"Yes, and I am sorry," Briwyn said. There was a look of deep knowledge in her eyes. One that told Isbet she well knew of her thoughts despite her preparation. "She never spoke of me to you?"

"Not that I recall."

"I suppose she wouldn't." The sorceress seemed to muse to herself. "We had a falling out. A silly thing, I don't even remember what it was about. How I wish…." She drew in a deep breath. "When we discovered you were traveling with the prince, I knew you were the perfect one to see."

Rajan spoke for the first time. "Forgive me, milady, but what is this all about?"

Her eyes never leaving Isbet, Briwyn moistened her lips before saying, "I'll come right to the point. The Celestial Vine – it is growing."

CHAPTER NINE

Bram understood nothing that was occurring, but this news seemed to distress Isbet.

"You say it's growing?" Isbet demanded, forgetting all protocols. "By what ground?"

"The Celestial Vine lengthens at least two feet per day and the tip now measures several hundred yards in circumference."

"So, it's true. Chira is at the tip."

Briwyn leaned back in her chair and closed her eyes. "It is underneath us."

"You have an idea what's causing it." It was a statement.

"Yes." Briwyn cast a withering gaze on Bram. "Your father, to begin with."

Bram didn't appreciate her tone. "I'm sorry, but I do not understand any of this."

"Nor I," Rajan said.

"You know of the Celestial Vine?" The queen raised one manicured eyebrow.

"I've been told the myths and stories of it."

"It is no myth, as you will soon see." Briwyn's lips thinned in displeasure. "The Celestial Vine is a conduit of all earth magic." She nodded to Isbet. "We sorcerers can draw power from it as well, although our main source of power comes from the heavens."

Bram said, "But such a thing can't exist. It would have to be thousands of miles long and its circumference—"

"Bram." It was the first time Isbet had addressed him by his first name. "I have seen the root at the province of Vine, which is its namesake. The root is at its center."

"He won't believe until he sees," Briwyn said.

"And as to that," Bram countered, "why do you believe Wilhelm is to blame?"

"He's not," Briwyn said. "But whatever magic he is dabbling in is a part of it. The Vine is reacting to his schemes here at the tip. Elsewhere there are others who are messing in magic that should not be."

"That is why," the queen began, "we could not join with Wilhelm. In fact, we...." Aimeli paused and glanced at her cousin. "Although my noble cousin doesn't agree, I allowed you to come here, Bram, to provide proof and to ask you to intervene on our behalf. Tell Wilhelm he must cease his actions and give us time to find the others who are causing the Vine to grow."

His words caught in his throat. Bram still didn't know what to make of the whole situation. "I'm sorry – I can't – I don't—"

"If you have no objections, we will take you below now." Briwyn stood. "Young Seth?"

The boy looked up. He had been silent, listening intently.

"Would you like to meet some children? My niece is about your age."

"All right," Seth said.

Briwyn called one guard, who escorted Seth out. Bram wasn't certain he enjoyed leaving the boy and said so.

"He can't go with us," Briwyn said, "until we discover his power. He may have an adverse reaction being so close to the Vine."

Briwyn then turned to Rajan. "You will need to write everything you see and hear. Since Wilhelm appears to trust your word above all else."

"Of course," Rajan said. There was something in Briwyn's manner that quieted Wilhelm's secretary.

The queen stood, and Briwyn held out her hand as Aimeli grasped it and the two women preceded them out. No one spoke as they walked. Bram's mind hummed with questions and his thoughts for Seth's safety. What if they planned to take the boy hostage if he didn't agree to their terms? He knew the answer to that with certainty.

Bram was uncertain how powerful Isbet was, but he figured Briwyn could best her. The sorceress was much older and seemed wiser. Isbet paid her respect of a better. Wilhelm, however, would consider Seth's kidnapping as an act of war.

Then he would summon the dogs....

Bram was so into his musings he looked at nothing around him; a small portion of him focused on following behind the group. Rajan seemed nervous, Isbet anxious. He wondered what being around the mythic Vine would do to her.

They were descending, it seemed, an infinite number of stairs, cracked with age. The light dimmed. It was as if they were going into the heart of the earth itself.

At the bottom of the stairs was an immense wooden door where two guards stood to attention. They didn't salute or move as Briwyn took a key from within her sleeve. She inserted it into the keyhole, turned it, and pulled the door open. The guards made no move to assist. In fact, on closer inspection, they didn't even seem to be alive. More like the wax dummies he'd see at the museum in Rhyvirand.

Beyond the doors was not a path or another set of stairs but a wooden box.

"Step inside, please." Briwyn motioned with one slim hand.

"In there?" Rajan's voice rose in fear.

"It's safe," Briwyn said.

Too intrigued, Bram said, "I'll go. I can note down everything that happens."

"Yes, but will Wilhelm trust your word?" Briwyn asked.

"Why wouldn't he?" Bram said. "I've given him no reason to mistrust me." He hoped nothing showed in his face.

Briwyn regarded him, her face impassive. "Very well."

They moved within the confines of the box and as Briwyn closed the doors, Bram's last glimpse of the outside was of the look of relief on Rajan's face.

There was a great sound of metal clanking together, followed by the unmistakable cadence of heavy rusted chains moving. The box gave a sickening lurch as it began its descent and Bram lost some of his hard-won confidence.

"Have you spoken with the Children?" Isbet directed her question to Briwyn.

Now Bram was even more confused. "Children?"

"The Children of the Earth," Briwyn explained, "those who live with the Vine and were birthed from it." She turned to Isbet. "Yes, I have spoken with them."

"And?"

For the first time, Briwyn seemed nervous. "They are aware of what's happening, and most feel no need to intervene."

"That offers no surprise," Isbet said.

For once Bram understood the gist of the conversation. "The Vine growing is to their benefit."

Briwyn rewarded him with a grin. "As the Vine grows, so does their power. I have told them of the danger from both sides. From the humans who dabble and the dark fey who grow stronger and may find that they are no longer satisfied with remaining in the Deep Earth."

Her words made him shudder.

"Since you know history so well, Prince Bram, then you must know of the legends of the Shattered Time."

"Yes," Bram said, "the time after the Fall of the Vine when the Riven Isles came to be."

She made a soft *hmm* of agreement, nodded as she folded her hands before her. "For example, when you dig deep into the earth, there are things there you'd rather not see?"

"Yes, but those things could never destroy me," Bram muttered.

"Indeed."

"The Children, they will not interfere in your investigation?" Isbet said into the silence.

"It's impossible to say," Briwyn said. "We will speak to our representative in Underneath, then we are to meet with the Shadow Council to get permission. It should go well since they don't care, but the dark ones...."

Bram was unsure why they needed permission if the mystic beings didn't care. Then again, it was only proper to ask permission before one went traipsing across the borders of one's neighbors. Bram could see the consternation on Isbet's face. He had little desire to go against dark fey himself, at least without an enchanted weapon. If anything happened to him....

"Lady Briwyn" – he feared asking but needed to know – "the dogs, are they dark fey?"

Briwyn assessed him, her face at first a blank mask, then a spark of emotion lit in her eyes – admiration. "This is the first time you've mentioned the dogs, my prince."

"We try not to speak of them."

"It will not bring them running." She smiled as though there was a hidden meaning behind her words. "They are not dark fey," she said. "But even the Children, who aren't dark fey, can hold animosity towards mortals."

"But," Isbet muttered, "it will turn back on them."

The realization confused Bram. Weren't the dogs dark fey? They were Wilhelm's tools. How could he control them? He had heard the whispers of some magical item deep within the estate vaults....

The sound of the box hitting the ground with a metallic report brought Bram out of his thoughts.

"What are you expecting, Prince Bram?"

Bram started at Briwyn's question. "I – I don't— I've heard the stories—"

Briwyn reached for the iron handle and tugged the door aside. "The stories will not prepare you."

Her actions had the proper effect.

Bram could only stare in wonder at the landscape that spread out before him. His heart could have stopped then and he would be forever certain that he'd seen everything life offered. They stood at the top of a slight incline at the base of a sheer rock wall, which, Bram figured, was the underground portion of the hill on which the royal estate sat. A pale blue light that originated to the east allowed them to see. Bram had expected pitch darkness. Still, it took his eyes time to adjust and when they did, new marvels appeared to him.

Another realm stretched out before him; one that formed a patchwork quilt of craggy ranges and valleys, bursting in a riot of tangled vegetation and glittering rock formations. There was flora there that had a look of familiarity, but it was hard to tell in the muted light. Others were nothing like Bram had ever seen. These glowed with an eerie foxfire that took on disturbing visages, like beasts leering at them.

Some sported leaves that could envelop several men. Others were covered in nettles, razor sharp, that put a finest-honed blade to shame. Some towered over them, rivaling their aboveground brethren, while their opposites were tiny delicate things that spread across the forest floor in a bristling carpet of silver. There were plants with bulbs that strained for a time before cracking open and spewing gigantic spores that adhered to everything around them.

Despite the dim light, they flourished, some with enormous trumpet blooms that gave off an intoxicating scent that drew any mortal to partake of their beauty. There were tall, bare trunks old and gnarled, awash with sweeping fingers, each nestled with tiny blooms.

It was some time before Bram noticed the three women were watching him and waiting. All had the indulgent looks of an elder matron humoring a child. Bram cleared his throat. "You were correct, Lady Briwyn, I was not prepared."

She laughed but there was no derision in it. "Please stay close, Prince Bram. You are a newcomer here and may draw unwanted attention. It would not do to have you spirited away for closer examination."

"With all due respect, milady, that does not fill me with confidence."

It relieved Bram to see a path of glowing stones just a few steps away from the rock wall. It cut through the silvery carpet, winding its way several hundred yards through the clearing in front of them, where it connected with a circle of stone smooth and without blemish. Identical paths branched out in the three other directions to disappear within the dense foliage, which closed in another perfect circle. Bram doubted it was a coincidence.

"The pathways are here more for our benefit," Briwyn explained. "The inhabitants of this realm have no need for such things."

"Did your ancestors come to some agreement to allow these here?" Bram asked.

"Something of that nature."

They made their way down the path and continued in the direction that Bram assumed was west, but he could never be sure. One thing he noticed was that when he stepped onto the stone circle, he felt a thrumming of power which raced across his skin, causing him to gasp.

"These circles are areas of safety." Briwyn didn't turn but continued. "As long as you're within one of them it is difficult for the Children to get at you." She glanced back. "They can wait you out and a powerful Child can shatter such enchantments."

"Is there any good news?"

Bram's confidence further waned when they passed beneath the canopy of vegetation. His skin crawled from the notion that thousands of eyes watched his passing. Once they were inside the canopy, he heard sounds like he'd never heard before, soughs and murmurings, guttural calls and screeches that didn't come from any animal he knew existed. Of these, he had the briefest of a glimpse. They would flit away on the moist air, duck behind branches or slip into the many dark ponds that dotted the forest floor.

"Triune, protect me," Bram whispered when he saw the stones, like jagged teeth two man-heights tall lining the edges of the path that kept them on their course. They came to another intersection but instead of a circle of stones, there was a gazebo with two long curving benches placed on either side. The light was better here; the stone itself glowed, although Bram couldn't explain how.

"We'll wait here for our guide to take us further," Briwyn said.

That suited Bram fine, as he had no desire to travel through this land without someone who knew its lay. The three women sat in silence, Briwyn and Aimeli on one side, Isbet on the other. Bram was too restless to sit. There wasn't much to see around the gazebo. Clusters of flowering plants on slim stalks resembling orchids, if Bram had to put a name to them, surrounded it. Again, he wondered how anything could grow here. Still, Bram could appreciate their beauty.

"Lady Briwyn," he said, "would there be any objection from the denizens of this place if I picked some flowers for three lovely women?"

He'd finally gotten the upper hand. The queen and Lady Briwyn flushed with murmured comments about how charming he was. Although her face was as red as the others were, Isbet was silent. Bram had to snap off the flowers from their stems with his fingernails. He carried his gifts to the three and gave a little bow as he handed one to each. He lingered before Isbet, hoping to draw some reaction from her. She took the flower and covered it with her slim fingers, setting her hands on her lap. "Thank you."

Her reaction disappointed him. Not that women hadn't rejected Bram before – he'd done his share of rejecting as well – but he couldn't quite fathom her disinterest. It bothered him. Perhaps he felt this as a challenge. Bram resumed his seat and tried to avoid staring at her. There they waited. Bram wondered who they were waiting for, but he didn't want to seem like some eager child, no matter how his curiosity protested. He wondered as well how their guide would know to find them here.

There was a rustling in the underbrush behind where Briwyn and Aimeli sat. Neither reacted to the noise overmuch except Briwyn, who squared her shoulders and adjusted her hands in her lap.

Bram supposed he should have taken that as it was, but he was nervous about being caught off-guard. Although in principle a man of the cloth, Bram had trained as a soldier. Of the many titles he held, Father Protector was one of the most familiar. So, it aggravated him when he reached for a sword at his hip and realized there wasn't one.

The being that emerged didn't appear a threat. She was a fine-boned, delicate creature, with glossy translucent skin. She stood only three feet in height, resembling a girl-child not long out of infancy. However, her insect-like wings, which glistened in the pale light, belayed any opinion that she was a mortal child. She wore a plain dress with no embellishments except it seemed to be silk and perhaps it was, as it carried a glossy sheen. The three women rose from their seats and to Bram's complete surprise, they bowed, and Briwyn motioned for Bram to copy them. Still, Bram hesitated before obeying the silent command. He was a prince of the realm after all and showed deference only to a king, but he figured it was only polite and safer if he showed her respect.

"I bid thee welcome always, girl-child."

Bram realized the being was addressing Briwyn.

"You honor us with your help, Revered Mother." Briwyn inclined her head. "May I present to you His Royal Highness, Prince Bram Greyward of Rhyvirand."

When those aquamarine eyes fell on him, swallowing became all but impossible. Bram had no idea what to say or even how to address her. What if he insulted her and she transformed him into something unpleasant? Why hadn't Briwyn schooled him on how to behave?

There was little to do at this point. "It is an honor and a pleasure to meet you, Revered Mother. I am in awe of your world."

There was a brief flicker of amusement in her clear eyes. "I am surprised to see you, Bram of Tamrath."

Her use of the name of his true homeland sent a shudder through him. Wilhelm's edict that he forsake everything that he was didn't concern them. "Why is that, milady?"

"I thought Wilhelm's little lapdog would be here."

"If you mean Rajan, he feared the chain box." Bram nodded back the way they had come. "Wilhelm has no reason not to trust my word."

Her eyes held secret knowledge. "He doesn't."

Bram had the uncomfortable feeling that she knew all about Jaryl's ruse. What would she do with the information?

"It does not matter," she said. "I am here to take you to the Vine's Head, and you will see for yourself what has been happening. And he is very unhappy it destroyed his house."

Her latter words had Bram lost all over again but Briwyn was nodding, her lips pursed in disapproval. The being turned to the path without comment.

Once they were far enough from the gazebo the light faded, and they had to make their way in semi-darkness. It was uncomfortable, as Bram once again had that sensation of many eyes watching.

It was sometime later that other clear denizens of this world joined them in the form of ghostly balls of bluish light which dipped and bobbed in their wake, dogging their footsteps and darting away when they turned their attention. Bram sensed that they were as sentient as the pixyish girl who led them. He glanced at Isbet and found to his surprise that she was smiling at them. She reached out to one; it brushed her fingers, and she laughed with delight. It entranced Bram. It was a side of her he'd not seen.

She noticed his regard and although her smile faded a little, there was wry amusement in her eyes.

"What are they?" Bram asked.

"You've heard of wil-o-wisp?"

"Yes, but—" Bram reached out a tentative hand. "I've heard they're – I mean we call them corpse-light."

"They can be dangerous," Isbet said. "As can all the denizens of the Vine."

They came out of the cover of the trees to another large open space. It took a few moments for Bram to realize they were in a cul-de-sac.

There appeared to be three separate structures, but Bram couldn't quite make out their shape. He realized why they looked so strange to him when he stepped further into the clearing. A mass of climbing vines hung on a wall, shaped with patient hands to form the dome of a hut. There were three separate dwellings, yet Bram could see how the vines formed twisted conduits between each. Smaller tendrils grew out of the main body of those same, pale flowers making them look like lacy curtains.

Stranger still were the windows carved within the loops and twists. Bright light spilled from each of them. Some windows were shaped in irregular patterns, mimicking the path of the Vine itself. Some were upside-down, making it necessary for one to walk underneath them to see into them.

Bram was so caught up in the fantastic sight that he didn't realize the others had gone on until Isbet said, "Coming, Your Highness?" She was staring back at him with the same amused look.

"Y-yes." He had to force his legs to obey his command.

Each cottage had a door carved of wood, which was identical in appearance. More of the supple vines formed a decorative arch above it on which a single lamp hung, burning with a comforting glow. It surprised Bram they permitted fire in this world.

Their guide stepped up to the door and knocked.

"Go away!" a voice growled from within.

"Browaing, you old coot, it's Minuet!"

"What? Well, come in, then!"

The door opened on its own and the group stepped inside. There was no one there. The sudden brightness caused Bram to squint.

"Call for me when you wish to leave. I will be nearby." Minuet inclined her head and slipped outside, twilight embracing her.

Bram was glad for the bright cheery room. Lamps adorned the walls and hung from the ceiling. An obvious receiving room, it was comfortable in the simplicity of its decorations and furnishings. Each piece was a carved and polished miniature version of mortal furniture. Bram doubted he could fit in the chairs. The couch had a hand-stitched afghan thrown over it, set against the wall to their left, and a circular table and chairs were on the other side.

A fire burned on the hearth, which again made Bram wonder. A black pot of something that smelled of spices and vegetables boiled within. Above the hearth, set on the mantel were several framed drawings of family and friends, no doubt.

What held Bram's fascinated gaze was the hand-drawn map that hung above the fireplace, framed within a shadow box. He stepped forward, his eyes adjusting at last. The land looked familiar, but—

It came to him. The map was of the Riven Isles, showing the length and width of the Celestial Vine as it wound its way beneath the Lands.

"So, it is true." Though Bram thought after all he'd seen the truth should be obvious. "The Celestial Vine exists."

He stepped closer, mindful of the pot and the fire. Bram marveled at the neat hand lettering. The Vine twisted and turned like a mighty river winding its way across the continent, divided into several large sections through the main body with at least several hundred other connecting lines, which Bram supposed to be tributaries.

"There are many rivers," Bram commented to no one in particular.

"Those aren't rivers." Isbet moved beside him. "Those are offshoots."

"Offshoots?"

"As a country has provinces or states, the Vine has offshoots or branches. Each branch is ruled by a different family and the branch takes that name. Here is where we are now." Isbet pointed to an offshoot labeled Aethewyn.

Bram saw a blank circle inked on the map to the right of the branch. "What's that?"

"The lake below the palace cliff."

"The lake is down here too?"

Isbet chuckled. "Something like that, as you'll see."

"Impressive, isn't it, man-child?"

Bram turned at the voice. The little being who stood there covered in bristling red hair had a face that was as knotted, wrinkled, and nut-brown as the vines that made his home. It made him look ancient, but his bead-like eyes burned with an inner fire. He wore a green tunic and shorts, and Bram noticed he was barefoot.

He shook a soup ladle at Bram. "What's the matter, man-child, ain't you never seen a kobold before?"

CHAPTER TEN

Isbet couldn't help but grin at the very confused look on Bram's face. *He can be so adorable*, she mused. Then she banished such thoughts.

"Uh, no, sir," Bram replied.

"Well, I s'pose it's expected," Browaing mused. "Do you want to eat first or see the damage?"

"We've eaten already, Lord Browaing." Briwyn, as always, seemed to speak for the group. "We want the prince to see all the damage, then we'll take him before the Council."

"Fine by me," Browaing said. He looked Bram up and down. "Yer sure he'll be safe?"

"Why wouldn't I be?" Bram directed the question to Briwyn.

"Well…." For the first time the sorceress seemed uncomfortable. "There are beings who would use you for their own purposes as Wilhelm does, and others…." She sighed. "Prince Bram, you may not realize this but you are a very attractive young man. Some will want you for other reasons."

Bram's stomach fell as heat rose in his face in the space of a few heartbeats.

"He would be a tasty morsel," Gaemyr said. He'd been so quiet since they had arrived in Underneath, drawing power from the Vine. Isbet knew when he came awake, he'd be at the peak of his power and so would she.

"Oh, hush," Isbet muttered.

"You don't agree?"

"Gaemyr," Isbet warned.

"What's this, Gaemyr?" Browaing demanded.

"Stating the obvious, forgive me, Lord Browaing."

"You can hear him, too?" Bram sounded incredulous.

"O'course I can." Browaing winked. "I am fey, after all – asides, the old boy and I go way back."

Now, this was a surprise. Isbet figured Browaing would know of Gaemyr, but this familiarity – Isbet wondered if Browaing was instrumental in Gaemyr's current state. No, that couldn't be it. Although Gaemyr had never been forthcoming about his previous life, Isbet had sensed bitterness with his lot in existence.

"And what of you, young witch?"

"Forgive me, sir?"

"You willin' ta take it upon yourself to step in if need be?"

Isbet breathed in, nodded once. "Yes, milord."

Browaing gave a curt nod, satisfied.

"Do I even want to know what that is about?" Bram mumbled.

"No," Isbet replied.

"Follow me then. Sooner I get this done, the sooner I can eat."

Browaing led them through a doorway to their right into a connecting corridor. Isbet stepped around a 'window' underneath her feet. Although she seldom questioned what motivated the Children to do such things, she still wondered why it was there. The corridor itself segued into an incline that forced them to lean forward to avoid any bumped skulls. After a time, the incline leveled out and Isbet released a sigh of relief for her aching back. This corridor veered to the right and ended at a flight of stairs.

Browaing kept right on going as though he hadn't a care, and whistled a tune while he swung the ladle like a pendulum. The next corridors were a maze of twists and turns, ending at last at another flight of stairs, only this time, a door kept them from proceeding further.

"Well, this is it. Hope yer ready." Browaing reached for the door latch.

Isbet didn't know what to expect or how extensive the damage would be, but this was beyond what she'd tried to imagine.

The kobold lord had opened the door into space.

There was nothing left of the side of the house but large splinters jutting from the original frame.

"Triune," she heard Bram mutter.

"Well, yer Highness, they brought you here for this, so come forward." Browaing motioned with stubby fingers.

"Let's see how brave the stripling is," Gaemyr commented.

Isbet shushed him as Bram moved past her. There was little room, forcing Isbet, the queen, and Briwyn to press themselves against the wall.

"Merciful Triune." Bram leaned over as far as he dared. It didn't look safe and Isbet whispered a spell to catch him if the timbers gave way.

"You wanna have a look down, witchling?" Browaing asked her.

Morbid curiosity got the better of her. Isbet waited until Bram was beside her before approaching the edge. She used Gaemyr to keep her footing by forcing him in between some surviving boards.

The Vine offshoot had sheared its way through the room, plunging it several hundred feet. When Isbet looked down from the dizzying height, she saw lanterns placed in a circle around the area of the wreckage. Leaning to the right, Isbet saw a second cottage like Browaing's, also damaged, the wall punctured through like a pin in cloth.

"Look there." Browaing pointed to the left and Isbet saw where the offshoot lay shorn. The area was also quite a distance away from the cottage.

"That offshoot was a mere sprig a week ago," Browaing explained. "Sure, I knew I'd have ta cut it, but...." The kobold shook his head. "It tore through the house a week later. That ain't right and ya know it."

"No, it isn't." Isbet worried her lower lip. For the Vine, even an offshoot to grow like that was impossible. Offshoots took years – sometimes decades – to grow a fraction of an inch.

"I take it the branch shouldn't have grown so fast?" Bram asked.

"Indeed." Worry edged Briwyn's voice.

"Let's go back now," Browaing said. "They said it ain't safe ta stand here anyway."

They made their way back to the receiving room, where Browaing bade them sit. The kobold served bowls of steaming vegetable stew and black bread, insisting Bram try some dark brown ale he brewed himself. For the women, he had water flavored with what tasted like mint, which could have been the case, since sometimes a Child would do business with the mortals aboveground. Isbet enjoyed brown ale herself and would have asked for a sample save for the supposed impropriety of such an action. Things weren't so much different Underneath.

"I am curious, Lord Browaing," Bram said as he sipped the ale. "Excellent!"

Browaing beamed underneath his beard. "Glad ya like it, sir. I know yer a hobbyist yourself."

"Oh." Bram flushed with pleasure. "My attempts seldom, if ever, come out so tasty. Although, some of the best ale comes from Tamrath."

Browaing laughed. "What's yer question, Highness?"

"Oh," Bram said. "If I remember the story, when the Vine was first sown, it took very little time to grow, so why is it so surprising that it's growing now?"

Browaing leaned against the table and crossed his arms. His grin was mischievous. "Why don't you answer that, witchling?"

"Me?" Isbet paused with her spoon halfway to her mouth. "But you would better be able to answer—"

"No. You, witchling."

Isbet held back a sigh of exasperation. The most she could do was give a theory. She guessed Browaing simply didn't want to answer the question for his own reasons. "From the mortal texts I've read, it reasons that as mortals do, when something is young and full of the vigor of life it sprouts. As it ages or if it becomes injured, its healthy development slows." Isbet leaned back in her seat and sipped her own drink. "We cannot be sure since this occurred before our great-grandparents' time, but on my travels, I have heard many tales."

"Such as?" Bram asked.

"You've heard the tales yourself, Highness."

"I've heard some," Bram said. "But I'd like to know what you've heard, please."

"How can I refuse such a gracious request?" Isbet's lips upturned. "Very well. I have read that the Vine took several years or decades to grow. That the Giant-killer was the great-grandson of the farm boy who first planted the seeds. Others say that the Vine grew within a night and the Giant-killer took years to climb it. Another tale says the Children took up residence within the Vine during this time and the boy – now a young man – had many encounters with them as he made his way Up Above. They also say the giants felled the Vine to kill him and guard their secrets." Isbet tapped one finger against her cheek. "Although, it is said the young man used the Woodsman's Ax to escape the giant's wrath."

"I'm finding all of this hard to believe," Bram muttered into his ale, just as there was a knock on the front door.

"Enter," Browaing called and the door swung open on its own.

Minuet stepped into the room. "The Shadow Council has summoned you. If you will, all, please follow me."

★   ★   ★

The wil-o-wisp trailed in their wake as the group followed Minuet.

On her travels, Isbet had seen the grand estates of those not human. Still, she was in awe when they arrived at their destination. Bram was staring like a schoolboy on his first time at the fair.

The seat of power within this offshoot of Underneath seemed to go on forever. It began with a rectangular open area that was the width and breadth of the Riven Isles themselves. The place was ablaze with the light of thousands of wil-o-wisp. They lay in a thick mass in their path and seemed unconcerned as the steps of the intruders disturbed their rest, floating for a time with the breeze of their passing then settling in place once again.

One couldn't call the structures she saw buildings per se, Isbet thought. The grand estate was a forest of interconnected vines woven in a pattern of lace orbs, which served as rooms. They carved large gems worth the ransom of several monarchs to serve as windows, some the size of a fist, others that of a full-grown man. These orbs hung by several suppler vines twisted into ropes thicker than the trunks of the oaks of Jack-In-Irons. Still others formed walkways between each orb so the inhabitants could traverse the many areas, although these drooped. Most walkways were open, others draped in a covering of the silver flowers, giving some measure of privacy.

It took a few moments for Isbet and the others to notice that the tallest man couldn't reach the lowest orb. There was obviously a way for them to enter, otherwise why bring them here? Isbet let her eyes travel upward until she could only see pinpoints of light in the darkness, which were obviously more orbs unseen within the limits of her vision.

"Suppose I need to get to the big hall." Browaing strode forward and, like Minuet earlier, he seemed to vanish into the shadows. "Minuet, make sure they're not late."

"Yes, Lord Browaing."

As they moved to follow Minuet, Bram spoke. "He's a member of the Council?" He clamped his mouth shut with an embarrassed gasp the moment the words left it.

"That surprises you?" Isbet smirked.

"Well – I – that is—"

Isbet couldn't suppress her chuckle. "Don't fret, Highness. I didn't suspect either."

"Oh," Bram said, his eyes wide. "Oh! Were you toying with me? Triune."

"You sound surprised."

"That is because you are full of surprises, Lady Isbet."

Isbet wasn't certain if she should take his words as a compliment or not.

The old staff rewarded her with a mocking snort.

"We seldom have visitors here from aboveground," Minuet said as they approached the base of one vine. "And we have no need for an entrance on the ground. Besides, the kings and queens of this land must be above us who walk on the earth below."

Yes, there were similarities to aboveground with monarchs. Isbet approached the base and laid a hand on the rough wood. "Gaemyr, shall I release you?"

The staff shuddered in her hand. "Yes, here is fine." Isbet doubted he knew of how respectful he sounded by the anxious tone of his voice.

"Lady Minuet, is that permissible?"

"I don't see why not." Minuet reached out and touched Gaemyr at the tip. "He is home."

"Thank you." Isbet pressed Gaemyr against the bark.

Gaemyr breathed a sigh of anticipation as the Vine drew him in. His face relaxed in its contentment. Isbet watched as he sank into the wood, becoming one with the magic that had created him. Moments later, he'd vanished, and the wood regained its original appearance as though nothing had occurred. Isbet could sense his presence as he moved along the vine to its heart, where he would drink of that power. He wouldn't need to feed for weeks once he partook, which always made things easier for Isbet.

"Now, I take it you two are not climbers." Minuet nodded at the queen and Lady Briwyn.

"I have enough power to carry us aloft," Briwyn said, "Afterward—"

"You won't need your power here," Minuet said. Then she turned to Bram and Isbet. "And you?"

"I can climb," Isbet said.

Bram's expression was wistful. "My brother and I rock climbed off the coast of Tamrath every summer." Isbet saw the pain in Bram's eyes. She couldn't look at him. She couldn't bear to see the despair mirrored there.

It couldn't be helped. Isbet firmed her resolve. She drew herself up. "What do I need to do?"

Minuet didn't answer at first. The look she gave Isbet caused her to shudder. She hated Minuet's clear insight. *It's none of your concern*, Isbet wanted to say, but knew she couldn't.

Minuet turned away and Isbet felt the unmistakable thrum of magic in the air. Above them, there was a rustling through the boughs and two thick vines snaked their way down until they were within reach.

"We'll meet you at the top." Minuet nodded once to them and the sorceress whispered an invocation that caused a wind to whip up from the still air and lift the queen and Briwyn off their feet. Isbet watched in fascination. All Gifted peoples shared at least one type of magic, but levitation belonged to the sorcerers.

When they found themselves alone Bram grinned with mischief. "Shall we race? First one gets the prize?"

"What is the prize?" Isbet said.

"If I win, we have one serious conversation and I get to learn more about you."

Isbet didn't like that one bit. "Whatever for? I'm not some adventurer or princess in disguise. You may find my life mundane."

"No," Bram said, tugging on his earlobe. "I believe you have quite a few interesting tales."

"And what do I get if I win?"

"What do you want?"

I want you to help me destroy Wilhelm.

Vine, where had that thought come from? She could imagine what Gaemyr would have said. Still, it made Isbet wonder – would Bram help her? He had no love for Wilhelm but how much more would he expect of her? He would want some noble reason such as love for her country, but Isbet had no interest in such things. She only wanted to give her grandmother's spirit the honor it deserved. If Wilhelm remained unpunished, her grandmother would never rest.

"Lady Isbet, are you all right? Did I upset you?"

Isbet released a breath. "No, Highness, you did not. Very well, I will make the wager with you. One conversation and I learn more about you."

"Done!" Bram grabbed his vine and Isbet followed suit. "Ready? Set. Go!"

Isbet took three running steps, hopped onto the wall, and pulled herself up hand-over-hand. She was strong and healthy and had climbed before, so it wasn't too difficult. But Bram had the greater strength and experience and was the victor, beating her by a body length. Isbet accepted his hand when she reached the top.

He was grinning at her. "You have many hidden talents, I see. I look forward to our conversation."

It surprised Isbet to find she did as well. "As do I."

Bram gave a start before blushing.

The queen and Briwyn waited for them, both wearing those knowing looks the elders seemed to favor when they suspected something was blooming between two young people. Minuet's face was an unreadable mask.

An almost overwhelming scent of flowers filled the walkway as the five negotiated its length. They were not alone there. Others traversed the narrow space and gave them curious glances. Some had skin as pale and translucent as the flowers, others as black and shimmering as polished opals. They had curved eyes and pointed ears. Some, like Browaing, had faces awash in a sea of wrinkles. One man stopped Minuet and spoke to her in whispers; his eyes traveled over their group with disdain. He was shirtless, dressed only in loose white trousers and slippers. His body was muscular and oiled, making his dark skin glisten in the glow of the wil-o-wisp. His violet eyes narrowed and his full lips thinned in displeasure. He continued his conversation with Minuet, but his gaze never left the visitors. Isbet noticed he lingered on Bram for a time, enough for it to be uncomfortable in her estimation, before he straightened and turned, going back the way he had come.

"Was that a Dokkalfar?" Bram said in an awed whisper.

Was there no limit to the many times Bram would surprise her? "Yes, that is their proper name."

"They govern this offshoot," Briwyn said. "Revered Mother, have we offended?" She directed the question to Minuet.

"No, no," Minuet said. "Serval is always like this. Everyone and everything that does not involve him is a threat."

"He is the queen's brother, is he not?" Briwyn said.

"Yes, but as you know, he has little say in such matters."

"Lady Minuet, I'm curious," Bram said. "I've heard that most fey beings don't like to give their true names. Am I correct in assuming that Serval isn't his? Your pardon, but just as Minuet isn't yours as well?"

"You are correct, Prince Bram." She glanced back at him with a slight smile. "We are very protective of our true names."

"Of course," Bram said.

"The Children will often choose a name that has to do with nature or something beautiful and valuable," Minuet continued. "A serval, for example, is a cat. The queen chose the name Calla."

"And yours has to do with beautiful music and dancing," Bram said. Minuet laughed with delight. "Ever the charmer, Prince Bram."

"Is Lord Browaing's name true?"

"No," Minuet said. "But he chose a kobold name from centuries ago. He feels it's insulting to separate ourselves from our true names."

They continued, passing under an archway to a central hub that branched off in eight different directions. This area served as a social meeting place. The din of conversation lowered as they passed. There were no seats but many circular wooden tables on tall thin stems, on which people leaned and placed drinks and various samplings of food served on silver trays.

"Since you have gained advance permission to have your say to the Council, you needn't wait with the others." Minuet motioned with a wave to the room behind them. "We have prepared a waiting room for you."

CHAPTER ELEVEN

The relative solitude of the waiting room relaxed Bram. The gazes, some disapproving, from the denizens of Underneath made him squirm like a child awaiting an unpleasant parental encounter.

Bram took a seat on one end of a stuffed couch, where he sank his rather tense muscles into the cushions. The queen and Briwyn sat in the two available chairs. After a few moments' hesitation, Isbet sat on the other end of the couch.

Minuet inclined her head. "I would recommend that you not leave this room until they summon you."

"We won't, Revered Mother, and thank you again," Briwyn responded.

"What will happen?" Bram asked once they were by themselves. He had seen enough of council meetings in his day to learn that one misspoken word could cause a long and bloody war.

"I will speak for us if they call us before the Court," Briwyn said. "I would advise against speaking out of turn and to only answer questions asked of you."

"Yes, of course," Bram said. He'd not intended to speak at all unless spoken to, let alone out of turn.

"We hope that they will focus on Briwyn and we may make our request," the queen said. "Their decision may not be immediate, and they may make us wait here."

Bram found little comfort in her words. Isbet spoke, drawing Bram away from his thoughts. "Do not worry, my prince, we will protect you."

"Triune," Bram muttered, his face heating from both embarrassment and shock. Isbet had made a jest. Bram didn't believe it possible.

Their wait was not as long as he expected.

Minuet returned, stating, "It is time."

Bram figured it was best to let the ladies take the lead, and he followed behind Isbet.

They traversed another less opulent hall but still the twisted limbs of the Vine formed a vaulted ceiling above them. The corridor ended at a set of curved double doors. Shards of smoked glass in various shapes and sizes made windows between gaps in the tangle. Once again, Bram found himself amazed, not at the architecture but at the terrible beings that stood guard.

Yet more of the many beasts of legend, the two balanced themselves on their serpentine tails, which curled beneath them, their scales polished. The powerful torsos were protected by breastplate and cuirass. Although they were soldiers, their faces held a defined nobility. Their eyes sent a shiver across Bram's skin; snake-like, their pupils were like slits in the dim light, within a yellow opalescence. Clawed hands gripped the shafts of their weapon of choice – a poleax.

Naga. Bram didn't dare say the word aloud.

They needed no instruction as Minuet approached them. With the barest inclination of her head as a command, the two moved with a sinuous grace afforded their kind and opened the doors.

At first, Bram saw nothing; the room appeared shrouded from floor to ceiling in fog. Bram supposed his eyes needed time to adjust, like from darkness to light. After a few moments he began to discern shadows taking form.

A line of them appeared as wraiths but as more time passed, he could see they were mortals, draped in hooded robes of royal blue. They sat at a long table, but Bram could not make out much else. Two more shadows stirred a few steps behind the tables and he realized they were also naga. They moved back and forth with a graceful, steady motion.

It was then that Bram saw Minuet was no longer with them, but soon another shadow joined the silent group. Continuing to follow Briwyn's example, Bram stood quietly between the queen and Isbet. Briwyn took three deliberate steps and bowed low. Bram and the others followed suit. Bram thought it was no surprise that these three women found curtsying not to be their fancy.

"I am Briwyn Galil, Lady Duchess, and cousin to Her Majesty, Queen Aimeli of Galith," Briwyn said. "I give greetings and thanks to you, the Shadow Court, for granting us this audience."

The hooded figure at the center of the group gave a slight nod. "You are our honored guests in our land, Lady Briwyn Galil." The female voice held an air of quiet strength. "Let's come to the point. You wish permission to examine the Vine. To what end?"

Bram had the sense that the hooded leader was aware why, but he supposed she had asked for her own reasons.

"The Vine is the keeper of all life in the Riven Isles," Briwyn responded. "It binds us all together as one, Overworlder and Underlander. The Vine is the source of our power and keeps our lands in balance. There are outside forces that have used the Vine for their own ends. They corrupt and distort its true purpose. This is a great insult to you and your people as keepers of the Vine."

Another nod and Briwyn took that as permission to continue, for she said, "We wish to find the culprits and halt their egregious actions. They are putting not only our world in danger but yours. Also, think of those beings of the dark, the denizens that the Vine keeps from your royal court. We know they are stirring from their imprisoned sleep and will seek to destroy you."

Bram didn't like the sound of that. There were many tales of those creatures from the deepest parts of Underneath. They dwelled in the rotting decay beneath the Vine's roots, feeding on death and misery.

"And do you not believe that we can handle our own affairs?"

The voice came not from one of the hooded figures. Bram hadn't seen the person who stood just to the left, a few steps away from the table, his body shrouded like those of the naga guards.

Briwyn opened her mouth to reply when the center figure raised her hand. "Serval." She spoke the name in rebuke.

"Majesty." Serval balled his fists. "I have a right to an answer. We have a right—"

"You do not hold sway in this council." The voice was still calm but the command in it was clear.

"I have the right by blood and birth to speak. To request the respect I am due."

Now that Bram saw better, he recognized him as the Dokkalfar that had pulled Minuet aside in the hall. Hadn't Minuet said he had little say in such matters? He guessed further that the central figure was his sister, the queen.

"And has Lady Briwyn disrespected you?"

"She disrespects us all by claiming that we are incapable of handling our own affairs."

"I don't recall Lady Briwyn even hinting at such a thing," the queen continued. "However, Lady Briwyn, is it safe to assume that was not your intent?"

"No, Your Majesty," Briwyn replied. "In fact, we have asked so we do not interfere with any plans you may have while we investigate." Briwyn drew in a deep breath, inclined her head. "We ask that you allow us, so we may save lives."

The members of the council conversed in whispers. Bram noticed that Serval stood with his arms crossed over his chest. The longer the whispers went on, the more tense the young man became. Bram could see it in the rigidness of his stance.

The queen's attention returned to Briwyn. "The council will retire and discuss the matter and advise you of our decision. We will summon you here again."

Briwyn bowed low again and they followed. "Thank you, Majesty. We await your decision."

They stood there as the queen rose and the council filed out. Serval, however, lingered and Bram realized with much discomfort that the man's gaze was on him. Bram's first impulse was to look away but that would have been a sign of weakness. When one naga moved in front of him, it spared Bram any further incident by blocking Serval's view. Two more of the scaly beasts did the same, each bowing to Briwyn and the other women.

The obvious leader of the group spoke. "I am Azai, captain of the queen's personal guard. She has entrusted me with your safety."

"Triune," Bram muttered and wondered why they deserved such an important official.

Azai turned to him and his lips upturned in a slight smile. "Do not fret, Highness, I take my duties with great regard."

Bram returned the smile. He had expected Azai and his people to be cold and aloof, but this man had shared a confidence that was meant to amuse and reassure. He noticed the women were also smiling and as always, that brought warmth to Bram's face.

"We have arranged separate accommodations for each of you. I hope you find them to your satisfaction."

"I am sure we will, Captain Azai," Briwyn said.

"My comrades will stand guard at the hallway entrance to your chambers," Azai continued. "Please request any help you need from them."

"Thank you."

The room given to Bram had the usual comforts and suited his style, as though the architect seemed to know that he liked dark woods and colors, warm brick facades and serviceable furniture. Bram shunned the great opulence that befitted his station. There was a nagi – Bram learned this was the female equivalent of a naga – who waited on him and was both dangerous and beautiful, her lower half glistening and black. He invited her to sit with him for a while. He learned her name was Timai and he enjoyed a conversation and the light repast with her as he settled in a comfortable leather chair, his feet resting on a stool.

Bram would have liked to explore once Timai left him but set aside that idea. He was still too unfamiliar with this world to want to risk stepping into some forbidden place or insulting one of its denizens. Bram chose a book, in the common tongue, from one of the many that lined a set of shelves against a far wall. It was the author's version of Underneath's creation, the same story they'd discussed at Browaing's home earlier about how the farm boy Jack had used the Vine to climb Up Above and learn the secrets of the race of giants.

The Woodsman's Ax was famous in its role and found its way in to many other stories of good over evil, including that of the Maiden in Scarlet. A lycanth had kidnapped her to consume her soul, having already done so to her grandmother. There was the tale of the good queen who knew her wicked stepdaughter was a witch bent on taking her father's throne but could not get her husband to believe her, so her loyal guardsmen had taken the mighty weapon, hunted her down, and disposed of her.

Bram loved these stories of heroes protecting the innocent. He'd been like that once. Bram banished these thoughts for they took him down a dark road. He chose instead to continue to read until his eyes became heavy.

Bram was dozing when a polite knock came. Bram didn't know how much time had passed, since he had no sense of such things so far under the ground.

It was a naga. "Your Highness, the council has once again summoned you into their presence if you would please to follow me."

"Certainly."

His female companions already awaited him in the hallway. They greeted him with smiles and nods that Bram returned. They seemed ready and calm. He had to commend them on that because he was shaking in his boots, as the saying went.

They did not speak as they returned to the room where the Shadow Court had gathered. The figures sat in their places again and Bram saw someone hovering in the background, who he figured was Serval. The doors closed behind them. There was a brief pause before the queen spoke. "We, the Shadow Court, grant your request."

It took everything Bram had not to release a sigh. The women had also kept their reaction to themselves, but relief was plain on Briwyn's face as she stepped forward and bowed. "Thank you, we are in your debt."

"That you are," the queen said. "We do not give this consent without serious consideration. Will you, Briwyn, and your royal cousin of Chira agree to our demands? One favor and you will consent with no argument?"

"Yes."

It sounded to Bram like they had already decided. His eyebrows knitted as he wondered, was he included in this agreement? He doubted Wilhelm would do the leaders of Underneath any favors. As uncomfortable as it might be, he needed to make this clear to Briwyn and Queen Aimeli.

"Very well." For the first time, Bram saw her fingers, long and slim, when she steepled them outside the sleeves of her robe. "Then this pact with the people of Underneath and rulers of Chira is established. We will discuss this matter further and come to agree on how you should repay your debt. Until then, please—"

"Your pardon, Majesty?"

All attention went to Serval as he stepped in front of the table where all could see him. "I have my own stipulations for this agreement. Am I not afforded that right as a member of the royal family?"

"This is between this Court and Chira."

"Will you strip me of all my rights? To have my pride thrown aside like so much waste? Majesty, I demand what is my due."

"You demand?" The queen's voice hardened.

One figure next to her leaned over and whispered something to her. After a moment, the queen nodded. "Very well, Prince Serval, what is it you desire?"

His next words shocked Bram into stunned immobility.

"I want the prince," Serval said. "I lay claim to Prince Bram Greyward."

Bram clenched his fists until his nails bit into his palms. He took a single step forward and opened his mouth to say – well, things that a father of the cloth shouldn't say – when he felt slim fingers close around his arm. Isbet's grip, solid and powerful, halted him. He would have never guessed she was that strong, but as her fingers pressed against his skin, leaving marks, Bram was sure of it.

The queen was silent for much longer than Bram would have liked, and when she spoke, his heart fell into his stomach. "I will grant the request of Prince Serval." Isbet's grip tightened. Bram thought she might break the skin. "Unless, by our laws, one of you lay claim to him."

Isbet released him and it was though an even greater connection ended. She stepped forward, next to Lady Briwyn, and bowed as the older woman had. "I do, Majesty," Isbet said. "I lay claim to Prince Greyward."

CHAPTER TWELVE

Bram felt it better to keep his own counsel as the naga escorted them back to their rooms. He was about to leave them when Queen Aimeli said, "Highness, if you would join us for a moment?"

Oh, I'll join you, and you'd better damn well explain yourselves. Bram would never speak such things aloud.

They'd stonewalled him in the council chambers, Aimeli and Briwyn moving to either side of him as Isbet made her declaration. Serval made his feelings clear on the matter until an admonishment from his sister caused him to move back in the shadows to sulk. Bram didn't give an ass damn. What he wanted was these women to explain themselves.

"Please sit." They had retired to the parlor in the queen's room and she motioned him to a chair. Bram didn't take it, although by all protocols that was insulting the queen. He was barely keeping hold of his civility at this point.

Bram went to the sideboard, poured a glass of red wine, and took a healthy swallow. "So, what is this about?" Bram made a sweeping gesture with the goblet. "Why am I being bandied about like a prized bull at auction?"

Aimeli folded her hands in her lap, her eyes downcast.

Briwyn responded. "We had hoped this would not occur. We noticed Serval's attention on you when we were in the hallway, but we never thought he would act on it." She released a long breath. "The laws, as I'm sure you know, are different here. We are fortunate that women hold sway, otherwise we would have lost you to them."

"I still don't understand," Bram said. "They expected me to just give myself up?"

"You wouldn't have a choice," Briwyn said. "Serval would have taken you by force, and what do you suppose Wilhelm's response would be? We could not attempt a rescue, not without endangering our pact and the lives of our people."

"And the pact is more important than my one life." Bram supposed he shouldn't have let himself sound so bitter.

"If there was any other way, we would have taken it." The queen raised her eyes to gaze at him. "But yes, protecting our people takes priority, as it does with you."

Bram knew she spoke the truth. He thought about his sworn oath to protect the common people. As for Wilhelm, Bram could well imagine what his response would have been. Bram's abduction would be considered an act of war.

"My apologies," Bram said. "Yes, you must think of your people."

"The only way to prevent Serval from having you would be if another female claimed you," Briwyn said. "I could not because I am married and although Aimeli could have done so, we did not want to take the risk that Serval would challenge her as she is not one of the Gifted. And again, they would take you."

Bram said, "So Isbet was the logical choice." For the first time, he looked at the young witch. Unlike Briwyn and Aimeli, she wasn't in the least bit contrite. She kept that damnable calm of hers that raised his ire. "So Isbet, how do you feel about all of this?"

"We discussed and agreed upon it." Isbet rose and moved to the sideboard to pour her own wine.

"So, you all decided upon this without consulting me?"

"And what would your answer have been if we had?" Isbet took a sip of the wine, her eyes assessing him over the cup.

Bram found he couldn't lie to her. There was something in her gaze that told him she would know. "I would have refused to cooperate."

She tilted her head to the side and smiled. Bram shook his head. He supposed they couldn't help it.

"This should keep you safe until we leave," Briwyn said.

"Which won't be until the council decides what the favor should be?" Bram said.

"Yes," Briwyn replied. "In the meantime, enjoy the queen's hospitality. You'll have much to tell your people waiting for you back aboveground."

Bram wasn't certain how much he'd be able to do so. He was certain Serval would not give up.

★   ★   ★

Bram returned to his room and tried to relax. He went back to the book, poured himself another glass of wine, which he sipped carefully. He needed something to calm his nerves but he had to be certain not to become too light-headed.

Insistent knocking made him start in his chair. Bram put the wine and book aside and approached the door. "Who is it?"

Bram had to take a step back when the door opened from the other side. Two naga came in who Bram didn't recognize. "How dare you?" Bram fought to keep his voice level. "You will pay me the respect I am due." There was nothing stopping them from accosting him, but he'd be damned if he'd let a servant disrespect him.

The naga ignored his ire. "Prince Serval commands you into his presence."

"Commands me?" Bram clenched his fists. A profane response rose to his lips, but he caught himself. Instead, he said, "I will accept Prince Serval's gracious invitation."

Bram moved around the naga, stepped across the threshold and waited. The second naga positioned himself in front of Bram while the first closed the door to his room and moved behind him. What did they believe he would do, try to escape? Where, by the Triune, would he go?

The naga led him back the way they had traveled when they went to meet with the Court, except this time they continued past the council chambers. There was no one in this area, which made Bram even more uncomfortable.

They came to a pair of double doors carved with the face of a cat with green gems for its eyes, the split traveling down the center of its face. The naga who had spoken to him glided forward and knocked.

A young nagi answered and she bowed low when Bram stepped into the room. At least someone was showing him the respect he was due. The room itself brought opulence to new heights. What caused Bram to raise an eyebrow was the surfeit of cat images decorating the room. They were everywhere. Paintings, sconces, carved in the furniture, painted on vases, and in the form of statues and figurines.

Bram liked cats well enough, and one of the manor cats was a plump old tabby that loved to sleep curled up at the foot of his bed at night, but this, he thought, was excessive.

"Your Highness, please make yourself comfortable." The nagi motioned to one of two plush couches that faced each other, with a low table set in the center. Bram took the couch, from where he could view the entrance.

"I will inform His Highness Prince Serval that you have arrived."

"Thank you." Despite the comfort of the couch, Bram sat at the very edge and rested his folded hands on his knees. He was not looking forward to his conversation with the prince since Bram felt he would hold a grudge about the refusal of his claim.

Bram sat and waited, noticing other things about the room. Although there were lamps lit by what Bram could only guess was sorcery, there were as many tapers as there were cats, situated all around, their scent cloying and thick in the air. It was a little too much for Bram. Servants, he assumed, had already set the low table with plates, utensils, and two small bowls containing towels in steaming scented water.

It seemed to Bram that he waited forever for the prince, but finally the set of double doors on the far left of the room opened. The nagi slid through first and lowered her head as Prince Serval entered the room. Bram had to admit Serval walked with the grace of the cat, his movements confident and measured. Serval wore nothing more than a pair of loose trousers of light silk. Purple gems adorned his hair, which he wore twisted on either side of his head.

Bram found himself fixated on Serval's eyes. The look in them, one of feral hunger, sent a chill through Bram. He now regretted accepting this invitation. Still, he remembered himself and stood at Serval's approach. Bram inclined his head. "Greetings to you, Prince Serval of Underneath."

"Greetings returned." Serval motioned for him to sit. "But there's no need to be so formal. I want to speak with you."

Bram took his seat as Serval did. Serval clapped twice. Four more nagi came through the double doors, each carrying trays of delicacies, their scents filling Bram's nose. The first tray had an assortment of sliced bread, toasted golden, surrounding a dish of what looked like melted cheese, or at least so Bram hoped. Another had a tureen of creamy mushroom soup and the third an assortment of fruits unlike any Bram had ever seen. They were of rich colors and unusual scents.

It was the fourth tray that had Bram taking notice. It contained several cakes of honeycomb – a favorite of Bram's and something he had not enjoyed for a long time. The nagi who greeted him at the door carried a silver decanter with two wine cups. She set them on the table and departed. Bram thought Serval would have them continue to serve them. He wasn't pleased being alone with the Dokkalfar.

"I hope you don't mind the choices I've made." Serval's smile was ingratiating. "I wasn't certain if you've had dinner. Please help yourself."

Bram couldn't resist taking one of the fine china plates and the supplied tongs, and lifting one of the honeycomb cakes. "This is fine. Thank you."

"You're very welcome." Serval lifted the plate of fruit. "I suggest you try this. It fits well with the honeycomb. Its taste is like your pomegranates."

Not wanting to appear rude, Bram took a slice of the deep-red fruit.

"I wanted to apologize for my earlier actions," Serval went on. "I didn't mean to cause you any discomfort."

Bram had trouble believing his words. Still, he said, "Apology accepted."

"I thought perhaps I should explain my actions if you'll afford me the opportunity."

"Of course."

"As you can well see, as a prince of this realm I am afforded certain luxuries," Serval said. "And anyone I choose as a lover will share my great fortune."

Bram paused, a piece of the honeycomb still in his grasp. His jaw fell at the words.

"And you need not worry about being ridiculed here," Serval said. "My people often take lovers of the same sex. Besides, no one would dare comment without facing my wrath."

"Prince Serval...." Bram put the honeycomb back on the plate and set it down. Instead of licking the stickiness off his fingers, he reached for one of the scented towels. "I don't believe—"

"In your capacity," Serval continued despite Bram's words, "you would not only share my bed but oversee my household and its everyday functions, and only I would be greater in power. You would accompany me during, as you call them, affairs of state and act as my personal steward. All this and wealth beyond your imagining, and you would be given the respect you deserve."

Bram opened his mouth to answer but realized he was in a difficult position. He knew what Serval wanted. Bram had no qualms with those who loved their own sex and in fact, there were important officials in court that did so. But even if he was so inclined, the mere thought of Serval touching him in that manner made Bram shudder in revulsion. "Prince Serval—"

"Serval." He reached for the wine and poured two cups. He handed one to Bram, who took it on instinct alone.

"I now must apologize to you because my answer must be no."

Serval leaned back in the chair and raised the cups to his lips. "Oh?" He took a sip. "Oh, I see. You're worried about the witch."

That was far from what Bram was thinking at that moment and he was sure he didn't like the tone Serval used when he referred to Isbet as 'the witch'. "I am not worried about Lady Isbet."

Serval continued as though Bram had not spoken. "I can deal with the witch if you like. I saw your reaction during the council. That whole situation displeased you. If you agree to my terms, the witch cannot lay claim to you."

Damn it. Without warning, Bram couldn't form a coherent thought. He set the wine down, even though he'd only taken a sip. "I'm not—"

Serval's gaze pinned him to his seat. "I want you, Prince Bram. And I will not allow some Overworld bitches to stop me."

"No." Bram rubbed his eyes. Fog enveloped the room and invaded his mind.

"I assure you I will make your nights pleasurable." Serval's lips lifted in a bemused smile. "And your days if you so desire."

"What's wrong with me?" Bram lay against the couch. He was sinking deep into the mire and struggled to get out. He was in trouble and he knew it, but he'd figured it out too late. There was only one explanation – magic.

Serval set down the cup and rose, ambling around the table. A nagi appeared from nowhere, carrying an engraved silver jewel box. Serval opened it and drew out a collar, strands of silver entwined around a night-black stone. "This is for you, a token of my affection."

"No…." Bram reached out, closed his leaden hand around Serval's wrist. "Get…away."

A sound broke through the lethargy. Bram grasped onto it like a lifeline. It continued, insistent knocking at the door and a voice demanding entrance.

"Damn it," Serval muttered. He straightened and stepped around the table to face the door. "I said no disturbances!"

Bram would never have a better opportunity. He summoned what little wits and strength he had about him and pushed himself off the sofa just as Serval turned back to him. Before the Dokkalfar prince could react, Bram balled his fist and swung.

It was a clumsy try, hampered because he still hadn't gathered himself, but it was enough to fill Serval with much satisfaction. Bram dropped back into the chair and waited for what was to come. Even the sound of splintering wood didn't draw Bram's attention.

"Serval!" Bram knew that voice. He squinted through the haze, willing his mind to clear. The presence of the female Dokkalfar filled the room and to Bram it seemed, cleared the air. She dressed like Serval in a full outfit of white silk. Gold bands encircled her well-defined upper arms.

"He struck me." Serval climbed to his feet. "The mortal bastard struck me. I want him executed!"

Others came into the room. Bram recognized the naga, Captain Azai.

"How is he?" the woman asked.

"He's coming out of it, Majesty."

"Sister," Serval said, his voice close to a whine. "Did you not hear me?"

"Silence." The queen crossed her arms and although not directed at him, the look she gave her brother caused Bram's stomach to clench. "It stinks of dark magic in here. Do not deny it, brother."

"Majesty." Bram found his voice. He reached out a hand and she moved around the room to curl her slim fingers around his.

"You're safe now, be at peace." Bram was reassured by those words. The last of the fog had been obliterated by some unseen force and calm settled over him.

"Captain Azai."

"Majesty."

"Escort Prince Serval to his chamber and confine him there. I will deal with him in the morning."

"Yes, Majesty."

Azai approached Serval and motioned him forward. Serval gave him a look of disgust but did not protest as he exited the room.

"Thank you, Majesty." Bram raised her hand to his lips.

"You are welcome, Prince Greyward," she said. "However, I must apologize, it is my doing that led to this incident."

CHAPTER THIRTEEN

"Majesty, what do you mean?"

Before responding, she poured herself a mug of wine. "My brother is used to having his whims catered to. Our parents indulged us both, but with Serval it came to a point where he considers himself entitled." It somewhat surprised Bram when she averted her eyes. "I suspected Serval would not accept my decision, but I hoped he would leave you be. I should have known better and I ask your forgiveness, Prince Greyward."

Bram straightened his shoulders, drawing a deep breath. He could not abide her taking the blame for her brother's transgressions. "Majesty—"

"Calla." She smiled at him.

"Calla." Bram returned the smile. "Such a lovely name. Please call me Bram."

The glow in her cheeks enhanced her beauty. "Thank you."

"Please do not apologize for your brother for I hold no blame against you." In somewhat of a bold move Bram reached over and squeezed her hand. "It is Serval's fault," Bram said. "Even as a man of the cloth, my faith trusts in taking responsibility for one's wrongdoings. There are those who will grant absolution, but the Triune teaches as the Father and Mother discipline the Child, we of the mortal realm should do the same. But that you let one follow their own path and face the consequences of where it leads them."

Bram wasn't certain how the queen would react to what he did next. "I absolve you of your responsibility to Serval. Your duty is to your realm and your people."

Calla seemed for a moment to observe Bram. There was a slight bit of merriment in her eyes and Bram found his own cheeks warming. "Thank you, Bram. Your words mean a great deal to me."

Suddenly shy around her, Bram twisted his body around and served up a plate of the honeycomb. "Would you like some?"

"Yes, it's my favorite."

"Mine too." Bram liked the beautiful Dokkalfar. She wasn't like many of the court women he met, unless they were soldiers or bodyguards. Although she was in silks, he could see her well-defined muscles. Bram thought if he put a sword in her hand, she'd give any opponent a battle.

"What are you thinking of, Bram?"

Bram rested an arm on the back of the couch. "How beautiful you are."

"Careful, Highness." Calla raised an arched brow. "Or I may have to seduce you."

"That would not be a bad thing."

She laughed. It was a throaty sound and Bram felt the spark between them. He kissed her. The kiss wasn't passionate, just a light touch of the lips. Bram caught her light flowery scent.

"No, it would not be a bad thing at all," Calla said. "You plan on seeing this through?"

"I-I don't—"

"You fear what Wilhelm will say? Yes, I know all about the war." She squeezed his hand. "I am sorry you lost so much."

"Thank you." Bram's throat tightened. He felt the darkness try to take him but something warm and peaceful filled him. A sense of how things were before Wilhelm had torn him from his home and his life. He knew it was Calla, using the same power as Serval, but it was to help him. He wanted her to know how grateful he was, but he couldn't find the words.

She seemed to know. "You are welcome." She reached for the wine cup again, refreshed their drinks. "Tell me about Tamrath."

Bram did and they talked of his true home and then Calla told him of the place where she and Serval had grown up, and even the few times when the two of them had shared some childhood adventure before things had changed between them. Bram also shared stories of himself, Jaryl, and their cousin and the frequent times they'd gotten into trouble.

It was well into the wee hours, when Bram yawned perhaps for the fourth time, that Calla said, "I think it is well past time you retired for the night, Bram."

"Please excuse me." Bram rose and offered her his hand. They walked to the door, where Captain Azai waited.

"Captain, if you will escort the prince back to his rooms?"

"At once, Your Majesty."

Bram bowed. "Good night, Your Majesty."

"It was for me, as well. Good night, Highness. It was a pleasure spending the evening with you."

As he walked down the corridor, Bram smiled at the memory of his conversation with Calla. It came to Bram then that he had not answered the queen's question. Would he see this through?

"You made the queen very happy tonight."

Bram started at the sound of Azai's voice. "She is a magnificent woman."

"That she is." Azai didn't look at him but Bram heard the admiration in his voice.

"Captain, I didn't thank you for your part in my rescue. I appreciate it."

Azai stopped, twisted around on his tail. "Do not mention it," he said. "Your Highness, I don't suppose I need to tell you it would be best to stay out of Serval's way. He will not take what happened without fighting."

"Trust me, I have no plans to be anywhere near him if I can help it."

"That is best. Avoid him no matter how rude it seems. If you see him coming, go the other way and if you need help, please seek me out."

"Thank you." Bram extended his hand and Azai took it in a cool grasp. He knew he could call the naga a friend.

★　　★　　★

The change was subtle, a slight chill of the air and an erratic movement in the shadows. Those little things woke Bram from his sound sleep. He frowned into the darkness and silence. The sound of his own breath was muted. Bram wanted to move, but his body refused to respond.

"My sister was correct." The voice that came out of the darkness had Bram drawing in a sharp breath. His heart dropped to his stomach. "I am accustomed to getting what I want."

How had he known what Calla had said? Bram realized that was not his biggest concern now. He tried again to move but the invisible bonds tightened around him. Magic, Bram realized. Serval had him in a spell.

"I must release you." Serval stood next to his bed. "I want you to enjoy this. I'll need your word that you won't fight. You will submit to me."

"Go to the nether-hells!" Bram forced the words through his teeth.

"I had hoped to not have to convince you." Serval held one hand over Bram's midsection. The bonds continued to tighten. Although still unseen, they changed shape and became thorn-points pressing against his skin to pierce his flesh. Bram didn't know if he bled, just that his body was on fire.

Bram opened his mouth to scream, but Serval made a quick movement over his mouth with his free hand. His scream was silenced.

Tears burned beneath his closed lids, escaping down his cheeks. If he could, he would have begged Serval to stop. Anything to have this awful pain cease. His stomach lurched, the gorge rising. He tried to force it back, knowing if it filled his throat, he would choke. *Please stop.*

"You've had enough, I see." Serval made a second motion with his hand. Air rushed back into Bram's lungs.

"Stop."

"Very well." Serval stepped back and the thorns receded, bonds loosed and fell away.

Bram lay there, once again in control of his body. He took deep breaths and concentrated on willing his stomach to quiet. A shudder passed through him, an aftereffect of the torture.

"Let me." The gentleness in Serval's voice filled Bram with disgust. The Dokkalfar prince passed his hands over Bram's body. Although there was no visible sign, despite himself he sighed in relief as the pain faded.

"Now," Serval said, "I hope we will have no more instances?"

Bram didn't respond, only turned his face aside.

"I did not lie when I said I would give you pleasure." The tenderness in Serval's voice was an affront. He seemed to think that Bram was a cherished lover, not someone he'd tortured to get his way.

Serval ran his hands across Bram's bare chest. The bile rose again as Serval pressed his mouth on Bram's stomach, his tongue tracing patterns. Bram swallowed.

Serval lifted his gaze. "You can call out my name if you like."

"Just get on with it." Bram's fists clenched around the fabric of the sheets.

"Come now, Bram, it won't be as bad as all that." Serval moved closer to the head of the bed and grasped Bram under his chin. "After this time, you will freely come to me."

A sharp *crack* reverberated through the room. Serval straightened, and Bram turned his head just as the door splintered and exploded, spewing wood fragments across the room. Light poured in and a figure stood in shadow against it, illuminated by the dozens of wil-o-wisp coming behind her.

"Bastard!" Isbet held her staff over her head. "You violate what's mine!"

The staff came down, Serval's body jerked in a single spasm, and then an unseen force threw him against the far wall. Bram scrambled to his knees on the bed and watched as Isbet advanced into the center of the room. She struck again, as Serval was gathering himself.

"Bitch! How dare you touch me?" Serval's rage burned through the air; Bram could feel it. Isbet fought, standing firm for a precious moment, her staff held in front of her, the face of the talisman alive, with red light pouring from its mouth and eyes.

Wounds appeared on Isbet's arms, like knife cuts across her skin. The dressing gown she wore ripped in places, exposing her. She didn't seem to notice. Her brow furrowed. Bram could even see the sweat gathering there and between her breasts. It was a battle of strength and silence.

Should he intervene? Bram couldn't move again, as though a little part of Isbet's magic kept him in place. *No*, Bram thought. *I can't, not in this.*

Another sharp *crack*, louder than the door shattering, and Isbet went to one knee. Serval was winning; Bram could see it in the wild look in his eyes and the manic grin that split his face.

Ancient wood groaned. The floor split, creating a great crack between the two combatants. Whatever force held Bram released him and he moved across the bed until his back met the wall. The bed was against it, underneath a circular window. Bram would have escaped through it and gone for help, but they were at least four stories up.

The battle continued. Serval was forcing Isbet backward. The crack lengthened, coming close to the bed. Bram wanted to call out to Isbet, to encourage her, but he knew that would only prove to be a distraction.

Bram willed her to win and he prayed to the Triune for her and for the strength of the Holy Family to fill her. If she lost this battle—

Isbet shifted the staff in her hands. Her movements were lethargic, and the force of Serval's attack hampered them. With a cry, she brought the staff down once again, driving the tip into the wood floor. It screamed, or was that Isbet? Bram couldn't tell. Another crack shot out from where the staff was embedded, crossing the larger crack, which expanded.

"Don't, you stupid bitch!" There was fear in Serval's voice.

Isbet wrenched the staff from the floor, held it aloft for a moment, and then brought it down again. The cracks split apart, and vines burst through the openings, forming a crisscross of interlocking branches, separating Bram from both Isbet and Serval. They continued to grow, shearing through the room like an ax blade. There was a ponderous groan like a giant turning and stretching after a decade's long sleep. A great crash and the room lurched backward, throwing Bram hard against the wall. He struggled forward, on his hands and knees, reaching for anything to hold on to.

The room split apart, the wood giving way, exploding into chunks and splinters. A cry erupted from Bram's lips as the section fell out from under him and hurled him into space.

CHAPTER FOURTEEN

Isbet lay on the bed, staring at the ceiling, watching the movements of the liquid light as it made its way along the Vine. She supposed some people would look at this display as the life's blood of the plant. Well, it wasn't blood per se, but it was life energy and the food that nourished the Vine.

The offshoot that she observed was a thick branch growing from a hole in the floor and had traveled its way in a great arch across the ceiling. Isbet wondered about safety, considering if this offshoot grew it would take a good chunk of the room with it.

Her worry wasn't what was keeping her awake. Isbet listened to the world that surrounded her. Because the Vine was everywhere, she could sense movement and hear the beating hearts and their breathing, slow in sleep. There was the soft touch of the wil-o-wisp as they alighted on the floor or attached themselves to walls, their glow always keeping some section of the palace lit. It was not peaceful, for Isbet also sensed the various magics that stole their way along the Vine's length. She dared not trace them back to their sources. Isbet didn't know where they would lead.

Isbet noticed then that something was different in the offshoot. A knot had appeared along the smooth branch that hadn't been there a few minutes ago. The wood was malleable, shaped by unseen hands. Isbet continued to watch, interested, as a dark brown face appeared.

"Well, it's about time," Isbet said.

Gaemyr screwed up his expression. "I was enjoying myself and not in the least bit of a hurry to return."

"So, I gathered," Isbet said. "Have you satisfied your hunger?"

"Indeed!" Gaemyr grinned. "I will not have to feed for weeks to come, barring any accidents or overuse of my power."

"I see nothing in the foreseeable future," Isbet said, but she hadn't prepared herself for a true scrying. "Do you sense the lines of magic traveling through the Vine?"

His expression sobered. "Yes, I do. The strongest is coming from far away, but whoever is meddling in things here is causing their share of damage."

Isbet worried her lower lip. "A favor, if you don't mind?"

Gaemyr must have been in high spirits, for he said, "Of course, my dear."

"See if you can discover anything further. If we find one of those guilty of this tampering, they may lead us to others," Isbet said.

"A novel idea," Gaemyr replied. "Perhaps I'll do more – ah – investigation?"

"Don't go skulking about where you don't belong," Isbet scolded.

Gaemyr made a noise of disagreement before fading back into the Vine.

Isbet blew out a breath. "How that damnable staff vexes me sometimes." Still, she supposed if Gaemyr found something useful it wouldn't hurt having the information, or so she hoped.

It seemed only moments later that Gaemyr returned "Isbet!"

"What? What is it?"

"You must come now! There are treacherous doings with your prince."

Isbet was off the bed in an instant, grabbed her trousers, and pulled them on. Gaemyr fell into her outstretched hand.

"Where?" Isbet didn't bother with her boots. On bare feet, she darted down the hall, her footfalls soft on the wood.

"His rooms," Gaemyr said. "He is there."

"Damn it to the nether-hells." Isbet stopped at the head of the corridor leading to Bram's room and pressed her back against the wall. With a quick look around the corner, Isbet saw two naga standing guard in front of Bram's room, both loyal to Serval, no doubt.

Now came the problem of how to get past the guards. Naga had their own type of magic that Isbet had studied, but she didn't sense those two had the Gift. However, there was still the problem of how to deal with them and get into the room.

"Gaemyr, I will need your power."

Gaemyr sighed. "Very well."

Isbet closed her eyes. Her breathing became steady and deep. She allowed herself not to fall but to step carefully into the world between. When she opened her eyes, the veils between worlds appeared as sheer gossamer curtains and yet they kept the entrance to the mortal plane and other worlds sealed off. They moved as though stirred by a gentle breeze as Isbet drew on their power.

Wil-o-wisp gathered about her, drawn by the gathering. Isbet spoke to them in her mind's eye and they obeyed. With Gaemyr in her grasp, Isbet spread her arms wide and sprinted down the short length of the hall, dragging the veils with her, wrapping them around her arms, shaping them to her needs, and the wil-o-wisp surrounded her, passing through them, bringing them alive with light.

The first naga turned, bared its teeth at Isbet, and lowered the halberd, the deadly tip aimed at Isbet's chest. His movements alerted the second but as he turned, Isbet flung the veils forward. The fabric wrapped around them in a silk cocoon. Isbet tightened them around the naga, securing them, then she brought her arms down and pulled the naga to the floor. Only another Gifted could free them.

Isbet did not slow. Now drawing on Gaemyr's own power, Isbet focused his energy and touched the tip of the staff to the door. Fissures appeared, pulsing with light at first, then the door blasted apart in great chunks.

Isbet only took a moment to assess. Serval stood by the bed on which Bram lay. The room stank of darkness and treachery and Isbet knew what Serval planned without explanation. He turned to her and even in the semi-darkness, she witnessed first surprise then hate in his expression. She had to strike now before he gathered himself.

"Bastard! You violate what's mine!" Isbet brought Gaemyr down in a violent motion, pulling more veils with her, melding Gaemyr's power with them. As with the naga, she surrounded Serval, binding him for a precious moment, then, focusing Gaemyr, she sent a pulse along the veils. Isbet pivoted to her right, the veils tightened, wrenching Serval off his feet and sending his body airborne.

Isbet could no longer use the veils. Manipulating them as she had drained her energy but also, if one of them moved aside, something unpleasant might escape into the mortal world and Isbet did not want that on her head.

Isbet drew on a different source, the deep earth that birthed the witches and was their true power. But Isbet hadn't figured that the Vine itself would surround her with the energy of its own volition. It was familiar and foreign at the same time, but Isbet wasn't about to question it. The energy smelled of the loam of the earth, gathered at Isbet's command, and her first strike sent Serval to his knees.

"Bitch! How dare you touch me?"

Serval also drew on the Vine and Isbet sensed his skill exceeded hers. She would die if she did not defeat him. Serval's initial attack bathed her in the fire. Gaemyr was her shield, but the spell punished him without mercy. Gaemyr's struggle was hers.

They fought in silence. There was no taunting or banter as the books and plays often wrote, nor attempts to distract or enrage so one would make a fatal error. Isbet always thought such writings were ridiculous. Spells took concentration, focus, and talking wasn't something you wanted to be doing. All her focus was on Serval.

Serval continued to batter her shield and Isbet searched for an opening, but Serval refused to give her the opportunity. One slip and she would have the advantage again. Small bits of Serval's power penetrated her defenses, like heated knives ripping across her flesh, tearing at her dressing gown. It was not her concern. She wasn't some virginal maiden embarrassed at a hint of exposed flesh.

Sweat gathered, pooled between her breasts, and ran in rivulets down her face. Serval was almost through. Isbet let go, dropping to one knee as the barrage caught her. The smell of her own burning flesh filled her nostrils.

Isbet was taking the full force of his power, and it threatened to rip her apart. She slammed Gaemyr into the supple wood, driving the point deep as she copied Serval, taking directly from the Vine and the source lines of magic she had seen. She knew the cost. If she disrupted the various magics, she could draw someone's, or something's attention, and she was uncertain if the Vine would allow her to delve deeper into its heart. She drew her power from the earth, but she was not a true Child of the Vine.

She had little choice.

The floor cracked, the jagged seam running across the room. Isbet tried to draw in a breath, but the surrounding air burned. She switched Gaemyr to one hand, her arms weighted down by the oppressive heat. She made Gaemyr her anchor by driving him into the floor again and drew on the same force that Serval used.

A sound filled her ears, its origin uncertain to her. It was as though she had fallen into the middle of a surreal dream which allowed her to see Serval's expression of shock. The floor split the opposite way, crossing the first crack.

"Don't, you stupid bitch!"

Isbet heard the fear in Serval's voice. The Vine was filling her with its power, drawing it away from Serval, and what Isbet feared would happen did as new growth burst through the cracks, fed by the magics that Isbet had drawn upon and by her own life.

She could no longer see Serval, only hear the ancient, ponderous sound of the old wood stretching itself out, seeking to expand after so many decades of dormancy. The room dropped from under her feet and Isbet leaped, the offshoots heeding her silent call. She had not expected them to obey her will, but they did. She climbed up the tangle of supple young vines, escaping death.

Then came the scream.

"Bram!" Isbet didn't think twice. She let loose of Gaemyr and dove from her safe perch. The offshoots and branches parted, allowing her an opening just as Bram fell. She reached for him. Her fingers brushed against his, her other hand reaching—

The Vine heeded her call again, or so she believed. There was something different in this power. It was not familiar to her as before. It filled her mind and body, intertwining with her soul where tiny seedlings sprouted and grew, nourished by that part of her.

It seemed for a moment they would both fall to their deaths, but Isbet reached with one hand – no, her hand had changed. It was smooth and strong, and it grasped Bram by the wrist, wrapping itself around. There was a violent jerk and Isbet was certain her arm would pull out of its socket, but she felt her muscles tighten and Bram's weight seemed of no consequence. Her other hand closed around a branch, but it seemed the distance between her and it was long.

Below them wil-o-wisp lit the open area. People were coming from their homes and rooms, carrying their own lights. The ground was close now, although her other hand still grasped the branch high above her.

"Oh, Triune," Bram said.

"Bram, I'm letting you go."

He looked up at her, his expression a mixture of concern and fear, but she nodded and untwined her hand from his. Bram dropped to the ground below. Isbet released the branch and dropped beside him.

"Isbet!" Bram rushed to her, catching her as her knees gave way. The familiar awareness that was her power was now entangled with the Vine around her soul. Her body had not adjusted to the change and it reacted as her stomach turned and it flushed her skin with fever. Her mouth and throat were so dry no words would come.

"Here!" Someone pressed a cup to her lips and cool water washed down her throat. So sweet and crisp, she'd never sampled such, and the Vine welcomed it.

"Isbet." Bram knelt beside her. He ran his fingers across her temple, brushing back her hair. Isbet would have never allowed such under normal circumstances, but she found his touch comforting.

"It's all right." Isbet wasn't certain why she said that. She supposed she looked strange to Bram. Her arms lay out on either side of her, stretched far out of proportion. It would have to do, however, for Isbet didn't have the strength to say any more.

CHAPTER FIFTEEN

The storytellers and the scholars were wrong. Bram did not witness his life flashing before his eyes. As the room broke apart and Bram fell into nothing, pitch darkness surrounded him. At least he wouldn't see the end coming.

Then light filled his eyes and fell like a waterfall out of the gaping hole. Not water but wil-o-wisp. They fell behind him by the dozens and a figure came behind them.

"Bram!"

A brief touch of her fingers. *At least*, he thought, *I have that.*

Then something caught him. It halted his descent as it wrapped around his wrist, jerking his arm. Bram closed his hand around it and smaller tendrils of it secured themselves around his fingers. Bram looked up and – Triune—? Isbet's arms, no longer skin, muscle, and bone, but a tangled length of vines, twisting and pulling taut as she fought to hold him. Her other hand reaching – no, supple stems, twining around a branch as the other did around Bram's fingers.

The stem lowered him to the ground. Isbet spoke to him but he didn't quite understand her words. His gaze was fixed on the disturbing thing she had become. He acknowledged her and she released him.

"Thank the Triune," Bram said aloud, although he figured he should thank Isbet. People came from all sides of the clearing. Bram kept his eyes on Isbet until she too was on the ground.

"Isbet." Bram caught her when she collapsed. Her brow burned with fever, but no sweat appeared. Bram touched her, hoping she would awaken.

"Here!" The voice made Bram jump a little. Browaing knelt beside them and handed Bram a wooden cup.

"Here, give her this. Let her sip it."

Bram cradled Isbet's head in his lap and took the cup from Browaing. He tipped the cup to her lips. She must have been conscious on some level because she took a sip.

"It will be all right," Isbet whispered.

"Yes, it will be," Bram said. "It has to be. Here, drink more."

"Stay with her." Browaing rose and turned. People moved just out of Bram's line of vision, gathering around to gawk at the spectacle. *Damn them all.*

"Bram." He didn't even look up at the sound of Calla's voice. Not until she touched him on his face. "I'm here to help her. Do you trust me?"

"Yes."

Calla laid hands on the tangle of vines of Isbet's left arm and hand. Curious despite himself, Bram observed as Calla drew her hands up towards Isbet's shoulder. As she did, the vines withdrew, disappearing back within themselves as though Calla had turned time backward, sending them to sleep.

As the queen continued, flesh and bone replaced the greenery. Isbet's hands appeared somewhat normal, except for what appeared to be a tattoo of twining vines around her wrist. A sound drew Bram's attention for a moment and he looked to his right. Browaing instructed those gathered in the cleanup effort.

Calla moved to Isbet's other side and completely restored her body. Once she'd finished, she stood and stretched.

Browaing approached them both. "Quite a mess," he remarked. "Prince Greyward, what in the hell happened here?"

Bram began to reply, but a voice rang out, "The bitch attacked me!"

Serval stepped into the clearing. Bram noted with some satisfaction that he had not survived the destruction unscathed. Serval pushed past some of the gathered people. He was a pitiful sight, with his fine clothes torn and his face dirty and bleeding.

"Without provocation?"

"Yes, sister!"

"That's a lie!" Bram tightened his hold on Isbet.

"You – you son of a whore! You dare accuse me of—"

"Serval!" Calla raised her hand.

"I will not be silenced, sister!" Serval said. "The witch has committed an act of war against me and our people. I say they should die here and now."

"Shut your mouth, arrogant pup!" Browaing snarled. "Have I not told you, you have no say in these matters?"

Serval didn't respond but stood there pouting like a child denied a favorite treat. Bram had seen the fear in his eyes. The Dokkalfar prince afraid of a little kobold? But then again Bram had a sense that Browaing had been alive many decades if not centuries longer than Serval. The life spans of the Children outlasted mortals and the older they grew, the more powerful they became.

"You disrespect Our Majesty." Browaing balled his fists.

There were murmurings within the crowd. Such situations could turn volatile. Would Serval cross that line?

No, for Serval held any words he'd intended to speak.

"Prince Greyward, what happened?"

"I—" Bram caught himself. He didn't want to lie to Calla but – Triune, he didn't want anyone to learn what Serval had done to him. He would never keep his dignity.

"You see, Your Majesty?" Serval spoke but kept his eyes downcast. "He knows I speak the truth."

"Isbet—" Bram swallowed the stone in his throat, "—came to my aid." Bram nodded at Serval. "They fought, Serval and Isbet. I can only guess the battle caused the destruction."

"You needed no aid, at least that is what you said when you invited me into your rooms." Serval looked at him now with the barest hint of a smirk.

"I did not." Bram looked to Calla. "He forced his way into my rooms. Your Majesty, may we further discuss this in private?"

"Your Majesty, what does Prince Greyward have to hide?" Serval said. "I ask that you consider how this may seem to our people, that you are showing undue favor to the mortals."

The mutterings grew louder. Bram looked from Serval back to the queen.

"You little—" Browaing began.

"No," Calla said. "Browaing, please have Isbet taken care of. Be certain she has everything she needs."

"Yes, Majesty." Browaing turned towards the gathered group. "You there, I'll need some help." He motioned to some other naga standing nearby. "Get me a stretcher, now!"

When Bram turned back to look at Calla, he saw not the kind, gentle woman he'd spent an evening with but the ruler of her people. Bram appreciated what it meant to be in such a position. Every monarch, no matter how powerful, must bow to the will of the people. Any impropriety may make that ruler seem ineffectual. Bram caught the slight change in her face. Her remorse. It only lasted for an eye-blink but perhaps Calla recognized he understood.

"Well, Prince Greyward, will you speak true?" Serval asked.

Triune, how he despised the bastard. As a man of the cloth, he shouldn't harbor such feelings against his fellow man, but as an imperfect human he did. "Prince Serval broke into my rooms and attempted to – force himself on me. I made it clear I did not want him, but he tortured me until I agreed. Isbet freed me from his spell."

"As she had the right." Calla regarded Serval as she spoke. "I needn't tell you, brother, it is our law. Lady Isbet laid claim to Prince Greyward. You had no right to him."

Serval made a noise of disgust. "So, what you are saying, Prince Greyward, is that you allowed me to take you like some helpless virginal lad and then you needed rescuing by a woman? Where are your cock and balls?"

Those gathered began to laugh and taunt him, but they did not get far.

"Silence, all of you!" The queen's hand sliced through the air in front of her. "If you do not help here, then return to your homes."

Some moved off but others went to help clear out the debris. Two Dokkalfar maidens approached Serval. One draped a silk shawl around his shoulders and the other presented him with a wineskin. They then fawned over the man.

"Yes, yes, my dears, I am not seriously harmed. No mere witch can best me."

Calla looked after him a moment before turning back to Bram. "Are you injured, Highness? Do you need attention?"

Browaing returned, followed by two naga carrying a stretcher. "Here, let us take her," Browaing said. "I promise, Bram, she will receive the best of care."

Bram moved away, laying Isbet down. She seemed to be conscious now, yet she remained still as the naga lifted her onto the stretcher. Bram thought to follow as he moved away but his legs refused to obey.

So, what you are saying, Prince Greyward, is that you allowed me to take you like some helpless virginal lad and then you needed rescuing by a woman?

The taunts and the sound of the laughter haunted him. He was the victim; they had no right to shame him as they had. He tried to push the memories away, but they continued to echo in his mind. *I am a warrior, trained in defense. I should have fought him harder.*

"Bram," Calla interrupted his brooding. "Come with me. I'll take you somewhere to wait, and besides, we need to see the queen and duchess."

He'd almost forgotten about Aimeli and Briwyn. Triune, he hoped no harm had come to them, but as much as he wanted to know for certain, as much as he wanted to know Isbet was all right, his pride wouldn't allow it. He couldn't face that, not now.

"I – I'm sorry, Majesty, I can't—" Bram turned and walked away. He thought Calla would call after him, but when she didn't Bram realized she understood his feelings.

Bram walked to the end of the clearing, where a path started into the woods, at first in semi-darkness, but as he went along, the wil-o-wisp followed him. His steps were further guided by plant life that glowed, great round bulbs filled with ghostly lights or mushrooms alive with phosphorescence.

Bram continued with no idea where the path would take him. He'd likely walk into something unpleasant, but he didn't care. He only wanted to escape that clearing, walking until only the natural sounds of this alien forest filled the air.

Although he had fled, his disgrace continued to dog him. It followed him even as he went deeper. Why had he come here? He should have refused, delivered Wilhelm's message and gone back home – no, not home – gone back to Rhyvirand and be done with it.

Bram didn't want to be in the middle of the bickering and intrigues of this world and its peoples, nor did he want to be a prisoner.

He wanted his damn life back.

Bram stumbled and nearly fell but reached out and steadied himself against the trunk of a tree. No, not a tree, a large and wrinkled plant although, like the trees from his world, it had branches that bore a round fruit at each tip. The branches themselves also glowed a soft green. Bram sank down at its base.

"Triune, why have you abandoned me?" Bram had not had these thoughts before, but as time passed and no rescue came, he began to call out to them, to plead with them. *Why am I still a captive? Am I not your loyal servant? Why have you turned your backs on me and my people?*

It came to Bram that this wasn't about his humiliation. When Serval had him captive, he'd been helpless to stop the man. Just like when Wilhelm had taken him. He couldn't fight. He'd given in. Bram just wanted the pain at an end. He balled his fist and slammed it against the thick trunk. It wasn't as solid as he expected, and his fist left an imprint. He supposed he shouldn't harm the flora here, but he didn't care. He slammed his fist into the surface again and again, and after a time and despite the malleable surface, his knuckles stung.

There Bram sat, aware of the tears but not in the least bit concerned. He leaned his head against the trunk and closed his eyes. "Let some beast of the Underneath come and take me, then." At least that would end his suffering.

* * *

"Wake up, Highness."

Bram came awake and drew in a sharp breath. "Who's there?"

"Up here, Highness."

Bram looked up. It took a few moments for his eyes to adjust but when they did, he could make out a face impressed into the wood of an overhanging branch. Bram had the strangest feeling of familiarity. "Wait – you're it – I mean him, the staff, Gaemyr!"

The face grinned at him. "Well, you are intelligent for a mortal man," Gaemyr said.

Bram said, "How is this possible? That you – that I can—?"

"Well," Gaemyr said, bemused, "I believe your first question is how am I here within this limb? It's simple, Highness. This is the Vine and I am of the Vine. Or at the very least this accursed form is of the Vine."

The revelation didn't surprise Bram. It was logical that Gaemyr was human once, but what crime could the being have committed that warranted such punishment? Was there no one to absolve him?

Gaemyr seemed unaware of Bram's musings. "And how can you hear me? Simple again, it's the Vine. You are not hearing me, but my voice through the Vine."

Bram nodded. "Wait, shouldn't you be with Isbet? How is she?"

"Isbet is fine. She asked me to look after you."

Bram almost said *I don't need looking after*, but he snatched the words back. He supposed he did, since he had no idea where he was. "How long have I been asleep?"

"Several hours. Don't worry, you have missed little," Gaemyr said. "And you seemed exhausted, so I figured I would allow you to continue sleeping."

Had the talisman been watching over him all this time? "Thank you, Sir Gaemyr."

"Now, there is no need for such formality." Despite the admonishment, the show of respect pleased him. "If you are ready, I shall lead you to Isbet."

"Yes, I am ready."

"Continue further up the path."

Bram nodded and walked. Whenever he came to a fork in the path, Gaemyr would appear and lead him in the right direction. Bram noticed they were going uphill. The trail then curved to the right and it surprised Bram to see light at the end, and even more so to hear voices.

"This way, Highness."

At the head of the path, the dense foliage opened into a cavern. Bram had never seen one so enormous in his life. But it wasn't the size that had him staring in wonder, but the cavern's ceiling, which was – Bram tried to put a description to it— It was as though a great gaping hole had been dug in the ground and a giant of old had stoppered it with a smooth gem from their immense treasure. It was of a blue opalescence, translucent and shimmering with light that fell in a shower over a pristine lake. The walls were covered with gigantic vines and blooms of deep purple.

Bram was trying to take it all in when he heard a cry.

On the opposite side of the cavern, a waterfall crashed over the cliff, churning the water at that end of the lake. Some clever hands had fashioned a slide at the top of the falls. A group of young people gathered there. Watching them enjoy themselves made Bram smile.

The youngsters lined up at the top of the waterfall, awaiting their turn on the slide. They were laughing and shoving against each other, much like the youth of his world did.

The next person in line stepped forward and Bram couldn't help the slight laugh that escaped him. It was Isbet. Without hesitation, she pushed herself forward, her hands over her head. She hit the bottom of the slide and flew out over the lake, disappearing underneath the water with a splash.

The people cheered when she surfaced, and with strong deliberate strokes she swam to shore. When she climbed out her blouse clung to her skin. Even from that distance, Bram noticed how beautiful and confident she was. Bram watched as she gathered her thin braids in her hands and twisted them, squeezing the water out.

"Well, what are you waiting for?" Gaemyr said. "Get your ass on down there. She's waiting for you."

CHAPTER SIXTEEN

The vision came to Isbet as the naga carried her away from the clearing. She was uncertain how it was possible that she witnessed what was happening to her, but Isbet watched everything around her, the crowd gathering, milling about, whispering and gossiping like a mess of old biddies.

Isbet heard Serval's insult and the cruel laughter. She swore from her place to make Serval pay but there was nothing she could do now. The scene was fading around her into dusk, drawing her, it seemed, within herself until she spotted the seedlings entwined with her soul.

This was not part of her plan. She could imagine Gaemyr chiding her now: *so much for staying out of this*. As she lay there pondering the future and how in all the nether-hells she would avoid any further distractions, the Vine spoke to her. Well, not speaking per se, but the seedlings entwined around her soul quivered as one tendril loosened its hold. Isbet reached for it and as the new leaf touched her fingers, she looked at – darkness.

It was blacker than pitch and stinking of everything decaying beneath the earth. Down, down the tendril drew her. Isbet struggled, but the Vine had complete hold of her now. The stench was unbearable, a mixture of the cloying sweetness of rotting fruit and rank filth of the long dead.

Isbet was in the bowels of Underneath, where all the creatures – the warped, deformed Children that the higher beings both ruled and feared – hungered to be free.

Isbet realized she would be in peril if any of them caught her. Even if she weren't there, they would still sense her presence. As she thought this, the Vine brought her back, pulling her from that place. Isbet did not resist.

"Damn it to the nether-hells," Isbet muttered.

A voice said in response, "What did you see?"

Sensation was returning now. The naga lifted her off the stretcher and she observed them with her own eyes now. They lowered her into a rectangular pool. The water was hot, and it went to work on her aching muscles.

The voice had been that of the Dokkalfar woman who had been in the clearing. Isbet's memory came back to her. This was the queen.

"Tell me, Lady Isbet, what did the Vine show you?"

The queen sat on a pillow at the edge of the pool. Two nagi moved around the room and one set a tray of food next to the queen and one by the pool within Isbet's reach. The Vine sent its message through her. "You have trouble coming, Majesty."

"Calla," she said, "and I thought as much."

"Then you have sensed this in the Vine as well?" There was little time for formalities, so she addressed the Dokkalfar as an equal.

"It has whispered to me that servants of the dark are stirring, but I'm uncertain why now."

"As am I," Isbet said. "However, the Vine showed me they are becoming aware. How long has it been since you have seen one of them here?"

"It has been centuries, even before my time," Calla said. "Browaing is the one to ask."

"They did not reveal their true forms to me," Isbet said. "Nor could I tell if they stirred because of the many forces of magic using the Vine. They do not reach that far."

"How do you know this?" Calla asked.

Isbet furrowed her brow. "I am uncertain. Perhaps the Vine told me. I am new to its...wants and needs."

Calla adjusted her position; she lay on her side, stretching out her long legs. "You are aware that you are now beholden to the Vine?"

"Yes." Isbet was not happy about the prospect. She'd known that there would be recompense for drawing from the Vine, or had that been the plan all along? Had the Vine felt a need for her and allowed her to partake? It was disturbing, and Isbet sank up to her neck in the tub.

"You are not pleased," Calla said.

"No," Isbet replied. "But we can do little about it now."

"You had a task that you set for yourself," Calla said. "But I did not invade your privacy. However, now your path has changed, Lady Isbet, perhaps for the better."

Isbet didn't believe so, but she had little choice. She expected Gaemyr wouldn't be any more pleased than she was. She decided a change of subject was in order. "How does Prince Greyward fare?"

Calla sat up and drew her knees to her chest, encircling them with her arms. "His body fares well but his spirit has taken a harsh blow."

"And what of Serval?" Isbet recalled his exiting the scene with no worry of punishment.

Calla didn't respond at first. Then she said, "It is a delicate situation with him. If I allow him to go unpunished, then—"

"Your people will look upon you without favor," Isbet said.

"So, I must deal punishment not only for this transgression but for others. I am sorry, but I may not mete out the punishment he deserves because he accosted a mortal, but I assure you he will face our law."

Isbet thought it impossible to sympathize with royalty, but she admired Calla and found it unfortunate that she had to be put in such a position. It was why she preferred her life as a wandering witch. To have your every move or act scrutinized.... It would drive her insane. "I am sorry I have brought this on your shoulders, Calla."

Calla shook her head. "There was no avoiding this. I would have dealt with Serval on some level. This incident is one of many, so do not concern yourself with it."

Isbet's concern was not for herself but for Bram. "Where is Prince Greyward now?"

"I...I'm uncertain. Serval does not dare attempt to accost him now."

"Majesty, I would appreciate if he were being looked after." Isbet pushed herself up and rose from the tub. One of the nagi rushed to her as she climbed out and draped a robe around her shoulders.

"Are you certain you're well enough to stand? I'm certain you've guessed the pool has healing properties?"

"Yes, Majesty." Isbet inclined her head. "And I thank you for its use."

Calla rose and stretched. "No thanks are necessary."

Isbet moved to the farthest wall where an offshoot of the Vine formed a part of the base. Isbet knelt.

"What are you doing?" Calla asked.

"Summoning Gaemyr." Isbet laid her hands against the smoothness of the offshoot. "Before the room split, I had to toss him away. He joined with the Vine again."

Gaemyr did not tarry as Isbet expected him to; he heeded Isbet's call, his face appearing in the Vine.

"Was that entire ruckus necessary?"

"What ruckus? I summoned you."

"Well, it seemed like someone was banging my head with a blasted club."

"You exaggerate," Isbet said. "I have a favor to ask of you."

Gaemyr sniffed. "From one thing to another now, is it?"

"Gaemyr—"

"Oh, lovely, what is it?"

"Find the prince and make certain that he is well. That no one accosts him."

"Oh, is that all? Fine." It surprised Isbet that he'd agreed, but then again perhaps it was because he would rejoin with the Vine.

"Extraordinary." Calla laid a finger against her cheek. "If you are ready, Lady Isbet, I have had new rooms prepared for you. There are also new clothes laid out and a meal prepared." She nodded to one of the nagi and she came forward. Clasping her hands, she bowed at the waist. "Osirha will escort you."

Isbet bowed to the queen. "I appreciate your kindness and generosity. I am now beholden to you as well and if you want a boon of me, you only need ask."

Calla approached her and, to Isbet's discomfort, framed her face with her hands. "I will need your assistance soon, but you will not be obligated to comply."

"I believe I will have no choice." With the Vine's influence in her mind and body, it would be doubtful she could refuse. There was no reason to dwell on it any longer.

"You had better not tarry any longer. Queen Aimeli and Duchess Briwyn have been wringing their hands in worry about you."

In all the commotion, Isbet had forgotten about Aimeli and Briwyn. She supposed there would be explanations aplenty. Osirha moved to the door and opened it, bowing again as Isbet stepped across the threshold. As soon as she did, the queen and duchess stood where they had taken seats on the floor. It irritated Isbet somewhat. Did no one have the decency to get them a damn stool to sit on?

The thought surprised her. She'd never been this concerned about the comforts of others before. However, she was not at her best and the Vine's influence affected her more than she wanted to admit.

"Isbet!" Briwyn was to her first. "We were so worried."

"No one would tell us what happened," the queen said. "Only that you were here."

"They wouldn't let us visit you. Are you well?" Briwyn said.

Isbet smiled. The two of them were acting like mother hens. "Yes, I am well now. They have given me new rooms."

The three of them started to walk, trailing behind Osirha. "And the prince? How does he fare?" the queen asked.

"He has also come from this unscathed, at least in the body. I have sent Gaemyr to look after him."

"We heard there was some – unpleasantness," Briwyn said, her voice hushed.

"Indeed." Isbet would go no further with that. She instead told them that Serval had attempted to accost the prince, and in the ensuing altercation she'd had to draw power from the Vine. Isbet thought it unwise to tell of Queen Calla's plans for Serval. She tried not to get into family squabbles under normal circumstances, and not with royals or the Children.

The nagi halted in front of a door. Isbet hadn't been paying much attention to where they walked but when she took a moment to examine her surroundings, she recognized they were in the royal wing near the Council chambers.

Osirha opened the door. Isbet looked at her companions. "Please come in."

This room was a sight better than the one Isbet had before. It was yet another place filled with too much opulence for Isbet's taste, but she would not say so.

As the queen said, food was available, and Isbet realized she was ravenous, but the first thing she reached for almost on impulse was the water.

"Lady Isbet, what is that?" Briwyn approached her. "May I?" She took Isbet's wrist and turned it, examining the mark. "This is—" her brow furrowed, "—the Vine?"

"Yes."

"What is it, Briwyn?" Aimeli now approached.

"It is a mark from the Vine. Isbet is beholden to it now. She must obey its call."

"Oh, dear," Aimeli said. "Isbet, we are sorry."

"By all the realms, why?" Isbet said.

"We never meant to involve you in this," Briwyn said. "I will ask Her Majesty if you and Prince Greyward may return to the surface."

Isbet blew out a breath and tugged at one of her braids. "No."

"But—"

"I can't leave, not now. I'm uncertain if they have made you aware but this place and these people are in danger." Isbet reached for the pitcher of water again, pouring herself another cup. "There are things stirring in their rotted dens attracted by the sources that are causing the Vine to grow."

Briwyn moved over to one of the plush chairs and sat down. "I must admit I did not expect this."

"How could you?" Aimeli also sat on a couch. "This is beyond a sorceress's knowledge and magic." The queen gazed at Isbet. "But not beyond that of a witch."

"Aimeli!" Briwyn chided.

There was no point in denying it. "The queen speaks true. Sorcerers rule the sky, but we rule the earth. And even if I did not want any involvement, I have no choice. However, if you would, take Prince Bram back to the surface?"

Briwyn stood and Aimeli followed suit. "Yes, we will."

"Please take care." Aimeli drew her fingers down Isbet's cheek. The intimate touch was something Isbet would not have allowed, but the queen departed before Isbet could respond.

She needed to speak with Calla. If she were to do this, she would need to learn what the Dokkalfar expected of her. She was still uncertain how the Vine would continue to communicate with her and her with it. Gaemyr had said she was causing a ruckus when she called him. Isbet would need to inquire more about what the talisman had heard.

Isbet finished her water and went to her bedroom, relieved to find her pack there and a new set of clothes, a midriff blue silk blouse and loose-fitting pants, laid out for her. There was also a small jewelry box of polished wood. When Isbet opened it, there was an assortment of bejeweled rings, bracelets, necklaces, and earrings. Isbet ignored them and removed her robe.

The silk was cool against her skin, although she preferred sturdier materials. Silk didn't do well on the road. Isbet was about to leave when she realized without Gaemyr she would need a focus for her power. She wanted to avoid drawing from the Vine if possible. She went back to the jewelry box and chose the most unobtrusive ring there was – a simple gold band with a deep purple stone – and slipped it on her finger.

Osirha was waiting for her by the door. She moved aside and bowed again. "Would you take me to Queen Calla, please?" Isbet would have preferred to walk by herself, but likely they assigned the nagi as her protection. Despite her quiet demeanor, Isbet guessed she would be deadly in battle. The nagi had a reputation for being fiercer than their male counterparts.

Osirha led Isbet back to the room with the healing pool but the other nagi attending said that the queen had gone out after receiving a message, but she didn't say where. Isbet worried her lower lip. She didn't want to be in her rooms all day and didn't want to wander around on the off chance of meeting Serval.

"Your pardon, milady?"

Osirha looked at her with amber eyes, her pupils half-full.

"Call me Isbet, if you please," Isbet said.

"Isbet." She smiled with pointed teeth. It would have been frightening if Isbet feared such things. "Perhaps I may escort you somewhere where you may relax and enjoy your time remaining here?"

Time remaining. Did she realize how ominous that sounded? "That's fine."

The nagi led her back through the twists and turns of the palace. There were fewer people about than when they had first arrived, and those who were whispered when Isbet walked by. Others looked at her with naked hostility. Isbet didn't worry, as they would not dare accost her as a companion of the queen and now a Child of the Vine.

They came to a balcony with vine ropes and Osirha wasted no time grabbing one and curling her tail around it, sliding to the ground with practiced ease. With Isbet, it took longer. She continued to follow the nagi down narrow pathways and arches of alien flowers until they came out at a large clearing filled with grasses tipped with white fluff. Isbet heard a multitude of voices from beyond a stand of rocks, which turned out to be the entrance to a huge cavern with a shimmering lake.

It took much to impress her, but this did. Isbet looked up, drawing in a breath at the immense milky gem embedded in the cave ceiling and the soft light that poured down, illuminating the water, dancing like silver fey across its surface. Huge purple flowers lay along the face of the far wall. Nearest to them was a small outcropping of rock. Someone had carved a set of natural stairs into the cliffside and at the top was a line of the various denizens of Underneath. Others sat along the grassy shore, sharing picnic lunches, or lounging while engaged in conversation.

The ones at the top of the cliff were taking turns swinging on a rope, out over the lake and dropping in, where they splashed and joked and were being young. Overworld or Underneath, some things did not change.

These younglings will not be the ones to battle, Isbet thought. *They should not worry over such things.*

"Please enjoy this place," Osirha said, and even as she did, two young Dokkalfar, a male and a female, approached her.

"You are the Lady Witch," the girl said. "Welcome!"

"We heard of the battle with Prince Serval. Will you tell us of it?" the boy asked.

There was a slight tug at her trousers and Isbet looked down to see a young faun, just out of infancy, looking at her with bright green eyes. "Would you play with us?"

"Yes, please come!" The girl took her hands, but Osirha moved beside them. The girl looked at her. "Please, Osirha, may she come?"

"It is up to Lady Isbet." There was a change in Osirha's voice, a slight air of command. "Do not make her feel obligated."

They looked so eager. Isbet was not used to celebrity, but she was not so cold as to refuse them. "I'll have a go at it."

"Splendid!" the boy said. "I am Sparrow, cousin to Her Majesty, Queen Calla."

"And you may call me Lark," the girl said. "We must give you a name."

Sparrow nodded in agreement. "Yes, you shouldn't give your real name as you do."

"It has never been a problem. I have safeguards against anyone using my name."

"Still," Lark said, "it would be safer. Spend some time with us and we will think of a new name for you."

"That's fine." Isbet took an immediate liking to the pair. As they introduced her to their friends, Isbet came to recognize the personality of each one. They treated her with as much reverence as Lark and

Sparrow, and although it was not spoken, Isbet also found there was no love here for Serval.

She would cast a spell of protection on them, on all of them, and she would keep them safe from the coming battle.

CHAPTER SEVENTEEN

The trail opened a crooked path down the hill, reminding Bram of the old nursery rhyme 'There Was a Crooked Man'. Although not quite a mile, it took a bit of time for Bram to make his way to the floor of the cave. He approached the group with some caution, and he swore to the Triune if anyone so much as snickered, he would go back to hiding in the forest.

Isbet had climbed the stone steps again and was waiting for her turn, so Bram sat on a flat, moss-covered rock and continued to watch. She seemed to be having as much fun as the youngsters were. For someone who had been up to this point serious and somewhat aloof, her actions were a mixture of surprising and amusing to Bram.

Bram watched as she executed an almost flawless dive, barely causing a ripple. The young people on the cliff cheered. Several of the others followed and splashed about in the water.

Bram nearly jumped out of his trousers when something pushed against his arm. A young faun looked at him with curious green eyes. Her body was covered in tawny fur. One ear twitched as though shooing away some imaginary insect.

"Hello, little one." Bram smiled at her. She didn't speak, just crawled into his lap and curled up comfortably. Bram had never had any dealings with fauns, although they dwelled both above and below. Bram wasn't certain of the protocol with them, but she reminded him of a young child, and he brushed his hands down her hair as he continued to observe the others at their play.

There was something soothing about just sitting there, watching everyone and cradling an innocent child. For a few moments, Bram could forget everything that had happened. He was somewhat content for the first time in many months.

Some of the young people were leaving. The tiny faun's mother approached, or so Bram assumed because her child seemed to sense her presence. She climbed from Bram's lap but before leaving, she kissed him on the tip of his nose. Perhaps someone as young as she knew Bram's soul was troubled.

When he turned his attention back to the lake, Isbet was just climbing out onto the grassy shore. Silhouetted against the light, the sight of her was magnificent. The wet silk clung to her well-defined body, giving shape to her ample breasts and the curve of her hips. Her nipples were hard and pressed against the fabric and Bram imagined they were as dark and sweet as she was.

Nether-hells, was all he could think. That and he had to thank the Triune for not making celibacy a canon of his station. As the Archbishop, he could honorably court and wed a woman, but it was generally accepted that he refrained from – *outside pursuits.* Still, he was a mortal man after all. It wasn't until she lifted an eyebrow that he realized he was staring somewhat rudely and lowered his gaze. "Lady Isbet."

"Your Highness."

"I said don't call me that," Bram said, sharper than he'd intended. "I mean to say, please call me Bram."

She looked at him for a moment, her expression unreadable. "All right, Bram."

She sat on the grass beside him, stretching out her long legs. Bram diligently kept his eyes on the lake. "Gaemyr told me where you were. He said you were expecting me."

"Did he?" Isbet went about twisting her braids as she had done before. "I asked him to make certain you were well."

"As well as I can be, considering." Bram still couldn't look at her, but not because of her beauty. "Thank you, Isbet. You saved my life—" *among other things,* "—though I wish you hadn't risked your life like that."

"I would not let a friend come to harm," Isbet said. "You are welcome."

Bram couldn't help but smile slightly. "But you're all right now? You were not gravely injured?"

"I am fine," Isbet said. "I am uncertain if you know but Calla granted Aimeli and Briwyn's request."

"Oh, I know," Bram said. "She told me last night."

He could see her head turn out of the corner of his eye. Bram exhaled sharply. He may as well tell her so there would be no misunderstandings. "Serval tried to entrap me earlier in the evening." Bram told her of the summons to Serval's rooms and how the Dokkalfar nearly caught Bram in his spell.

"You will be relieved to know Calla plans to punish Serval, although she advised me it had been a long time coming," Isbet said.

Bram could well believe that.

"Besides, I knew you did not want Serval and the trouble it would cause if he took you by force," Isbet went on. "It would have gone badly later on."

"What do you mean?" Bram asked.

"I am sure you have heard stories about mortal men and women falling in love with fey creatures?" Isbet said.

"Yes," Bram said. "Always in the fairy tales, they either are willing to go or are carried off into Underneath. The stories usually end happily, or the person misses the sunlight so much they leave."

Isbet shook her head. "At times they are happy here if they were gravely unhappy while on the surface. However, once you have been intimate with a fey creature, you become incapable of leaving them. Your very soul joins with theirs whether it is consensual or not. Yes, a great majority of the time the mortal cannot stand being in the darkness and hungers for the light, but the fey will not allow them to leave."

Bram shivered, wrapped his arms around his chest. "Serval said once he'd – taken me, I would be his."

"Yes, unfortunately," Isbet said. "And if a mortal does manage to escape, they would not be able to live Above Ground either, for their bodies would crave the touch of their fey lover. So, depending on how physically and mentally strong that person is, they may be able to fight or come to accept their situation, but there are a few who go mad. Then the fey will cast them aside and they will be unwanted in both lands. Forever branded a pariah."

"Triune," Bram said. "Then I suppose I have even more reason to thank you."

"You would more than likely have been able to fight off Serval's influence," Isbet said. "You strike me as having great strength of spirit, Bram. More than you apparently realize."

Bram didn't know what to say, completely in shock from the compliment. He was thinking the exact opposite after allowing Serval to take him so easily.

Bram noticed how quiet Isbet had gotten. He could see by the slight frown and the tightening of her features that she was pondering something. "Isbet, what are you thinking of?"

Her face relaxed just a bit. "I suppose I should tell you. There is trouble coming to this land because the rogue magic's making the Vine grow. The Vine gave me a vision of things to come."

"It's going to be bad, isn't it?" Bram said.

"Yes, but I believe this is merely the start of things. This will just be a mere skirmish, but people will die."

Bram could hear the sadness in her voice as she gazed at the youngsters who continued at their play. "I placed a luck touch on each of them. It is a simple spell many of the Gifted know, and it's not powerful, but perhaps it will protect them."

"Do you believe they will truly have to fight?"

"I hope not," Isbet said. "But I will fight either way."

Bram's head snapped to the side. "You're...going to fight?"

"Yes." Isbet didn't elaborate.

It didn't take Bram long to come to a decision. "Then I will fight as well."

Now Isbet looked at him. "There is no need for you to do so. Likely Calla will send Aimeli and Briwyn back up to Overworld. You should go with them."

"I owe you and the queen a debt," Bram said. "It must be satisfied." Bram noticed a naga approaching, dressed in the breastplate that Bram recognized identified the wearer as one of the queen's personal guard. He moved with that smooth grace and inclined his head when he came to them. "Lady Isbet, Your Highness, Her Majesty Queen Calla requests your presence in her personal study. Please feel free to stop at your rooms to refresh yourselves. If you would please follow me?"

"Thank you." Bram held out a hand to Isbet, careful to avoid looking at her body. *Damn that silk outfit.* "If I may?"

Isbet took his hand and he pulled her to her feet. They followed the naga back to the palace and through the many hallways until they came to the royal apartments.

"If you need any assistance, please ask of anyone."

"Again, my thanks," Bram said, "Please inform Her Majesty we will be there with all speed."

Bram wasn't certain if he wanted to be somewhere where he could possibly run into Serval again, but Isbet had said the queen was planning to deal with him, so Bram doubted she would let Serval near him.

Bram was in a rather messy state, he noticed, when he was alone in the room. He'd been given some new clothes as well, nothing elaborate but serviceable, made from the same filmy material as Isbet's clothes had been. There was water and a washbowl on the dressing table and Bram made use of it by washing his face, then reaching for a jeweled brush and running it through his hair a few times. He wasn't perfect but, he thought, acceptable.

The hall was empty when he stepped out of the room, but Bram had an idea of where he needed to go. He only needed to ask someone and they directed him. Although two naga stood guard, the double doors to the study were open. He greeted the naga and they returned the greeting as he stepped into the room.

The circular room had a high-domed ceiling. The room was lit by dozens of wil-o-wisp floating unobtrusively above them and was decorated in blush tones, including the desk that sat at the top of the room. There were paintings of other Dokkalfar hung on the walls. The largest was of a handsome older couple. Bram guessed they were Calla's parents. He could see the resemblance in their features.

Aimeli and Briwyn were sitting on a couch to his left and Calla sat in a chair beside them. There were tea and cakes on a small table. They were chattering and laughing like old friends and it was a few moments before they noticed Bram.

"Your Highness." Calla smiled in greeting. "Do join us."

Bram greeted each woman and kissed their hands before sitting in a chair opposite Calla.

"Isbet will be along shortly," Calla said. "I understand you spent some time with her today?"

Bram willed himself not to blush. "Yes, I did. I beg your pardon, Majesty, but she informed me that there will be a skirmish very soon."

Calla's expression sobered. "Yes. I will have my most loyal servants escort Queen Aimeli to the surface."

"Majesty," Briwyn spoke up. "I wish you would reconsider our offer. We could have an entire company down here at your service."

Calla shook her head. "They would not arrive in time, I assure you, and I cannot guarantee their safety, but I appreciate that you are staying."

Briwyn gave her a wry grin. "I will never shy away from a good fight."

"Majesties, Your Grace," Bram addressed the three women, "I have decided to stay and fight as well."

"I already figured you would, Highness." Calla smiled again. "In fact – *ah*, here we are." She nodded at something behind Bram. He twisted slightly in his chair to see five nagi enter. One carried a tunic, the second a pair of trousers, the third boots, the fourth a headdress, and the fifth a sword. Not just any sword, but a Holy Sword. It wasn't until Bram saw the sword that he realized what it was they had brought him.

"Triune." Bram pushed himself out of the chair and approached the three with an almost cautious reverence. "Are these…?"

They were his vestments. The clothes of his station. Pure white cloth, and royal blue cinctures and neckband, the colors symbolizing the purity of the Triune. Bram reached out, stroking one of the embroidered sleeves. Incomprehension was stealing upon him again. Did Calla know what she had done? She had given him back a piece of himself he thought lost. "How did you…?"

Calla did not answer his unfinished question. "I am in your debt, Arch-bishop. Please accept this as a token of my gratitude."

Bram couldn't stop touching the material. "No, thank *you*. You don't – I mean to say—" Bram supposed it would be better to stop now before he started bawling like an infant.

"Place take these things to His Highness's chambers."

The five exited just as Isbet came in. She carried Gaemyr as usual and Bram was surprised to find her in a set of fine leather armor. He saw her gaze track to the items.

"Such a magnificent sword."

Bram could only say, "It's my sword. *It's my sword.*"

Isbet inclined her head, then to the three women she said, "They are coming."

"Then we must make haste." Queen Calla rose. "Majesty, Your Grace, if you please?" Calla turned to him. "Arch-bishop, prepare yourself. I will send Azai to you."

"Yes, Your Majesty." The last thing Bram had expected was to be in a battle. He only hoped he would not fail, and the Triune would not punish him and these people for his doubts.

CHAPTER EIGHTEEN

The nagi helped him dress. Bram tried to focus his mind on other things and not the fact that the last time servants had dressed him was before he'd gone to battle and become a prisoner. It wasn't long after the death of his father. Jaryl came in to keep him company. He looked like a true leader – like their Patriarch.

Bram had been uncertain what would happen or if the Triune would even answer him. He'd had his doubts when his time with Wilhelm began to stretch out and no rescue was forthcoming. He'd prayed to the Triune to deliver him from his enemies. He had tried not to think that his gods had abandoned him.

The nagi presented his sword. Bram gripped the hilt, cool to his touch. It fit in his palm just as he recalled it. The blue gem in the pommel glowed of its own volition. He released a breath. *Just let me be. For one moment, let me just be.*

"Your Highness?"

Azai stood at the door. The nagi moved from the room, each bowing to Azai as they did so.

"I will escort you to the field of battle." To Bram's surprise, Azai bowed to him. "Thank you, sir."

"Azai." Bram clutched the naga's hand. Then Azai stepped aside and Bram went out before him.

★   ★   ★

Azai led him to a section of Underneath on the far side of the lake where they'd watched the young people play. The clearing was like the one Bram had fallen into, yet instead of foliage, there was a space in front of them where there was – nothing.

It was a great void, for no light escaped it or reflected in its depths, despite the light filling the clearing, glinting off armor and swords.

"What is that?" Bram asked.

"An entrance forced through the veils, linking our world to theirs. The Vine would never allow them to come from the depths, so they must find another means. Although how they did this...." Azai shook his head. "It is the rogue magic. That is all it can be."

An assortment of beings gathered were there that Bram had never encountered in his lifetime. Besides Dokkalfar and naga, there were kobolds, fauns, bogies, gnomes, brownies, and others beyond description. There were also dwarves, with one shaggy female in deep conversation with Calla and Briwyn. The Duchess of Chira appeared formidable in her borrowed Dokkalfar armor. Since he'd not seen any dwarves around before, Bram assumed Calla had asked for their aid. They could travel anywhere Underneath and were the ones who tended the Vine, its offshoots, and the tunnels.

Bram was fascinated by all that was around him, but soon he wondered where Isbet was. After some searching, he found her atop a rock cleft, amid a group of Dokkalfar and naga. He wanted to ask Azai if he could be near her, but the naga placed him on a small hill at the very rear of the lines of soldiers.

"Does this suit your needs?" Azai asked.

"Yes, this is fine, thank you, Azai." It gave him a clear view of the battleground below.

Azai motioned to some naga nearby and they approached. "Stand with His Highness."

"Yes, sir!"

Then Azai joined Calla and Briwyn and the three of them walked down to the clearing. They faced the blackness. It came to Bram as he stood by the guards; Calla had pre-arranged for them. Bram walked a different path. He was the Father Protector. His station allowed him to take a life only if it was in defense of another.

He drew his sword and plunged it into the soft earth with the gem facing towards him. When Bram was certain the blade was secure, he carefully knelt on the soft earth and waited.

An unexpected silence fell. Calla stepped forward and drew her sword. She spoke and Bram realized it was in the language of the Dokkalfar, but he understood every word. He guessed another spell.

"Come out, filth! Crawl from the darkest fen and show yourself to me!"

Bram kept his gaze fixed on the darkness. It moved, bubbling like hot tar as a black tendril of it stretched out and ejected a blob of something whose rank smell carried across the clearing, making Bram want to gag.

The thing moved, rearing upward, taking a shape not mortal, but there were the features of some little beast, with knobby arms too long for its stunted body. Its face was almost bat-like. Its large, rounded ears twitched. Bram did not understand what it was, so he quietly asked one of the naga.

"It is nothing," the naga replied. "It is a messenger. A vespere."

The vespere approached Calla and spoke, and the sound of its voice sent a chill down Bram's spine. He didn't understand the creature's guttural language, but the meaning behind its words became clear. Whatever was in that darkness wanted blood and death.

Calla finished with the thing, brought her sword down and cleaved it in two. She raised her sword again, pointing the blade at the void. "Did you not hear me, filth? Come out!"

The darkness was a seething cauldron, rippling and boiling across its surface. Bram bowed his head, closed his eyes, pushing that little piece of doubt away. The words of the prayer, so practiced in his youth, fell from his lips.

"I beseech thee, Triune, Father, Mother, and Child,

Fill this unworthy vessel with your will, your power.

As Father Protector, I ask a boon, to protect the lives of the innocent.

Be my strength, my eyes, and my soul. Come to me, oh Blessed Triune.

Please, do not forsake me. This is not for me, this is for them."

There came a presence. It was slight at first, like a gentle breeze, carrying a sweet perfume. It washed away the last of the stench the vespere had left. Through his closed eyes, Bram sensed the gem glowing and with it a sense of being embraced by loving arms.

It was She, the Mother. Her face and form had been captured in paintings in their cathedrals, but Bram experienced her true being. Warmth, sacrifice, caring, and a fierce protectiveness of her children, as any mother would feel.

Bram drew the power to him. It was his to make use of. Not a magical power, for it was not his. The Mother would fight; Bram was a conduit for her, not at his command, for Bram would have to continue to pray and pay attention to the battlefield.

More tendrils emerged from the blackness, and the things that came from them were the beasts of nightmares, some so hideous Bram had to fight not to be sick at the sight of them. They would kill without mercy, or suck out a man's soul without remorse, leaving him an empty shell to wander for eternity, never knowing peace again.

They came, it seemed, in an endless wave and Calla called for their troops to go forward to meet them in battle. Meanwhile, those gathered on the clefts, including Isbet, cast spells that caused some of the enemy to wither and die, while others burst into flame. Isbet held Gaemyr aloft and seemed focused on the void, and Bram saw the edges of the Vine growing over the space, entwining with agonizing slowness, but Isbet worked to seal the void. Bram focused his concentration on the battlefield. The stone allowed him to differentiate friend from foe by showing their auras, and he focused the Mother's Holy Fire on them. His friends received the benefit of her blessing, while their enemies received her wrath. Calla and Briwyn fought in the middle of the fray and Bram had to admit they impressed him.

As for the enemy? With a mere touch of the Light, they tore apart, and whatever made up their dark souls, the Mother crushed with her mighty hand.

Bram continued to pray, the words coming fast, his breathing, for now, steady and deep, his nerves alive with the Holy Fire. If the battle went on too long, he would have to replenish himself. The dark ones didn't seem to pay Bram much attention at first, until they realized what he was, and as the Mother walked among them, they retreated, but evil can't escape the light, the pure. The Mother found them every time.

Bram noticed ghouls sneaking up on two of the youths he'd seen at the pond. The ghouls wielded bows and arrows and used them with deadly precision. Bram reached out with the Mother's hand and touched each one. They disintegrated, their wails of agony lingering then fading to nothing.

Still there were more, goblins, revenants, incubi and succubae, duppies and Duine Shee and, to Bram's surprise, witches. They focused their attention on the group of magic workers on the cleft. Bram raised a wall of protection between the witches and his allies, but it used most of his power. He was leaving the rest unprotected, but—

Something rushed through the field towards him. Bram recognized it as it gave out death easily. Bram had only moments to react before the Red Cap was on him, its evil eyes burning crimson, its claws wet with blood. If the Mother's love was not still protecting him from the attack he would have perished in a most gruesome way. Her Light burned the clawed hands of the beast, and Bram changed his prayer to one for that horrid creature – and it disappeared.

Lycanths came next from the void. Although they were not denizens of Underneath, perhaps they escaped those who would kill them. Whoever or whatever it was, they were obviously under someone's command. Bram felt sorry for the men and women caught in the curse. He almost didn't want the Mother to touch them, because they would die, yet they would be free.

The gem showed him the spirit of a woman imprisoned by the curse. When the Mother's Light caressed her, the wolf form tore away. It held her for a moment. She smiled at Bram before the Mother took the woman into her embrace and to her rest.

Something drew Bram's attention to the void again. Isbet was still working on sealing it and the witches were relentlessly attacking, but Bram noticed a figure off to the side. Was that – Serval? Was he insane? Did he have something to do with this? The Dokkalfar prince made no move to fight, but he watched with undisguised glee.

Bastard, Bram thought, but he wouldn't allow Serval to distract him. Unless Serval joined the fight, he was of no consequence to Bram. He continued, letting the Mother's Light flow through him, but it was taking its toll. Bram was mortal, and to have the power of a goddess coursing through him sapped him of energy.

Already his brow and chest dripped in sweat. His vision began to blur, and his head ached between his eyes. He wondered who was in command of their enemies? There was no plan or procedure. The beasts just came and fought, throwing themselves into the fray with no rhyme or reason. Bram directed the Mother towards the hole. His curiosity got the better of him and through the gem, he could peer inside the darkness.

Something looked back.

It was without description, but more the presence of everything in a man's nightmares. It locked eyes with Bram and it leered.

Bram screamed.

"Sir?" The voice of the naga seemed far away as the Mother stepped between him and the presence. He fought to gain control again. It cost him a great deal, and his head was pounding now, and the power of the Mother faded. *They must finish this.*

A thick growth of foliage covered the void. Creatures crawling underneath a narrow space retreated before the Holy Light, but others threw themselves at it in what became an act of suicide. The remaining Vines joined, closing off the void. There would be no help for the enemy now.

Bram's whole body ached, his muscles cramped, his legs weak from being on his knees. No longer able to stand it, Bram said the prayer that would pay homage to the Mother as she approached him. He sensed her regard, and it was of hope and peace.

"Things will change," she said as she kissed him on the forehead.

Bram wanted to straighten from his position, stretch out in the grass and sleep for several months. He looked now at the scene with his own eyes and they burned and filled with tears. Calla's troops were prevailing. Some denizens of the void tried to escape past the battlefield but the moment they were full in the light coming off the pond, they vanished, or Azai's troops stopped them.

Bram searched for Isbet, but she was no longer on the cleft, having moved down into the clearing, fighting with a viciousness Bram never thought possible. She'd gone straight for the witches and they fell before her. They had power, but Isbet had the Vine and she used it to its fullest. Those that did not fight with magic, Isbet fought hand to hand, wielding Gaemyr like a weapon. Bram thought he heard bones breaking.

With the more human-like creatures, she held Gaemyr before her, and streams of light would rush from their mouths and into Gaemyr's. Moments later, they would be nothing more than withered corpses. *Soul Eater*, Bram thought.

Isbet fought with a style Bram had seen a long time ago, when he'd gone on a diplomatic mission to the other end of the Riven Isles, to the province of Jack-In-Irons. It involved a series of timed kicks and punches. Isbet would leap into the air and bring her leg around, smashing her foot into whatever vulnerable area she aimed for.

"Sir? Highness?" Bram realized the first naga he'd questioned earlier had been trying to get his attention. "Do you need help? Please tell us what to do."

Bram's aches and pains returned. "Yes, help me up, please."

The naga did so. "Come," he said. "You no longer need to be here. You have fought well, Your Highness."

Bram gave him a smile and allowed them to lead him away. He didn't want to leave but he was no more use to them now. He looked back once more to watch as Isbet faced another combatant. He thought, *she is magnificent.*

The battle was nearing its end and they were the victors. Bram, however, did not witness its conclusion.

CHAPTER NINETEEN

"To my Lady Witch!"

"To Isbet!"

The dwarf warrior filled the wood cup that Isbet held. It was sort of an amusing situation. The battle won and the wounded cared for, their dwarven companions had broken out a cask of their finest nut-brown ale. A warrior passed cups around and filled them to overflowing.

Isbet sat and drank while she watched their stout companions link arms and sing a bawdy victory song. *Gaemyr is going to be sorry he missed this.* Isbet had released him into the Vine once again for, despite feasting, the battle had drained him completely, and although he could not directly partake, he still enjoyed a raucous celebration.

And raucous it was, as they toasted Calla and Briwyn, but Isbet wasn't certain she was deserving of such accolades. Well, she had fought and protected her compatriots, so she supposed it wouldn't hurt if she joined them in their celebrations.

Isbet felt they should celebrate. Although there had been quite a few injuries, they had suffered no casualties. Just some cuts and bruises and a few broken limbs. A few of the Dokkalfar were poisoned but they had their natural immunity and Isbet, being a witch and having to deal with various herbs and poisons, had developed immunity to most over time.

Still, she'd gotten a rather nasty cut across her hip, courtesy of one of the lycanths she had faced. They were under the influence of five witches who had joined in the battle. She would not turn, thanks largely to her Gift, which protected her.

It infuriated Isbet that witches were there; however, if they believed she would not destroy them they were sadly mistaken.

Isbet was not naive. She was quite aware of witches who coveted the darkness and she'd come to despise them for their foolishness. She'd had her encounters with overzealous witch-hunters and Light-bearers who weren't at all concerned with whatever path a witch followed. To some of them, all witches were evil incarnate and deserved to be destroyed. Too many times, Isbet had to escape some village or tiny hamlet because of that belief.

Isbet decided to set her anger aside for now. There was little point in spoiling the celebration. Besides – Isbet allowed herself a smile – she enjoyed dwarven ale. Most thought it too strong for their tastes.

"To you, Queen Lienna. Your assistance is greatly appreciated." Calla held out her cup and Lienna refilled it.

"T'wasn't hard." Lienna burped without apology. "All the mess that's goin' on down here. Glad we got here in time."

Isbet couldn't help an admiring smile. The hearty dwarf queen was slightly taller than her companions, her face round, with a puckered scar adorning her left cheek, and when she smiled, it showed broken teeth. Her dirty-blonde hair was done up in two thick braids on either side of her head and Isbet knew among her people she was considered quite a beauty. She had many consorts in her commons, but none had taken her heart quite yet for her to make him a dwarf prince. Queen Lienna of Rild Commons did not seem in much of a hurry to marry.

"How's that cut faring, Lady Witch?" she asked.

Isbet set her cup aside, grasped the edge of her shirt and raised it slightly to reveal the crisscross of new vine that had sewn the broken skin together. The Vine had reached out to her, to protect its chosen and Isbet had found it unnecessary to use her own Gift to heal the wound.

Lienna shook her head and her braids swung back and forth. "Incredible." She extended a hand. "Let's get you up now. We could all use a good bath, eh?"

"Agreed," Isbet said as Lienna pulled her up. Dwarf strength was legendary.

As the four women walked towards the royal quarters, Queen Lienna said, "I've gotten some strange tales of trouble with the Vine. Well, I suppose I can't call 'em tales. I can feel the Vine's hurt just like you."

"It is as I said," Calla replied, "men meddling in the affairs of Underneath."

Lienna halted, reached out and grasped Calla's wrist. "I'm afraid it's more than that, Calla-girl."

Now they all stopped walking. Isbet had sensed something herself more than just the rogue magic in the Vine, and as she looked at Calla, she realized the Dokkalfar queen knew.

"I became aware of its presence during the battle when the vespere came. The enemy stank of this...*thing*."

"I suppose that's all you can call it for now," Lienna said. "Don't know where it came from. Did the rogue magic make it? Or wake it up?"

"Wait," Briwyn said, "you mean to say there is something more we have to deal with now?" Isbet heard the concern in Briwyn's voice. "I sensed nothing."

"Do not fret, Lady Duchess, we will still allow you your investigation," Calla said. "It appears we will need all the assistance we can gather."

"B'sides," Lienna said, "you wouldn't know it, bein' a sorceress and all. If this thing was somethin' of the sky, you'd know right out."

"Then this will be a task where we will surely need assistance," Briwyn said. "I will speak further with my cousin when we return to Overworld." Briwyn turned to Isbet. "This is now a matter where we must make this known to all the peoples of the east. If we stop it here it may not affect the Vine throughout the Riven Isles. I will also speak with Prince Greyward. Perhaps he can carry a message to the other kingdoms. Perhaps if he convinces Wilhelm how serious this is, he will allow Bram to warn Tamrath and Morwynne."

"Let's get inside," Lienna said. "I know our Isbet will want to know how her handsome prince is faring even if she keeps that stone-face of hers."

Isbet tensed as all three women looked at her. "I— Bram is a companion, so yes, I am interested in his well-being."

All three women laughed, and they walked again. Now she was grateful Gaemyr was absent. He would have truly gained much amusement from her predicament.

★   ★   ★

The maps were old – *ancient*. Were the need not so great, Isbet doubted Queen Lienna would have brought them. They showed the original tunnels, caverns, and caves that formed when the Vine first fell. The dwarves fashioned them with the assistance of another denizen of the Underneath – Knockers.

"This is the area where the greatest concentration is." Lienna outlined a portion of the map near the Morwynne Islands off the coasts of both Rhyvirand and Tamrath. The three women leaned in closer. Isbet knew this would greatly distress Bram. As though her thinking of him was some type of summons, there was a knock at the door and Bram came in.

"Welcome, Prince Greyward." Calla smiled at him. There was a mischievous sparkle in her eyes.

"Majesties, Duchess." Bram inclined his head and immediately approached Isbet. "Are you all right?" He took her hands in his.

Isbet resisted the urge to pull her hands away. He'd washed and changed, his dark hair slicked back on his head. He'd shaved also. He was dressed in his everyday uniform of the Arch-bishop. "I am well, and so are you, I see."

"I was told what happened at the battle after I was taken away. I am sorry I could not remain."

"Don't be sorry." Isbet couldn't help a smile. "You protected the peoples of Underneath."

"And we will always be in your debt," Calla said.

Bram looked as if he realized too late they were not alone in the room. He released Isbet's hands and turned to the table. "There is no debt to be paid. I am honored you trusted me enough to allow me to fight beside you." A look of urgency crossed Bram's face. "But there is something I must tell you. Something I saw during the battle."

"If you mean that thing in the darkness, we know of it," Queen Lienna said.

"You do?" Bram's eyes widened.

"We of the earth were able to sense its presence."

"I was unable to," Briwyn said.

"But why?" Bram said. "Oh yes, I see, because your Gift is of the air and sky. But I don't understand. I don't have the Gift. Why did I see it?"

"You truly don't know?" Both Calla and Lienna looked confused.

"You are a Light-bearer, Prince Greyward," Isbet said.

"A what?"

"He wouldn't be familiar with the term," Isbet explained to the others. "Recall it hasn't been used since the time of the Vine and is only now coming back into favor."

"Wait," Bram said. "Yes, now that I think of it, I have heard that term before in an old song. Mostly children sing it. It's been so long I'd almost forgotten."

"Whatever that thing is, it is both of the earth and the supernatural," Calla said. "As Lienna has stated, it could have been created recently or was dormant until the rogue magic awakened it."

"What did ya see, Highness?" Lienna said.

Now all eyes were on the prince, Isbet's included.

"I saw…." Bram paused. "I didn't really *see* anything." He closed his eyes. "It was more of a *presence*. It had no form yet, but we were a source of amusement. I thought I saw a face, but it was more like a trick of the darkness." He opened his eyes. "Do you know how when you close your eyes after looking at something and a ghost image of whatever it is stays under your eyelids? That's what it was like." He let his gaze travel to each of them. "I apologize that I cannot be of more help."

"Actually, you've given us much more than we had," Isbet said. "Thank you."

Bram flushed in that endearing way of his and said, "You're welcome."

Isbet tried to ignore the knowing looks of the other women in the room.

"Highness," Calla said, "before you entered, Lienna was advising us that the worst concentration of whatever is infecting the Vine is in Morwynne."

"Oh no," Bram said. "What of Tamrath?"

"I'm afraid we don't know yet," Lienna said.

"Highness, if we may request yet another favor of you?" Briwyn asked.

"No concern, Lady Briwyn, it is fine," Bram said.

"I will speak with my cousin when we return," Briwyn said. "We will, of course, remain with our original plan, but now it is imperative that you convince Wilhelm. In addition, I will have an emissary visit the Dhar of Morwynne. Hopefully, we can convince him that he must act or, at the very least, allow us to investigate."

"Your Grace, allow me to speak with the Dhar," Bram said.

"Highness—" Briwyn didn't complete her thought.

Isbet knew why. Bram was a prince and it was unseemly that a prince delivered messages.

"Neither Rhyvirand nor Tamrath have attempted to open political relations with Morwynne for quite some time," Bram said. "Emissaries are often turned away, as you know. They are a very insular people."

"But perhaps if a prince of the realm made the request?" Briwyn nodded in understanding.

"Send your people," Bram said. "Give them documents of introduction for me. At least the Dhar will know I am coming so there will hopefully not be any misunderstandings."

"As ya do that," Lienna said, "I'll have my people look around a bit, see if this poison is anywhere else. This means all our lives if it goes too far."

Isbet released a long slow breath. This was not why she'd returned to the eastern provinces.

Bram took her reaction to mean something else. He gently touched her shoulder. "Do not worry, Bet. We will come through this, I promise."

A nickname. No one had ever given her a nickname. For some odd reason, she didn't mind it coming from Bram.

The other women were looking at the two of them again. "I was not worrying," Isbet said and left it at that. One task she had set for herself, and fate had taken her on a different path altogether. It was damned annoying.

CHAPTER TWENTY

"Bram!" Seth ran into his arms. His young ward seemed happy and in good health.

"I worried about you," Bram said.

"Why?" Seth asked in all innocence. "I had a very fine time."

"Did you?" Bram said. "Why don't you tell me all about it?"

"No!" Seth jumped up and down. "Tell me all about Underneath!"

Although he should have scolded Seth for behaving in such a manner, he couldn't help but smile at his enthusiasm. However, before Bram could speak, a familiar voice interrupted.

"Your Highness!"

Rajan was rushing towards him, his arms full of books and papers. Bram wondered what he'd been doing. "I'm pleased to see you."

The sincerity of Rajan's voice was unexpected. Bram wasn't certain how to react so he said, "Likewise."

If Bram was surprised, Rajan looked as if stunned. "I—"

Bram supposed Rajan hadn't expected such camaraderie but then again, he had no real fight with the steward and Bram figured he could use more allies than enemies. "I have much to tell you both." Bram lifted Seth into his arms. "I have to refresh myself first. The queen has requested our presence in her study."

"May I invite Mila?" Seth asked.

She was the niece of Briwyn, who, as the duchess had said, was around the same age as Seth. The two had become best friends. "I don't see why not."

Bram set him down and he dashed off.

"I've heard rumors there was trouble Underneath."

"I'm afraid it is much more than trouble," Bram said. "I will tell you everything. It is important that you dictate the truth."

★   ★   ★

The queen and duchess were waiting for them. The map spread out before them across the scarred wood table was like the one they'd examined in Underneath. There was food and drink set up as usual. Seth and Haeven sat on a plush rug near the expanse of windows, engaged in a game of Nine Men's Morris.

Bram was famished, he realized, but he waited until they served the royal ladies. Isbet came in last, with Gaemyr strapped to her back like a sword, but offered no apology. If it upset the queen or duchess, they didn't say.

"Highness." The queen waved one hand and a servant stepped through the door, keeping himself or herself unseen until the queen granted them leave to enter. "These are the documents you will present to Wilhelm and these to the Dhar of Morwynne. They have my personal seal and you may speak in my name." Another nod and a second servant entered, carrying a small chest. Inside, there were two rings nestled in satin.

"Take these as a symbol of our friendship and a sign that I take you as members of the Royal Family of Chira."

"Thank you, Majesty, I am honored," Bram said.

There was a brief hesitation on Isbet's part. She looked at Aimeli. "My deepest apologies, Majesty, but I cannot accept this gift."

Bram turned his head and stared wide-eyed at the young witch. To refuse such a boon was a grave insult, which would usually find the perpetrator on the chopping block.

The look on the queen's face confirmed her offense by the refusal. "Are we not friends, Lady Isbet?"

"I consider myself your friend, Your Majesty, but I – will not pledge my loyalty to Chira."

"Did I ask that of you?" The queen thinned her lips.

"No, Your Majesty, but will you not expect it? Will this ring not convey that message?"

Bram looked to the queen and back to Isbet. Didn't she know what she was doing?

"It will convey you have my trust. Is that not good enough for you?"

"Aimeli, wait." Briwyn laid her hand on her cousin's forearm. Briwyn went around the table and approached Isbet. "I know as one with the Gift you have seen many of our kind who have sworn loyalty to a kingdom, and have found themselves in a rather precarious situation when your Gift no longer suits the needs of those who demanded your loyalty. You have my word that will not happen here. Will you take my word and Aimeli's on this?"

Isbet inclined her head. "Yes."

Bram had to keep from breathing a sigh of relief.

"If we break this vow then you have every right to retaliate, and we will not seek retribution."

"Agreed," Isbet said.

The release of the tension in the room was tangible. The queen said, "Trust me, Isbet. Trust in the friendship we have made."

"I will, Your Majesty."

Bram stepped forward. "We will return to Rhyvirand, and I will speak with Wilhelm. Then I will travel to Morwynne and deliver our message." Bram noted his use of 'our' pleased them both. He wanted them to know they had his full support.

The goodbyes were heartfelt. Bram promised to return whether with good news or not and let them know of his progress. As they started their journey back, Bram rode beside Isbet. He couldn't help but ask, "Was that worth it?"

Isbet raised an eyebrow. "I assume you mean not giving my allegiance?"

"The queen is a friend. I don't see why it was such a problem."

"You recall what Briwyn said?" Isbet said.

"Yes, but you realize neither Aimeli nor Briwyn would treat you that way?"

Isbet didn't respond at first. She looked out onto the road ahead. "Are you familiar with Draydea of Innrone?"

"I believe so." Bram furrowed his brow and pinched the bridge of his nose between his thumb and forefinger. "Wait, yes. She was a witch appointed by the duke and duchess to be in their court." Bram noticed the faraway look in Isbet's eyes. "They executed her because—"

"Because of the death of their son," Isbet said. "She was in their court since the age of sixteen. Her Gift was the most powerful in the Isles. She believed the duke and duchess were her friends. Draydea thought this because she sat at their table, advised them, and predicted their fortunes. The duchess insisted they go everywhere together, and they dined and bought each other lavish gifts." Isbet's grip had tightened on the reins. "The duke even had a man executed who'd tried to molest her."

"It sounded like they cared for her," Bram said.

Isbet shook her head. "The duke and duchess had been trying to give birth for years and it seemed after a time that the duchess was barren. She pleaded with Draydea to help her but no Gifted, be they witch, sorcerer or necromancer, has the power to bring about a human life unless it is through dark means, and I assure you what was brought forth was not mortal."

"There were many rumors after that."

"Rumors that Draydea brought forth a child of darkness and it caused great pain and suffering to the people. Rumors that the baby came out deformed and died and the duchess went mad from grief. But the duchess had hired a warlock and when the baby came, Draydea realized what it was and tried to warn them, but they wouldn't listen.

"They dismissed her from her post, but they wouldn't allow her to leave their manor. She was a prisoner in a cell, albeit a luxurious one. It was a short time after that they found the child dead."

"They blamed Draydea?"

"She had nothing to do with it." Bram caught the bitterness in her voice. "But they imprisoned and tortured her, visited the worst atrocities upon her before—" he saw her shudder, "—they put her to the stake."

"Damn it to the nether-hells," Bram swore.

"That isn't the only instance of that nature," Isbet said. "It is bad enough when some brain-addled villagers want to take our lives because of what we are, even worse when someone you served and gave your loyalty to tosses you away like entrails."

Bram wasn't certain what to say. The persecution visited on witches depending on where they were in the Riven Isles was a common occurrence. It startled Bram when Isbet sighed.

"However," she said, "it was wrong of me to include the queen and Briwyn in my suspicions. It did not differ from witches being judged."

"I believe they understood." Bram gave her a reassuring grin. "It was fortunate that Briwyn was there to stay the queen's anger." Bram averted his eyes. "Isbet, I also consider you a friend of Tamrath." He realized what a risk he was taking by speaking the name of his homeland, but for once Bram didn't care.

Isbet's lips upturned; she was clearly pleased. It warmed Bram's soul that he had her trust.

★   ★   ★

Although Rhyvirand was not his home, it relieved Bram when they set off to return to the estate. He was eager to speak with Wilhelm and convince him of the urgency of the situation. He had to convince Wilhelm to allow Isbet to be Seth's instructor.

Not just for him, but for me as well....

Bram stole a glance at her. Triune, where had that come from? He admired the witch for her aura of strength and self-confidence. She seemed to live by her own complex code of honor, where she could be aloof one moment and the next show a deep affection for a little boy. Not to mention, she was beautiful.

I think Wilhelm will like her, Bram mused. Another thought occurred. Would Wilhelm try to use Isbet and covet her power? No, he couldn't consider that. In fact, he already had the answer to his own question – Wilhelm would not and if he tried, Bram didn't doubt that Isbet could deal with it.

There were no incidents as they passed through Tamrath. Captain Maive had been furious when she found out that Bram had gone Underneath without consulting her, but she didn't scold him. She reminded him that Wilhelm would have held her responsible had anything happened to him. Bram offered her apologies because he realized she was right and that she feared her punishment more than Bram's.

She kept a close eye on him during the journey but didn't speak to him. She rode between him and Seth, to his left, for which Bram was glad since he wouldn't have wanted Seth to hear Isbet's story about Draydea. Bram supposed he couldn't blame her for being offended.

Bram stared straight ahead, not allowing himself to meet the eyes of his people. He lowered his head as they passed by the cathedral. He tried not to wonder if Jaryl was watching. The aborted escape attempt seemed like decades ago. The only thing that kept him from breaking into pieces again was their task. This would be as much for Jaryl and his people as it would be for him.

★   ★   ★

Bram had long since ceased to care about the entourage. He lifted Seth off his pony and helped Isbet off her horse. Rajan had just dismounted when Bram said, "Rajan, we need to see Wilhelm now."

Rajan said, "Yes, Highness," and rushed off ahead of them.

Despite Bram not having said for her to come along, Captain Maive followed them into the manor. When they entered the royal wing, Bram entrusted Seth to his nurse. "Refresh yourself and have something to eat," Bram told him. "I will visit you later and tell you what happened."

Seth seemed to understand how important this was, "Yes, Bram."

"Lady Isbet, would you like to refresh yourself as well?"

"No, thank you, Highness," Isbet said. "We need to see the king now."

Bram nodded in agreement. They continued down the hall. Bram figured Wilhelm would be in his private study this late in the afternoon as he would be through with the day's petitioning.

Rajan met them coming back. "I see you surmised where Wilhelm would be. He has a guest and old friend of yours, he said."

"Of mine?" Bram's eyebrows knit.

"Yes, yours and Lady Isbet."

He exchanged a glance with Isbet, who seemed as perplexed as he. She grasped Gaemyr and pulled him from the strap, perhaps in preparation for what they might find. He doubted Wilhelm would let anyone from Tamrath visit. The only other people they had been in contact with were the Chir and the denizens of Underneath.

He rushed past Rajan, not stopping to see if he and Isbet were following. The guards were at their usual places but the doors to the study stood open in welcome. The queen lounged on a nearby couch, dressed more casually than Bram had ever seen her. She watched her husband and his guest and smiled, her shoulder positioned so the silky camisole dipped low to reveal what would be a scandalous amount of flesh, in obvious invitation.

Wilhelm, as always, appeared relaxed as he showed off a pair of dueling sabers that were a part of his private collection. He presented one to the dark-skinned man who stood before him. The man held the weapon at an angle, running his thumb along the blade in almost a caress as his eyes locked on Bram.

"Ah, Bram, you have returned," Wilhelm said. "Well, don't stand there, come in. And this must be the lovely Lady Isbet." He gestured. "Your friend Prince Serval has told us an amazing story. It seems we have much to discuss."

CHAPTER TWENTY-ONE

The stench reached her before she even entered the room. Isbet tightened her grip on Gaemyr, desperately drawing strength from him to keep the unpleasant hum along her nerves at bay.

Gaemyr made a noise of derision. "It stinks of dark magic here!"

That was a huge understatement. The air was thick with it, the cloying scent of corpses rotting in the sun. It burned Isbet's throat and settled in her stomach, making it quiver.

Isbet couldn't respond of course, and she could only hope Wilhelm couldn't hear the talisman. *Grandmother, it is worse than we both thought. What a fool this man is.* Now, finally seeing Wilhelm, the man who had murdered her grandmother, she wanted to rush forward and strike him down with the full strength of her Gift behind her anger.

When Wilhelm moved closer, Isbet's stomach clenched. She held Gaemyr against her chest.

"Don't fret, I have you," Gaemyr said.

She was doing the hells of a lot more than fretting. She clearly saw the aura of black blood and a putrid green surrounding Wilhelm's body, concentrating at the center of his chest. A line of it flowed from the middle of his back, twisting snake-like across the room and through the wall. Something had hold of Wilhelm. Something Isbet knew.

Wilhelm embraced Bram and she saw him shudder. Isbet was aware that, although Bram couldn't see the miasma that surrounded Wilhelm, he would sense it on a primal level. Bram would know it for what it was as well. He needed no warning.

Isbet turned her attention to Serval. He was doing a poor job of hiding his obvious fear. The smirk he'd tried to hold faltered as his lower lip trembled. *You see it too, you son of a harlot. Perhaps you should have stayed hidden in Underneath.*

"Lady Isbet, if you would follow us, please?"

Her attention was brought abruptly back to Bram and Wilhelm. She'd been so engrossed in her own thoughts that she hadn't heard a word of the conversation. She had to take a moment to gather herself. "Yes, of course, Your Majesty."

They stepped ahead of Wilhelm outside onto a wide circular balcony. Wilhelm closed the doors behind them.

"Sir, I don't know what Serval told you—" Bram began.

Wilhelm waved a hand. "No, no, dear boy, no need for that." He stepped forward and laid his hands on Bram's shoulders. Tendrils of the aura reached out and brushed across Bram's cheeks.

Isbet turned, pivoting on one foot, ready to bring Gaemyr between the foulness and Bram, but Gaemyr halted her in mid-step. "No!" Isbet froze. Neither one seemed to notice her actions.

"That person told me such a fantastical story and it was most amusing," Wilhelm went on. "Of course, I didn't believe a word of it."

"Sir?" Isbet was as shocked as Bram.

"Really, son." Wilhelm stepped back, folding his arms as he shook his head. "Did you truly believe I'd take the word of some bottom-dwelling whoreson over yours?"

Bram's jaw dropped. He looked at Isbet for a moment. She wasn't certain if he wanted her to say something. "I'm sorry, Father. Thank you."

"The bastard's muddled his brain," Gaemyr said of Bram. "You'll have to put a warding on him as soon as you're alone."

I don't know if that will even work at this point. Still, she would try.

"Now, sit down, you two. I know you're tired and hungry, so I'll have something brought out." Wilhelm was already striding briskly towards the door. Isbet moved towards Bram. She knew she was taking a risk, but she touched him briefly at the center of his forehead. She managed to lower her arm before Wilhelm returned.

"Isbet—" Bram whispered.

"Later," Isbet said.

"Now, Bram, I want to hear what is true."

They told him, and after a time servants brought out a cart of food with little cakes and wine. Bram told Wilhelm of their time in Underneath. Of the trouble that came to them and the battle they had fought. Wilhelm leaned forward in his seat and listened intently. The cord had followed them outside and Isbet could see it pulsing with the foul light as though feeding on the words Wilhelm was taking in.

Bram then showed him the messages from Queen Aimeli and Duchess Briwyn and advised Wilhelm that he had agreed to speak with the Dhar of Morwynne. Isbet had to admit, Bram was quite the orator; his voice was sincere, and not once did it have a pleading quality. It retained its strength the entire time.

When Bram ended his tale, Wilhelm leaned back in his chair and steepled his fingertips. "That is dire news indeed." His eyes unfocused for a moment and a huge pulse of red filled the cord, then it returned to its original state. Isbet could only guess what that meant. "However, I will give much thought to how to handle the matter. I will say this evil, whatever it is, must be dealt with."

"Thank you. I appreciate your trust."

"You will, however, travel to Morwynne and speak with the Dhar. Present my case first and then you may speak with him about Queen Aimeli's request. But be certain you convince him it is better to ally with us."

Isbet saw Bram's jaw tighten imperceptibly. Despite his feelings, Isbet knew he would have to do what Wilhelm said, no matter how dire the situation was.

"Now, as for you, my dear Lady Isbet," Wilhelm smiled as he stood. "If you are agreeable to be young Seth's teacher, I would appreciate it. There will be a healthy salary attached. You will have your own suite, and would you need a workplace?"

"If it pleases His Majesty."

What seemed to please Wilhelm was Isbet's deference. "Then you shall have it. My advisor Ancer Fallor will see to it all. Now then, would you please come with me? I would like to reward you for your service."

"Your Majesty is too kind, but no reward is necessary."

"It is as far as I'm concerned." Wilhelm took her elbow and the cold threatened to pervade her. Isbet had to focus her Gift to keep it at bay. "Bram, you won't mind if I steal some time away with Lady Isbet?"

Isbet could see he did, but they both knew he had to keep his own counsel. "No, Father."

"Splendid." Wilhelm led Isbet inside, through the parlor, and out the double doors. "We'll pay a visit to the exchequer's office and by then, your suite should be ready."

Isbet had visited royal houses before but never one as gaudily designed as this. It was a thief's dream. Everything was made of precious metals and jewels or draped in gaudy silks and lace. Isbet knew some very accomplished thieves and grifters who made a nice living and others for whom these riches would make their living better. She never judged, and the thieves respected her for it.

Wilhelm had been chatting all the way as they walked and Isbet had only been half-listening. Wilhelm was telling her his plans for Morwynne. Why he trusted her with that information she wasn't certain, but although Wilhelm didn't say it outright, he intended to take the Islands by force if they didn't agree.

Just as they did to Tamrath. To Bram, Isbet thought.

"Here we are," Wilhelm said. A heavy door stood open and inside Isbet saw three immense desks of carved wood. An almost painfully thin woman in thick spectacles that swallowed her eyes and a good portion of her face occupied one of them. She wore her hair in two long braids, which swung wildly when she stood. "Your Majesty! I wasn't informed—"

"This is an informal call, my dear, no need to worry." Much to Isbet's relief Wilhelm detached himself from her arm. "This is Lady Isbet and I would like to give her an opportunity to choose a reward."

"Yes, of course." The woman took a moment to extract herself somewhat clumsily from behind the desk. She bobbed a quick curtsy before moving to the other side of the room. There was another door, as heavy as the first, and the woman in a not-so-subtle manner dug into her dress top and pulled out a ring of keys. She chose one, and as she went to pull the handle Wilhelm stepped forward. "Allow me, my dear."

The woman's cheeks went scarlet as Wilhelm pulled the heavy door open.

Yes, charming, but it's all an illusion, Isbet thought. *The magic surrounds you. Making you appealing, especially to the easily persuaded.* Isbet could see the woman was very enamored of Wilhelm.

The hall beyond the door was narrow, smelled of mildew and was semi-dark, as the only light was at the other end. However, to Isbet the cord filled it with light. How far did that thing reach? Isbet wasn't certain she wanted to know what was on the other end.

Two burly guards sat on stools on either side of a second door. They didn't move or even acknowledge their presence. The woman opened it.

She stepped in first and Wilhelm followed. Something made Isbet pause. There was a spell here, but she wasn't certain if it was sorcerous or necromantic. It certainly wasn't witchery. She clutched Gaemyr tighter and for once, he was oddly silent.

Unlike in the stories told and songs sung, there were no piles of treasure, gold, or jewelry lying haphazardly about. Square wooden chests were arranged and stacked against the walls. There were lock boxes and cabinets, all seeming organized and marked with various symbols. There were two more closed doors, one to her left, and the other across the room and slightly to the left.

"You may leave us now." Wilhelm nodded to the woman, who blushed deeper as she gathered up her skirts and left them alone.

"Don't be nervous, my dear, it's fine. Feel free to look around and choose whatever you desire, as much as you desire," Wilhelm said. "And consider yourself a friend of my realm. I am at your service."

Isbet stepped across the threshold and a sense of power both familiar and dangerous struck her hard. It froze her steps and nearly stilled her heart. Her throat closed and Isbet forced a swallow. She knew that power, masked though it was, cloaked with whatever magic permeated this room. Isbet's eyes locked on the door opposite them.

It was there, Isbet knew, right behind that door. The Tinderbox was there.

"Is there something wrong, my dear?"

Wilhelm's voice brought her abruptly back. Isbet stepped into the room. "It is just that your generosity is overwhelming."

Wilhelm looked at her before he threw his head back and laughed, rather boisterously. "I don't consider this overwhelming."

Now, just what did that mean? Was he so consumed by greed that what he kept in this whole room was nothing? Or was he referring to the one true treasure? She didn't want him to become suspicious, so she began a cursory search of the area. She was not much for jewelry unless she could use it to work magic. She did choose a few rings with the notion to have them be-spelled later.

Coins were always useful and some of the chests had these neatly wrapped in burlap, their denominations marked. Isbet took several of the bags, and then continued her walk. When she came to the first door at the right side of the room, Wilhelm said, "You'll find some very nice things in there."

He was correct. There were rolls of silks, wool and cashmere, soft satins and fine intricate lace, as well as bales of fine leathers and cotton, which would be perfect for armor and some suits. Isbet asked about this.

"I'll have the seamstress sent to your suite tomorrow."

Isbet approached the second door and the sensation of the familiar, of home, surrounded her. It carried her back to that time in the woods with the dogs running and playing in the semi-darkness with the scent of the loam in the air.

"What," Isbet said, "is in here?"

There again was an imperceptible change – a slight widening of the eyes, a heated flush on his face, and Isbet saw what she knew to be fear. It was gone in an eye-blink. If she didn't know the Tinderbox was within before, Wilhelm confirmed it then.

"In there—" Wilhelm whispered, "—is my greatest treasure. It means more to me than life itself."

Isbet believed him. She stepped closer to the door and pressed a hand gently against it. Fire bloomed in the pit of her stomach that quickly spread all over her body, flushing her face hot and drying her throat. That voice that gave her guidance in her mind shouted out, "...now is the time! The dogs are here. Kill him! Strike Wilhelm with the very heart of your Gift. Only then will your grandmother rest...."

"What is it?" Isbet forced the words.

Wilhelm wagged a finger. "That is my secret, my dear."

He made a point of walking forward and placed both hands on her shoulders, purposefully turning her away from the door. "Now feel free to choose more if you like, and if not—" The message was clear.

Isbet dared not wrest herself from his hold, as repulsive as it was. "I am pleased and quite grateful, sire."

"You're welcome." The amiable tone had returned.

As he led her from the room, his hands still on her shoulders, Isbet felt the slight brushing of power. The same he'd exposed Bram to. Again, she called on her Gift, called on Gaemyr to keep the darkness at bay until she was out of Wilhelm's reach.

*　　*　　*

Gaemyr spoke for the first time since the treasury. "The Box was there!"

"I know." Isbet frowned. "You think I didn't? You think I didn't want to kill the bastard—"

A polite knock stopped Isbet's tirade. She'd been unable to sit still after the servant girl had shown her to her suite, which, like everything else in the palace, was gaudy and overblown. "Come in." Isbet worked to modify her voice.

"Isbet?" Bram stepped through the door. Isbet realized he had bathed and changed. She must look a sight, but Isbet wasn't the least bit concerned with her appearance.

"I'm glad you're here. We must talk."

"Yes, I thought you may wish to."

Isbet had thrown her pack on a nearby chair. She went for it now and drew out the doll. Then she realized what Bram had said. She turned towards him. "Why did you believe I wanted to talk?"

He smiled slightly. "We've been companions for quite some time. I like to believe I can read you at least a bit."

Isbet couldn't resist the upward tug of her lips. "Why don't you sit, then?"

Bram sat on the couch. He watched as Isbet set the doll on the sideboard and opened its mouth.

"I remember that," Bram said mildly, motioning towards the doll.

Isbet sat beside him. "Are you aware that Wilhelm reeks of dark magic? That he has been using it to manipulate you?"

Bram frowned. "I knew there was something. It was only a feeling, but at times when he touched me or spoke to me—"

"This whole manor is permeated with it." Isbet told him about the cord attached to Wilhelm's back.

Bram paled. "That's – I can't find the words."

Isbet could see he was greatly disturbed, and she supposed he had reason to be. "I need you to tell me more about Wilhelm. How did he come to be king?"

Bram sat against the couch back and crossed his left leg over his right knee. "I can only tell you what I know from the rumors we'd heard and the intelligence we gathered. When Wilhelm arrived in Rhyvirand—" Bram paused. "Well, no one quite knows when he arrived here. Some say he was merely a commoner, others say he was a rich squire who'd been traveling an awfully long way, for he had scuffed boots and old clothes. But he presented mysterious riches and was soon welcomed by the nobility."

Isbet leaned forward, intent on his words. She rested her chin on her entwined hands. She knew where these mysterious riches had come from.

"The romantics figured he was escaping assassination or someone wanting his place," Bram continued. "The thing was, after being the center of attention in the city, he disappeared."

"But that was not the last of him."

"I have heard that he was…inappropriate with the princess."

"The queen?"

"Yes," Bram said. "That he had kidnapped her and had been with her, so the king commanded his execution." She saw Bram shudder. "But on the day he was to die he summoned the dogs. They say he had them rend the king and queen and all the nobility to pieces and left their corpses to rot on the street."

"And the people made him king."

"What choice did they have? He was a lunatic. And the queen – that is, the princess – married him willingly. She only cared that her lavish lifestyle continue. We thought he would be satisfied with this until his envoy visited us with his…request that my father consider unifying Tamrath with Rhyvirand."

"But the Patriarch saw his true intentions," Isbet said.

"My father was a brilliant man and devoted to his people."

She could see the deep sadness in his eyes. *Wilhelm has much to answer for.* "He sent the dogs."

"Not at first. He had his army invade. He came in secret, and we had little time to prepare but enough that we managed to keep them at bay." Bram pulled both his knees against his chest. "My father didn't want me on the battlefield, but he knew I was Father Protector to our people, and it was my duty."

Isbet drew in a soft breath when tears began to trickle down Bram's cheeks. "The dogs came right for me. I couldn't – looking at them – into their eyes—" Bram suddenly pushed himself off the couch. "Damn it, it was all my fault! Why couldn't I fight them?"

Isbet stood as well. She approached Bram and framed his face with her hands. "Now listen to me, Bram. It was not any fault of your own." Isbet knew she was possibly opening a Pandora's Box, but she said, "The dogs were born from an ancient and powerful magic, well before the time of the Vine. No mortal man can resist them, especially when they are ruled by such a vile man as Wilhelm."

Bram wiped the tears away with the back of his hand. "You must think me a man of very weak character."

Isbet huffed in exasperation. "I am thinking no such a thing."

"Thank you." Bram managed a smile.

"Now—" Isbet moved away, "—I am going to create talismans for you and Seth. Keep them on your persons and they should help to combat Wilhelm's influence, but I can give no guarantees."

"All right," Bram said. "Isbet, I will appreciate anything you do." He raised her hand to his lips. He closed his eyes, his grip tightened. "Bet—"

She wasn't quite certain if she expected him to kiss her. He released her hand and buried both of his into her braids. He gently tipped her head back and guided her forward. He wanted to kiss her and Isbet was a bit surprised to realize she wanted the same. Isbet didn't resist. His lips were soft but firm. There wasn't a hint of weakness in his actions. She opened her mouth in acceptance and his tongue invaded.

His arms went around her, pulling her close, and she could feel his arousal pressing against her stomach. Isbet allowed her arms to snake lazily around his shoulders. She felt her own response, a pooling of liquid heat in her own sex. Isbet was not without experience or talent, a fact made known by previous lovers. She genuinely believed in indulging. Bram was handsome and intelligent and if he wanted her then as much as she wanted him, she would not be averse to agreeing.

When she saw the smoldering lust in his eyes, Isbet traced her thumb along his bottom lip. "Bram, what is it you want?"

He seemed to come to himself again, his eyes going wide. "Oh, Triune—" He didn't make any efforts to pull himself from her embrace. "Isbet, I'm sorry."

She couldn't help teasing him. Isbet raised an eyebrow. "You're sorry?"

"Yes – I mean no – I mean – oh, damn—"

He ran a hand through his hair. "Gods, Isbet. I've wanted to kiss you for – forever. I want to do more than that to you."

Isbet initiated the second kiss. Unlike those swooning maidens, if she found a man attractive, she acted on it. "Then feel free, Highness. I find you handsome and appealing."

She could tell he was pleased by her words but still a bit wary. "I – don't want to take advantage."

Isbet suppressed a laugh, certain Bram would take it the wrong way. "I am not some virginal maiden who concerns herself with reputation."

"And that is what I find so appealing about you," Bram said. "Isbet, I want – let me—"

She waited. Bram finally sighed. "I want too much from you. I want to be with you. I want to make love to you, Isbet."

"But?"

"What will that mean? I don't want you as a mistress. I respect you too much for that."

He was such an impressive man, Isbet had to admit, but she didn't want him to feel obligated to take her as his wife. As deep as her feelings were for him, she didn't want that – and what kind of life would that be? Damn it all, why couldn't he have been some spoiled moronic noble? The last thing she had expected was to fall for Bram Greyward.

She could imagine what Gaemyr must be thinking. *Well, this certainly causes one hell of a complication.*

"Then I suppose we must leave things as they are."

"Yes." He did not sound convinced. He stepped back. Turning away, he said, "You must make haste with the talismans. Wilhelm wants us to travel to Morwynne by week's end."

CHAPTER TWENTY-TWO

It relieved Isbet to be away from the manor and the stench of darkness. The entourage had increased by several more and they did as the rest, clung like leeches to Serval.

"Pathetic," Captain Maive muttered. Her dislike for Serval was clear. It raised Isbet's opinion of the guard captain even more.

As for Serval, he was enjoying the attention, flirting with both the women and men, taking gifts of jewels and fine clothes. Every so often, he would look their way and grace them with a smirk but nothing more. At these times Bram was nervous.

"He dares not say anything against you," Isbet said.

"I'm not concerned with what Serval says but more what he plans to do."

Serval had told Wilhelm he was eager to assist in his plans to unite the Riven Isles. He went on to Wilhelm about his concern for the safety of his people and how his sister had sent him to begin negotiations, a blatant lie, one which incensed Wilhelm further. Isbet had to at least, if not admire Wilhelm, laud him for his dislike and mistrust of the Dokkalfar prince.

"Serval is of little consequence. He is a child, an infant throwing a tantrum because he wants and does not receive," Isbet said.

That brought on a slight smile. "That he is."

They had not spoken of their kiss, but she had caught him smiling every so often. There was no awkwardness or hesitancy. They both accepted their mutual attraction, but what to do now? Isbet still had her plan, or at least she had until a few nights ago.

"Stop dwelling on it," Gaemyr said.

Isbet didn't reply since it would draw attention. Gaemyr had been admonishing her for most of the afternoon until he fell silent with a huff after eliciting no response. It wasn't that simple – now that so much had changed.

Ancer Fallor had perished at her hands.

The tension at their first meeting had filled the air. Fallor made it quite clear what he thought of her and those with the Gift. Isbet wasn't in the least bit concerned with how he judged others. His instructions had been to show her to the basement rooms that were to be her laboratory. Ancer seemed pleased by the fact it was to be in the basement, but it suited Isbet fine. This way she wouldn't have any unwanted guests.

"I hope this meets with your approval," Fallor said.

"It does." Isbet didn't bother to thank him.

Ancer sniffed. "Very well," he said and left.

"Pompous ass," Gaemyr said. "Still, this is impressive."

"Yes," Isbet agreed. It rivaled many of the places of research she had used in the past. "Wilhelm will expect just as impressive results."

"Seth is an intelligent lad. He'll come about his Gift."

"Indeed."

Isbet spent some time in looking around. Another discovery was the grand library Wilhelm kept. There was already a surfeit of older books on magic stacked on supplied bookshelves to her work area. Isbet guessed Wilhelm kept secret the newer tomes.

It was a bit too easy to see the books Wilhelm had taken a special interest in, because that aura of darkness still clung to their pages like wisps of red fog. She found Wilhelm was in fact obsessed with magical objects.

One thing Isbet noted was that Wilhelm had that familiar habit of making notations on the blank spaces of pages – one that annoyed Isbet no end – and it gave her some additional insight into what Wilhelm sought. That knowledge increased her ire.

Some items Wilhelm had brushed aside as useless, such as the Seven-league Boots and the Steel-driver's Hammer.

However, he seemed interested in Dragon's Teeth and worse yet – was Wilhelm that much of a fool? – the Bottle Imp. If Wilhelm used it, it would send him to an eternity of torment. It made Isbet wonder what drove this man. She surmised she would need to find out and perhaps use that against him.

The second night she stayed in the manor, Isbet left her suite and went to walk among the veils. She hadn't done so previously, for when she arrived she'd spent that first night preparing for their journey to Morwynne.

What she saw now made her anger burn white hot. Wilhelm did not understand what he'd brought about. It would be almost impossible for her to explain it to Bram, although with training, Seth would bear witness to the horrors. Isbet was glad he didn't have the ability yet.

Some weaker veils hung shredded as if something vicious had taken claws to them. Isbet also saw these things, walking among the veils or caught within them, struggling to break free of their imprisonment.

Most of the beasts and apparitions were of a corporeal form. Some were translucent and others Isbet saw right through to the blackness that bled from within their souls. They crawled or slithered between the cracks and crevices, hung on the tattered remains with ragged claws, and some walked on their bare knuckles, their bodies solid and muscular.

Some saw Isbet. She couldn't fathom why the larger ones didn't attack her, except perhaps the mark of the Vine and her own Gift served as a shield. That did not cause them to cease their mewling and grunting, or their stares of pure hungry malevolence.

"This is—" Gaemyr said. "We should leave this place. Now."

With Gaemyr's words, Isbet realized how dire things were. The staff feared little and mocked many, but this – it disturbed even him. She was not one for hesitation, but she did, long enough for Gaemyr to say, "Isbet!"

"No." She straightened her back and firmed her resolve. "We cannot just leave things like this."

"Why is everything so complicated?" Gaemyr huffed. "Very well then."

Isbet continued to move, smiling at the staff. She noticed the further she moved away from the royal wings the more solid the veils were, but even that would change.

The good thing was that she could move, using the solid veils to hide her from the guards roaming about, although she could feel them quiver, affected by the change.

Isbet came to the door of the exchequer's office, locked this time of night. She leaned forward, whispering to the mechanism. It didn't give at first, but the spell wasn't so strong that Isbet couldn't break it after a time.

Wrapping herself in the veils again, Isbet moved towards the second door with the same results when she tried the lock. The two guards were at the end of the tunnel. Isbet wrapped their faces in veils, capturing their sight and hearing. These veils Isbet pinned so they wouldn't loosen and then sent the guards with a whispered command to have a taste of the new wine. They walked away. Isbet then went to work on the lock, which was much harder than the first two but it too gave way.

"Yes," Gaemyr said. "They are still here."

Isbet nodded once. This was her new wine, the intoxicating scent of the dogs. Isbet approached the door. There were seven spelled locks, each sealed with a different magic. Isbet was certain she had never seen such a collaboration and wondered how Wilhelm had gotten this group of Gifted together.

Sorcerous hands crafted the first three locks, witchcraft sealed the next three, and necromancy the last.

"Seven locks and the seventh being the hardest to break." Isbet leaned closer to examine it. "Damn it to the nether-hells."

"It appears we must seek a different course of action," Gaemyr said.

"Isn't there anything you can do?"

"No," Gaemyr said. "I couldn't say if this was being cautious or paranoid, but Wilhelm knows enough to protect what he considers his greatest asset."

Isbet stood Gaemyr straight up on his tip, where he stayed balanced. Drawing on her Gift and whispering a prayer to the Vine, Isbet leaned in close to the first lock, feeling the spell out at first, knowing it would become harder but also knowing she had to succeed. Isbet began the incantation.

"Stop!"

A figure stood at the door. The light from the lamp he held cast warped shadows across his features, stressing the fury burning in his eyes. "Witch!"

Isbet then saw what he had in his other hand – an iron fireplace poker.

Ancer Fallor advanced across the room. "I suspected you were about some treachery!"

"I am a guest of your king and a friend of the prince—"

That did nothing to cool his hatred and Isbet saw he was willing to risk the king's – and Bram's – ire. Fallor meant to kill her.

Isbet didn't give any thought to her next actions or their consequences. She reacted. She reached her free hand behind her, the magic of the locks sending pinpricks along her fingertips. Necromantic power raced along her nerves, and as Fallor raised the weapon, the veils responded to her silent command. They caught Fallor by the wrist, binding him.

Fallor halted, his mouth open wide. His head turned towards his arm, which hung suspended in the air. "What – is – this?"

"Ancer Fallor, I wish you no harm. Let me by and I will release you."

He didn't seem to hear her at first. He continued to stare at his arm. His brow furrowed as he pulled against the veil, which did not give.

Then Fallor seemed to come to himself again. "You rancid bitch! What have you done to me?"

"If I have your word, you will not accost me again…?"

"You'll have no such vow from me, witch!" Fallor swung his free arm and the veils, now more guided by Isbet's use of the necromantic power, bound that arm as well.

Fallor started to bellow like a frightened mule as he struggled against his captivity. "Stop, stop! By the names of the gods, I rebuke you, witch!"

Had Bram said those words, Isbet would have been in serious pain, but coming from Fallor, they meant nothing.

"Keep him quiet!" Gaemyr growled.

She had to use Gaemyr to grasp the other veil because it was beyond her reach but once she did, Isbet pulled the end taut then wrapped it around Fallor's head. She waited and listened, hoping no one had heard him. When there was no sign of any interference, Isbet leaned against Gaemyr.

Fallor still struggled, but the veil muffled his cries. He slipped and fell back but the veil held him, making him appear like a doll on invisible strings.

"You know what we must do."

Isbet did. Fallor would run to the nearest guard and have her arrested if she released him, and no amount of reasoning would cause him to do otherwise.

She had a herbal formula that would cause him to forget, but she didn't have it with her and there was no way she could get back to her suite, retrieve it, and come back before someone discovered Fallor. Isbet stepped forward as Fallor's struggles waned and held Gaemyr over him. When he finished, she released the now inert body. Isbet didn't need to do anything else. The beasts that roamed the halls, attracted by the smell of death, came, and saw. They paid little attention to Isbet. A live witch was more of a threat than a corpse, an empty shell. Still, there were beasts who fed on the soul; they gave the body a haughty sniff before turning away. However, others converged in a heated frenzy, tearing what was left of Fallor to bits. Everything went, flesh and bones. What the beasts didn't devour scavengers did, feasting on the remains until there was nothing left of Ancer Fallor.

★   ★   ★

Rumors abounded about where Fallor had gone. His wife, a fat matron, wailed that she had suspected her husband was having an affair with a young servant girl. Whether it was true or not, it explained his disappearance. Although the king and queen indulged the possible affair, the remaining nobility could not and the offenders could very well find themselves shunned by polite society.

Isbet could have left well enough alone and Gaemyr had told her she should; the death of one man would not cause her much concern, but now....

"Isbet?"

She turned to Bram and caught herself before she could speak a coarse word. "Yes?"

"Is something troubling you? You've been quiet."

Then Isbet heard herself say, "Yes, there is something troubling me." She reached over and touched Bram's elbow. "I will tell you of it later."

He nodded once, satisfied. Isbet occupied the rest of her time by calling Seth over and teaching him the basics of magic and explaining how each Gift manifested itself.

They continued their journey. At night when they camped, they told stories around the fire. The captain and her soldiers gathered around Bram, unlike what Isbet had seen in the past, where the nobility separated themselves from the commoners. It was quite displeasing to the nobility traveling with them since they had hoped to garner Bram's attention. Even Serval's presence didn't improve the situation, much to Serval's displeasure.

Isbet didn't sleep much that night, choosing to remain by the fire, but in all honesty, it was so she could watch Bram's tent. Serval and his followers had been drinking all night and Isbet didn't want to take the chance that he might decide to accost Bram again. She had spells and herbal measures to keep her awake and chase away the fatigue. She would sleep when they arrived on Morwynne.

★   ★   ★

It took hours for them to board the small ferry, and after a while, the captain became so incensed that she ordered a good majority of the entourage to stay on the mainland. They didn't like this but whining to Bram did no good; the prince himself was past annoyance and wished to dismiss the lot of them. The only one who Bram opposed to having stay behind was Serval. The captain didn't like it at first, until Bram explained that both he and Wilhelm didn't trust the Dokkalfar and wanted him watched, something the captain was more than willing to do. Therefore, it was Isbet, Bram, Seth, and Captain Maive with four of her most trusted guards – and Serval.

Isbet had never been to Morwynne, so she had no idea what to expect. She told Seth this when he began to ask questions. "I can only tell you what I've heard, brother wizard—" a name which pleased Seth no end, "—Morwynne is not the island's true name, but the name given to it by an explorer and his party centuries ago."

"The island didn't have a name?" Seth asked.

"Yes, it did, but the party had so much trouble with the language and the words, he took it upon himself to rename the island and its people."

"That doesn't sound decent."

"You are correct, it was not," Isbet said. "The man didn't bother to learn of them or from them. He and his party were only interested in their wealth and beautiful dark women."

Seth blushed a little when Isbet mentioned the women, but she didn't believe in hiding such things from children. "Dark women like you?" he asked.

He was so endearing. "Well, thank you, Seth." The young man's blush deepened. Isbet went on, "It was because of the actions of the explorer and his party that Morwynne cut themselves off from the rest of the continent. It took them decades to bring their home back to the way it was, and they are very protective of it."

Seth pondered this for a moment. "What if they don't want us there?"

Isbet sighed. "Then we will leave." She glanced at Bram, who nodded once in agreement, but she read in his eyes what the consequences would be. Morwynne would suffer the same fate as Tamrath and Avynne. "However, the letter of introduction may cause the Dhar and Dharina to be more amiable."

"I hope so." Seth surprised both Isbet and Bram when he said, "I don't want the same thing to happen to them that did my country and Tamrath."

Neither she nor Bram spoke at first, but Seth was looking at her. "Well said."

★   ★   ★

It came as somewhat of a surprise to them when they landed on the shores of Morwynne to find an entourage of five guards waiting to greet them, which raised Isbet's suspicions. Even if the queen's message had reached them, how had the leaders known when they would arrive? The tallest man Isbet was certain she'd ever seen approached. She wondered if there was some giant's blood in him. The last true giant died at the felling of the Vine.

The man was tall and muscular, at least nine feet, his skin coal black, his well-defined muscles shining from the scented oils he had applied. It was necessary, for there was little shade on the desert island. Bram approached him first and the giant bowed. "Welcome, Your Highness."

One of the other of his party, a lovely fair-skinned woman, repeated his words in their native tongue. She was the only one of the entourage with light coloring. History said that the explorer and his men had taken many of the island women as their wives. Some went to them of their own free will, while others weren't given a choice.

Bram also bowed. "Greetings returned. I am honored to set foot on your soil."

"The honor is ours," the man replied. "Let us make haste to the House Royal."

"Indeed," Bram said.

Isbet wasn't about to miss an opportunity to have a good look around. Homes were small and modest, not grandiose. They were open and airy, made of sand-colored bricks. Instead of windows or doors, gauzy material in a variety of colors adorned every opening. Their dress was as airy, light fabrics covering the areas of the body. There were hats galore; most everyone had one on and they were as colorful as everything else.

However, one thing remained universal; as in every other kingdom, town, or province, men and women were hard at work, children were running about in play, and merchants calling to potential customers to buy their wares.

As they came closer to the House Royal Isbet noticed some houses were more opulent, with actual netting over the windows and doors. There were also precious stones and metals adorning and decorating the homes. Even the bricks under their feet seemed better placed. They passed through a marketplace and Isbet took in the various scents of meat, spices, and sweet things. She could see very well that both Bram and Seth wouldn't have minded sampling the fare.

The House Royal sat above everything else on a tiny hill. One of their guards whistled as they stood at the line of stairs ascending to the columned opening. The Morwynne entourage then began to jog up, leaving their party no choice but to follow. Bram lifted Seth into his arms and started with Isbet right behind them. They were all winded and sweating by the time they reached the top. The entourage was used to the climb in the heat. Even Isbet didn't prefer to be in this condition, especially when she was about to meet with a royal.

The guards gave them no time to catch their breath. The leader and his group started down a long hall with a vaulted ceiling and a floor of gray marble. As always, there were servants or officials moving about. There were open-air offices on either side and several smaller rooms filled with groups of students. It surprised Isbet to notice that they all had the Gift.

They came to the throne room, where the vaulted ceiling had a mosaic of clear glass depicting what Isbet assumed was their deity. It bathed the air in dozens of colors. The man turned and the group halted.

"Majesties, I present to you Prince Bram Greyward of Rhyvirand and his party."

Bram stepped forward, motioning for Seth to stand beside Isbet. She could tell the situation frightened the boy, so she took his hand. Bram approached the dais and went down on one knee. "I give you greetings from my father, King Wilhelm, and from Queen Aimeli and the Duchess Briwyn of Chira."

The Dhar spoke. "I am Dhar Aman Damerae. My first, Her Royal Majesty Anya Damerae. We have received the message of introduction from the queen."

"I hope she conveyed the urgency of our visit?"

"She did, although it was unnecessary. We are aware of the situation with the Vine and we will deal with it on our own."

Isbet glimpsed a look of almost desperation flash across the Dharina's face. Something was amiss here.

"I am at your service," Bram said. "What may I do to assist?"

The Dhar didn't respond. His gaze moved to the woman who had just entered the room from a door on the other side of the Dharina's throne. She stopped next to it and bowed, then leaned down and kissed the Dharina on the cheek.

"Sorceress," Gaemyr said, though he didn't have to.

"Yes," the Dhar said to an unasked question. "Do you and that bastard Wilhelm take me for a fool?"

His anger shocked Bram. "Majesty, I don't—"

"Be silent!" The Dhar came off his throne. "You believe that because we keep to our own affairs we are ignorant of what has occurred on the mainland?"

Bram made no response. The Dhar was not asking for one.

"I know all about the fate of both Tamrath and Avynne." The Dhar's voice carried across the room. "And now I can only assume Wilhelm has set his greedy sights on my land and plans to take it with his foul magic."

Again, Bram didn't reply. They both knew it was the truth.

"You are now a hostage of the Dhar, and I will kill you, Prince Bram Greyward, if need be." The Dhar's voice had gone deadly soft. "We will not allow Wilhelm his victory."

CHAPTER TWENTY-THREE

"How dare you!" Serval called out. "I am a prince of the under-realm and am no man's hostage! I came here to warn you—"

"Did I not tell you to be silent?" The Dhar waved a hand and their escort turned and drew their curved swords and advanced.

"Your Majesty, this is not right," Bram said. "What type of man do you call yourself—"

At the same moment, Captain Maive and her guards positioned themselves facing each direction and drew their own weapons.

"Stay your ground!" Captain Maive said. "You will not hurt His Highness."

This was moving too fast for Bram. Didn't the Dhar realize what he would bring upon his people? "Please do not do this."

Seth wriggled from Bram's hand and pushed past Isbet and the circle of protection. "You leave Bram alone, you big bully!"

The guard nearest to him stepped up to the child and raised his hand as though to strike him.

"Don't!" Bram lunged forward.

Isbet got there first.

She swung Gaemyr upward in a violent motion, catching the guard under the chin with such force Bram heard the crack of bone. Never had he seen such a thing. Isbet was a fit and an able fighter but this seemed almost too incredible to believe. Yet there was the guard, on the floor and in obvious pain.

"How dare you attempt to injure my charge?" Isbet stood over Seth, Gaemyr lowered. She seemed intent on spearing the guard with it. "Is this how a man of honor behaves?"

It was the angriest he'd ever seen Isbet. Bram realized she cared for Seth and that only increased his admiration of her.

The other guards, first stunned into immobility by the scene, came back to themselves. Bram tried once more to keep the peace. "Majesty, you claimed an awareness of what Wilhelm is capable of. What will happen if you harm us?"

Isbet now stepped forward, facing the guards. Although nothing had changed about her, he could sense her gathering her Gift. Bram didn't expect Serval to fight and Serval didn't disappoint. He moved behind one of their guards.

One of the House guards attacked their right flank, spurring his companions on. Their mistake was ignoring Isbet. The captain moved back to Bram. "Stay behind me, Highness." They both realized it would do no good. As the guard lunged to attack, Isbet cracked Gaemyr across his skull and he fell flat. Isbet then brought Gaemyr down in one sharp motion, striking the tip on the marble floor. There was stark silence for a moment; even the clang of steel faded.

The floor beneath them trembled. Something hit against what should have been unyielding marble and a crack formed. Bram feared what it was.

"Cease this!" The sorceress stepped down from the dais. Whether she had broken Isbet's concentration, or she was agreeing, Bram couldn't tell. Although the trembling had ceased, Isbet kept her stance and her gaze stayed pinned on the sorceress.

"Marjani—" the Dhar began.

Marjani raised one hand and after an annoyed murmur, the Dhar went silent. Bram had to admit the sorceress was beautiful, her skin a warm sugar brown, her eyes deep set and as black as the long braid she wore down her back. She dressed in a halter top and loose-fitting trousers. He realized from her mannerisms that she reminded him of Isbet. "What is your name, Lady Witch?"

Isbet remained on her guard. "Isbet, milady."

Marjani smiled at that. "May I see your hand, please?"

Isbet extended her right hand, while keeping a tight hold of Gaemyr in her left. Marjani examined the tattoo on Isbet's wrist for a few moments. Then she turned to the Dhar and spoke in their native tongue.

The Dhar responded, in obvious shock during the exchange, which went on for several minutes. The Dharina, who had been silent to this point, said in land-speak, "Please let them try, my husband."

The Dhar released a breath. "Very well." He nodded to Marjani. "My second has informed me that the Vine chose you as its speaker."

"It did," Isbet said.

"Then you are a Child of the Vine and to injure you would be sacrilege."

"And what of my companions?" Isbet said.

"I do not trust them," the Dhar said, "but because of you I will not injure them. However, while I will treat you with the respect afforded your rank, you are still my prisoners. Your release will depend on whether or not you can help us."

"What would you have us do?"

"You will know in time."

Isbet seemed ready to speak further but relaxed her stance and looked to Bram, who said, "Captain, stand down."

Marjani said, "Set aside your arms. You—" she pointed at one guard, "—take him to the healer." The second guard helped the injured man to his feet. "I am reducing your rank to Able Guardsman. Lady Isbet is correct. A man of true honor would not attack a defenseless child." Marjani turned to Seth and smiled. "Although one with the Gift, no matter how small, is not defenseless."

Seth flushed scarlet at her words and ducked behind Bram's knee. Bram thought that woman commanded a great deal of power.

"Have rooms prepared for our guests," the Dhar said, "and food and drink."

"Sire," Serval stepped forward, "it is imperative that I speak with you in private."

Dhar Aman gazed at Serval for a moment. "Yes, we will speak in private. My Dharina and I will join you when it's convenient."

Bram had seen the look of desperation on the Dharina's face before. Now there was some relief. What did they have to do with that?

★   ★   ★

A suite of adjoining rooms separated by filmy curtains made their temporary accommodations. Bram was thankful for the curtains as they kept insects out. He wondered how these people bathed without worrying about prying eyes, but he soon found out certain parts of the room had folding screens that opened in a semi-circle. Still, the possibility of becoming an unwilling exhibitionist embarrassed Bram since Seth would share his space.

They had set food out, an assortment of grilled fish and vegetables, and Bram asked that Isbet and the captain join him in his room. The three made themselves comfortable and Seth sat on the floor next to Bram. He'd found a game, or what he'd assumed was one, but the instructions were in the native language, so Seth amused himself with stacking the smooth wood blocks on a marked board.

"So, I am open to opinions or suggestions," Bram said. "Any thought on what they have in store for us?"

The captain glanced at Isbet before saying, "Only that they wish for us to perform a task. Did you both notice the Dharina's distress?"

"Yes." Bram nodded to Isbet, who returned the action. "And how she asked the Dhar to let us try. I can only assume there is something amiss here in the palace."

"But," the captain asked, "does it need the force of arms or magic to resolve?"

★   ★   ★

They found out soon after. They were summoned to the royal quarters, where they found the Dhar and Marjani sitting on opposite ends of a long couch. The Dharina was absent.

"Please sit," Marjani said.

Bram allowed Isbet and Captain Maive to sit first, then he and Seth bowed, the boy doing so at Bram's instruction before they sat.

"I have spoken with Prince Serval," the Dhar began without

preamble. "He has quite a story to tell, which, I am to understand, you refute?"

"It depends on what he said." Bram knew not to agree to something without all the facts.

The Dhar smiled. "A very sound response. What he said is that you were my enemy. That you instigated a battle to seize control of his sister's kingdom and that you escaped prosecution in Underneath. He said you also planned to trick me into letting my guard down so that Wilhelm will take my land. He also said Lady Isbet attacked him because she grew jealous that you were – amid coupling."

Heat rushed to Bram's face. "That's. A. Lie."

"All of it?"

"Yes, gods damn that bastard. It's all a lie."

"Then tell me what the truth is."

Bram did. He told the Dhar all – including Serval's trying to force him, as embarrassing as it was. He expected the Dhar to laugh, but he did no such thing. In fact, he nodded, keeping his gaze on Bram. And knowing he was risking all, Bram confirmed Wilhelm's plan and the consequences if the Dhar refused his initial request. A look of anger crossed the Dhar's features for a moment, but he didn't respond.

Finally, Bram said, "I leave this to you, Great Dhar of Morwynne, to choose who speaks the truth, but I ask you one favor. Allow the women and young Seth to leave and I will stay."

The Dhar exchanged a look with Marjani. "You have my faith, Prince Bram Greyward. I believe you."

Bram released a sigh and let his shoulders drop. "Thank you." He should have let things be, but curiosity getting the better of him, Bram said, "What made you decide in our favor?"

Both the Dhar and the sorceress grinned. "I am a good judge of character."

"Stop being immodest." Marjani shook her head. "I could see the treachery on Serval, eating away at his soul. I saw him to be a deceiver."

"You're a diviner," Bram said.

"I'm not being immodest, wife," the Dhar grumbled. "Any fool could see he was a liar. A mewling child who thinks the realm owes him some due."

It didn't surprise Bram that Marjani was also his wife. What little information they had of Morwynne had told them that they allowed the Dhar three wives and no more.

"So now this situation begs the question, what should we do with Serval?"

Lock him up, was Bram's first thought, but he knew it wasn't up to him.

"We should confine him to his rooms for now," Marjani said. "Although he no longer has his power, he could still cause trouble."

"He doesn't?" Bram said.

"Yes," Marjani said. "Lady Isbet, you will see when you next lay eyes on Serval."

Isbet nodded.

"And now, we shall ask the favor of you." The Dhar stood and extended a hand to Marjani. She took it in hers as he helped her to stand. "Please follow us."

The two led them through an entryway, through additional rooms until they came to a closed door where a single female guard stood. She saluted the Dhar then knocked, stepped aside, and opened the door. It was a bedroom. The Dharina was there, sitting at the bedside of a little girl about Seth's age. The Dharina went to rise, but the Dhar moved across the room. "No, my dear, you need not get up."

There was the smell of illness there. Of sweat-soaked covers and bitter medicine. Bram could only watch as the Dhar stood at his wife's side and rested his hand on her shoulder. "May I present my daughter, the Princess Tiyah."

It surprised Bram when the child opened her eyes and gave them a hesitant smile. "Greetings."

Observing that poor child in such a condition made his throat close, but Bram found he didn't have to say anything. Seth crossed the room and approached the bed. "My lady, I am Prince Seth, once of Avynne."

She drew an emaciated hand from beneath the covers and Seth took it, kissing it. "You have a fever. Would you like some water?"

"Yes, I would, thank you."

Bram watched with pride bursting through his chest as Seth crossed the room to a dresser, where there was a cask of water and some tiny crystal cups. He filled one and carried it back to the princess. "Here." He held the cup as she drank. "Better?"

"Yes, thank you."

As the scene unfolded, not one adult in the room had moved or spoken. The only signs of the Dhar and Dharina's devastation were the tears making silent tracks down their faces. She looked up at her husband and nodded. The Dhar left her side and went to Bram. "The princess is ill. I asked Serval this and he refused, but I know you will help."

"What is it?" Bram said.

"She is a witch," Isbet replied, not looking at them, fixated on the princess. "It is not an illness. It is poison."

"It is a taint, a bitter Rot that infected the Vine and cursed her. It is spreading beneath us," the Dhar said. "All my people are at risk, however—" The Dhar lowered his head for a moment and when he raised it again, his expression was hard but his words desperate, "Please, I beg of you. Please save my daughter."

CHAPTER TWENTY-FOUR

"Majesty, I am uncertain how—?"

"How did this come about?" Isbet stepped forward and grasped the Dhar's forearm, an action that would have received severe punishment under normal circumstances, but that was the least of the Dhar's concerns.

"There are many caves on this island where the children play," he said. "The Vine lives in all of them and protects them, or at least—" The Dhar drew in a ragged breath. "It did. My daughter and some House children were playing in a cave and when they went deeper inside, my daughter sensed the wrongness there. There was darkness where there was light, and out of this came a tendril of the Vine, but it was black with the disease. My daughter warned the others not to come near, but they did and when she called upon her Gift to protect them, the Vine reacted. It took hold—"

"It will be fine, I give you my word." Bram laid a reassuring hand on his shoulder. "Please continue."

"It took hold of her with thorns that tore at her flesh. It forced her to use her Gift to sever the hold, but it took so much of her that—"

"How did she escape?"

"The children ran off to get help. They just left her there." There was a bitterness in the Dhar's voice. "As fortune would have it, Marjani was nearby and could keep the horrors at bay while other elders carried her out."

He turned and looked back to the bed where Seth now sat on a little stool and was whispering to the princess. "When I received Queen Aimeli's message, I wasn't aware of how far the taint had spread and why." He turned back to Bram. "My sincere apologies for suspecting you."

"No apologies are necessary. You spoke true. I will give you the same vow I gave to Chira – I will try to convince Wilhelm that this is more important than his plans for conquest."

"You are an honorable man, Your Highness." Now the Dhar turned to Marjani. "Take them to the caves."

★　　★　　★

"We were fortunate," Marjani said as they walked the path through the palace gardens. "These caves adjoin the royal grounds so no one else may enter. The people are not aware of how ill the princess is."

"You have sworn the servants to secrecy?" Isbet adjusted her backpack on her shoulders.

"No. We depend on their loyalty. Besides, only those most trusted with the princess know the truth and they will not break a confidence."

Bram supposed the closeness of this secular people was the reason such loyalty developed. Had they been in Rhyvirand or even his beloved Tamrath, there would not only have been gossip but intrigue upon intrigue, and everyone from close relatives to the lowest servant would have been scheming to take advantage.

There was a short stone staircase descending onto a secluded beach. A group of the guards was there. Two were in a small fishing boat, while one tended a fire. A fourth was chopping at one of the many palm trees that dotted the island, and the two remaining stood at either side of the entrance to the cave.

They acknowledged the group but didn't leave their tasks. Beside him, Isbet muttered an oath. Marjani stopped, turned to look, and continued.

"What is it, Isbet?"

"You'll know soon enough," Isbet said.

It wasn't, however, until they reached the entrance of the cave that what Isbet had sensed caught him as well and he realized it was the same. Bram would never forget that cold chill and the smell of decayed things.

"Dear Triune," Bram said. "This is much worse than the Vine growing."

"The growth only gives this Rot greater power," Isbet said. "But you are correct, this must take precedence. If this thing infects the Vine to the root...."

"Now you both see," Marjani said. "Witch or Light-bearer, only you can help us. This thing is immune to sorcery. A Child of the Vine or a Vessel of Gods can stop this."

"We will do what we can." Bram couldn't help but wish he had his sword and vestments.

"Perhaps I should enter alone."

His gaze went to Isbet. "You'll do no such damn thing."

"One moment." Marjani signaled to the guard tending the fire. He approached and she spoke to him in their native tongue. The guard undid his sword belt and handed it to Bram.

"Take it," Marjani said. "It is not your Holy Sword, but it should suffice."

Bram looked up at her while buckling the belt. *I keep forgetting, she is a diviner.*

"And now this." Marjani raised her hand as though to reach for something above her and when she lowered it, a light rested in her palm. It coalesced into a shining ball. Marjani repeated the action three times. "These will guide your way."

They were like the wil-o-wisp in Underneath. Bram went to reach for one but Isbet grasped his hand. "Ball lightning."

He'd heard of the phenomenon but had never seen it. Bram didn't fear, for Marjani seemed to have complete control over it.

"Thank you," Bram told the sorceress.

"Wait!"

All eyes turned to Serval, who was making his way down the path. Bram saw the look on Marjani's face, part annoyance, and part anger. *So much for him remaining in his rooms,* Bram thought.

"I've decided to assist," Serval said as he ran up.

"Why?" Marjani didn't hide the suspicion in her voice.

"Is this not the honorable thing to do?" Serval said. "I realized that I was mistaken before, besides—" he raised his hand and pointed a finger at Bram, "—I've warned you about their treachery!"

Bram kept his peace since he already knew they had gained the Dhar's trust. Isbet must have thought along the same lines for she said, "It is fine. Let us go now. Standing here does no good."

Isbet entered first, despite Bram's reservations. He prepared a prayer as they stepped into the cave, which swallowed the outside light. They would have been in complete darkness were it not for the lightning.

"What an awful stench," Serval said.

He was stating the obvious, so Bram ignored him. The lights went before them. At first, there was nothing but the rough stones sparkling with the minerals reflected by the light.

"Wait!" Isbet put her hand out to halt their progress.

"I don't take commands from you, wi—"

"Quiet!" Isbet said.

Bram strained to listen. After a time, it came to him from just beyond the range of his hearing – breathing and the slow beating of the heart of some slumbering beast.

"Do you hear it now?" Isbet said to Bram.

"Yes," Bram replied.

They continued and came to a sharp curve in the path. There black vines beginning as tendrils thickened as they walked deeper into the cave.

"There is a light," Serval said.

It was dim, but they noticed a pale blue luminescence. A hint of movement sent Bram's gaze to the ceiling. The vines writhed and undulated, their flesh bursting open as they dragged themselves across the jagged edges. The wounds dripped a green ichor.

"Triune." Bram was so intent on this, it was a few moments before he noticed that they had reached the source of the light. The path had opened out into a small cavern where a huge branching had pierced the cave wall through a massive crack.

"What can we do?" Serval asked. "This is beyond us. We should leave this place now."

"You can leave if you wish," Bram said. "Isbet?"

"For once Serval is correct. There is little the three of us...."

Her words faded and Bram followed her line of sight to the gaping wound in the cave wall. Something was moving within it.

The thing came, gaunt and serpentine. Its skin was the unhealthy pallor of a body riddled with sickness. It dragged itself along the rotted length of the Vine, its snake tail wrapped around the putrid flesh. Dark hair clumped and tangled, half-concealing a hard-boned face. Black eyes, appearing as empty sockets, stared at them with malice, and when it smiled, it showed ragged pointed teeth.

"Holy Triune, what is that?" Bram moved beside Isbet. "Not a nagi?"

"No," Serval responded. "It's a lamia."

Bram knew of the vicious demons. Related only by their serpentine tails, nagi hated being confused with lamia. Normally possessed of a sinister beauty, a lamia tried to ensnare as many unfortunate males as possible, then devour their souls and bodies.

"She is cursed," Isbet said. "Whatever is infecting the Vine has poisoned her."

Bram took a few steps forward. He then noticed the wriggling form, once hidden by the woman's hair. It was an infant. It grunted as it suckled, making a watery, gurgling sound.

"No," Bram murmured. He noticed that Isbet and Serval had moved beside him.

"We must kill it," Serval said. "It is an abomination."

Bram didn't know if he meant the lamia, the baby, or both. It wasn't until moments later that another sound came to them. Mewling cries like newborn kittens came from the hole. A face peeked out beyond the darkness.

"There are more of them?" Bram couldn't tell how many.

"They must die. She will steal the children of this place to feed her own," Isbet said.

Bram had also heard that legend about them. It made him sick to think it was true.

"Allow me to exorcise the curse," Bram said.

"No," Isbet said. "You cannot. The lamia and her brood must die."

Bram said, "I will not take the life of a child."

Isbet turned to him, her face a sculpture of hard lines, and fire burned within her eyes. "They are not children. They are demon spawn. You know this to be true, Highness."

"Enough of this debate." Serval strode forward, closer than any of them had yet tried.

The lamia hissed again and crawled back on the branch, keeping hold of the infant.

"Away with you, vile one!" Serval stretched out his hand, palm up, and then balled it into a fist. Bram sensed the vibration around them as it charged the air and ran along Bram's nerves. He remembered it.

The force hit the branch. Although Bram couldn't see it happen, he knew it had when it exploded into a mess of flesh and ichor. The lamia screeched, and she-demon and baby fell.

She hit the rotting loam and the infant landed beside her. Its mewling cry assaulted Bram's ears. The lamia pushed herself up and raised on her tail to full height. Her intent was clear but, even though they all knew she would attack, Bram was not expecting her to move with such blinding speed. Before he could even draw the sword, she was on him, the tail wrapping around his legs and jerking his feet out from under him.

Bram landed hard on his back, the air forced from his lungs. The knotted and clawed hands grasped at his throat. The pain brought him out of his shock. Bram slammed his hand against the lamia's forehead, pressing down with his fingers, and shouted, "Be gone, she-demon!"

The Triune did not forsake him, just as it hadn't during the battle at Underneath. The lamia released him, rearing once again upon her tail. Her head went back, and her arms spread wide as the mark – the sigils of the Triune – burned onto the flesh of her forehead. She whipped around, her tail slipping clumsily on the mud. The lamia turned back to them when she believed she was at a safe distance. She kept one hand on her forehead. She hissed at them while black tears ran down her cheeks.

Bram could find no purchase to climb to his feet. Isbet came to his aid, not having any trouble moving about. She grasped his arm and pulled him up with little effort. "She is gone," Bram said. "If the touch of the Triune did her harm, then there is no bringing her back."

"I know," Isbet said.

Knowing he was risking himself, Bram stepped forward, a simple prayer on his lips as he approached her again. The lamia stood her ground at least for a time, as she edged to the side. The infant reacted to Bram's words and started to scream. When Bram was within an arm's reach of her, the lamia bolted, somehow finding traction. She crossed Bram's path and went straight for Serval. The Dokkalfar had the good sense to have another spell ready; again he made a motion, and the lamia came to an abrupt halt. Her tail seemed to go out from under her.

There was a sound of wood cracking, and the severed end of the Vine exploded with new growth, not the healthy color of the earth, but blackened with sickness. The Vines twisted and intertwined, like fingers reaching and groping.

"Serval!" Isbet's warning was futile for the vines tangled his body within their grip.

Isbet slammed Gaemyr into the ground, grasped the staff in a white-knuckle grip, and then her head lolled back, and her eyes rolled up into her head. She was choking, fighting for breath.

"Isbet!"

"Help me!" The Vines were pulling Serval into the opened end, which proceeded to consume him as though it were a snake. "Help me!" It wasn't a plea but a command. Serval wanted Bram to choose – him or Isbet. For Bram, there wasn't a choice.

He saw the lamia had retreated to underneath the damaged section of Vine, but she seemed calm, a smile on her lips. Bram turned back to Isbet and saw the change, saw the sickness traveling up her arms, across her face, saw her whites darken into inky pools.

That thing had possessed her.

Bram steadied her head in his hands, pressed his forehead to hers, and said, "Get thee out! Get thee out, demon, release her!" He heard the lamia scream again. She was coming for him; he could see her out of the corner of his vision. Still, Bram concentrated, said the words again, put all his force, his being behind it, until Bram felt the lamia relent, felt it drain from Isbet's body. Another force joined him in his fight and he somehow knew it was Gaemyr. The thing had taken him as well and now he was fighting to bring Isbet back.

Isbet's hands loosed from around Gaemyr. She fell limp against him. Bram thought the lamia would take them both but when he looked where he thought she was, there was nothing left but a putrid, empty shell.

Isbet coughed, pushed back from him and vomited black bile.

"Isbet?"

"Gaemyr," she said.

Bram picked up the staff and gave it to her, watching as she knelt in the filth, her chest rising and falling with deep breaths. She looked up at him and Bram couldn't imagine seeing eyes as beautiful as hers.

"Thank you, Bram."

Bram went to his knees and pulled her into his arms. "I thought I would lose you. Please never scare me like that again."

She didn't respond and Bram thought she didn't have to. She did not stay in his embrace for long. "Serval."

Bram helped her to her feet. The diseased Vine engulfed Serval's body. The outline showed as it pulled him deeper into its heart.

"Is there anything we can do?"

"I don't know," Isbet said. "Follow me."

Isbet walked to the wall, where the crack was. She chose hand- and footholds to climb. "We must see to the other offspring first."

"Isbet," Bram said. "Let me."

"No," Isbet said. "Although they are beasts, I do not want their blood on your hands."

"It is my duty," Bram said. Isbet didn't respond. She was looking at Gaemyr, her head tilted to one side as though listening to him speak. Bram figured he could no longer hear the staff because he wasn't connected to the Vine, or because they were no longer in Underneath, or both.

"Very well then, we will continue on," Isbet said. "Are you certain you will resist this time?" she asked Gaemyr. "I don't want to lose you, you rotted old piece of kindling."

There was a pause before Isbet laughed. She then approached the part of the Vine stretching the length of the cave to pierce another wall, from where there came a faint greenish glow. She pressed Gaemyr to it and the staff melded through the flesh. "He will take care of the offspring and then try to determine Serval's whereabouts. We should move on."

"Agreed." The decision did not need discussion.

CHAPTER TWENTY-FIVE

Isbet trod carefully across the slippery floor of the cave as she made her way to the opposite end, which opened into a cavern. Her skin prickled with an involuntary shudder.

Your overconfidence was your downfall.

Isbet had thought to call on that part of the Vine not yet taken by the Rot, but it was far away, further than Isbet had imagined, which meant the Rot was far worse than they realized.

The presence was there, faceless, yet familiar. She recognized it, and it her.

It chose Gaemyr first, taunting him, knowing that he was once a man, now nothing more than a freakish thing. Gaemyr was a product of the Vine and therefore a slave to it or in this case, the presence. It had filled Isbet with its poison, seizing her body and mind with its will. She fought and it laughed.

Then a light blazed a path through the darkness in her mind. The fire burned her and then the presence. It was enough for Isbet to break free and although Bram had not injured it, he had done enough to force the presence to retreat.

Marjani had spoken true. Child of the Vine and Light-bearer, they were both needed. It sounded like some blasted prophecy. Isbet halted at the egress. Her hand rested against the slick rock face. She drew in a deep breath.

"Isbet?"

"I will be fine." She needed to reassure Bram. "Arrogant and foolish of me. I thought to call on the Vine not affected by this Rot."

"It is worse than we realized, isn't it?"

"Yes," Isbet said. Then she reached out and laid her hand on Bram's forearm. "It would have taken me, were it not for you. Thank you."

Bram cupped her chin in one hand and lifted it before kissing her on the lips. "I will protect you."

Such a declaration would have amused her in the past but now she understood Bram's sense of honor made him who he was, and she wouldn't make light of that. It was, as always, appealing. Bram followed close as Isbet stepped into the next cavern. Here, like in Chira, their way was lit by a pale luminescence. There was no wil-o-wisp. They needed to choose their footing with care.

There were several thick offshoots attached to the ceiling, marked with the Rot. Each one disappeared on the far side of the cavern. It was not light enough to show if there was another exit but Isbet supposed there had to be. Clumps of overgrown flora dotted the cave floor. Like the Vine, they had the taint of the Rot. They no longer possessed eerie beauty; they seemed like ugly, stunted things that, had they been sentient, would attack with nettles and poison.

Isbet lifted her gaze, allowing her eyes to adjust. She wished Gaemyr were with her. The cries of the infants had long since faded and Isbet knew Gaemyr had finished his grim task. Somehow, she spotted a slight disturbance in the shape of the Vine's flesh. She pointed upwards, directing Bram. "There, do you see?"

It took Bram a few moments. He squinted then said, "Yes."

"We should continue on," Isbet said. "We don't want to lose sight of him."

They resumed their journey with no difficulty. Every so often Isbet would look up to follow the movement again. Serval's struggles were becoming less noticeable. Still, the outline remained, and they followed until they came to the opposite wall of the cavern. There were several cracks in there. However, the one where the offshoot went through proved to be too narrow for the two of them. Isbet might squeeze through but not Bram.

Isbet shook her head. "This will not work. We must choose another way and hope we find him again." Isbet examined the closest fissure. "There, do you see?"

"Yes, a faint light."

The fit was rather tight there, but they managed. As Isbet stepped into a smaller chamber, she realized the light came from enormous gems, like the one in Underneath, but what they revealed was a wasteland. Whatever lived was alien in appearance. Some bent towards them as they passed. "Take care not to get too close," Isbet said.

"I have no intention," Bram replied.

They could no longer see the offshoot that trapped Serval's body. There were several offshoots, but if Serval was in one of them, it was impossible to tell even with the light from the gems.

"I'm sorry," Isbet said.

"Let's not give up hope yet," Bram replied. "We should keep going."

There was a makeshift trail in front of them. Isbet figured others had traversed this place, but it had to have been a long time ago.

"Where do you suppose we are?" Bram said. "In relation to the Island, I mean."

"No idea," Isbet said. "I have never been to Morwynne." She turned back and gave him a reassuring smile. "However, I believe we haven't traveled far."

They had some climbing to do. A search of the wall revealed no way out, but Bram spotted a jagged hole in one gem. Since light didn't pour in, it had been hard to spot. Bram had Isbet go first as they made their way with some precarious hand- and footholds. The hole was just large enough for them to squeeze through.

"Triune," Bram whispered behind her.

Spread before them to their left was a range of rocky hills. The beach where they had started was far to their left and figures moved around below, mere dots. The island landscape continued to the right.

What had Bram muttering in shock was the thick branch of the Vine rising out of the sea in an arch. Several offshoots wound across the cliff face, all black with the Rot, but the main trunk remained healthy.

"I wonder if Marjani knows about this," Bram said.

"If she does, I'm sure she would have told us," Isbet said. "It's difficult to believe, but this is a good sign. It means at least the heart of the Vine is unaffected."

"Shall we continue?" Bram said.

"Yes."

They crossed the rocks until they were closer to where the trunk curled at the topmost part of the arch. Isbet nodded to herself, gauging the distance. She walked several steps back.

"Isbet?"

She broke into a run, leapt.

"Isbet!"

She landed on the trunk at a crouch, then stood. When she turned back to Bram, he was looking quite put out, but after a few moments of fuming he followed Isbet's actions.

"Never do something like that again," he said when he landed beside her.

Isbet rolled her eyes skyward. "Bram."

Now that she was there, she had a clear view of where the bottom of the arch disappeared back under the water. This puzzled her. "Why are the offshoots rotted out, yet this part of the Vine is whole?"

She'd been speaking more to herself, but Bram answered, "I couldn't say."

Isbet sat cross-legged on the trunk and laid her palms with her fingers spread wide on the surface. It came to her, the sense of a battle, a massive struggle between magic and wills. So far, the Vine was keeping the Rot at bay but there was no way to determine how long it could go on. Moments later, Isbet's question received a response.

"The Vine has split," she said. "We can't see it, it's underwater, but it's working its way back into the healthy area." Isbet stood and arched her back in a stretch. "If only there was a way to sever the rotted portion of the Vine."

"The Islanders are renowned for their diving skill—"

"No. It would be too dangerous for them. We need a creature of the water."

There was a small offshoot, about as tall as Bram, curling in the air. Isbet approached it and grasped with both hands. "Gaemyr!"

It took much longer than Isbet expected but the offshoot quivered in her hand, a section of its stem reshaping into Gaemyr's face. "I was searching for you. Blasted Rot is all over the place," he said.

"You had me worried."

"Humph," Gaemyr grunted. "That Serval is paying for his treachery. I heard him screaming all over the place."

"Can we still save him?"

"Not likely," Gaemyr said. "He was already halfway gone. Try. Your prince there will want to." His gaze fell on Bram.

Isbet ignored the way Gaemyr referred to Bram as *her* prince. "Then you're aware the Vine has split below us."

"No man would survive down there, no matter how fine a swimmer he is."

"So I gathered. I will need your assistance."

"Very well."

Isbet turned to Bram. "I will call for help. I will need to concentrate."

Bram nodded and sat, pulling his knees up to his chest. Isbet sat as well. She held Gaemyr up, his tip resting against the Vine's flesh. Isbet allowed herself to fall into that place between worlds. The veils were there too. With Gaemyr as her guide, Isbet grasped one veil, drawing it aside. Water swirled around her, filling her vision, green and inviting, promising to wash away all that was impure.

Isbet called out. Stretching her arm, she beckoned. The water spirit heeded her call. It was young and had not the power to resist her. Isbet did not want to insult the denizens of the water, so she asked the spirit for her help, begging her to understand the urgency of her request.

An Undine. She rose up out of the water with a crystal spray, glistening from the setting sun. Isbet took her other hand, bonding them together, and let herself fall forward into the very soul of the sea creature. Isbet was the Undine now. She dove back underneath the cool water, at home there. The murkiness and the shadows were of no consequence to her. It was as clear as if she were on the land during the mid-day.

There! The rotted section of Vine. The Undine part of her shuddered at the poison leaking into the water. Isbet swam through the blackness, feeling the sea creatures crying out in pain. The Undine wanted to go to their aid. It was the first time Isbet imposed her will. First, they needed to halt the poison, or they would all die.

Isbet came to the submerged cliff face, deeper than any swimmer could reach. The rotted Vine emerged from a sea cave at the base. Uncertain where she was, Isbet approached it, sensing the malevolence. She hesitated, drawing her Gift around her. This beast would not take her again. Isbet closed her hands around the Vine and pulled. There was a slight give. Isbet propped her feet against the cliff wall and pulled again, putting all her strength and her Gift and the supernatural power of the Undine into it.

A scream filled her head and her ears. The rotted Vine came alive, writhing and twisting in her grasp. Thorns burst out of the festering skin, piercing Isbet's hands. She bit down on her lower lip hard, willing herself not to scream as the fire of the poison traveled through her veins.

The water exploded into a torrent of froth and bubbles as something grabbed at Isbet, winding its way around her arms. She knew what it was as it gripped tight and tugged. There was a second scream as the rotted Vine tore away from the base. A blackness flowed from the wound. Isbet released it and the Undine took that moment to flee beyond the veil, leaving Isbet in darkness, her lungs burning for air. She flailed for a moment until she sensed a presence nearby. Gaemyr took hold of her and pulled her through the darkness.

She wasn't going to make it. She had to breathe. Isbet opened her mouth and the water flooded down her throat. She thought she would drown, but then she broke the surface, coughing up bitter water through her mouth and nose.

"Isbet—" Bram reached for her and pulled her to safety atop the trunk. At the same moment something black and twisted rose from the water behind him. Isbet cried a warning before the thing came down like a fist and struck the Vine where they stood. The shock caused the Vine to whip upward, pitching Isbet and Bram from their perch, and both plunged into the darkness of the sea.

Now blind, not knowing which way was up and to safety, Isbet thought that her life had ended.

Forgive me, Grandmother. I have failed you and I have failed my friends.

As her chest threatened to burst, the surrounding water swirled and boiled, the force of it propelling her body forward. She did not understand what was happening until she felt the familiar grip of the Vine. It dragged her along through the murk until her body encountered the rough surface of the cliff. Isbet felt around for any handhold, but her hand passed through a void. It was an opening in the rock. Isbet was faltering, her lungs burning. As she felt the darkness creeping around her vision, she also felt strong arms embracing her. Firm muscles worked and sliced through the water. As she saw the first hint of light, Isbet blacked out.

CHAPTER TWENTY-SIX

Isbet jerked awake in a painful spasm and her lungs expelled what remained of the water. She coughed until a hand was laid on her chest, which seemed to quiet her.

A young man looked down at her. Isbet had only seen a being such as him from afar. The selkie gazed at her with eyes round and black as precious opals but still, Isbet could see the question in them. He blinked and then turned and spat out a mouthful of water.

He nodded to Isbet's left. She saw a female holding her open mouth over Bram's. Her cheeks extended as water spilled from the corner of Bram's mouth and like the young man, she turned aside and spat water. Again, she covered Bram's mouth, her cheeks filling out. She spat a second time. Then Bram was awake, caught in a fit of coughing. She laid a small hand on his chest, stopping him.

"Who—?" Bram began.

"Thank you," Isbet said to the young man. "We owe you a life debt."

"Isbet, what – who are they?" Bram said, his voice hoarse.

"Selkies," Isbet said. "They saved us, perhaps in gratitude for destroying the rotted Vine." Whatever their reasoning was, Isbet was ridiculously glad to be alive. It appeared it hadn't been her time after all, or Bram's.

The male selkie bowed low at the waist then held out his hand to the woman, whom Isbet assumed was his mate. They took their seal forms and slipped without a sound back into the water.

Bram moved up beside her. "I've never seen a real selkie before."

"I have, but it's not a particularly good idea to go near them," Isbet said. "They lost many of their people to greed or men wishing for a compliant mate. The males lure daughters away and when they tire of them, deposit them back on land to a family who think them tainted and unmarriageable." Isbet took in their surroundings. "At least we are in a much more pleasant place."

They were in another cavern, this one lit by the same phosphorescent plants they had seen in Underneath. Isbet recalled many of them and realized a few of them were edible. As if on cue, Isbet's stomach growled. Bram chuckled and then his stomach followed suit.

"Perhaps we should find some food."

"That will not be an issue." The main Vine had several offshoots rising and falling, creating small overhangs that hid depressions in the rock. Isbet figured one of these would be a good place to rest. That gave her an idea. "We must not forget our task."

"Of course," Bram said. "But what can we do at this point?"

"The princess became ill after being affected by the Rot. Perhaps if she consumes some unaffected flora—"

"Ah, I see." Bram frowned. "Do you believe we're still in Morwynne?" He flushed. "My apologies, I don't mean to continue to ask questions, it's just, you seem so much worldlier than I am." He grinned. "You've even seen selkies before."

"They are common among the shorelines," Isbet said. "And Bram, do not cease to ask questions. I am glad you trust me enough to seek knowledge from me."

He seemed relieved. Isbet hid an amused grin.

They found themselves in another cavern much different from the last. Here the Rot didn't seem to exist. The flora was lush. The cavern floor was carpeted with tiny green flowers. Their star-shaped petals glowed and filled the cavern with a cool light.

There was also a line of caves on the far wall in front of them, with cobblestoned paths leading to their entrances. On each side were towering plants as tall as trees. They somewhat resembled the palms that Isbet had seen swaying in the wind off the shores of Giant's Spine. The bristly crowns on their heads gave off a ruddy light.

There were four moss-covered arched branches, draped with long trails of ivy, creating makeshift alcoves underneath. These branches had also pierced the far wall above the tunnel entrances, like sentinels guarding doorways to the unknown.

"This can't be natural," Bram said. "It seems man-made."

"I believe it is." Isbet's attention returned to the pool as the water began to churn. Bram moved to stand in front of her, but it was only the male selkie. He grinned and drew Gaemyr from the water. Isbet walked forward. "Thank you again," she said as she grasped her staff.

"Of all the blasted—" Gaemyr went into a tirade of rather unpleasant yet colorful profanities that would have had any other maiden swooning. Isbet had heard it all before. Ignoring him, she bowed to the selkie. "Sir, my apologies, but I need to ask another favor. I am aware you did not have to assist us—"

The selkie shook his head and placed a finger against Isbet's lips. Then he stepped back and nodded.

"Know you the House Royal of Morwynne?" Isbet asked.

He nodded.

"I need for you to take something to some fishermen on the beach. It is to cure a young girl who is ill. I will be in your debt."

A second determined nod.

"Bram, please follow me." Isbet drew off her sodden backpack and set it down just as Gaemyr ceased his tirade.

"Are you through?" Isbet asked.

"No to the hells, I am not through!"

"I take it he's upset?" Bram grinned.

"A bit." Isbet looked up. "Some of these mushrooms made into soup may help and perhaps tea steeped from the leaves of these trees. The water shouldn't damage them overmuch now that the rotted branch is severed."

They went about gathering what they needed. Isbet pulled out some twine from her pack and wrapped what they'd gathered. Then she gave it to the selkie. "Tell the fishermen to take these to Marjani. She needs to make soup or tea, understand?"

He nodded, smiled and then the selkie disappeared below the surface again.

"Could he not speak?" Bram asked.

"I only know what I've been told," Isbet said. "They communicate somewhat the same way whales do. I'm assuming he is one of those, but it appears they still understand the common-speak of the country where they dwell."

"Amazing," Bram said.

"I suppose we'd better choose a way out."

They followed the nearest path until they came to the cave mouth. "Look at this." Isbet stepped inside the cave. Some talented hand had worked the walls smooth.

"Dwarves?" Bram inquired.

"Without a doubt," Isbet said. "If we are fortunate, there are commons nearby. In the meantime...."

They gathered more of the mushrooms and found a small trickle of fresh water coming from a crack in the walls, likely to become a waterfall in the decades to come. It wasn't much, but it was enough to quench their thirst.

Gaemyr had gone quiet when Isbet explored one alcove. Several wil-o-wisp floated and moved around, unconcerned with their presence.

"We should rest a bit," Isbet said. "Then we shall see if we can locate the dwarves."

Bram didn't argue but sat, stretching his long legs out before him and leaning back on his palms. "I find all of this so hard to believe."

"Never thought you would be in this position, did you?" Isbet smiled.

Bram chuckled. "Not in my entire lifetime."

"Let me feed, gods be damned," Gaemyr said.

"Oh, all right. Gaemyr, you're like a fussy old crone."

Gaemyr snorted as Isbet raised him above her head. He joined with the branch, dissolving into its flesh. Isbet sat cross-legged.

Bram asked what had been on both their minds. "What will we do? What *can* we do?"

For once, Isbet didn't have a ready answer. The thought disturbed her. "I am uncertain."

Bram didn't press her and for that, Isbet was glad. She sat pondering the situation. Her original plan – to avenge her grandmother's murder – seemed so far away now. She disliked how that thought made her feel.

Isbet didn't realize she'd been nodding off until the soft rustle of Bram's approach alerted her. She tensed as he reached for her. Her first thought was to go on the offensive. What was he trying to do?

"You're exhausted. Come here."

She realized she was and yawned. He indicated she should lie down on the carpet of moss. It was soft and had a faint scent of ripe apples.

"I'll keep watch," Bram said.

"No need." Isbet was half-asleep as she cast a warding, but she could see it taking hold as she dropped off.

★　★　★

Isbet woke to a slow and steady breath against the back of her neck. One muscular arm was draped around her shoulders. How much time had passed? Bram was snoring, which told Isbet that he felt comfortable enough to know that he could sleep.

As to the position they were in....

Isbet smiled. "Bram?"

He muttered, tightened his hold on her, and continued snoring. Isbet dislodged his hand. Bram rolled over, his face peaceful, his expression softened in sleep. He was a handsome man. Isbet straightened her body over his, leaned over and kissed him on the lips.

Isbet wasn't expecting him to wake up so abruptly, although his eyes were still unfocused with sleep. She kissed him again.

"Isbet," he murmured.

She didn't know what or why she was doing this, only that she wanted him as she had when he'd first said he wanted her. This time when she kissed him, he opened his mouth, accepting her tongue inside. His arms encircled her shoulders. Isbet savored the taste of him. It was like the finest wine.

"Isbet—" Bram whispered into her mouth. "I won't be able – I can't—"

Isbet reached across for her pack. She felt around inside it and drew out dried brown stalks. She offered one to Bram. "Eat."

He accepted her offer. Isbet ate the second stalk. She then uttered a brief invocation. "Now I may have you as I please, Bram Greyward."

Bram didn't argue. He was intelligent enough to figure that, first, Isbet wouldn't harm him and second, she was taking precautions. They kissed again, Bram trying to take the lead, but Isbet wasn't having it. She straddled him and undid the ties on Bram's shirt. Understanding she was in command, he raised his arms as she removed it.

His chest was smooth. Isbet traced the planes and lines with her tongue. Bram drew in a sharp breath. "Triune."

Isbet smiled with confidence, familiar with bringing a man pleasure. Bram's expression and body language were quite pleasing.

She ran her tongue around his dark brown nipples. He reacted with a grunt. Isbet continued to work her way down his torso, kissing and nipping with her teeth. He was hard in his trousers. Isbet undid the ties, freeing his erection. An eyebrow raised. "You are well endowed, aren't you, Highness?"

Bram responded with a short breathless laugh that ended on a gasp as Isbet took him in hand. She took her time, stroking his length. It was hot and smooth in her grasp.

Bram lifted his hips as Isbet pulled down his trousers and removed his boots, laying them both aside. She stretched again as Bram watched transfixed. She drew her blouse over her shoulders. Bram's jaw dropped. Almost mesmerized, the prince reached for her, palming her breasts. Most men had little knowledge of how to touch a woman; Bram seemed skilled in that area as he rolled her dark nipples with his fingers. Now Isbet moaned.

Bram sat up, placing an arm around her waist. He pulled her to him, closing his mouth around one dark bud. Fire shot down from his touch to her sex, setting it alive. Bram did marvelous things with his tongue.

"Triune, you taste as sweet as I imagined."

She laughed, cupped his chin, and lifted his face. They kissed again, their tongues warring. Isbet pulled away. She stood, baring herself to him. Bram didn't hesitate. He was on his knees, both hands grasping her buttocks. He brought her forward.

Isbet's back arched and she plunged her hands into Bram's hair. She couldn't stop the low moan coming from her throat, couldn't stop her hips from circling. Isbet seldom called on gods, but this time she did. This man was talented.

Bram knew where and how to touch her. After a few moments, a single finger went into her warmth and a cry burst from her lips. "Gods be damned, Bram."

He laughed. It was a sound of pure male satisfaction. He continued torturing her with his fingers and tongue until the heat culminated in one great spasm of pleasure that tore through her, causing her cry to fill the cavern.

Her legs no longer supporting her, she fell against Bram and he guided her to lie down again. She looked up at him. His eyes were wild, feral, and they sent a shiver of anticipation through her.

"I'm not through with you yet, my Lady Witch," Bram said. "My sweet Bet."

She reached out her arms and he came to her. His arm went underneath her right thigh, pulling it forward.

"Do not wait. Take me," Isbet demanded of him.

He did, thrusting himself deep within her. He growled between his teeth, holding himself there for a moment before pulling out. Isbet had forgotten how long it had been. How good it felt to have the hot length of a man inside of her. A man she cared for. "Bram." Her arms went around him, pulling him close, clutching at him as though she might lose him.

However, Bram was there, his muscular body pressed against hers in an intimate dance, his hips moving against hers. He took her with his sex and with his fierce kisses and the heat built again.

When he reached completion, Bram thrust into her as his seed filled her. He growled like some caged beast. Isbet followed him; they cried out together.

They lay, arms and legs entwined, their breathing labored. Isbet enjoyed the pleasant sense of the pulse at her sex. It was a while before her heart quietened.

"Isbet," Bram said. "Stay with me, please."

Isbet was not one to assume things. "In what way, Bram?"

"I…" Bram said. "I don't know. I just want you to make my home yours. You promised to stay and teach Seth but—"

"So, I am to be Seth's teacher and your lover?"

He sighed. "Whatever you desire I will give it to you. I will marry you and make you my princess. I just want you to stay with me."

When she didn't answer, Bram said, "You don't have to decide now. Let's lie here together for a bit. You feel so good."

"As do you."

They lay there, drifting in and out of sleep. At one point, they made love again, this time slow and languid, taking their time with each other. They slept again, waking later to eat some mushrooms. As they sat there sharing their dinner, Isbet decided.

"Bram," Isbet said without preamble, "if I am to stay with you, then I must be honest with you about everything."

"Isbet, I'm not concerned—"

"No." Isbet held up her hand. "There are things I need to tell you."

He leaned back, resting his elbow on his knee. "All right."

Isbet told him everything. About finding her grandmother dead and discovering Wilhelm's hand in it and her plans to make the man suffer. How she planned to take back what was hers – the Tinderbox. She even confessed to Ancer Fallor's murder.

"And I must warn you," Isbet said, "the meddling Wilhelm has done into the arcane has damaged the veils that protect our world."

"Veils?"

She forgot how little he had learned of magic. "I will try my best to explain this but I'm uncertain I won't simply confuse you further."

"It's all right, Isbet. I'll try to understand."

She smiled. "There are…safeguards that separate the ethereal from the mortal realm."

He nodded.

"To a Gifted who can see them, they look like veils – curtains that one can draw aside to see into the ethereal realms. But these veils are strong enough to keep the denizens of other realms out of ours."

"Until some careless mortal does something that damages them," Bram said.

"It's not just mortals," Isbet said. "Also fey, who choose the path of darkness. Some still have a mind to repair them, while others leave them as they are."

Isbet adjusted her position and spread out her legs, leaning back on her palms. "When these veils are damaged, the beings will walk among the…corridors…the places in between the veils. A Gifted can see them as corporeal images but mortals may feel a shiver or a sense of foreboding."

"I have within the estate," Bram commented.

"You are fortunate none have been able to breach the veil into our world."

His brow creased in confusion. "Something I don't understand… if you can see them, doesn't that mean they've already entered our world?"

Again, Isbet chose her words carefully. "No. Imagine a large house with many doors. You are outside the house, but you can see everything through a window. Now beside you is the main entrance, bolted. As long as what's inside the house doesn't open that door, you are safe."

He frowned. "But they can see out the window. Were you in danger?"

"Not from those beings. They weren't strong enough to do me any injury."

"Not then," Bram said. "Promise me, you'll be careful."

"Don't worry, I will," Isbet said. "Did I explain it well enough?"

"Yes, I believe so."

"If we return you to Rhyvirand, you must hire a necromancer to effect repairs."

"I will."

"If Wilhelm is still in power, he may try to prevent you from doing so."

Bram looked away. "I will figure something out."

Isbet decided not to pursue the subject further. "Shall we continue then? What other questions do you have?"

He asked if agreeing to train Seth was part of the plan. "No, Seth needs training, or his powers might run amok." What of her feelings for him? "I care for you, Bram. You are not like other men I have come across in my travels. You are unique."

"I care for you, but you figured such," Bram whispered. "But one thing troubles me, Isbet. Why didn't you just tell me? You realize I have no love for Wilhelm."

"Not at first," Isbet said. "I have been away for a long time, Bram, and am only now learning of the situation."

"You were in Jack-In-Irons?"

Isbet lifted an eyebrow. "What makes you say that?"

"During the battle, you used a fighting style that comes from Jack-In-Irons. We had some delegates visiting and I spent some time with the princes. They tried to teach me, but it just didn't take, I'm afraid."

"That occurs from time to time," Isbet said. "It's no reflection on you. So, what are you thinking, Bram?"

"That I wished you had trusted me from the beginning, but you were right." Bram pinched the bridge of his nose. "But how could you, with so little information about me?"

Isbet smiled at him. With each passing moment, her admiration increased.

"As for Ancer Fallor?" Bram's lips pressed into a thin line. "It may be cruel of me to say, but he deserved his punishment. I was not fond of the man and you being a guest of the royal family, he would face execution for attacking you anyway."

He straightened and looked at her. "As a prince of the realm, I pardon your crime. As the Arch-bishop, I absolve you of your sins." He made the sign in the air.

Isbet bowed her head. "Thank you." She knew how important his rank and status were to him.

"Now come here, woman," Bram said, "and have your penance."

Isbet grinned and obeyed.

CHAPTER TWENTY-SEVEN

Bram watched as Isbet checked everything in her backpack. The herbs she kept well sealed, so only a few of them suffered water damage. She also removed several articles, talismans, that Bram guessed were used in her work.

Bram continued, as he had for the past hour, entertaining thoughts of their lovemaking. It had been as incredible as he had expected. Isbet had not been demure and shy like what he'd encountered with other women. There had been something wild, feral about her. It had driven Bram to near insanity. She was as sweet as he'd imagined, better than new wine. He was developing an affinity for dark-skinned women.

Bram supposed the fact that she didn't tell him of her plans should upset him but then again, she had been right. Until they had spent this time together, she couldn't risk trusting him. But she trusted him now, of that he was certain.

There had also been no declarations of love from her, or him. He cared for her, but love? Perhaps in time he could win her heart. For now, he was glad she had come into his life. That thought came with a sudden epiphany. *All this time*, Bram realized, *I thought the Triune had forsaken me, leaving me to be a captive, but perhaps she is the answer to my prayers. Perhaps They sent her to me.* Bram was so certain of this, he felt hope for the first time in years.

He was so busy staring at her, he was a little surprised to find she had finished and now sat cross-legged in front of him. "So now, Bram, shall we discuss business?"

"First," Bram said, "I wanted to say I am sorry for your loss."

Her expression softened. "Thank you." Then her look became intense. "Now we must figure a way to take the Box from Wilhelm."

"You said earlier that it was in the vault guarded by a — what did you call it?"

"A seven-tiered lock," Isbet said. "Seven is a powerful number when you're dealing with magic. Tell me, do you recall a parade of necromancers, sorcerers, and witches at one point?"

"Yes," Bram said. "I didn't think much of it at first, because I was more involved in escaping, but I recall such a group meeting with Wilhelm behind closed doors. This was before some servants and officials began to trust me, so I never could find out what was going on."

"I had just started work at the locks when Fallor discovered me," Isbet said. "But it may not have mattered. The locks become stronger."

"You don't believe you can break them all?"

"Not without help." Isbet drew in her lower lip. "Gaemyr can help me through the first few but after that...."

"What else would you need?"

She smiled as she leaned back on her arms, planting her palms flat. "The Woodsman's Ax or the Steel-driver's Hammer would suffice."

Bram shook his head, managing a wry grin of his own. "You wouldn't know where either of those items are?"

"Only through rumor and speculation," Isbet said. "The Ax is still in the hands of the Giant-killer's family and the people of Jack-In-Irons won't even discuss the matter. As for the Hammer, I was once told it rests with the Steel-driver, but no one knows where his grave is, and even if I were so inclined to desecrate a grave, which I am not, the tales say, although dead, the Steel-driver's corpse will awaken and protect his resting place."

"I could ask Wilhelm to show me the Box," Bram said. "I'm certain I could wrest it away from him."

"Are you certain he will consent to that? That he won't have guards around?"

"He says he trusts me." Bram averted his gaze, embarrassed.

"And despite everything," Isbet said, "you are not comfortable betraying that trust."

"Am I insane or just a complete dullard?"

"Neither." Isbet stood. "Let's focus on what we may do now. Escaping this cavern and finding out where we are."

She stretched and Bram followed suit, getting the kinks out of his stiff muscles. He nodded towards the line of caves. "Any idea which one?"

"The center, I suppose." It seemed as good a choice as any other.

Although the wil-o-wisp followed them inside, Bram found that the walls of the tunnel itself glowed a soft silver.

"Dwarf magic," Isbet said. "It's like witchcraft, but they have control over stone and metal, although no one outside of their own people can explain why."

"And it's safe to assume they don't tell?"

"Such a revelation would have the person torn from their commons and exiled to the surface."

"Drastic, isn't it?"

"Perhaps, but there are obvious reasons for it," Isbet said. "It's possible that someone revealed their secrets and it caused trouble or suffering among the dwarves."

"Likely," Bram said. "Then again, think of what an enemy could do with such knowledge. They say dwarves know how to make the earth tremble and level cities."

"Hmm." Isbet nodded. "Wait."

They hadn't gotten far, at least Bram didn't think so. Now what trouble awaited them?

Isbet pressed her ear against the wall and leaned in close. Bram didn't make a sound.

"Come here, listen."

Bram also leaned in to listen. At first, he heard nothing but then.... "It sounds like someone is knocking!"

"Let's go further. If it's what I think it is, there are dwarves nearby."

They continued for a few hundred yards until Isbet stopped and they listened again. This time there was a more pronounced knocking with a rhythm to it. Isbet stepped back from the wall. "Knockers."

Bram had heard tell of them. "Aren't they responsible for causing mines to cave in?"

Isbet shook her head. "Only the malevolent ones. Knockers lead miners to the richest deposits, and they are helpful companions to the dwarves."

As they moved forward, the sounds grew louder and then came the hammers, the pickaxes, and the sounds of crumbling stone. Light – greater light – filled the entryway and the tunnel opened to a smaller cavern, only large enough for about ten men to fill it, or in this case fifteen dwarves. They worked at the walls, chipping away, their work lit by several lanterns. Bram also saw two thin, stunted beings, their skin pale gray and their faces rather craggy. What Bram noticed was their hands were at least twice as large as his were. Knockers.

"Hail, Children of the Vine!" Isbet called out.

Several turned to look at them for a moment and went back to their work, save one – a stout female with flaming red hair and a face full of freckles. She carried a pickax that she rested on her shoulder as she approached them. "Well, what do we have here, two humans?" She squinted. "A human and a witch. What brings you to these parts and how?"

Bram stepped forward and bowed. "I am Prince Bram Greyward of Rhyvirand, and this is the Lady Isbet."

"Well, I'll be bashed and tattered," the woman said. "Know you Queen Lienna?"

"Yes, she is a good friend."

"Well, she sent word of that battle in Queen Calla's realm and said that a Prince Bram and a witch named Isbet helped her," the she-dwarf said. "She was mighty impressed. I'm Luana Kgar, Master Miner of Sickle Path Commons. Now, you have a story to tell. Are you hungry?" Luana turned and started walking. "Our commons aren't far from here and we have some good food always brewing." Luana pointed to a nearby she-dwarf. "You there! Take over while I see to our guests."

Bram and Isbet had to run to catch up, for, despite their solid stature, dwarves were nimble, especially the females. Luana led them through a network of tunnels until they came to an immense open cavern that held her commons. Like the Dokkalfar, they used what the earth and the Vine had blessed them with to make their homes and businesses, although the dwarves were more likely to use stones than branches. In the center of the cavern was a circular pool, which Bram realized as they approached wasn't a pool at all but a well, the water in it coaxed from deep within the earth. Women and children came to fill buckets and thirsty citizens dipped cups in the dark blue and drank with much pleasure.

"Have a seat right here," Luana said. "I'll have something brought back."

They weren't the center of attention, or so they thought, but they got a few curious glances. Dwarves were often too busy to ponder much on new arrivals unless they were there to cause some mischief, at which point the perpetrator may find themselves on the business end of an ax or hammer.

After a little while, Luana returned, followed by three other dwarves with trays filled with various fruits and vegetables and a big hunk of some unidentifiable meat. Bram decided it was best not to question what it was. Their hosts invited them to eat first and off the same plates. Every so often, some dwarves would approach and take a share of the food.

Luana sat and a mug of dark ale appeared in her hand. "So now, let's hear the story, eh?"

Bram was too busy enjoying the fare, so Isbet began the story. Someone brought them mugs of ale and while Isbet drank, Bram finished the tale.

"I'll be bashed," Luana said again. "Someone was lookin' out for ya, that's for sure." She took a long drink, burped and someone appeared with a tankard and gave her a refill.

"Where are we, Lady Luana?" Bram asked.

Luana snorted. "What's with this Lady Luana? I ain't no royal. Call me Master Luana if you like, plain Luana if you don't." Before Bram could respond, she went on, her expression sobering, "Yer underneath Tamrath."

Bram's drink caught in his throat, and he broke into a fit of coughing. "Tamrath? Oh dear, Triune." His appetite fled. Bram set the drink aside and stood.

"We need ta get ya topside," Luana said.

"We – I can't." Bram looked around, but he wasn't certain why.

"Bram," Isbet said, "we have to. There's no other way. It's unlikely we'll be able to get back to Morwynne soon."

"But if Wilhelm discovers I'm there—"

"I'm seein' ya have little choice," Luana said. "Why don't I send a message topside? I have some friends up there, so we can make sure the Patriarch is expecting you."

"Luana is correct." Isbet stood, moved next to Bram, and laid her hand on his arm. "We have no choice."

"Very well, but I'll send a message to Wilhelm as soon as possible."

"Then let's git ta work." Luana raised her mug in a toast. "And then we'll git ya into the sun again."

★   ★   ★

The response came after dark, which was what Bram expected. Jaryl didn't come, as Bram also expected, as it would be too difficult to explain his sudden need to leave the manor. However, they sent Captain Tamair with a trusted guard and a single mount for them. They could explain one horse but not two? Isbet would ride with him. Bram greeted the captain and they embraced like brothers. Tamair said, with much conviction, "Welcome home, Arch-bishop."

A dry well was their egress back to Overworld. The dwarves had carved hand- and footholds; however, Tamair had brought a rope ladder. Before they made the climb, Bram went down on one knee before Luana. "You may not be royalty, but you are a true lady in my sights."

She flushed and her freckles stood out against the red. "You human males, only have one thing on your brains."

Bram grinned. He raised Luana's hand to his lips. "Thank you."

Isbet knelt and embraced the dwarf miner. Luana whispered something to her that Bram didn't quite hear, and when Isbet drew away she nodded and said, "Don't worry, I will."

Bram allowed Isbet to go first. Gaemyr was complaining about something and Isbet shushed him several times. Bram started the climb soon after. Tamrath. He was home. He only hoped his being there wouldn't bring trouble to his family and that Wilhelm would understand. He had said he trusted Bram. Now Bram would see.

CHAPTER TWENTY-EIGHT

Isbet learned that they were not traveling to the palatial estate, but in fact to a cathedral a few miles outside of Bishop's Lane named the Cathedral of the Three. Churches were not a place that Isbet liked to be.

"What will you do?" Gaemyr asked.

"I suppose I must find other accommodations." Isbet had dismounted and moved away from their tiny group. She grasped Gaemyr.

"Isbet, are you coming?" Bram called quietly to her.

"My apologies, Highness, but...."

A confused expression crossed his face, and then he said, "Oh, I see. Listen, it's all right. You are a friend of the church."

They entered through the church gardens to a postern gate. A robed monk was there to greet them. He clasped his hands and bowed low. "Your Most Revered Archbishop, we are pleased to have you here."

"Is my brother here?"

"Yes," the monk said.

Bram turned to Tamair, "Thank you, Captain, for everything."

"My pleasure, Highness." Tamair then turned to Isbet and held out his hand. Isbet laid hers in his and he kissed it. "And thank you, Lady Isbet, we are in your debt."

"You are no such thing, Captain. Your friendship is all that I require."

"Then you have it." Tamair turned and bowed to Bram once again.

"If you will follow me, Highness," the monk said.

Isbet hesitated as she gazed at the monk. To her surprise, he looked right at her. "You have done a great service to this church, and you are welcome here. No harm will befall you," he said.

"Recall I absolved you, Isbet." Bram reached out his hand. "Do you trust me?"

Isbet placed her hand in his. "Of course."

Perhaps because Bram was a man of the cloth and this was his church, Isbet felt a measure of trust with him and that she wouldn't come to harm. He was the first person to invoke such feelings in her.

The cathedral itself was immense, but they seemed consigned to the back hallways as they walked. Isbet didn't have any idea where they were going until the monk said, "We have prepared your living quarters, and there is food and a fresh change of clothes for you."

"Thank you, Father."

They passed a few servants in the hall who would bow or wish them good evening. Their eyes were full of secret merriment as though they were pleased to be in on some grand scheme.

They stopped at a cul-de-sac of doors, reminding Isbet of Wicayth. An indoor fountain stood in the center of the open circle. Isbet looked it over with mild interest. The sculpture was of the Triune. Father and Mother stood embracing the Child, who poured water from a decorative urn.

The monk paused before the center door. "I will inform the Patriarch of your arrival. He is in the chapel praying for your safe return. Archbishop, we are all happy to see you again."

"It's good to be home." Bram embraced the old man. "Thank you." He turned and grinned at Isbet. "I have guest quarters next to mine… if you like."

Isbet arched one brow. "What makes you believe I'd want that?"

Then came that familiar blush. Bram turned and opened the double doors. The furnishings were modest as Isbet expected for a man of the cloth. The room was to Bram's taste, not ostentatious.

An acolyte was in the sitting room, setting up trays of food. She straightened and bowed to the monk. "Your Most Revered. We have prepared the guest room for milady and baths for you both."

"My thanks."

"With your permission, milady, if you would please follow me." She bowed again and motioned with her hand towards a door to her left. Isbet walked behind her and waited until she opened the door. It led to another central area, where a food tray had been set up. When the acolyte escorted Isbet into the bedroom, a bath was also waiting.

An acolyte's robe lay on the bed. "I am sorry, milady, it is all we have here. I hope the size suits you?"

"It's fine," Isbet said.

"If there is anything else you need, please summon me by pulling the cord." She nodded to the cord attached to the ceiling by the bed.

"I will, thank you."

She bowed again and exited.

"I suppose this place will suffice," Gaemyr said. "And won't you look divine in that robe?"

"Oh, stuff it." Isbet tossed him on the bed.

"My, aren't we cranky?" Gaemyr was silent for a moment. "By the by, concerning Prince Greyward, you have my approval."

Isbet halted as she lifted the robe up. "And that means what?"

"You're very aware of what." Gaemyr gave an exasperated sigh. "You tell him I said to see that you're not injured."

He was silent after that. Isbet smiled and mimed a kiss to him. He responded with a less-than-true harrumph.

★   ★   ★

Bram grinned when Isbet entered the sitting room. For the first time, she felt her own cheeks go warm. "This was all they had on such short notice," she explained.

"I see." Bram raised his eyebrows.

Isbet harrumphed that time.

Moments later, there was a knock and one acolyte opened the door. A man dressed in the rich robes of his station stood there. Despite her having been in Tamrath before, Isbet had never seen the Patriarch face to face.

Bram was off the couch and went to embrace him. Seeing them, Isbet felt her throat tighten. It reminded her of her grandmother and the close relationship they had had. It was not one of true affection between relatives, but a mutual respect of teacher and student. But sometimes Isbet had gone to her because of some sadness or illness and her grandmother had been there to comfort her. So perhaps it *was* more.

"This seems so familiar." There was a sob in the Patriarch's voice.

Bram stepped back and smiled at him and at the tears running down his cheeks.

"Please tell me you're staying this time," the Patriarch said.

"Jaryl..." Bram embraced him again. "I'll try. I promise."

The Patriarch's gaze fell on Isbet with a mixture of curiosity and welcome.

Bram turned. "Patriarch Jaryl Greyward, may I introduce the Lady Isbet."

Patriarch Greyward moved across the room and went down on one knee before her. He took her hand and kissed it. "My Lady, I and Tamrath are in your debt."

Isbet shook her head. "You are not. You and your brother have given me your friendship and you have not judged me, which I appreciate."

Jaryl released her hand and stood. "We have a royal sorceress and diviner here. We do not shun people who have the Gift. Please don't let experiences color your perception of the holy orders."

"I will not," Isbet assured him. "You both have my utmost respect."

"I thank you." Patriarch Greyward turned back to Bram. "Let us sit and talk, dear brother. Aune will be here soon." Jaryl said to Isbet, "Aune is our cousin. She now holds the title of Mother Superior, but I'll wager you'll get along."

"Oh?" Isbet smiled. Her gaze darted to Bram and his blushing was her reward.

Bram and Jaryl began to talk, catching up on all that occurred since they had last seen each other. As the conversation continued, Isbet sat, speaking only when Bram asked questions of her. Isbet had thought several times of leaving them in private but neither had asked that of her. She realized she had made the right decision when the Patriarch said, "After they took you, I sent out more spies into Rhyvirand. They say Wilhelm is once again preparing his army to march."

"Morwynne." Bram rested his chin on his closed hand. "I gave the Dhar and Dharina my word that I wouldn't let any harm befall their kingdom. They gave me my freedom for it."

"From what you've told me," Jaryl said, "he is beyond reasoning with."

"What else may I do?" Bram said. "I want to at least try."

"What do you think, Lady Isbet?" Jaryl asked.

"That Wilhelm is beyond saving," Isbet said, "but if I know our Arch-bishop, he will try anyway."

"I must," Bram said. "If it is true, if he is beyond rational, then I will use whatever means in my power to return."

"You must take great care."

They looked towards the door when a knock sounded. Another acolyte opened it from the outside and a woman stepped in. She wore a nun's wimple with plain white blouse and leather trousers.

"Aune!" Bram ran into her embrace. He lifted her up, swung her around and kissed her on the cheek.

"Welcome home, Arch-bishop." Aune took his hand and led him back to his seat. Then she turned to Isbet. "And you must be Lady Isbet." Aune held out her hands as she walked towards Isbet. Isbet raised her hands in response and grasped Aune's. "Have these cousins of mine thanked you? I think we both know how forgetful men can be."

Isbet grinned at her. She liked her. "They have, Mother Superior."

Aune released her hands and placed a finger on Isbet's cheek. "Call me Aune. Now, don't I seem rather young to be a Mother Superior?" Before Isbet could reply, Aune said, "We must find something more appropriate than those awful acolyte robes. I have the perfect thing. Come to my quarters." She grasped Isbet by her hand and pulled her up. "What an interesting staff. Is it the sentient?"

Isbet looked back at Bram and the Patriarch.

"Don't worry, you know Aune will take care of you, Isbet," Bram said.

"That," Aune said, "and Coline wishes to meet her."

"Coline is here too? We'll need her to send a message to Morwynne," Bram said.

"You tell me, my dear cousin, and I'll relay it."

As Isbet followed, Aune talked about how glad she was Bram had returned and thanked Isbet for her part in it. "We hope you both can stay, but did Jaryl tell you of the rumor that Wilhelm is on the march?"

"Yes," Isbet said.

Isbet expected Aune's rooms to be sparsely furnished with little decoration, until she saw it for herself with its homey touches, warm colors, and shelves lined with books. Aune continued to converse with her, while rummaging through chests and closets, settling finally on an outfit like the one she had worn when first meeting Queen Aimeli, save it was in black with silver trim.

"This should do!" Aune pointed to another door to her left. "You may change in there."

The outfit was a bit tight on her, but it worked well enough. Isbet was in no hurry to meet with Coline, but she figured she should get it over with.

After leading her through several corridors and down a flight of stairs, Aune stopped at a single unadorned door and knocked. An acolyte opened the door a crack. Unlike the others Isbet had seen dressed in the royal colors, this young man was all in blue. "Greetings, Mother Superior. Mistress Coline is expecting you and the Lady Isbet."

Isbet realized this young man was more than an acolyte and in fact was Coline's apprentice, and a sorcerer. When Isbet stepped across the threshold, she drew in a deep breath. The room itself was bare except for two curtains on either side blocking off sections. In its center there was a Diviner's Globe. Isbet had never seen one used by sorcerers. She coveted one, but only a privileged few received a divination from them.

Like a normal globe it was set in a circular holder, allowing it to turn in any direction. At first glance, it was translucent marble. Floating in the center were blobs of metallic blue and gold, dancing and entwining. Runes carved in the polished gold of the holder seemed to flicker with their own light. The script wasn't one Isbet recognized, so she figured it was a language known only to the sorcerers. Each branch of the Gifted had their own secret dialect.

"Please wait here while I ask Mistress Coline to join you." The acolyte shuffled off and disappeared behind the curtain to the left.

"Amazing," Isbet said.

"I'm told it's called a Diviner's Globe," Aune said.

"That is correct," Isbet said. "It's a rare and powerful talisman of magic."

"So I gathered."

There was movement to their right as the acolyte appeared and drew the curtain aside. The woman who stepped between the silk folds took Isbet back to the guard that had greeted them on the shores of Morwynne. She was dark and muscular, her hair in myriad braids like Isbet's, except they swept the floor. The acolyte gathered them up and held them like a bride's train. Like her apprentice, the woman was all in blue – overcoat, shirt, and trousers, although her feet were bare.

She stood at least eight feet tall.

"Giantess." Isbet breathed the word.

"Well, I'll be damned," Gaemyr said.

The woman's dark gaze fell on Gaemyr. "And why would you say that?"

Isbet figured this was one of those cases where discretion was the better part of valor. She bowed, keeping her gaze lowered. "We have seen one of the giant's blood only from far across the land, mistress."

"We are rare," Coline said. "You are Lady Isbet?"

"I am at your service." Isbet could feel the woman's power, much greater than hers, charging the air.

"So," Coline said, "should I kill you now?"

"Coline!" Aune said.

Isbet kept her gaze down. "I could not stop you, mistress."

"Wait," Aune said. "What is this?"

"The witch knows what this is," Coline said. "Did you believe I was unaware of your presence?"

"I—" Isbet said. "I had hoped you would ignore me."

"Well, I did not," Coline said.

"Coline? Please tell me what the matter is," Aune said.

Coline's voice softened. "I am sorry, Aune. Would you trust me? This is something between the witch and me."

"She saved Bram's life," Aune said. "She brought him back to us."

"I know," Coline said. "I take that into consideration." Her attention came back to Isbet. "Does Bram know?"

"Yes," Isbet said.

"Then I suppose that is something," Coline said. "Do you recall our attempt to rescue Bram? This witch and her actions are why we failed. Although I don't know why she did such thing."

"That – that was you? You told Wilhelm's guards where Bram was?"

Isbet raised her head and met Aune's gaze. "Yes. I had my agenda, but now things are different."

"Different?" Aune's brow furrowed, then it seemed realization dawned, and her eyes sparkled with knowing. "Oh, I see." She grinned. "So, Coline, I believe we owe Isbet our forgiveness, do we not?"

"If that is your wish, Aune," Coline said. "Although I believe we should punish her."

"You'll do no such a thing!" Gaemyr challenged.

Now Coline's gaze fell on the staff. "And what do you propose to do?"

"Protect her," Gaemyr said. "I will keep her from harm, even if I have to give my soul to do so."

Coline's lip upturned. "And so you would."

"So, the staff is sentient," Aune said. "I thought as much. I can see the life within it."

"With all due respect, Mother Superior...." Isbet wanted Coline's attention away from Gaemyr. "The prince has absolved me."

"He has?" Aune said. "Then why are we still discussing the matter?"

If Isbet liked Aune before, this had her completely taken.

"Coline, Bram needs you to contact Morwynne."

"I have tried before and their diviner has turned aside my efforts," Coline said. "She and I are almost similar in skill."

"Her name is Marjani," Isbet said. "Tell her you speak for the prince and Isbet."

"You have befriended her?"

Isbet nodded. So did Coline. She sat before the globe and motioned for Isbet and Aune to join her. "You will come with me, Lady Isbet." Coline placed her hands on the globe. "Do as I do."

Isbet placed her hands, palms flat, on the globe as well. She hadn't expected it to be warm. Coline closed her eyes and began to whisper an incantation in what Isbet supposed was a language of the sorcerers. The colors moved faster, flickering like flames. They expanded to fill the whole of the globe, blurring, turning into smoke, swirling and bubbling for a few moments, then like the clouds after the storm, they cleared.

The image was that of the Riven Isles as the giants viewed it from Up Above. Coline moved the globe with a gentle motion of her fingertips and the land rushed by, past the provinces of Vine, Bale, Avynne, Rhyvirand, and Morwynne.

"Stay by me." Coline joined with Isbet's consciousness, as though taking her hand, as they approached Morwynne. "Lady Marjani."

Isbet had the sense of standing behind Coline and moved to stand next to her.

"Speak to her, Isbet."

"Lady Marjani," Isbet said. "It is Isbet."

There was a hesitation. "Isbet, prove to me that it is you."

"You know me," Isbet said. "You know Gaemyr." Isbet touched her staff to the globe surface.

"Ah, yes," Marjani said. "We worried until we received your message from the selkie—"

"The herbs, did they work?"

"Yes," Marjani said. "The princess is recovering. I am rather angry with myself for not thinking of it."

"Do not fret over it. I am happy to hear she will recover," Isbet said.

"And perhaps," Marjani continued, "there will be a betrothal."

"Excellent. I am glad they are getting on so well. Please tell Seth that the prince and I are thinking of him."

"I shall," Marjani said. "And with your permission, I shall begin his testing. He's just starting to assess his power and the sooner, the better."

"Agreed," Isbet said. "Now we must speak of business. Know you that Wilhelm is preparing to march?"

There was a pause. "Yes, we know."

Isbet thought they might. If Tamrath had spies in Rhyvirand, then it made sense Morwynne would. "The prince and I will try to stop him, but you must prepare for the possibility of war."

There was a sigh of resignation. "As we thought."

"The prince's entourage should still be on the mainland," Isbet continued. "Take them to the island and use them as leverage."

If the suggestion surprised Marjani, she didn't show it. "Very well."

Isbet saw the sweat gathering on Coline's temples and her fingers trembled. "I must go. If we can contact you after we finish this, we will. If not...assume we failed."

"Perhaps fate will be kind," Marjani said. "I wish you well. Be safe, the both of you."

"And to you and your house."

Coline broke the connection. Her apprentice brought her a drink and when she finished it, he helped her up. Coline turned to look at Isbet. Her face was pale, her expression tired. "There is a great evil following Wilhelm. You know this," Coline said. "You had best prepare yourselves."

Coline leaned on the acolyte as he helped her across the room and drew back the curtain. Coline moved behind it.

"She will need to rest." Isbet stood and stretched her legs. "Aune, I will need to ask a favor of you."

"Anything," Aune said.

"There are things that I will need." This would be a vastly different battle.

CHAPTER TWENTY-NINE

"Make haste with these messages," Bram told the guard. "Give them to Wilhelm only. Let no one else see them, understand?"

"Yes, Arch-bishop."

The three guards galloped away from the cathedral with their precious messages secreted away in their coats. They had received another intelligence report – that a man was accompanying Wilhelm in his personal entourage – a young Dokkalfar male.

"Serval." How he made his way back to Rhyvirand was unknown, but Bram wasn't so much concerned with that as he was with what Serval had told Wilhelm to cause him to break his supposed trust with Bram. And that wasn't the only thing that troubled him.

Three nights after they learned of Wilhelm's movements, Jaryl had called him to his office. He offered his brother a seat and poured them two glasses of a rice liqueur that had been a gift to him from the royal family of Jack-In-Irons. Then Jaryl joined him on the couch. "Bram, I have been in touch with Chira through Coline and advised them of our situation."

"You have?" Bram's brow creased in confusion. "Shouldn't you have told me?"

"Yes," Jaryl said. "I am sorry, but I knew it would upset you."

"Upset about what?"

"Captain Tamair will escort you out of the city," Jaryl said. "The queen and duchess have agreed to give you asylum."

"Jaryl, why are you doing this?"

"I don't want to lose you again."

For a moment, Bram lowered his gaze to his hands fisted on his thighs. "I'm not leaving."

"Bram, what if the same thing happens again? What if Wilhelm just takes you?"

"Do you think my running away will change things? Besides that, I will not hide like a coward while my loved ones fight."

"We can send Lady Isbet with you. At least with her, you'll be able to—"

"The answer is no," Bram said. "Jaryl, how could you do this?"

"You know why." Jaryl grasped him by the shoulders. "Please."

Bram held him by the back of the neck with one hand. He kissed Jaryl on the cheek. "No."

Then Bram walked away. He rubbed at his eyes, trying to stop the tears that threatened, not because he was angry with Jaryl, but because he feared that Jaryl was correct, that Wilhelm would just take him, and he'd never see his home and family again.

As Bram returned to his rooms, he saw Isbet walking down the corridor from the opposite direction. She caught his gaze and Bram could see by her expression that words were unnecessary. She knew it troubled him and perhaps somehow knew the reason. Isbet hastened her stride towards him, took his hand, led him into the sitting room, and guided him into a chair.

There she left him for a moment, although he couldn't guess what her intentions were. When she came back, she stood before him, undoing the buttons on her blouse.

"Isbet." They made love, he on his back and Isbet mounting him, and for a little while, Bram forgot everything.

★　　★　　★

A week passed after the messengers had left. Coline once again spoke to Marjani, who advised her that Bram's entourage were their special guests and meanwhile, Captain Maive and Rajan were on their way to Tamrath. That Rajan was coming there and not returning to Rhyvirand surprised Bram a bit, but it also relieved him that they had earned Rajan's trust. Besides, Marjani had advised them, Rajan had said that he found Serval distasteful.

Jaryl never mentioned his leaving again, although Bram knew his brother well enough to know he wanted Bram out of harm's way. To Bram, it mattered little. Two more days passed, which made everyone nervous, for Wilhelm should have arrived long before now, but then it depended on when he'd left Faircliff.

Then one messenger arrived at the cathedral steps. He was bloody and battered and his eyes were coal black – no white, no color – just a darkness that caused all those to see him shudder. The guards who found him sent for Bram and Jaryl, but Coline and Isbet were with them so they all went to assist.

When they tried to take him into the cathedral, he began to scream and flail, trying to free himself from the hands that held him. When he spat a yellowish bile, they removed him from the holy place and to the adjacent garden. He calmed somewhat but they could still see his distress.

Coline examined him. "He has the taint. He will die if we attempt to take him inside again."

Bram, Jaryl, and the guards laid him down on one of the stone benches. Isbet knelt beside him. "They poisoned him with the Rot."

"Is there anything either of you can do for him?" Bram asked.

"No." Isbet looked at Coline, who shook her head. "But I can ease the way home for him."

Jaryl knelt beside Isbet and leaned his ear in close to the man's mouth. "What is your name?"

The man said something that Bram didn't quite hear. It was only for Jaryl to know. They watched as the Patriarch continued to whisper to him. When the man replied, Jaryl would nod in response, and the whole time, Jaryl never let go of his hand.

"Please, have someone bring me what I need," Jaryl said to no one in particular, and Bram heard the movement beside him as one of the other guards walked away. Jaryl's attention was on his charge.

When the guard returned, he handed Jaryl a wrapped bundle without a word. Bram knew what it was – a bottle of blessed oil, a clean white handkerchief, and a smooth black stone. When Jaryl went to touch the blessed oil to the man's forehead, Isbet said, "Don't."

Jaryl looked at her, his expression calm. Bram knew he understood. "I have to."

It seemed the guard was too far gone. His only movement was the ragged rise and fall of his chest. Jaryl placed the items on the guard's body. The stone for the strength of the Father, over his heart, the oil for the Mother, and the purity of the handkerchief for the Child, which Jaryl draped over the guard's eyes. It signified how the Child sees everything with innocence. When it ended Jaryl stood, his face grim. "Lady Isbet, if you would."

Seldom without her pack, Isbet reached into it now and withdrew a cameo pin, but Bram saw the portrait itself was of an ugly old woman, her mouth open in a soundless scream. Isbet laid the cameo on the soldier's chest, then one hand over his eyes and bowed her head, her lips moving in what Bram suspected was an invocation. She then balled her fist and drew her hand up, almost as if she were pulling at something. And then something appeared. A black worm-like creature entwined itself around her fist.

Bram drew in a breath as he could see Isbet caught in a silent struggle. The worm twisted and writhed in her grasp, which Isbet tightened around its body, crushing the life from it. This seemed to go on for an endless time, but finally the worm ceased to move and a moment later, it became ash falling through Isbet's fingers. The guard took one last breath, then went still.

Jaryl stood there, his fists clenched. Aune approached him and touched his forearm. "I will see to his proper burial and ensure that his family is cared for."

"Thank you." Jaryl pointed to the remaining guards. "You there, assist the Mother Superior. See that he has a burial with honors."

"Yes, Patriarch!"

Bram had not seen that look on his brother's face for a long time. It was the same one of bitterness after their father died. "Jaryl?"

"Let's go inside." Jaryl began to walk, without seeing if they followed him.

Jaryl led them to his own quarters. Two acolytes were there but when they saw Jaryl, they scurried away like two frightened mice, and perhaps that was appropriate.

"Jaryl, what is it?" Bram said. His brother stood with his back to them. "What did the guard say?"

"He said that Wilhelm is coming. He...comes to claim you."

Bram thought he should feel something – fear, resignation – at that information, but he did not. He was just.... He supposed a strange serenity filled him. "I see."

"Bram—" Jaryl began.

"It's all right, Jaryl." Perhaps what he was feeling was not serenity; he was simply accepting it. "I will see what he wants."

"He wants you!"

"He didn't bring his army all this way for just me," Bram said. "Did he say something else?"

"Yes, something that made little sense."

"What was it?"

"He said something about a box. It was plain and didn't seem to have any value, but Wilhelm coveted it," Jaryl said. "He said the king and the Dokkalfar quarreled about it right in front of their men."

Bram inhaled. He turned to Isbet. "It has to be."

"Yes."

"Wait, does this mean something?" Jaryl asked.

"The Tinderbox," Isbet said. "Have you heard of it?"

Jaryl shook his head, but Coline said, "I have. There are many rumors surrounding the Box and its power. You know of its power?"

"Yes," Isbet said again. "It belonged to my grandmother. I am familiar with its use. It is what Wilhelm used to summon the dogs."

"Those hideous beasts that took Bram? Wilhelm means to use them again?" Jaryl strode to Bram. "Now you *have* to go. Please, Bram—"

Before Bram could voice his protest, Coline said, "Lady Isbet, how may we control them?"

"Only by possessing the Box." Isbet turned to him. "Bram, I will go with you when you go to meet Wilhelm."

"You will take it from him," Bram said matter-of-factly.

Bram noticed whenever she was afraid or uncertain, she clutched Gaemyr and held him close to her.

"I will try," she said.

"Isbet—"

"And what will we do if you fail?" Coline said.

"We'll fight," Jaryl said. "I will—"

"Don't." Bram approached Jaryl and rested his arm around his brother's shoulders. "Do not involve our land in another war. If we cannot wrest the Box from Wilhelm—"

"I will not give in," Jaryl said. "You know our people will fight."

"I will fight," Coline said. "Now that I know the source of Wilhelm's power, it may be possible to stop him. We do not want other lands to fall."

"Coline speaks the truth," Jaryl said. "If we don't stop Wilhelm here and now, thousands will be enslaved or die. I know you don't want that."

Bram blew out a long breath, lowered his gaze, and then nodded. "Contact Duchess Briwyn, tell her of our plight. Perhaps they may send help in time."

"Yes, Arch-bishop." Coline bowed.

"Bram," Isbet said, "give me a horse and I will ride out to the well. Perhaps I can ask for help from Luana."

"All right, but please take care."

"Of course." She laid a hand on his shoulder, pulled him forward and kissed him. "I will be back as soon as I can."

When he was alone with his brother, Jaryl said, "She will take care of you. I trust her, Bram."

"Thank you." Bram pressed his forehead against Jaryl's the same way he had done before. "As do I."

★   ★   ★

It was quiet around the cathedral, which suited Isbet fine.

"Doesn't appear to be anythin' goin' on." Luana licked her thumb and pressed it against her ax blade. "Looks like we got back in time."

"Thank you again, Luana."

"Now, didn't I tell ya, we're even? Ya got my queen's blessin', you got mine."

Isbet smiled at the she-dwarf. "Prince Greyward is waiting."

A stable hand took Isbet's horse. He looked uncomfortable with a few dozen armed dwarves surrounding her. Isbet supposed she couldn't blame him. It was doubtful he'd ever even seen a dwarf, much less one girded for battle.

After much back and forth, Luana and her people set up a makeshift camp in the church gardens, despite there being enough room for them in the cathedral. Luana had waved the offer away. "My people and me, we'll stay outside under the stars. Now, don't ya fret. Besides, we want to be at the ready."

Several acolytes served the dwarves and saw to their needs. Isbet didn't envy them their tasks for, despite their present situation, the dwarves were a rowdy bunch, drinking, singing, and dancing, and Isbet knew it would continue into the wee hours.

Once the dwarves settled, the Patriarch summoned Isbet to his living quarters once again. When the acolyte opened the door, Isbet walked in as Jaryl was saying, "We'll try to keep them away from the city."

Bram noticed her first. "Isbet!" He ran to her and she welcomed him into her arms.

"I'm so glad you're safe." Bram traced her lips with the pad of his thumb. "I—"

Isbet placed a finger against his lips. "Later, love." He released her.

"Lady Isbet, it is good to see you," Jaryl said. "The dwarves are here?"

"In the gardens."

Jaryl nodded. "Good. We were discussing how we might draw Wilhelm away from the city and here to the cathedral. I am loath to send more messengers—"

"We can use my suggestion now that Isbet is here."

"The reinforcements from Chira haven't arrived yet." Jaryl turned to Isbet. "Bram wishes to meet Wilhelm before he arrives at the city."

Isbet nibbled on her thumbnail for a moment. "It doesn't matter that the Chir army arrives in time. If we fail there will be little they can do, beside fighting alongside our remaining forces. However, an idea occurred as I was riding back. I think we should take Luana's troops with us."

"Isbet?" Bram asked.

"Recall their power over the earth." Isbet smiled to herself. "And as you know, I am not without power to command the earth. But the dogs are also creatures of earth magic.

"Your Eminence, Prince Bram and I need to prepare. There are things I will need if you would supply them?"

"Of course," the Patriarch said. "But what is this scheme?"

"What we decided," Isbet said. "I – we will approach Wilhelm under the pretense of negotiations and then, I will attempt to take the Box from him." There was more to it, but Isbet doubted anyone would approve.

★   ★   ★

Isbet watched as Bram shared a brief farewell with his family. She recalled last night, how she had lain in Bram's arms, enjoying his feel and scent. She never thought there would be someone like him in her life, someone who made her as content as he did. To Isbet that was more important than happiness.

Luana and her dwarf troops armed themselves and awaited the order to march. They were rowdy and eager as usual. Isbet had stolen away from the cathedral last night, loath to leave Bram's arms but needing to talk to the Master Miner.

When she had returned to Bram's bed, he was awake, as she knew he would be.

"Where did you go?"

"To speak with Luana. I know how I will attempt to wrest the Box from Wilhelm and I will need her help."

Bram had drawn her close. "Will you tell me?"

She did, and she could see he didn't like it, but he agreed to it. They were long past the point where he'd treat her like some simpering maiden, commanding her to stay behind.

"Well, this is all unexpected." Gaemyr broke into her thoughts.

"Agreed," Isbet said. "But I have no regrets."

"Why should you?" Gaemyr said. "You've kept your word. You will destroy Wilhelm. It may not be by the method you first devised, but you have acted true."

"Thank you, my friend," Isbet said. "Thank you for staying by my side."

Gaemyr snorted. "Is that not the task given to me?"

Isbet didn't reply, but allowed herself a secretive smile.

★　　★　　★

Bram moved his horse beside hers. "Let's be off."

Isbet nodded. "Are you up to this, Highness?"

"Yes," Bram said. "This has to end. I must face Wilhelm. I have been complacent too long."

The last scouts who had returned to the cathedral reported that Wilhelm and his troops had camped a few miles away, between the borders of Rhyvirand and Tamrath. As far as they could tell, it was not the first time the army had stopped, which was why it had taken so long. They had also reported that there weren't as many troops as expected, a mere quarter of what Wilhelm had during the last battle.

They brought what could be some more good news. There was some dissension among the leadership. They verified that Serval was there and the arguments between him and Wilhelm were often and loud. One thing was clear, Wilhelm didn't want a battle.

They rode on, and as they came closer Isbet felt a chill begin at the base of her spine.

"What is it?" Bram said.

"There is great evil here." Isbet swallowed, her throat dry. "The Rot permeates this place – it infects everything."

"Yes," Bram said.

Luana, who walked beside them, spat off to the side and said, "Ack! What stinks around here?"

There was Wilhelm's encampment, spread across a large clearing in the trees. As far as Isbet could tell, there were no guards posted and most of the men and women were milling around or sitting before their tents, minding cook fires. A few of them were even off near the edge of the woods imbibing, though it was only past noon.

"What a disgusting mess of a camp this is." Luana shook her head. "We could slaughter 'em easy and not break a sweat."

"I don't understand," Bram said. "Does Wilhelm think this group could even take the cathedral?"

"No," Isbet said. "I sense that neither Wilhelm nor Serval is in control here."

"The Rot?"

"If I were to venture a guess. Wilhelm may be still fighting it, which would explain why he hesitates to act. Serval wants to fight. The Rot has filled him with its hunger."

Bram didn't comment. For a moment, he seemed far away. "Lady Isbet, stay here with Master Luana's troops."

Isbet turned towards him, keeping her expression impassive. She thought, *He isn't going to—?*

"There's no need for us both to go and if I am taken captive then you have the dwarves with you to carry out your plan," Bram said. "Attack at the first sign of trouble. I'll take care of myself."

"You had better!" Gaemyr said. "The last thing I want is to deal with a crying woman!"

To her complete astonishment, Bram nodded to Gaemyr and said, "I will, sir."

He left Isbet gaping.

Gaemyr chuckled. "Well, I'll be damned."

★ ★ ★

Bram dismounted and led his horse through the center of the camp, heading straight for the big tent. Some of the soldiers looked at him with mild interest. They seemed normal enough, but there were others.... Bram saw the taint of poison in their eyes like in those of the poor messenger who had risked all to tell them of Wilhelm. Their black gazes followed Bram as he walked, and seemed to pierce his very soul. He shuddered, trying in vain not to let it affect him. Only when he whispered a prayer of strength did the soothing influence of the Mother, who watched over all her children, calm him.

"Bram?"

Bram spun at the sound of a familiar voice. His stomach heaved painfully as the man approached. His eyes were all black, like those others with the taint, but he seemed not bothered by it.

"Bram Greyward!" Serval opened his arms wide. "It's so good to see you again!"

Bram clutched the reins with one hand, his fingertips digging into his palms. His breath caught in his throat, his chest squeezed tight.

"It's all right." Serval took his free hand. "We've been waiting for you. That is, Wilhelm and me."

Bram looked down at his hand as though it were an alien thing, grasped by Serval's. "Come with me."

Bram dropped the reins as something, more than just Serval, took hold of him, moving his legs like a puppet master. Bram knew what it was, and he struggled against it as if he were in a nightmare and trying to wake up. Serval drew the tent flap aside. "Your Majesty, your son has arrived."

Serval released him and moved away. It took Bram's eyes a few moments to adjust to the dimness of the tent. There, sitting at the long table, was Wilhelm and before him, on its rough-hewn surface, sat the Box. His fingers curled around it protectively. Bram didn't know what he expected the box to look like. Certainly, larger than it was. He'd imagined something more ornate, made of gold and encrusted with jewels. But no, it was a plain metal box, dull gray, with no markings to make it look different from any other. Bram held the sharp breath that he'd almost released. No, he couldn't let Wilhelm know his attention was on the Box. Then again, it was not only Wilhelm. The thing that had taken hold of him sniffed at the back of his mind like a starving mongrel after food. He fought to keep it at bay, to distract it somehow.

Bram took a cautious step forward. "Wilhelm?"

Wilhelm lifted his head and Bram met his gaze. Wilhelm's eyes were normal and yet his expression said he was, much like Bram, engaged in his own private battle. "Bram."

Upon hearing his name, Bram took another hesitant step. "Sir, are you all right? Do you know what's happening?"

Wilhelm nodded. "I'm sorry. This is not—" he grunted in pain, his eyes squeezed shut, "—what I wanted—"

"What do you mean?" Bram went to his side, touched him on the shoulder.

Wilhelm started at the action. "Don't touch me!" He shoved back from the table, tipping the chair over. "No, no – you shouldn't be here."

The Box was within his grasp. The mongrel was getting closer, intent on its hunger. All he needed to do was reach out....

"You're in pain. I can see. Please tell me what I can do to help." Bram knew Wilhelm didn't deserve his help but there was something in the way Wilhelm looked, like a lost soul hoping to fill a void. Perhaps Wilhelm suffered that true pain, looking for something to make his life meaningful by surrounding himself with a false sense of family. Now perhaps he realized it was all a lie.

"Nothing," Serval said. Bram had almost forgotten he was there. "All he has to do is give himself over."

Wilhelm was fighting the Rot, but to what end? "Wilhelm, you must continue to fight. I don't want more innocents hurt. I give you my word, I'll help you."

Wilhelm didn't look at him. "I want you back home."

Home was not Rhyvirand. This was Bram's home, and he would do anything to protect it. "And I'll go if you swear not to attack Bishop's Lane."

Wilhelm released the Box for the first time. He planted his hands on either side of his head and shook it, as though attempting to rid himself of something in his skull. "I – not Bishop's Lane or the cathedral. I knew where you were."

Bram realized they must have gotten information from the messenger.

"This isn't so bad," Serval said. "I fought too at first. I felt so alone and betrayed. All that sorrow coming from Wilhelm and others in the Riven Isles. I didn't want to give in to that." Serval moved carefully around the table, letting his fingertips slide across the surface. "Then I realized how good it could feel, allowing that power to flow over me. It was so very intimate. The being behind it told me of its wants and needs. It doesn't want to destroy, Bram. It wants what we all do, life, nourishment, and freedom. Doesn't a being such as this deserve the same?"

He stood before Bram and he could see the darkness moving about in Serval's eyes, like worms crawling within the blank sockets.

"I know I behaved badly." Serval slid his arms around Bram's waist and a shudder of revulsion raced over Bram's skin. "And for that I'm sorry." Serval drew him close. "But if you give yourself to me now...." Bram drew in a breath and Serval's mouth brushed his ear. His gorge rose, searing his throat. "I promise you it will be the sweetest agony imaginable."

Bram choked and bile filled his mouth, forcing him to swallow. He had to awaken from this nightmare. Everything around him was going dim. "Mother, give me your protection."

Fire engulfed him. It blazed around him, lighting up the tent, and Bram forced it into his hands. He placed them on Serval's chest and shoved. "Get away from me!"

Serval fell and laughed as he did. He didn't seem concerned that Bram had rejected him once again. "Bram, you need to trust me."

A hand closed around Bram's wrist. Wilhelm struggled to rise from the chair, his eyes blacker than a well. "Go—"

Bram didn't hesitate. He ran, ripping the tent flap aside. The bright light of day caused him to shield his eyes. It had been much darker in that tent than he imagined. The soldiers approached, but there was no anger or malice in their expressions, just that eerie smile of welcome, and they stared at him with their awful eyes.

"Do you see now, Bram, the service we have done?" Serval's voice was behind him. "Pain, loneliness, sorrow, all it wants is to feel.... To be in the light. To give others pleasure and fulfill their wants. Wilhelm and I, we are its greatest triumphs."

Bram drew his sword. "By the Triune, keep your distance!" The influence of the Mother and Child was about him, but the Rot was there too, filling each lost soul, and it came to Bram that he could not cause these innocents injury, despite them giving themselves over to the Rot, and who was he to say that they had? Perhaps, like Wilhelm, they no longer had the strength to fight. How could he punish someone for finding solace from pain and sorrow, even if it were from some foul being?

"I knew you would show mercy," Serval said. "That is why I want you so."

Serval was on him when Bram noticed a faint tremor in the earth. At first neither Serval nor the soldiers reacted to it, until the rumbling gained voice and momentum, jarring the earth, making it buckle and crack.

"What is this?" Now there was fear in Serval's voice.

The earth beneath him rose, split open into a yawning hole. His sword dropped from his grasp and fell into the darkness, Bram following.

CHAPTER THIRTY

First, there was darkness.

Then the sensation of traveling along on a thick wave, and Bram clawed with his fingers, realized it was dirt, soft and malleable. He feared at first he would die, this place becoming his unmarked grave. The air was hot and thin, and he struggled to breathe.

The ground trembled again, the motion shaking his body, making his head ache. Then light poured in and blessed air with it. His forward momentum was slowing.

"There he is!" a voice cried out.

"Let's get 'im up here, then!"

Luana? What had they, *how* had they—?

Hands grasped at his shirt, pulling him up, and the sunshine had never felt so good on his face.

"Sorry about that, Highness." Luana grinned at him. "Thought mebbe it would be better if we jus' got ya out of there."

Dwarf magic.

"It ain't as easy as goin' through water, but we manage."

"Thank you," Bram said. "Isbet?"

"Here." Isbet knelt before him and draped her arms around his shoulders. "You're safe."

He kissed her, and the dwarves cheered and hollered.

"We have to leave," Bram said. "We're not safe here. We have to get to the sacred ground."

"I know," Isbet said.

"Can ya stand? That's a good boy," Luana said. "Let's get back ta that fancy church of yours."

Bram looked around and saw they were a bit of a distance from the camp. What people he could see in the camp were dashing about in a seeming panic.

"Don't worry, they'll be busy for a while," Luana said.

One of the other dwarves brought him his horse. They rode hard at first, until they felt they were a safe distance from the camp, and then slowed their horses to rest. Bram told Isbet what had occurred.

"The place stank of the Rot," he said. "Serval was already taken but Wilhelm seemed to be fighting it." Bram chose his next words carefully. "He had the Box. It sat right there before him and I didn't take it."

"Why?" There was no accusation in Isbet's voice.

"Because...." Bram hesitated. "Isbet, I think I truly know what we are dealing with now.

"Serval kept saying how lonely he was, how Wilhelm was gripped by sorrow and that he didn't want to feel that." Bram went on. "I can't say if Wilhelm's meddling brought this to life, but I understand now. Wilhelm isn't a ruthless conqueror. He is just a sad old man, wanting to have something to take away whatever sorrows he must live with. And for a moment, I felt sorry for him."

"You once said you didn't know where Wilhelm had come from," Isbet said.

"When I was being pulled into their thrall, I could see Wilhelm, lost and alone like an orphaned child. The being who was at the very bowels of Underneath was also searching for an escape, and Wilhelm provided a conduit for it."

"That would explain the lines of magic I saw attached to him," Isbet said.

"But I also had the sensation from those soldiers that there were more with so much sorrow." Bram lowered his gaze. "Isbet, I'm sorry."

"Whatever for?"

"I can't kill them. Do you know why?"

"Yes," Isbet said. "They are not evil men, but whatever grave unhappiness they suffer, the being behind the Rot takes that all away. It is like when you indulge in too much drink or narcotics."

"How can I punish them?" Bram heard the plea in his own voice. "Tell me what I can do."

Isbet breathed deeply. "They willingly gave themselves to the Rot. They are no longer mortal and deserving of our mercy."

Bram squeezed the bridge of his nose. "But when someone is possessed by drink, we know they are not necessarily bad, just in need of help."

Isbet shook her head. "This is not the same. There is no going back for them. Soon even Wilhelm will succumb if his sorrow is great."

"He warned me and gave me a chance to escape," Bram said.

Isbet was silent for a moment. "He was stronger than he believed but he has no faith in himself. The being will eat away at that strength unless Wilhelm uses it to break free."

Isbet pulled the reins and brought the horse to a stop. She took Bram's wrist in a painful grasp. "Will you be able to act when the time comes? If not, say so now and *I* will deal with Wilhelm and Serval."

Bram considered her words. He carefully weighed them against everything Wilhelm had done. The war, the deaths of his father and uncle, Seth, his home and his father's dishonor. All so Wilhelm could fulfill some twisted wish to belong and to wipe his sorrow and loneliness away. And it all came about before Wilhelm had released the being, as inadvertent as that was. No, one warning would not make up for that.

"I will do what needs to be done," Bram said.

★   ★   ★

Jaryl met them at the bottom of the cathedral steps. "Our scouts said you were on your way back. What happened?"

"We don't have much time," Bram told him. "Wilhelm does not plan on attacking Bishop's Lane. He's coming here. He wants me, or so he says."

"We won't let him have you."

"I don't plan on letting him have me," Bram said. "After what I saw, I thought perhaps here on sacred ground would be a better place to fight them."

"And it keeps them away from the city." Jaryl nodded.

"I'll need another sword," Bram said, although he wondered if it would do any good.

"I'll have one brought," Jaryl said.

Bram spoke to Aune, asked her to gather her sisters to pray. Aune said they would settle in the garden. Bram had Coline attempt to ascertain where Wilhelm might be, but all she could tell him was a dark cloud hovered over the land and as far as she could see, that was where Wilhelm waited. However, she would call upon all her power to keep them safe and to keep a watchful eye on the city.

An acolyte brought him a sword, like the ones the soldiers used. It would have to do. Bram then gathered their soldiers and told them what to expect.

"You must put aside any sorrows or guilt," he told them. "I know I am asking a lot of you, and I know it will be difficult, but if you have something that will feed this being, it will try to consume you. Tell me now if there is anything that weighs too heavily on you."

Three of the soldiers took him aside and told him of their troubles. One had just lost his father to an accident. They had been awfully close, and it was taking all he could do to cope, which was why he chose to work instead. The second, a young woman, had found her husband to be unfaithful, while the third had a wife who was terribly ill, and he hated to be away from her. The soldier with the ill wife Bram sent home. To the other two, he said, "I will assign you to protect the Mother Superior and her sisters. Be certain no harm comes to them."

Coline reported later that same day that Wilhelm was now on the move and a scant few hours from the cathedral. She also divined that the Chir soldiers would not reach them in time. It was what both Bram and Isbet had expected.

Led by Jaryl, their soldiers would provide the last line of defense against Wilhelm reaching the cathedral. Jaryl looked the part of the Patriarch of Tamrath, resplendent in silver armor. His face was set in hard lines. Bram looked at him with pride and wasn't surprised when Jaryl turned his way and gave him a brief nod. As for the dwarves, they would be at the ready with their earth magic. Isbet rode beside him, as grim and determined as he.

They knew when Wilhelm and Serval were nearby. The stink of Rot preceded them, sour on what little breeze that stirred. There was no structure to the marching troops. They walked in a muddled group, almost at their leisure.

"I don't see Wilhelm," Isbet said.

"Bet that coward ran off with his tail b'tween his legs," Luana said. She stood at the head of the line of dwarves, a few feet behind them.

"No," Isbet said.

Something in her voice made Bram turn to her. "What is it?"

"Wilhelm is here, so is Serval." Her gaze seemed unfocused at first, then she came to herself.

"Look." She nodded towards their enemy.

The milling soldiers had stopped and suddenly split their ranks, creating a makeshift aisle. Something stirred at the back, low to the ground, appearing out of nothing. It coalesced into a dark fog that moved up to the head of the column, filling the space. Bram saw it and remembered its color and stink. He knew what it meant. "Triune, no."

Isbet grasped his hand. "Courage."

"You know what that is too, don't you?" He couldn't stop the hammering of his heart or the sweat that gathered at his brow. He hadn't expected this to happen to him. He could not stop himself from trembling.

"Bram," Isbet said as she squeezed his hand, "focus on me."

Bram did. He let the pain and her touch occupy his mind, but still, there was that little edge of fear that he fought to suppress.

They came, the three of them, walking with slow deliberate steps. The dark fog swirled around their massive paws, their movements causing wisps of the darkness to rise from within, clinging to their legs. They were as terrifying as Bram recalled.

...and there came three dogs, one with a pair of eyes as large as teacups, the second with eyes as big as millwheels and the third with eyes as big as a tower....

Isbet slid off her horse, slapped it on the rear, and watched it run for a moment. Bram breathed in deeply, gathering what he could of himself and praying to the Triune for strength and protection. He dismounted as well, and his horse needed no urge to flee.

Wilhelm and Serval rode in the wake of the beasts, and even from where he stood Bram could see the Box, nestled in the crook of Wilhelm's right arm. The talisman seemed brighter than anything nearby, slicing through the darkness as though wanting to make its presence known, to declare it was an instrument of power.

"Wilhelm!" Bram called. "Cease this. Go on your way."

He didn't know if Wilhelm heard him. His face had taken on an eerie cast from the light of the Box, his eyes, now black as Serval's, reflected the silver fire. Wilhelm dropped the reins and raised his hand. He made a broad sweeping motion.

The dogs broke into a run, the fog trailing them. Bram drew his sword, but Isbet stepped in front of him, raised Gaemyr high over her head, and brought him down, plunging him deep into the earth. "Now!"

Behind them, the dwarves moved in unison, one fluid motion that belied their stockiness and temperament. It became a dance of great strength and power. A yawning crevasse split the earth in two, but Bram knew it wouldn't stop the dogs.

Isbet grasped Gaemyr, her lips moving, and the swell of power was so great, even Bram experienced the fire along every nerve. As the dogs went to leap the crevasse, a wall of thorns broke from the opening, green and supple, yet knife-sharp, their tips deadly points. Bram knew this was the true Vine, not tainted by the Rot, but the dogs, unimpressed or perhaps without choice, leaped into the midst of it and impaled themselves.

They howled, almost as one, and the noise itself was a rasping sound dredged up from the foulest places of Underneath. It assaulted Bram's ears and made him want to flee for his life. He forced himself to remain, tensing his muscles and taking a rigid stance. It was all he could do to hold on. The thorn patch continued upwards, spearing the air in every direction and trapping the dogs in the greenery.

Behind them, the dwarves were moving again, unaffected apparently by the howling, and the ground now undulated in time with their movements. The thorns began to sink back into the crevasse, taking the dogs with them as they struggled, rending flesh and drawing black blood.

It was then that Isbet cried, "Now, Bram!"

Bram did not hesitate. He drew his sword and charged forward. The dwarves were behind him, their ranks split, and the ones who stayed with Isbet continued with their dance. Bram leaped a section of the thorn wall that did not grow as tall from within the crevasse, and when one of the enemy soldiers saw him, he cried a warning to his companions. Some heeded his cry. They were the ones who had not yet succumbed to the Rot, and perhaps they felt the need to act out of duty, Bram guessed, but they were too few and found themselves outmatched by the dwarves and the Tamrathi soldiers who had come to fight alongside them, including Captain Tamair. They plowed a clear path for Bram to Wilhelm.

The Arch-bishop approached his false father, where he sat astride his horse. Now that he was near, Bram truly realized that it was over for Wilhelm. He had given in. Bram felt a pang of pity, but it soon faded. Out of the corner of his eye, he saw Serval on his own nervously dancing mount, but the Dokkalfar prince did not attempt to come near.

"Bram," Wilhelm said, his voice disturbingly calm, "you came back to me."

"Wilhelm, the Box. Give it to me."

"I can't." Wilhelm clutched the Box against his chest like a child refusing to relinquish a favorite toy. "Without this, I'm nothing."

Bram kept his own counsel on that. "I asked you to cease this."

"Wilhelm." Serval moved his mount closer. Gone was his welcoming smile. Except for his eyes, he seemed his own bastard self again. "Don't let him distract you. Call the dogs and command them to kill him."

"No!" Wilhelm buried his face into his chest and hugged the Box closer. "I won't."

An expression marred Serval's features, and his skin reshaped like wet clay. Mottled gray pockmarks burst through his flesh. It was just for a moment but it seemed to last forever. Bram recognized the visage. That one he'd seen before, leering at him in the darkness. "Very well."

The earth trembled once again, but this time there was something different in the sound and the feel of it, something beyond even the dogs. Its force sent Bram to his knees. Serval was not immune to the power. His horse screamed and reared, throwing him off its back. Another crevasse opened directly behind Wilhelm, who was struggling to calm his mount but only succeeded in having the horse unseat him as well. A second wall sprouted but the Rot had tainted it with black thorns bleeding ichor.

The walls climbed skyward, arching over their heads. Bram had his last glimpse of the gray sky. In the now semi-darkness, he heard a scream of agony. A light exploded at the base of the wall. Bram pushed himself to his feet, half stumbling and half crawling towards it.

The Box. For an eye-blink, it was in Wilhelm's grasp, but he dropped it and turned his head to the right, to stare in confusion at the thorn that had pierced his shoulder. Another cry burst from Wilhelm's throat and black blood soaked the fine silk shirt he wore. Bram continued to move, guided by the light. He concentrated on that.

"Bram, help me—" The last word ended on another scream as a second thorn impaled Wilhelm's thigh. But the Box was nearly within his grasp.

"No! You will not have it!" Serval was coming for him. His face still held the image of the Rot. Bram drew his sword. Then the unexpected occurred. The thorn wall sprouted healthy offshoots. They effectively blocked Serval's path and separated him from Bram. The Arch-bishop sensed what had happened. *Isbet.* But was she well?

He had to finish this now and go to her. He bent down and took the Tinderbox in his hands. A vision appeared in his mind's eye, of the dogs freeing themselves from the thorns, their eyes now on Isbet, who stood helplessly, caught casting her spell.

"Bram—" Wilhelm hung like a rag doll on the thorns. "Please."

It went against everything he stood for to ignore a soul in need. He hoped the Triune would forgive him, but after all, he was just a man. Bram went to his knees, fumbled with trembling fingers to strike a spark. He kept dropping the firesteel, as the vision of the dogs going for his precious Isbet continued to fill his mind. He succeeded in striking it once against the tinder and the flame burned bright.

"Stop!" Bram cried and the first dog did.

He struck a second, then a third, and commanded them all.

"Oh Triune!" Bram clutched the burning Box with both hands, staring into the tiny flames. He could barely hold it steady, his body shaking.

Now that he possessed the Box, confusion seized him, trapping him between what was right and what was wrong, what he wanted to do and what he needed to do. He could destroy Wilhelm and Serval, take back his home and make Rhyvirand and all its peoples his. He could truly rule the Riven Isles.

No. The thought forced its way to the forefront of his mind. No, no, *no!* That was the Rot, filling his mind, tempting him with power. Bram realized it was the Box that had provided the opening for the Rot to infect Wilhelm. From there it had tainted him and those around him.

Bram stood. "Come to me now."

In an eye-blink, the dogs stood before him in all their greatness. Fur dark brown and bristling, teeth sharp and yellow stained, and claws that dug ruts in the dirt. His old fear returned, but it was only for a moment. Bram was beyond that now and he wouldn't let it stop him. He pointed to the first and largest. "Fetch Wilhelm." The greatest beast bounded far over Bram's head and returned in an instant, bearing Wilhelm by his shirt collar. He seemed to be unconscious.

To the second, Bram commanded, "You, fetch Serval." He pointed to the first, then the second. "Take them both to the steps of the cathedral." Then Bram pointed to the third and smallest. "You, take me to Isbet."

The third approached him and knelt and Bram climbed on his back. Then the dog was leaping in the air, flying past the forest of thorns, and over the scene of the battle, where the soldiers who weren't dead had run away. A third wall impaled the soldiers taken by the Rot. Bram felt little sympathy for them.

Then he was there, next to his love. Isbet was still in her stance, her expression twisted in both pain and concentration. Sweat ran in rivulets down her face and stained the front of her blouse. *Why had she not completed the spell?*

Then he saw why. At first there were new Vines at her feet, surrounding her in what he assumed was a circle of protection, but there suddenly appeared splotches of black, eating away at the new growth, and Isbet was fighting to hold her spell and to keep the Rot at bay. It had gotten this far, and sacred ground or not, it wanted Isbet. They surrounded her in the circle of poison, trailing up her legs and rending her clothes. She screamed.

Bram drew his own sword and called upon the Mother, but she was already there. "Be gone from this holy place!" he commanded. He drove the blade into the ground and as Light-bringer, her blessing flowed through him as it had in Underneath, branching out into golden strands that Bram entwined around the tainted Vine. He forced the purifying light into the earth, until he came to its base and tore it asunder. The black thorns receded, shriveling into death and freeing Isbet.

"Isbet." Bram ran to her. The dwarves had stopped their dancing, but they didn't approach right away. Bram noticed the first dog was there, still holding the fabric of Wilhelm's collar between its great teeth. When the dog saw Bram, it came to him as tame as any house pet and dropped the sobbing, pitiful heap of a man at his feet.

His eyes were still black and shed dark tears, but now Wilhelm seemed to Bram like nothing more than an errant child crying for something he had lost. Right then, Wilhelm was beneath Bram's notice. "Isbet?" She was unconscious, yet she still grasped Gaemyr in her right hand. He drew her to him and cradled her in his arms. She bled from many wounds, the worst on her legs and feet. She would bleed to death if he didn't do something now.

Bram placed his hand on one of the wounds and her warm blood seeped between his fingers. "Mother of the Triune, I beseech thee, lend me your power to heal her. Find favor with this, your loyal daughter."

Again, the Mother came. She smiled at him as she laid her hands over his, and the power flowed through him, into Isbet and with it some of Bram's soul as well.

When the Mother withdrew, the bleeding had stopped and there remained scars all over Isbet's body where the wounds had been. It was possible she would never lose those scars, but that mattered little to Bram. His Lady Witch was safe.

"Look there!" someone cried, but Bram couldn't see who. All eyes turned to the thorn wall, and a being, half-naked and bleeding, was now within its heart. Serval. The thorns pierced his flesh and secured his flailing body.

There were other things too – things that Bram knew lived in the bottom of Underneath. They crawled and slithered from the crevasse, shadowed shapes that had no form and still others he did recognize. They did not tarry or fight but made their escape. These things were now loose in the world.

"My soldiers!" Bram called. He knew they were exhausted, but they had no choice. "Pursue those foul beasts and be certain none of them are left alive!"

"I have them, brother, follow me!" Jaryl cried out and their soldiers rushed in pursuit.

Now to this matter. Bram looked as the second dog approached and sat as calmly as the first and waited with expectant eyes. "What happened? Why didn't you take Serval?" He knew there would not be a verbal response. The dog huffed almost indignantly and moved closer until Bram could feel the heat of its fetid breath. Bram cautiously reached out his hand and laid it against the dog's muzzle.

The vision came to him as clearly as the first had. The second had taken Serval, carrying his struggling body between its teeth, not a very clever move on its part. It was about to do as Bram had ordered when the Rot had claimed Serval for its own, snatching him away, but not before the dog had bitten down and taken off Serval's arm. Since Bram had given him no further instructions, he had returned to his new master – the keeper of the Box.

Bram didn't know if the being behind the Rot was greater than the dogs. But the Vines had injured them, and they did not want to be hurt again.

Then the thorns that held Serval began to recede, dragging him down into the darkness. Serval laughed, and they heard it despite the distance. It was somewhere between hysteria and triumph. It stayed with them long after the ground swallowed him, and the sound faded away.

Luana had come up behind him. "Looks like somethin' wanted him more than we did."

"Indeed." Bram once again turned his attention to Wilhelm. He did not want that vileness in the cathedral and doubted Wilhelm would be able to enter at any rate. "The three of you, guard him," Bram ordered the dogs. "Do not let him escape or allow anything to take him."

The dogs surrounded Wilhelm and sat, as still as statues.

Bram lifted Isbet in his arms and carried her inside.

CHAPTER THIRTY-ONE

When the thorns pierced her flesh, Isbet had never experienced such agony. Through the Vine, she had seen when Bram had taken the Box from Wilhelm and how Serval had tried to take it from Bram.

She didn't need to tell the dwarves to act. They were Children of the Vine and the Vine was fighting back. Isbet called on the power, and the Vine, supple and new, heeded her call. Thorns as sharp as any sword burst from the Vine, forcing their way upward. Isbet took hold of them, pulling them from deep within the earth. They blocked Serval, keeping him from her Bram.

She noticed the soldiers tainted by the Rot were gathering themselves to fight. Isbet drew on every ounce of will, causing a third thorn wall to come to life. The soldiers did not have their instincts and training to assist them and they succumbed.

Something caught her attention, out of the corner of her eye.

"Isbet, beware!" Gaemyr warned her.

Then Isbet saw him. Serval. The thorns had taken him, but he did not struggle against them. He suffered a grave injury when one of the dogs severed his arm. Serval laughed as they impaled him, pushing into his flesh, nettles and rotted offshoots taking twisted hold of his soul. Black blood dripped onto the supple stems that Isbet had formed and the Rot spread, eating away at the life pulsing within them. Serval laughed again and it was the sound of a man gone mad. He opened himself to the Rot without so much as a protest.

"You will not!" Isbet placed herself between the new Vines and the Rot, but it continued to spread. Isbet was losing ground. Now that Serval had given himself over, he was no longer a mortal being. One great push from him and the Rot drove forward and claimed what was once good and new. The Rot took a burning path towards her.

When it reached her, Isbet had little strength to fight. The thorns and vines surrounded her, stabbing at her; they bled the Rot, which forced its way deep into her, threatening to blacken her own soul. She vowed to take her own life before she gave in.

Then came a new power much greater than the Rot. While the Rot came from the sewers of Underneath, this power came from Up Above.

The Mother. Isbet knew her. She smiled at Isbet and took her into a gentle embrace. The Mother's light filled her soul with contentment. There was no more pain, no more Rot burning her insides. It recoiled at the Mother's touch. The Mother spoke reassuring words to Isbet and she sensed she had the Mother's favor. Perhaps because of Bram? Isbet did not question further.

Serval cursed her but his words held no power. The Mother stood by her now and with her blessing, Isbet drew on the last remaining bit of power she had. The Mother then drew a third presence near her that at first Isbet didn't recognize until he made himself known. Gaemyr. The Mother stepped aside, faded into the ether once more and Gaemyr took her place.

Always beside me, always my friend.

You have other friends now.

He'd spoken the truth. Isbet smiled. She could feel them nearby, focused on her.

As for Serval, the Rot dragged him down into the depth of Underneath. The way he continued to laugh, it was as though he welcomed this gruesome end.

It was no longer Isbet's concern as she focused on removing the taint from her own body. If Serval wished to live in the entrails of the beast, so be it.

A poor choice, Isbet thought.

★   ★   ★

The Mother came to her again. Isbet wondered if she were dreaming. Perhaps she was, for at first she was floating in nothing, then the light of the Mother surrounded her.

"Thank you," the Mother said. "Thank you for protecting my child."

"I did only what you asked of me." Isbet did not understand why she'd said that, but she knew it to be the truth.

"And now you must go back to him. He asks a boon of me and I shall grant it. Your life, Lady Isbet."

Bram was there; Isbet sensed his presence.

"Live, dear Isbet," the Mother said. "Live and fare thee well."

★　★　★

Isbet came awake when the sun warmed her face. She was in her bed in her room in Bram's guest quarters. She pushed herself up and frowned as her gaze went around the space. Where in the hells was Gaemyr?

Isbet pulled the cord by her bed. She heard nothing, but supposed there was a bell somewhere, because an acolyte came rushing into the room. Her eyes bugged when she saw Isbet. "You're awake! Thank the Triune."

"Girl, where is my—"

However, the girl ran out and yelled, "She is awake, Lady Isbet is awake!"

"Oh, by everything that's good and decent." Isbet yanked back the covers then hesitated when she saw the scarring on her legs and feet. "Damn it all," she muttered. She swung her legs around and sat up. "How in the hells long was I asleep?"

Isbet heard running feet and a tiny figure halted before her door. "Isbet!"

"Seth!" Isbet held out her arms and the little boy leaped upon the bed and climbed into them. Isbet held him tight, breathing in that scent of the outdoors that only little boys had. "I missed you," Isbet said as he snuggled against her chest.

"You did?" He looked up at her, with all the love and admiration he had. "I missed you too and you'll never guess – Coline tested me. I'm a wizard."

"You are?" She grinned and hugged him close. "I'm so proud of you."

"You'll still teach me, won't you?"

"Of course."

More running feet and Bram's muscular frame filled the door. There was such a look of relief on his face that it melted Isbet's heart. She had missed him too, even if she had only been unconscious for a short time. She needed Bram Greyward with her. Not to mention, he held Gaemyr in his grasp.

"Isbet," Bram said.

Seth looked up and the little urchin grinned. "I'll come back later, Isbet. I'll go tell everyone you are all right."

He hopped off the bed and scurried out the door, closing it behind him.

Bram walked carefully towards her as though he thought she would bolt like a frightened deer. He knelt before her and handed her Gaemyr.

"How are you faring?" Isbet asked the staff.

"Not good at all!" Gaemyr said. "It's about time you woke up! Lazing about, leaving us in a fit of worry."

"I missed you too." Isbet smiled. "And thank you."

Gaemyr harrumphed. "Well, then have your prince carry me out of here. I suppose you two will want to go at it."

"Gaemyr, you are incorrigible."

"And your first sign of that was...?"

Bram was looking at her with questions in his eyes.

"Thank you for bringing him," Isbet said to Bram. "Would you take him into the other room, please?"

Bram took Gaemyr into the common room. He closed the door behind him when he returned. Now Isbet opened her arms to him and he came to her and kissed her, drinking her in like a man dying of thirst. She could feel him growing hard as his length pressed against her stomach and she laid her hand over him. He moaned and grasped her hand. "Damn you, woman, you scared the shite out of me."

Isbet laughed, pulling him to her again. The first time they made love had a harried, almost desperate sense of urgency. The second they took their time, caressing each other as though learning each other's bodies again.

They slept for a time and when they awoke Bram left her and went to the kitchen. He returned with a tray laden with food. Isbet wasted no time. She ate while Bram told her of the goings on in her absence.

"I sent Rajan back to Rhyvirand," he said. "He will inform the queen that Wilhelm can no longer fulfill his duties as king. I made him my new advisor."

Isbet buttered a biscuit and drizzled a bit of honey on top. "You will continue to rule Rhyvirand?"

"For now," Bram said. "I cannot leave its people without a king." He picked up a strawberry from a small bowl on the tray, took a bite, and chewed. "I have asked Captain Maive to search out any relation of the old king and queen. They would be the true heirs."

Isbet nodded, taking a welcome sip of hot coffee. "Where is Wilhelm?"

"We were right to assume he couldn't enter sacred ground. We tried to bring him into the cathedral, but he started screaming so we returned him outside, guarded by the dogs."

"And you have the Box?"

"I want you to have it," Bram said. "It belongs to you."

"Thank you," Isbet said. "Do not concern yourself with Wilhelm's punishment."

"I thought you may wish to deal with him," Bram said. "He is yours."

Isbet nodded, then asked, "And what of Avynne? Will Seth stay here?"

Bram smiled with affection. "He refuses to leave either of us, so...." Bram hesitated. "I have sent a message to his uncle, leaving it up to him who he wishes to rule Avynne until Seth comes of age." Bram moistened his lips. "You will stay, won't you? Stay and continue his teaching?"

"I have already promised him."

"I could use your counsel." Bram didn't meet her eyes.

"Only my counsel?" Isbet tilted her head to the side.

"You wouldn't have to do anything else." Bram's voice was soft. "As I have asked of you before, just stay with me, Isbet."

"I will." Isbet took his hand. "You didn't doubt, did you?"

He grinned. "Of course not."

★   ★   ★

Isbet struck the tinder in the Box. One, two, three times, and the dogs, silent and still, awaited her commands.

Bram and Seth were there. Seth had refused to let Isbet out of his sight, although he knew enough about the world not to make himself a nuisance when she and Bram were together. The boy had become proficient at making himself scarce at the most appropriate times.

The Patriarch, Coline, and Aune stood on the cathedral steps. They had deferred Wilhelm's punishment to her. The dwarves had gathered there. They too wanted to see what punishment Isbet would mete out. The soldiers from Chira had arrived the day before. They returned home, laden with gifts, messages, and kind wishes from the Patriarch. Bram and Isbet were to visit Chira again as there was much to discuss. They would visit Underneath while there to tell Calla of Serval and decide what they should do if he appeared again.

The Dhar and Dharina agreed to journey to Tamrath. There were things that needed settling and a new alliance to forge.

Bram had brought the Box to her earlier that day. As he handed it to her, he said, "Isbet, do you suppose...I mean, do you believe Serval is alive?"

Isbet nodded. "Yes." She had to be honest with him. "Or at the very least he is still in this realm as the Rot consumed his soul. We, or someone else, may have to deal with him again."

They spoke no more of Serval after that.

Isbet walked to where Wilhelm sat in front of a small, tattered tent. He never partook of the food and drink given to him. He rested his head on his chest but when Isbet approached, he lifted his gaze to her. His eyes were still black, and his face streaked with dried, oily tears.

He looked much older than he had as the many enchantments he had placed on himself began to fade when he could not renew them. He was nothing more than a pathetic old man.

"Wilhelm, do you recognize me?"

He nodded.

"And do you recall the old woman from whom you stole this Box?"

At first, he made no movement. Isbet could well imagine him searching his old memories. Wilhelm nodded again.

"She was my life. Someone I cared for. Someone I loved," Isbet said. "You sought all these years for love and companionship and in doing so, to feed your selfish needs, you took away people who mattered most to someone. My grandmother, Bram's father, and Seth, his people. So...." Grasping the Tinderbox, she stepped back. "I will let them decide your fate."

The first real emotion flickered across Wilhelm's face.

"Heed my command," Isbet said. "Open the veil. The True Veil. Let those he destroyed come and judge him."

The dogs raised their shaggy heads and howled all at once. Isbet stepped nearer to Bram and felt him shudder at the sound, but to Isbet it was such a familiar thing that it caused her no bother.

There was the sound and the feel of the earth trembling once again, but it was only where the dogs stood.

"Are those the dwarves?" Bram asked.

"No." Isbet nodded and the ground before them buckled and rose into a mound of rocks. A hole opened in its midst, torn by invisible hands. Though invisible to Bram, out came the wraiths, all of those who had died at Wilhelm's hands. There standing in judgment were Bram's father, her grandmother, the soldiers, the people. They came and pointed accusing fingers at Wilhelm. They surrounded Bram's father with a holy fire, making him the most fearsome of them all. The Triune stood behind him.

Wilhelm's mouth opened in a silent scream. He struggled to his feet but stumbled and fell to his knees. "No, please!"

"I see nothing," Bram said. "What is he afraid of?"

"Be glad you don't see," was Isbet's answer.

Wilhelm half crawled, half stumbled over to where Isbet and Bram stood. He reached up a hand as though to grab on to Isbet's blouse, but Bram stepped forward and slapped it away.

"Bram – son – please – they want to take me – don't let them take me—"

Bram shook his head. "I don't...." Isbet saw him faltering, pity in his expression. She waited.

"No." Isbet heard the firm resolve in his voice. "Whatever you are seeing, Wilhelm, it's what you deserve."

"But I never meant to hurt you," Wilhelm said. "I only wanted—"

Isbet took Bram's hand. "Do not falter. It will give him power again."

Bram gave a curt nod; his voice was grim. "Go, take your punishment."

"I won't!" Wilhelm sounded like a petulant child. "You can't force this fate upon me."

"Go, Wilhelm, or let the dogs take you," Isbet said. She could see what Wilhelm saw. Not only the wraiths but also what they had in store for Wilhelm. He would suffer in torment, dragged to the deepest of the nether-hells. Isbet turned away. "Well?"

Wilhelm opened his mouth as though to voice one last protest. The blackness drained from his eyes in the form of more tears. Even the Rot had forsaken him. It had no use for Wilhelm now. She could see the resignation and the way his shoulders fell. Wilhelm climbed to his feet, his face without expression as he turned and began to walk.

"Will the dogs go too?" Seth spoke up.

Isbet had known of his presence but she had shielded him from the sight beyond the veil. "No. They will come back and then return to their true home."

Seth walked forward.

"Seth, no!" Bram moved to stop him.

"It's all right." Isbet put her arm across his chest. "Watch."

Seth called to the dogs and they came to him like obedient pups. All three towered over him but he petted them on their powerful forelegs and they lay at his feet. He ruffled their shaggy manes and scratched each behind the ears. The smallest licked him on the face, hands, and arms.

After a time, the dogs moved away, and Seth took his place beside Isbet. Wilhelm hesitated, looked back one last time. Isbet wasn't certain if it was to plead for mercy or if he was taking one last look at the living world that he would never see again. Then he disappeared behind the blackness of the cave. Isbet saw the wraiths crowd in behind him, shielding him from her view. The veil closed and the mound of earth sank until it once again became part of the soil.

*   *   *

"Will you be gone long?" Bram asked. They stood on the balcony, the same one where he'd often had discussions with Wilhelm at the palatial estate of Rhyvirand.

Isbet looked out at the land that Bram now ruled as prince regent. "Until next season. I will introduce Seth to those who taught me. When he is older, I will take him back again. Soon he will receive a reward as I received Gaemyr to prove his prowess with the Gift."

Bram framed her face with his hands. "Try to come back before the season changes."

There was a polite clearing of the throat and they turned to find Rajan at the door. "Highness, we have settled the queen in her new home."

"Very well. Thank you for handling it, Rajan." His new advisor was performing his duties well. They'd developed, if not a friendship, at least a mutual respect.

When they told the queen about Wilhelm, it seemed it made little difference to her as long as she had her wealth and her lovers. Bram didn't want her influence on the estate, so he agreed to construct a private manor for her in the country outside of Faircliff, consigning the princess back to her copper castle. Bram provided her with a nice monthly allowance, which was very pleasing to her.

The people accepted him as their ruler. Bram never realized that he'd gained quite a good reputation with them, and that there had been some talk among various factions regarding Bram seizing control of the kingdom. Now it was a moot point but the people were satisfied.

Bram would rule well while Isbet was away and when she returned – well, Isbet had her own plans in mind for that. She'd taken some time to locate a necromancer to repair the veils within the estate. The woman had advised them it would be a long and arduous process and it was likely she would need to call in help. Bram advised her to do whatever she needed to do, and he would supply her with everything she needed.

★   ★   ★

Isbet and Seth started their journey early in the morning, about two weeks after the battle. They would ride the best horses from the estate stables and bring a pack mule laden with supplies. Before they left, Seth squeezed Bram right around his middle. The boy had grown some inches. "Make me proud," Bram said.

"I will," Seth replied as Bram lifted him up onto his horse.

Bram turned to Isbet, pulled her into his arms, and kissed her with abandon. "Take care. Come back to me soon, my Lady Witch."

"Of course." Isbet mounted. "Fare thee well, my prince. We will return home soon." They rode through the estate gates and into the sleeping city.

"Please tell me you'll stay out of trouble this trip," Gaemyr said.

Seth giggled and raised his hand to his mouth to stifle it.

"Oh, hush up," Isbet said.

Gaemyr did not hush, as they left the city and crossed the farmlands. At one point, Isbet sang a bawdy song Gaemyr was fond of, and he belted it out in his off-key voice. Seth was blushing through the whole thing.

They stopped at Wicayth and spoke with Magistrate Edolin. Isbet told him of the happenings in Faircliff. He nodded as she completed her tale. Isbet had a sense he'd been expecting something of that nature to happen.

One last stop before their journey began.

The tree was there in all its majesty and would be there still when she returned. Seth did not question her as they stopped, and Isbet slid off her horse and removed the Tinderbox from her pack. With the Box under her arm and Gaemyr in her free hand, Isbet approached the long split in the trunk of the tree.

She called on the Vine again, entwining many offshoots in a crude staircase, which she used to descend into the depths of the tree. Her steps were familiar as she returned the Box to its rightful place, and without her having to command them, the dogs returned as well. Isbet stood, drinking in the familiar sights, and then she said to them, "Let no one take you again but me and my folk. Let no one take the Box from its place. Let it be hidden until I come for it."

The three bowed their shaggy heads and, as Seth had done, she approached them each, ruffling their bristling fur, and burying her face in it, inhaling scents just as familiar. Then Isbet stepped back and gave each of them a nod, and they stared at her with strange eyes that told her much.

Isbet ascended aboveground. She used her Gift and laid a hand on the great tree. The Vines wove themselves across the opening, hiding it from prying eyes. Isbet mounted.

"For now, we are finished," Gaemyr said.

Isbet nodded again. "All right, Seth. It's time to go."

EPILOGUE

Three months later

Bram had taken to walking out on the balcony every morning since receiving the letter from Isbet that they were on their way home. Since Isbet hadn't revealed where they'd gone, he couldn't guess how long that would take, but Bram made certain to check. He wanted to see them first. Not find out later that they'd arrived.

He thought about how much had changed since she'd come into his life, which was now on a course he hadn't expected. Bram didn't mind.

He'd received word from Calla. There had been no sign of Serval. The growth of the Vine had ceased for the moment, at least in her realm, but there had been other reports of concern elsewhere. His newfound friends were all keeping a watchful eye.

Still, Bram thanked the Triune every day for their blessings.

Something caught his eye, far on the horizon but drawing closer. Yes, he was certain it was a horse and rider – no, two horses and a—

Bram knew it was they, although he still couldn't quite make out their forms. He left the balcony, dashed through the parlor and out into the hall. "Rajan!" he yelled. "Where are you?"

"Here, Highness." He was just coming from another hallway. "Is everything all right?"

"More than all right," Bram said. "Prepare a feast of welcome. My family has come home!"

Bram didn't wait for a response. He hurried down the corridor for the entrance and ran to welcome those he loved home.

ACKNOWLEDGEMENTS

This will be my first time writing acknowledgements, so as always, bear with me while I get this right.

First, my love and thanks to my Big Brother aka Lance Flemmings and my best friend and soul-sister, Kelli Riffle, and my friend Charlotte J. Parker. I appreciate you and your continued support – and incessant hounding *wink*. How many times did I want to quit? To chuck every page in the recycle bin? Every time you were there for me, encouraging me to continue, no matter how difficult I was. You have my gratitude.

To my literary agent, the fabulous Anne Tibbets of the Donald Maass Agency. You will never know how much it means to me you took a chance to become my advocate in the business. How you are always there answering my questions with patience and understanding. I sincerely appreciate you.

To my publisher, Nick Wells, and editor, Don D'Auria, of Flame Tree Press. Thank you for taking a chance on me and my work. For helping me bring *Tinderbox* into the world. I have waited so long for this opportunity. I hope we will have a prosperous business relationship.

Also, Don D'Auria and Michael Valsted, thank you for catching all those little things I missed, so that *Tinderbox* can be at its best when it's on the shelves. Without the two of you, it would have been an awful mess.

Thank you to the wonderful cover artists and the publicity team at Flame Tree, especially Sarah Miniaci, for your wonderful work and how you made me look good!

And, of course, a thank you to Mr. Hans Christian Andersen (1805-75).

FLAME TREE PRESS
FICTION WITHOUT FRONTIERS
Award-Winning Authors & Original Voices

Flame Tree Press is the trade fiction imprint of Flame Tree Publishing, focusing on excellent writing in horror and the supernatural, crime and mystery, science fiction and fantasy. Our aim is to explore beyond the boundaries of the everyday, with tales from both award-winning authors and original voices.

•

You may also enjoy:
The Sentient by Nadia Afifi
The Emergent by Nadia Afifi
American Dreams by Kenneth Bromberg
Junction by Daniel M. Bensen
Interchange by Daniel M. Bensen
Second Lives by P.D. Cacek
The City Among the Stars by Francis Carsac
The Haunting of Henderson Close by Catherine Cavendish
The Garden of Bewitchment by Catherine Cavendish
Vulcan's Forge by Robert Mitchell Evans
Black Wings by Megan Hart
Stoker's Wilde by Steven Hopstaken & Melissa Prusi
Stoker's Wilde West by Steven Hopstaken & Melissa Prusi
The Widening Gyre by Michael R. Johnston
The Blood-Dimmed Tide by Michael R. Johnston
Those Who Came Before by J.H. Moncrieff
The Sky Woman by J.D. Moyer
The Guardian by J.D. Moyer
The Last Crucible by J.D. Moyer
The Goblets Immortal by Beth Overmyer
The Apocalypse Strain by Jason Parent
Until Summer Comes Around by Glenn Rolfe
A Killing Fire by Faye Snowden
Fearless by Allen Stroud
Resilient by Allen Stroud
Screams from the Void by Anne Tibbets

•

Join our mailing list for free short stories, new release details, news about our authors and special promotions:

flametreepress.com